FLESH

David Galef

THE PERMANENT PRESS
Sag Harbor, NY 11963

Library of Congress Cataloging-in-Publication Data

Galef, David.
   Flesh / by David Galef.
      p.   cm.
   ISBN 1-877946-55-9 : $24.00
   1. College teachers—Mississippi—Fiction.
   2. Obese women—Mississippi—Fiction. I. Title.
PS3557.A41148F58   1995
813'.54—dc20   94-11245
                                                                                    CIP

Lyrics to Robert Johnson's "Terraplane Blues" copyright 1978 King of Spades Music. Used by permission. All rights reserved.

The characters, events and physical details in this story are partly real but wholly imaginary. This is my working definition of fiction.

First Edition, April 1995—2500 copies

Manufactured in the United States of America

THE PERMANENT PRESS
Noyac Road
Sag Harbor, NY 11963

I would like to thank the Yaddo Colony for its generous assistance during the writing of an early draft of this book. And love to Beth, for everything from expert copy-editing to well-timed hugs.

All flesh is grass.
—Isaiah 40:6

1

During a typical Mississippi summer you can boil and fry at the same time, and maybe even smother if you're wearing anything heavier than cotton. Going through my desk that morning in 1989, I found all my postage stamps stuck together and transferred them to the refrigerator. My first memory of Max is from one of those mid-July afternoons gone crazy with the heat and humidity, so that cars and trees and even people shimmered in the distance, half-apparitions until they came within hailing range. The sun seemed to expand as the day progressed until it was one huge yellow field-tent, enclosing everything. About the best thing to do is fool the heat by smiling as if you enjoyed it. Susan and I were sitting on what we called our front porch, really a concrete stoop overlooking the scrub grass and Jimson weed around the apartment block. We were keeping cool by planning the purchase of an air conditioner.

The rumble of a rental truck from around the corner made me sit up. You can always tell the sound of those vehicles because they're noisier than a car, but without the heavy purr of a professional rig. This one sounded like at least a medium-sized van, and I wondered who was moving in. As the gray U-Haul came up our street, it seemed to experience a moment of hesitation, like a pachyderm suddenly unsure of the location of the burial ground. After idling for a moment, the truck lumbered ahead, then reversed and did a creditable parallel parking job right beside our Honda Civic. The engine died, and the next moment a short man wearing mirror sunglasses came out of the cab. Susan waved, a habit that I as a former Northerner still had to get used to.

The man smiled, though I wasn't sure he saw us at first. He stared up at our apartment block, which is only two stories high, but on a hill that condescends to the curb. He stared down at something that flashed silver in his hand, probably a key. His figure shimmered at the edges—it was hard to get a fix on him until he came closer.

Susan nudged me with her knee. "That's got to be the new tenant for next door. It's been two months already."

I nodded, trying not to drip sweat. Susan remained unwilted in her sleeveless blouse and shorts, her auburn hair coiled gracefully at her nape, but then she was a native.

Susan nudged me harder with her knee. I got up from my wicker chair, which creaked and groaned like a lost soul, even in this humidity. The man was walking this way, following the path up to our building. He was slightly built but wiry-looking, dressed in tight black jeans and a polo shirt. His thick brown hair formed a thatch over his angular face. If there was anything particularly noticeable about him, it was that face—not the features, but the expression. It seemed to have a strong element of bluff to it, as with a poker player determined to make a go of two pair. When he took off his glasses, his eyes looked like what I'd call true blue.

"Hello, there," said Susan, putting on what I recognized as her hostess face.

"Hi," he said, and abruptly the poker face was replaced with that smile, warm and ingratiating "You live in C-8?"

Susan and I nodded as a couple.

"Well, if I'm in the right place, and this door opens. . . ." He inserted his key, which turned easily enough in the lock, but the faded white door had swollen from the humidity. He pushed at it; it wouldn't budge. He tried again. The veins in his arms stood out like packing cord. Suddenly, he put all his weight against it hard, as if deliberately knocking someone down. The door groaned open, and he grinned in victory. "There! It looks like I'm your new neighbor." He pushed the door all the way open and then back-stepped onto our stoop, which was just an extension of his. "My name's Max Finster. I'm new in the history department."

I suspected a hand-crushing grip, which I got. He was just as hard on Susan, and she winced a bit. I told him we were Don and Susan Shapiro, which was true, and that we were delighted to meet him, which was semi-plausible. At least it was nice seeing someone new on the block. Our neighbors on the right had gone down to the Gulf for a week, and C-7 had been empty since June. In mid-July, there's not much going on in Oxford, except the tail-end of summer school at the university. Dinner parties become incestuous with the same round of people, mostly faculty members who have elected to stay here for one reason or another. Susan was bored by this, and I suppose she had a right to be. In our case, we couldn't really afford a prolonged vacation, so we had compromised with a week at Susan's parents' place in Georgia, and a resolve to take off for a weekend or two in August. Mostly, we spent a lot of time out on our porch.

Max's first reaction when he stepped inside his apartment was a low, prolonged whistle. "My God, I could sublet this to three other New Yorkers and still have my own room. Or I could rent somewhere else and be an absentee landlord. Does it really go back as far as it looks?" His voice grew muffled as he disappeared into one of the walk-in closets. C-7 was about the same size and layout as our apartment, but I'd forgotten how cavernous it was compared to something urban. There were four large rooms radiating out from a short corridor, like a quincunx, with one room obviously intended as the kitchen and another as a bedroom. The place was rife with closets, including two walk-in caves and a modest kitchen pantry.

"Are you here by yourself?" asked Susan, my matrimonially-minded wife.

"Hmmm? Oh, yes, all by my lonesome, junior faculty, degenerate bachelor habits, you know the type." He had a voice owned by a certain type of actor, engaging with just an edge of abrasion. He re-emerged from his new habitat with a loose grin for Susan. I beamed back: I'm an English professor, and on the whole I prefer talkers to non-talkers. They provide text.

"Well. . . ." Here Susan prompted me with a nudge. "Would you like some help unloading?"

Max considered the offer. You could tell he liked doing things alone, including driving over 1,000 miles in a rented van. "Tell you what," he said finally. "Let me move what I can. There are just a few big pieces I may need help with, and I'll shout if I'm desperate. Okay?"

"Sure." Susan tried to signal me into arguing, but I ignored her. If a man wants to show off, it's probably healthier to let him. So Max went back to the van and began to carry out the first of many, many book crates. You could tell they were heavy as hell, the cords in his neck huge with the strain. In fact, we couldn't sit out on the porch anymore, since we felt ridiculous just watching someone struggle like that. So Susan went inside to make some iced tea, and I finally strode over to the van to see what I could do in spite of the restraint order.

Max had succeeded in carving out a large hole in a wall of boxes that surrounded a clump of furniture. Nothing exciting: a blond bureau, two mammoth bookcases, and a distressed cabinet. Over on the far side of the van were two bicycles with a blanket between them. Max was more or less in the center, disentangling a matrix of bungee cords that had kept things from sliding. He was sweating handsomely, damp patches plastering the shirt to his chest.

I leaned halfway in. "You about ready for a hand? You know, it's hard to watch you go it alone—and it's a downright breach of Southern hospitality."

A chuckle. "All right. When in Rome."

I was going to point out, in a hideous drawl, that he was in Miss'ippi, but he heaved me one of the last book boxes, and I staggered out of the truck and up the hill. He followed with a stuffed laundry basket that had a frying pan sticking out of some sheets, with a plaster cast of a Greek statue half-swathed in foam rubber on top. Only the head and groin were visible, but it was a rather prominent groin. The genitals were almost as big as the head.

"Who's that?" I asked on the way back.

"Who's where?"

"Up there." I pointed.

"What?"

I felt as if I'd stepped into an Abbott and Costello routine. "On top of the frying pan. In the basket."

"Oh, that. Statue of Priapus. Sort of a conversation piece."

"Sure looks like it."

He shrugged, and I realized that was all he was going to say about it. We heaved out some furniture from the truck. On the two-man items he let me lead, but made sure to carry more than his share of the weight, mostly by holding his end higher. Soon I was perspiring over my regular sweat, a sudatory spectacle. But with two people, the work went a lot faster, and in about half an hour the whole gray interior of the truck was visible. The last items to go were the two bicycles, one of which Max just got on and rode up the path. When I had a chance to look at them more closely, I could see that one was obviously an expensive machine, while the other looked like the brown bomber I had when I was a kid. Max rode the bomber.

"Racing bike and truck bike," Max explained as he pedaled away. He had the disconcerting habit of not looking at you half the time he spoke. When he did gaze at you and talk to you at the same time, you felt oddly honored.

"What's a truck bike?" I called after him as he rode right into the foyer of his new apartment.

He emerged on foot. "I use the racing bike for distance, for training. The truck bike is for transportation. Going to the supermarket, things like that."

"No car?"

He walked down the hill to fetch the other bike, stretching a motley bungee cord between his hands. "No, I haven't a car in the world. I'm more of a two-wheel person." He snapped on a grin.

"Maybe, but you're going to need a car around here. No public transportation."

It was hard to tell whether he was pleased at the solitude or annoyed at the inconvenience. He nodded vaguely, laying his hand over the handlebars as if soothing a fretful horse. I was going to offer to help him sort out the boxes we'd moved, half from courtesy and half from curiosity, when Susan poked her head out the screen door.

"If you two stevedores are finished unloading, how about some iced tea?" This was Susan's version of half courtesy and half curiosity. There was also a plate of sugar cookies. Soon we were all sitting in wicker chairs on our mutual porch, sipping the Southern beverage that Susan always made a bit too tart—like Susan herself, I sometimes thought. In any event, she did know how to extract information. In a few minutes, she'd obtained a thumbnail biography. Thirty years old, Ph.D. in British history from Columbia, avid cyclist, single and available. I could see Susan's mind churning around prospects, which are not so numerous in Oxford, unless you're willing to join the church or prey on the academy. Susan was a graduate student floundering in journalism when I met her here. After we got married, she switched off to community volunteer work.

When I said that I had a friend at Columbia still plugging away on her dissertation, Max pointedly didn't ask her name. Not that they would have known each other, being from different departments, but he seemed to want to leave the subject of New York altogether. It wasn't that he shut down; rather, he turned the conversation around as if we were the new arrivals. He nodded after each answer as if we'd made the right choice.

After about fifteen minutes, Max stood up abruptly, thanked us for being neighborly, and said he really had to get back to his boxes. Just outside the stoop of his apartment, he drew out a pen and a wad of paper from his pocket and jotted down a note to himself.

"What do you think he's writing down?" I asked Susan.

"I don't know—'Don and Susan—must remember their names'?"

" 'Get back deposit on truck,'" I suggested. I also thought of Priapus and his phallus. Our new neighbor, I foresaw, would be a fruitful object of speculation.

For about two hours, we heard the shuffle of corrugated cardboard on linoleum, with an occasional thump and a muffled curse. At about three-thirty, when I was thinking of getting some work done at my desk, the screen door to C-7 sprang open and Max emerged in skin-tight cycling shorts and a banana-yellow jersey that read "MERCIER." I saw him divided up through the front blinds, my view on the outdoors when I've withdrawn to the world of literature. He had cleats on his shoes that made him clop as he walked, but he lost all awkwardness when he mounted his bike. His cleats fit into the pedals, and as he rode down the walk, he hunched over in a catlike crouch. The bike was the same color as his jersey and shone like a yellow mirror.

By the time he hit the asphalt, he was moving fast. He accelerated downhill and passed right through the red light at the bottom intersection. I wondered where he was going in a place he didn't even know yet. He zoomed straight past the fire station and down the bend in the road by the municipal pool, never hesitating. The pace he kept looked brutal and unstoppable, his thighs pumping like pistons. I watched him through the blinds, as I often did from that day on, until he disappeared from sight. Like a vanishing godling. I knew I couldn't possibly have kept up, but turning away from the window, I half-wished I were along for the ride.

2

Most people take a while to move into a new place, but Max settled in overnight. He did this through a combination of effort and laziness that I came to recognize as Max-efficiency. That is, he put a lot of energy into something in order to get it over with, and then he lost interest. As he told me later, he simply unpacked what he had and didn't bother much with additional furnishing. Since Max had lived in a typical graduate student apartment in New York for the past six years, that meant three or four sticks of furniture now spread out over 800 square feet of linoleum. He had one chair in the kitchen and one in his study. He did buy a cheap formica-and-steel desk from Dale's Office Supply, as well as an additional bookshelf, both delivered the second day he was here.

He also got an air conditioner, which prompted us finally to go out and buy one ourselves, a Whirlpool the size of a small refrigerator. It was expensive and powerful and it worked beautifully, but it was almost a shame, since then we had to find another topic for discussion. We settled on our new neighbor.

We had seen him in town a few times, riding around on his truck bike. It had a wide rack in back, and it was amazing what he could haul with the aid of those bungee cords. On his first Sunday here, I saw him toting a full-length mirror and a fold-up chair from the local Wal-Mart. Susan offered to drive him a few places, but he thanked her in a way that made her stop asking.

He didn't get around to buying a car. I asked him about it one day, and he told me he'd gotten as far as Cheswick Motors, a Chevy dealership at the top of University Avenue. "I pedaled right into the lot, thinking maybe I could pick up a small used car and get the hell out. But you know how it is. I was halfway through the door when a salesman in a checkered vest shook my hand, said how glad he was I came, and he knew that I would be, too."

I didn't recall anyone at Cheswick wearing a checkered vest, but I allowed for anecdotal license. I nodded as if I'd had exactly the same experience.

"Anyway, when I mentioned I was looking for a cheap used car, his eyes lit up like a cat's. He tried to show me a Pontiac convertible owned by a sorority girl who sold it the moment her boyfriend got a Mercedes, only used it for formals. I don't need that kind of crap.''

"Uh-huh." I took in his dismissive tone, resolving something for myself. I was learning to read him, a little. "You didn't really want to buy a car, did you?''

"What?" If he was annoyed, he quickly recovered himself. "No, you're right. I'm pretty happy with a one-wheel drive.'' He got on his brown bomber, which was waiting submissively by the apartment stoop, and rode off in the direction of the campus library.

"Just let us know if you want a ride anywhere!" I called after him, helplessly echoing my wife.

I'm not sure why I offered. He was cheerfully self-sufficient, sometimes arrogantly so, and though women often see this as a challenge in men, I wasn't a woman and I had enough challenges in my own life. I guess I was curious as to his limits. He didn't seem to have any. He cooked for himself, too, the smell of his dinner invading the evening like a spice brigade. Once the scent of onions was so strong and tantalizing that I walked around back to where his kitchen was, the window wide open. Max was attacking a frying pan with a spatula. Then he took a knife that looked like a Japanese sword and minced up something large and helpless—I think it was an eggplant—on a cutting board. Either the stove or Max was sizzling, maybe both. I took one last sniff and walked away before he saw me. A few days later I smelled something like old sweat socks on fire. "Cumin," said Susan, wrinkling her sensitive button nose. "Cumin and cayenne. He's probably making chili.''

Every afternoon, at precisely three-thirty, he would dart out of the apartment on his racing bike, usually headed toward Sardis Lake. He usually rode for at least an hour, coming back with his jersey almost translucent from sweat. Susan worried for his sake about accidents, but he showed her his helmet, a black plastic half-moon with a styrofoam lining. It had a sticker inside guaranteeing his safety.

Susan wasn't impressed. "And what if some drunken frat boy drives right into you?''

"Student drunkenness? Around here?" He assumed what we came to call his LOUR: Look Of Utter Respectability. "I'm shocked, ma'am, simply shocked.''

"Well, just keep an eye on the road.''

"I'll keep both of them on it."

Then he disappeared into his apartment. After the sounds of a shower, the radio came on: NPR's *All Things Considered*, which we also listened to, with an odd stereo effect from the two adjoining apartments. Mostly he was a model neighbor, quietly industrious as he worked on his course preparation for the fall. He'd installed his desk and computer in the front room and spent a lot of time in front of the screen. He did library and supermarket runs on his bike and picked up his mail in the early afternoon like most academics.

Since the history and English departments share a communal lounge in Bishop Hall, I took him there to introduce him to some of our faculty. I figured he'd met the history people already. As it turned out, only our crowd was there, prolonging a cup of coffee into a discussion of local real estate. Melvin Kent, a gnomish gentleman whose field and manners are medieval, extended a hand. So did Bob Hammer, who purports to do something with linguistics but whose real interest is bird-watching.

"Pleased to meet you." Max was good at picking up the local intonation.

A stentorian voice from the other side of the lounge spoke up: Franklin Forster, a transplanted New Englander who looks like a bear. His expertise is American Gothic, which includes an air of menace supplemented by a bushy beard but a high, oddly querulous voice. "And *have* they given you an office yet, *Mr.* Finster?"

"Yes, in Bondurant."

Franklin exchanged looks of bereavement with all of us. Bondurant was the property of the sociology department and considered inferior quarters. It happens to be where my office is.

Max spoke up. "Actually, I don't intend to spend much time there. I do most of my work at home."

Franklin nodded with a smile that exposed his crooked yellow teeth. "I *take* it, Mr. Finster, that you are *not* a married man."

That got assorted chuckles. Franklin, now in his hale fifties, had recently remarried for the third—or was it the fourth?—time. Whichever, it was the second time he'd married a student of his, and we all felt slightly sorry for the woman involved. The teacher-student relationship had a nasty way of reasserting itself at odd moments. We would have felt more sympathy for the woman involved, a dyed blonde named Jane, if she'd been less like Franklin.

Meanwhile, Susan was plotting to invite Max over to dinner, but she wasn't going to do it until she had a suitable woman lined up. "What about Darleen?" she asked me one night. Our own domestic crisis had passed: the new air conditioner was humming happily away, and we were getting ready to go to bed.

I thought about Darleen, who taught Southern Studies. I thought about Max. "Too much the Southern belle. She'd drown him in jasmine perfume."

"Hmm."

"But what about Marjorie Bingham? The one in the psych department."

"Got engaged. Just last month."

"Oh." How do women pick up these facts—osmosis? Probably a gender-specific talent. Finally, Susan thought of a relative unknown, Marian Hardwick, a recently hired member of the fine-arts program. Neither of us knew much about her, except that she seemed bright and attractive. She drove a snazzy red Camaro and had a certain cosmopolitan air that might appeal. We discussed the other prospects a bit more, but finally settled on Marian. I don't know why we were so concerned. Maybe it was Susan's matchmaking impulse, or the anticipation of vicarious pleasure. We had entered that period of marriage known as the second-year lull. To prevent claustrophobia, we needed an outside interest. Or maybe we just wanted the best for Max. He seemed to bring out an aggressive mothering instinct in people.

Unfortunately, it wasn't clear just what Max wanted. He'd made one or two comments about a former girlfriend in Manhattan, but nothing specific, not even a name. I gathered he wanted to make a clean break, so I didn't push it. On the other hand, he was no monk. I was fairly sure he wasn't getting any action in Oxford because there isn't much action available, not for someone his age. Hang out in laundromats here, and all you get is your clothes cleaned. If your mind is really set on matrimony, on the other hand, your best bet is to join the Baptist church. Somehow I didn't see Max as the type for that.

I did feel he could use some sexual companionship. As it happened, the far wall of my study was also the wall of Max's bedroom. Judging from his lack of furniture, I imagined he kept the room fairly spare: the pine dresser I helped move, and maybe a reading lamp, the fold-up chair from Wal-Mart, and his box-spring mattress and wooden frame. All the objects were inaudible, except for the bed that creaked in a masturbatory rhythm in the early afternoon or late evening. Priapus was obviously there, as well.

If I hadn't been so curious, I would have left the room. Of course I never said anything about it. But I wondered whether he was using what they call visual aids, and if so, what they were. Sleek models in sports cars, or bike sluts? Perky breasts or big boobs? When I was growing up in Philadelphia, some boys used the old Sears catalogue, but part of being an adult means buying your own pornography. I had a few magazines myself, my first two years here, until I met Susan (after that, they got shoved into a locked drawer).

It was the sounds Max made that set me off. They were a cross between grunts and moans, sometimes with an odd cachinnation. Did he see himself on top or bottom? What particular body type or clothing set him off? Sometimes, working late in my study, I would think of questions like that. Eventually, I would pad into the bedroom where Susan was still half-awake and stroke her body all the way up and all the way down. Regular stopping spots included her pear-shaped breasts, her fuzzy blonde nether lips, and the delicate area of the inner thigh where the skin turns plum-colored. We didn't talk much, but when her sighs reached a certain pitch, she would reach out and do more or less the same to me, making me feel slightly epicene, especially since Susan had narrow hips and slender thighs. Our bed, with a new foam-core mattress on a steel frame, made barely a sound.

The dinner party seemed like plotting, in a way. Susan issued the invitation for that Friday night, and just so it wouldn't seem a set-up, we also asked the Pearsons, a faculty couple made up of half English department and half psychology lab. This pairing sounds disastrous, but in fact they get along perfectly well, both as a couple and with others. Gina Pearson, *née* Taglieri, is our resident Faulknerian, possessed of the idea that Faulkner committed suicide but otherwise reasonably sane. Her husband Stanley is an experimental psychologist who talks informatively about the hypothalamus and neural matrices, but he likes a beer or three and is also surprisingly knowledgeable about literature, especially in my field, which is British Modernism. Not that specialized fields matter much: at faculty dinner parties, we usually spend all evening complaining about the administration and the students.

Dinner was supposed to be at seven, and Susan spent over an hour preparing some complicated chicken dish whose name I've forgotten, but I remember that it smelled of tarragon and lemon juice. There was also saffron rice and lima beans. I was in charge of the salad, which I desultorily kept adding to until I realized I'd created a towering pyramid of greens in the bowl. Max was the first to arrive, promptly at seven. As our next-door neighbor, he didn't have far to walk, but I had the feeling that if we had announced dinner at 7:06, he would have come six minutes later.

He was wearing a pair of khaki slacks and an open-neck shirt, which is about as formal as you can get at this time of year and still breathe. He presented us with a bottle of California chablis, sweating in its paper bag. I started in on my hostly duties by pouring him a glass from another bottle, already open. Susan bustled about the kitchen, mostly because she liked bustling about in front of guests. I asked Max how many miles he had ridden that day.

He showed the kind of tough grin an athlete flashes when you ask how the training is going. "Thirty today. My bicycle almost melted on the way back." Max, it struck me, was the kind who needs a certain amount of pain in order to enjoy life.

Marian came five minutes later, dressed almost identically to Max and bearing the same brand of wine. The two contestants shook hands and embarked on a game of "Who Am I?" Then the Pearsons arrived, bearing another bottle of the same chablis—the B & G package store must have been having a sale on that wine.

Gina was all excited over a discovery about the coroner's inquest after Faulkner's death. One of her main arguments has always been that the attending doctor altered his story between the time he talked to the family and the time he wrote out the official report. Now she was trying to find out if the coroner was still alive. He was the one who had administered morphine to Faulkner after his riding accident, and there was a question about the dosage.

"Well, morphine wasn't so scientifically administered in those days," put in Stanley, academically. He then proceeded to put us straight about just how they did administer it, since Stanley knows a great deal about psychotropic drugs and their neurological effects. He sounds just as authoritative in other areas, though it's always a bit unsettling how he relates them all to neurology. When anyone in the vicinity is moody, for example, he's likely to suggest mood-altering substances.

"I thought Faulkner's wife was something of a morphine addict," put in Max from the sidelines. Gina rewarded him with a smile of complicity.

"She was a rather bad painter, I know that," said Marian, extending her glass forward to be refilled. "No sense of perspective."

"True—she married *him*." This was my contribution, though all I got was a look from a Susanly direction. This led to a discussion about what the demands of genius are, and since I'd already heard Gina on this topic, I went to set the table. When I got back, the discussion had shifted magically to the problems of the academic administration. Our current chancellor, in the grand tradition, tends to treat teachers as disposable.

We sat down to eat half an hour later, segueing to a conversation about some of our feebler students. Gina had vehement opinions on the subject, having labored in the classrooms of Ole Miss for fifteen years. I'd been around for only three, but there seems to be some correlation over time between teaching the students and resenting them. Stanley could probably have pointed out what part of the brain controls resentment. Marian kept guardedly neutral, and Max had no opinion at all, not yet having taught his first semester.

Dinner was delicious, as we told Susan over and over, and we were already halfway through the meal by the time someone asked Max the inevitable question about adjusting to the South. They used to ask me that, too, my first year here, until I learned to stop answering the question and say I liked it fine. By this time Max must have been asked that over a dozen times, but he managed to sound spontaneous, and it was then I realized that he must be a good teacher. "Actually," he began, "I like it a lot here. It's a welcome change from New York. The pace is more relaxed, the people seem friendlier. . . ." He went on, trotting out the points Mississippi residents expect to hear. But he ended with a slightly peculiar observation. "There's something about the women, too . . . they seem more womanly, somehow—I can't quite put my finger on it."

Marian put her elbows on the table. "You mean more ladylike."

"You're talking about the genteel manners and the dress. No, it's more than that. I saw an older woman the other day bicycling along in shorts and a sleeveless blouse. Flapping in the breeze, not demure. She wasn't ashamed to be showing so much of herself; she looked me right in the eye."

Marian, who also happened not to look demure, propped up one elbow with her hand. "What's your point?"

"Well, the women here seem more . . . at ease with themselves."

Marian snickered. "Maybe. The men all act like Ed, your friendly gas station attendant."

This led to what Susan called a gender-bender, as we tried to sort out sexual roles in the South. Of the six of us, only one was originally Southern, and that was Susan, who was born in Macon, Georgia. Gina was from a large Italian family in New Jersey, with Stanley a steadying influence from Wisconsin. Marian had ten minutes ago revealed that she grew up in California. And Max and I were both from up North. I mention all this because it's always non-Southerners who seem to be clarifying Southern manners and morals to the natives. Susan politely held her tongue when this happened, though in private she had some choice words to say on the subject. Two of them were *pigheaded* and *ignoramus*.

It was an edifying discussion to anyone who hadn't already heard Stanley on the subject. What we eventually concluded was that the South was a politeness and shame society, but without the neurotic guilt that characterizes New York. Stanley and Max disagreed on typicality and test-subjects, but then Stanley is the kind of person who would feed the same diet to a group for ten days to see whether their shit all smelled the same. Max, on the other hand, seemed to applaud eccentricity. Then they got on to whether there was a typical kind of Southern eccentricity. Max took out his wad of paper and wrote a note at the table, proving his own eccentricity.

"What's that you're writing?" asked Gina.

"Note to myself," Max answered disingenuously. He finished quickly and slipped the pen and paper back into his pocket.

"About us?" asked Marian.

"Not necessarily."

Susan brought in a huge angel food cake just then, and brightly announced coffee. The conversation took up with "ladylike" again and shifted to what was meant by "gallant." Susan said she thought the proper word was "mannerly."

"But all this gallantry—" Marian protested with one hand while accepting a slice of cake with the other. "What about all the rape and incest you read about—well, in authors like Faulkner." She looked to Gina for support.

"The return of the repressed," murmured Gina. It was her favorite etiology, used to explain any human behavior from shyness to deer-hunting.

"Overactive hormones," said Stanley.

Marian frowned. A moment later, with a clumsy motion of her hand, she somehow catapulted her coffee spoon from her cup. It flew through the air in a liquid arc, landing between Max's chair and hers. They both made a grab for it, but Max got there first. He handed it back to her with a mock flourish. "I believe this is yours, ma'am."

Marian flushed slightly. "That's gallantry."

"Civility," he informed her.

"Patriarchal gentility," she insisted, missing the deliberate exaggeration behind his gesture, as well as the coffee spots now adorning his slacks. For some reason Max didn't bother to enlighten her. Instead, he made some crack about matriarchy—he might as well have spilled hot coffee in her lap. The following invective was about as scalding. Gina tried to intercede, and Susan ladled in a comment about the weather, but Marian was talking heatedly about the double standard. Max, who hadn't been initially engaged, now took up the challenge and was detailing varieties of sexism. Stanley tried to introduce a relevant note by citing the relation between stimulants and sexual harassment, but it didn't help. Susan had gone to the kitchen for a sponge to wipe off Max's trousers, but he refused it. Susan sat down again and stirred her coffee helplessly, around and around, as she watched the dinner party come unraveled.

"Admit it—the kind of woman you go for is svelte, brainless, and subservient." Marian rested her arms on the table, and I couldn't help noticing that she was rather broad-hipped. The loose pants mostly hid that part of her figure, but she filled the chair when she sat down.

Max shook his head slowly, almost sadly. "It's not true." Then, as Marian was about to respond, he held up his hand. "For example, I'm quite attracted to you."

The flush on Marian's face deepened and spread downward. She opened her mouth to say something, but bit her lip instead. She looked suddenly like a flustered teenager. She searched the table for support, dwelling on Gina, who was maintaining a guardedly neutral expression. She turned back to her tormentor. "Okay, but that doesn't let you off the hook."

"I know." Max smiled ruefully, presenting a boyish face to match her girlish look. His true blue eyes didn't hurt the act. "But I'm not as simple as you think."

Since we were a dinner party of six and not a candlelit table for two, the conversation at that point took the safe way out. No one is as simple as you think, I put in, and then Susan remembered her cousin Betty, who was far more complex under the surface than you'd imagine—though maybe this wasn't the best example, since Betty eventually became a severe manic depressive and had to be institutionalized. In any event, the moment was defused, and we ended up in the living room, talking about that favorite topic of apartment dwellers, real estate.

Max and Marian were in facing bridge chairs, continuing their gender conversation for a while. At one point, I think they were comparing male and female legs, his placed against hers with their pants hiked up. Hers was plump, pale, and shivery smooth; his was tanned and hardened, with a brutal jut at the calf muscle. Max put out his hand to touch, and their voices sank too low to hear. I lost track at that point: I don't always hear or see what I should. Gina was talking about adding a porch to their house, and Stanley was describing how the workmen should do it. Susan described her dream-house, ante-bellum and out of reach. The evening broke up around ten, and we saw the Pearsons off from our screen door. I expected Max to travel the few steps to his place, but he must have made some discreet arrangement with Marian, because they walked down the hill to her car.

Susan clutched my arm, which she did whenever she felt she had something important to confide. "That was weird, back then."

"Uh-huh." I was wondering what kind of operator Max was. He seemed so forthright, but then, operators always do.

We stood in the doorway, dissipating the cool air from our apartment into the muggy outdoors. We saw Marian open the door for Max: female gallantry? We saw him get in; we saw her circle to the driver's side. Susan put her arm around me, and we held on to each other as Marian and Max sped away in her Camaro, into the humid black night.

3

I saw Max on his brown bomber a few days later pedaling over to Villa Flats, a bouquet of red zinnias carefully strapped on the back with a yellow bungee cord. A lot of new faculty lived in Villa Flats, I knew, and Marian was one of them. That weekend, Marian's red Camaro came over for dinner—next door. Max must have literally cooked up a storm, because an hour later a huge thunderburst blew out all the fuses in our apartment block. I imagined the two of them having dinner by candlelight. I imagined them moving from an inspection of their calves to more intimate parts of their anatomy. As Susan noticed, though, the red Camaro didn't stay there overnight.

But I saw them going to a movie together, which, considering the trash the local Cinema 3 shows, constitutes more a pretext than a cinematic experience. Max and Marian were becoming what in my high-school days we called a hot number. That came as no great surprise, though they certainly weren't an average couple. To begin with, they quarreled loudly and frequently. It usually had something to do with gender, and whose sex it was, anyway. Max had a way of twisting the argument so that perfectly reasonable statements sounded absurd, and vice-versa. In fact, I think one of the reasons Marian stayed with him was the chance to come out on top, if not in debate, then maybe in bed.

The first evidence that Marian was sharing Max's bed came not from protesting bedboards but from a protest in Max's bedroom. It was about three weeks later, and I was working late in my study, re-rewriting a paragraph in an essay about synecdoche and metonymy in Joyce. People mistake parts for wholes, or parts for others parts: this is my view of life. When I write about it in literature, it's called research. Usually, I can write good, scholarly prose when I'm "on," but this afternoon my mind had been elsewhere. Now I was compounding my ineptitude by refusing to call it a day. I wasn't so much shaping the paragraph as bludgeoning it. Susan had wisely retreated to the bedroom with an Ayn Rand novel. I was quietly pleased to see she was reading more, no matter what her choice of texts.

I had just about given up on the essay for the third time in five minutes when I heard the door to the bedroom slam. When you hear that on the other side of a wall, it sounds like a muffled cough. Marian's voice, on the other hand, came through clearly.

"It's a substitute," she announced. "It's an excuse, too, I think."

"Substitute for what? Sex?" Max made some kind of derisive sound, a muted Bronx cheer. "Hell, I thought most women liked men who're in shape."

"I *do*. It's just that—well, why do you have to do it every afternoon?"

I figured they were talking about Max's bicycling, not his masturbation. Parts for other parts. Though Max seemed to be continuing both steadily.

"It's a habit. Don't you have habits?"

"Yes, but not so inflexible."

"Besides, it's good for me. Boosts my cardiovascular system." There was something that sounded like a sigh in reverse, and I realized that Max was sucking in air.

"Hmmm. You know I like your chest."

"I like yours."

"Thanks. But see that? I could stand to lose about ten pounds."

I nodded reflexively at the computer screen. Almost all women think they need to lose ten pounds. Susan had said the same thing to me yesterday. When I reassured her that she looked fine—as Max was now saying to Marian—I got the same answer as I now heard.

"You're just saying that to make me feel better."

"No, not at all." There was a peculiar wall-penetrating fervency to his voice. "But maybe this will make you feel better."

"What is that going to do? You shouldn't. . . . oh. Ohhh."

That last "ohhh" hung in the air like a sob. A few seconds later, it was joined by another, somewhat lower-pitched.

The dialogue got hard to follow at that point. Something about riding, but I don't think the reference was to bicycles. It's hard to read body language through a wall. Besides, I began feeling like a voyeur, or maybe an auditeur. I saved what was on my screen, turned the machine off, and tiptoed from the room. It occurred to me that if I could hear them, the reverse might be true, as well.

Susan was still up, though no longer reading. She looked up expectantly as I came in, as if waiting for a progress report. "Finish?"

"Finish what?"

"Your essay. Isn't that what you were working on?"

I could have mentioned the distractions from next door, but I didn't feel like getting into that right now. So I grunted non-committally and lay down heavily on the bed, the professor returned from his exertions. My back hurt, I let it be known. Scholars are prone to lower-back pain.

Susan kindly offered to give me a massage, and though she never does it hard enough, she has a pleasant touch. I rolled over and she straddled me, keeping most of her weight on her knees. She began around my neck and slowly worked her way down my spine, using her fingers and the heels of her palms.

It felt good. I told her my lower back felt especially stiff, so she reached a little further down. After a minute, I expressed my eternal thanks. Susan nodded and kept it up. Like the bartender listening to the drinker, or the priest giving absolution to the sinner, the masseuse is a confessor figure. After another minute, I let out, "You know . . . *unh* . . . Max and Marian are really hitting it off."

"I know. I saw them in Kroger's the other day." Susan giggled a bit, rocking me, as well. "They were arguing over what to put in the shopping cart. Milk or half and half."

"*Gnnuh.*"

"It looked serious. For a moment, I thought she was going to hit him."

"*Ummmph.* Shows they're ready for married life."

Susan thumped me hard on the side, and I retaliated by arching upwards and toppling her. This wasn't difficult, since she weighed only about 115 pounds. I rolled on top of her, but I didn't press too hard, since I was always a little afraid of hurting her. We usually made love missionary style, but that night I thought of Max and made her ride me, holding onto my arms as she pumped up and down. Afterwards, we lay spoonwise the way young lovers are supposed to, with me snug against the curve of her buttocks. This was the way we had spent our first night together, after a party where I danced with no one but Susan. I had just spent six monastic years doing graduate work at the University of Pennsylvania, worried that life lay elsewhere, and here it was. At some point we quit dancing and started kissing—she said she had to, to stop me from stepping on her feet.

I liked her sense of humor. I always had, though it was beginning to fade. When we started going out, Susan was more fun, the kind of woman who sticks her feet out the car window when it's too hot, the kind of woman who bought me a Moon Pie and stuck a candle in it for my thirty-first birthday. She liked men with brains—actually, she said she liked a man who could think after sex. I liked Susan because she was such a switch from the Ivy League type, a sassy breeze instead of the huffy Northern wind. We just hit it off so well, we decided to get married. That changed things.

Maybe it was becoming a faculty wife that did it. Susan was increasingly restrained, or alternately cute, the two sides of a typical Southern wife. (I can hear Stanley muttering about the size of the sample, but I think it's representative.) Probably I was becoming something, too: reverting to the bookish, myopic type. As in the past, what I read often seemed more engrossing than the life I was leading.

I was about to drift off to sleep when something brought Susan back to the original thread of our conversation. She nudged me. "You know, it wouldn't hurt if Marian lost some weight."

I pinched the nearest piece of Susan, her right arm—no excess flesh there.

"*Ow*! You know what I mean. Around the hips, a little." I said nothing, and she continued her train of thought. "I think that's what they were arguing about in the store, actually. Honey, don't you think I should lose a few pounds?"

"You?" I was feeling tired, so I borrowed a line from *Mister Roger's Neighborhood*. "I like you just the way you are."

"Flatterer." This was said without inflection.

I reached out and placed my hand on her gently rising chest. She laid her arm over mine. I could feel our double pulse, merging into one hematic tide. Slowly, as in some sort of nocturnal osmosis, my body fused with her body and the bed and the blackness of the night, and I slept. Usually, my post-coital images were of Susan and me. That night, I dreamed of Max and Marian in some configuration as yet unknown to me.

When I woke up, it seemed, it was already the end of summer. Or at least the beginning of the semester, which amounts to the same thing. It was something almost palpable in the air; I could feel it as I shaved in the bathroom that morning, scything the white foam from my cheeks. Susan had bought me a straight razor last year, so I had learned how to use it. The problem was that I could never look too long at myself in the mirror: my bland features and receding chin, my mouse-brown hair thinning on top. Susan says I have a kind face, but I harbor a secret desire to look sharp, a fantasy fulfilled only when I'm preparing for class and think of myself as The Professor. I'd missed that during the slackness of summer.

That Saturday morning cars were parked along the hill. Improvised clothes racks hung from the back seats, dragging sweaters and blouses and dresses, and I knew the sorority girls had returned. In the afternoon, I heard Beta Gamma's new song-rhyme to *Gamma*, "Oh, how happy I am a," heralding the advent of fall rush. The songs are invariably accompanied by synchronized dancing on the sorority lawns, looking like mass-calisthenics. Since the Northgate Apartments are just across the street from Sorority Row, the spectacle is hard to miss. It would be sexier if the display weren't so drill-like, but it's still exciting to see forty or more late adolescent girls baring their midriffs in an arm-stretching cheer. Members of the young nubility. A few times I saw Max out on the porch, staring unabashedly.

Picking up my mail at the Student Union, I ran into a horde of tanned blonds and blondes, including a former student of mine who recognized me before I recognized him. The only seemly thing to do in those circumstances, which happen all the time to someone who teaches upwards of ninety students a semester, is grope. I left the Union still not knowing his name, though I remembered why he remembered me: he was the one in my introlit class who began every essay, "This is just my opinion," which in my opinion merited a C+.

An academic always feels ambivalent about returning students: on the one hand, they're the purpose of the university; on the other hand, they can take up all your time and energy. This, of course, is fatal at a research institution, where publish-or-perish is the eleventh commandment. Still, I can't see entering academia if you just like scribbling. So during the school year, most pre-tenure academics perform a balancing act that would put any trapeze artist to shame: teaching preparation, committee meetings, independent research, classroom time, grading, office hours—all somehow worked in and around your family and leisure time, though usually it's your family and free time that get worked in at random moments. I envied Max his blocks of freedom, and maybe a few other things.

The unsettling aspect of all this work is that, apart from classroom teaching, there's no particular schedule to it. And teaching is just the visible tip. The submerged iceberg of class preparation, for instance, can take hours and hours, but you cut it up any way you want. If you want to go to five movies in five nights, you can—as long as you realize that you're headed for The Lost Weekend. One faculty member in our department, a night-owl named Greg Pinelli, regularly woke up around noon, taught his class at two in the afternoon, and got down to his paperwork around midnight. He was a bachelor with a bachelor's habits, which included cooking a lot of Italian dishes with garlic. The departmental secretary, Mrs. Post, looked down on him as a non-Episcopalian and a sybarite, but he rarely saw her on his schedule. He had a key to the department office so he could pick up his mail at lunchtime, which for him was around seven p.m. His only fear was the threat of a morning class.

At first I thought Max was that type, but I soon realized the error of my presuppositions. From my own experience, I know that living alone can render you soft and petulant, or else turn you rock-hard and disciplined. It really depends on which part of you takes over in isolation: your id or your super ego. I tend to waver. My first year here, living alone in an apartment a mile away from campus, I found myself getting up later, going out to eat half the time, and cleaning up only when absolutely necessary. When I started going out with Susan, even she was properly appalled. "The Northern barbarian," she called me, and insisted on scouring the kitchen sink when I had her over for dinner. I tend to be guided by outside regulation, and I soon reformed. The rest was marital.

Not so with Max. I couldn't actually tell you what he did all the time, but he was always engaged in some activity. I know he got up around six and listened to the radio. I know because I started having early-morning dreams that incorporated the NPR *Morning Edition* theme-song. I also know he spent a lot of time in front of his word processor, framed by his front window. The window was in the opposite direction from my route to school, which meant I had to have a reason to be going that way. Once or twice, I feigned nonchalance and just glanced in: it looked as if Max were having a staring contest with his computer screen. His usually excellent posture bent as he bit his lip so hard it turned white. Sometimes he would type rapidly for twenty or so seconds. Then—this was my third peek—he saw me and waved, and I felt like an intrusive fool. I never did find out whether he was putting together lectures, writing letters to friends, or composing some dark opus of his own. Usually around mid-morning, he would go off somewhere on his truck bike, but he'd be back by lunch, which he ate at home. Of course, there was the invariant afternoon ride, and cooking dinner. I don't know how he structured his evenings—it occurs to me that I don't know what most people do with their evenings.

The point I'm trying to convey is that Max was constantly active, and always with a goal. If you saw him walking or riding, he always had a coming or going look. During the long hot summer, when the high point of the day was picking up my departmental mail, Max seemed to function on some internal schedule. Of course, all academics do, or we'd never get any work done. After all, no one is saying, "You *must* write that essay on Joyce," or "Okay, time to hit the library!" No one except an internal voice that snidely implies we've been slacking off, or which brightly suggests one more footnote for the road. Still, given that we all have to toe some invisible line, some are quicker off their marks— I think I've hopelessly garbled the metaphor here. To return to my basic point: all academics are moved by a combination of egotism and impending despair. Max just seemed more so. He outclassed even the people I knew in New York, land of the driven.

I thought about all this in mid-August as the department office changed from a ghost-store with one customer a day to a thriving concern with the phone ringing off the hook and Mrs. Post fielding messages with one hand and typing memos with the other. Mrs. Post is a respectable woman in her fifties who used to work for the army, and she occasionally wonders out loud why she ever quit the service. I think one of the things she longs for is a chain of command, but all we're able to provide in that area is a work-study student to help out with photocopying and mail-distribution. This year's edition was named Travis Peterson, a tow-headed guy in an olive-drab T-shirt he rarely changed. He had sloping shoulders and a sloping forehead. Travis would do things like copy your manuscript with one blank page, or deliver your mail to the adjoining box. His favorite activities were eavesdropping on faculty conversations and getting in people's way. We were trying to get him transferred, but in the meantime it looked like another semester with Travis.

Soon I began getting notices in my mailbox (or the adjoining one) about upcoming committee meetings and high administrative nonsense. At home on the word processor, I put the finishing touches on my syllabi for the three courses I was to teach: one graduate-level class in British Modernism and two sections of Introlit (English 200, required for all liberal arts majors). Forty impressionable minds contemplating Shakespeare, as the professor runs once more unto the breach. The Modernism seminar was both easier and harder: it had a cap of fifteen students, but the approach to the material was far more abstruse.

As junior faculty in the history department, Max had the same workload, three courses a semester, though not the same boss. Which was a pity, since our department head, I say without fear or favor, was a shrewd, humorous native New Jerseyan named Ed Schamley. An ex-newspaperman who had worked for six years at the *Miami Herald* before turning to academia, he wore a bright red bow tie to all faculty meetings to underscore the clownlike nature of the enterprise, and he had a healthy dislike of the establishment. A few of the veteran faculty members, the ante-bellum crowd, were annoyed that a Yankee was at the helm, but it saved us from a lot of what Marian would have called gentility.

The head of the history department, unfortunately, all but wore a white suit and a string tie. Henry Clay Spofford III, specialist in Southern history and religion, was the kind of chairman who would have ridden a white horse to work if allowed. He spoke with what I would swear was an exaggerated drawl, though I could never prove it. His wife Emma prized gossip above gold, most of it picked up or dispensed at the same volunteer group to which Susan belonged, the Ladies' Auxiliary of Oxford. I kept urging Susan to switch to some other organization. At the moment, they had her reading to prisoners. In an attempt to make me feel guilty, she said this was her substitute for having children. "Not now" was my usual response to that.

As to why Max had accepted a job with us, at first I assumed he was lucky. Ever since the Seventies, the job market in the humanities has been as small as any simile you can come up with. To give you some idea of the odds: a year after I was installed, Schamley casually let me know how many applicants there had been for my job. *Two hundred.* And that's at Ole Miss, which, though by no means a bad school, is no Stanford or Yale. Faculty who haven't been on a hiring committee in years don't really appreciate the situation, don't know what the hell's going on. Stanley Pearson, for instance, asked Max the inevitable question that night at dinner: "So, why did you pick Ole Miss?" At the time, I thought Stanley should have known better. Only later did I realize what a shrewd question it was.

Max replied without batting an eye. "Because that's where I got a job." Which may sound like modesty, but was really a clever put-off. Max's specialty was modern British history, coincidentally the same as my field in literature. But his publishing record showed no such thing; rather, it ran the gamut from Augustan politics to Jacksonian democracy. This was peculiar not just because everyone specializes nowadays, but also because it's unusual for graduate students to publish much at all. He'd also written fiction—or so he told me once, and then never referred to it again. About his work, he was either matter-of-fact—when I asked about it, he simply produced his curriculum vitae—or somewhat self-deprecating—he waved away his publications as too scattered; he really had to focus more; he had just gotten a break in a few cases. I couldn't quite decide whether this was false modesty or the genuine articles. I did look up one or two, and they checked out, but I found myself wishing I knew someone in the history department at Columbia. You know how it is: you get interested enough in a person, and you want to know not only what he's like, but also what he used to be like.

In the days during registration, we met from time to time in the hallways. I kept feeding him information about the university, such as how to get a faculty parking sticker (and then I realized he had no car) and how to order books for his classes (he'd already done this from the large, inefficient university store, but for next time I told him to use the excellent bookstore in town). I was going to tell him to hang out at one of the local bars, Ted & Larry's, if he wanted to meet women, but he already had Marian. I asked him, cautiously, how that was going.

"How's what going?" False modesty, or the genuine article?

There's a certain type who would have nudged him in the ribs, or given him a huge, dirty wink. I'm not the type. But I was curious. "I thought you were seeing Marian Hardwick."

"Oh, that." He chuckled a bit, and I realized I was seeing a new side of Max, one that chuckled. "She can be fun to be with. She can also be a real pain in the ass."

"Really?" A prompter I sometimes use in class.

"Yeah. Sometimes I think she actually tries to provoke me, just to see where it'll lead."

"Really?"

"Mmm . . . other times she goes all meek." He looked away, slightly guilty. "It's the provocation I like, actually. There's something about a dominant woman, and Marian—" he cut himself short. "Anyway, we'll see. So what are you teaching this semester?"

I told him. I think he genuinely appreciated hearing details of this sort, especially when he could pick up something new. I know he used a few remarks of mine about teaching poetry, but that was a while later, and under the circumstances I almost felt like an accomplice for reasons that will become self-evident if I'm telling this right.

When I finished my course descriptions, I asked him the same question. He was due to teach a graduate seminar in England before the Great War, along with two sections of "Europe from the Decline of the Roman Empire to 1648." If it's Tuesday, this must be the sack of Constantinople. I told him to expect only half his class the first week, since Ole Miss schedules its first classes before Labor Day weekend.

"We'll see. I take attendance in my class, you know."

"Oh, you have to around here. I call it a learning device." And since I didn't see any way to steer the conversation back to Marian, we talked a bit more about pedagogical tricks. We soon separated, me for the elevator up to the departmental copying machine and he for the stairs. I should have known that Max wasn't an elevator type. Before the elevator door closed, I saw those strong legs start up the staircase: two steps at a time, quick march. I knew he was going to beat me to the top.

4

The next scene is of Max dressed immaculately in a gray linen jacket, silk paisley tie, and pressed khaki trousers—clipped at the cuffs, so as not to get tangled in the chain as he bicycled to school on his first day of teaching. I waved back when he waved to me, at first wondering who the hell it was. I'd never seen Max in anything dressier than a short-sleeve shirt and slacks. The brown bomber bike made it doubly incongruous, but then, that was Max. I watched his trousered legs pumping furiously down the hill as he swooped past Crosby Hall, a women's dormitory. There were two women at the crosswalk, but he swerved rather than slowing down and rode right between four legs.

So Max was off to make his mark. My own first class of the semester was at one in the afternoon, though I had already passed my period of apprehension. Like most other people who perform, I get nervous at the approach of opening night, but I also have a shut-off time beyond which I stop fidgeting. I had fussed the previous few days, revising my introductory address five different ways. I envisioned all the perilous scenarios—lecture notes left at home, no chalk, a rip in my trousers—and then I simply resigned myself to whatever would happen. Actually, I was more curious as to how Max would fare.

I didn't see him around when I got to Bishop Hall at a quarter to one. I walked into the men's room, checked myself (I once taught an entire class with my fly wide open), and took the stairs down to my assigned classroom, where I could already see students milling around. The year before they'd all looked as if they were about fifteen years old, and this year, so help me, they looked about fourteen. It was still summer as far as they were concerned, and I saw a lot of shorts and tank tops. Bodies of all shapes and sizes, from pallid, bespectacled ectomorphs to sprawling giants deprived only of foreheads. Fresh-faced, clean-limbed—and here I was, about to inflict knowledge on them. This is not entirely metaphor: English 200 is a required course that drags in everyone from business majors to football players. My graduate seminar, a far more rarefied group, wouldn't meet until next week.

I walked to the lectern and dumped my bag at its foot. Then I bent down to rummage for my attendance sheet, notes, and text. It helps to let the class know the teacher can bend. When I straightened up, I smiled at the class, and recalled one reason why I like teaching in the South: the students smile back. They may not mean it, but there's a lot to be said for politeness, even if you define politeness as a civilized lie. Or gentility.

I don't hold to the practice that nothing gets done the first day. I took attendance, handed out syllabi and course requirements, and gave an introduction to the course. Since the word *literature* is enough to induce either panic or yawns in students, I always ask them for a definition of the word. And I call on people, which may be slightly scary at first, but it beats the tedium of a lecture.

I asked a baked blonde in a striped Zeta Tau Alpha T-shirt. She placed a red-nailed hand on her chest. "Me?" I nodded sympathetically. No safety in numbers. She screwed up her pretty face. "Gee, I don't know . . . poetry?"

"Could be," I murmured, and wrote that on the board, under block capitals spelling out LITERATURE. Next was an "Ed the gas station attendant" clone, who allowed that plays might also be included.

"How about movies?" I shot back.

"Naw."

"*Some* are," protested a girl in the front row, with glasses so heavy they looked as if they were amputating her nose. And then someone in the back weighed in with the inevitable, "Dull stuff by dead people that we gotta read," and we were off and running. Fairy tales, maybe, but not the filler on the back of some cereal boxes. How about if Shakespeare wrote a sonnet for Cheerios? We discussed the matter for a good ten minutes and finally decided that literature covered a lot of ground. Then, just as they were getting restless, I gave them something to read. Yesterday, I had made forty copies of Kate Chopin's "The Story of an Hour," which has two crucial literary attributes: it's only two and a half pages long, and it's in the assigned anthology. Since most hadn't bought the book yet, I passed out these copies and sat back to let them go through it.

I noted a lot of silently moving lips. Mississippi does not have an enviable literacy rate, and while all the students I've known here have been able to read, this literature stuff is a bitch. Then we talked about the story, which has a neat twist-ending to make it fun and a feminist message to make it subversive for most of the class. Since I had no names associated with faces on the first day, I just pointed. Near the end of the class, I asked a broad, barnlike individual who clearly hadn't been called on in years. I took note of his name: Tom Fallon. Tom looked half-embarrassed and half-flattered, and I resolved to keep trying.

One conclusion I've come to in the South is that, if anatomy isn't destiny here, it sure comes close. I mean, sadly enough, that if a girl is cuddly cute, she usually hasn't got too much upstairs, and when I see a bespectacled runt scratching his bad complexion, I know he'll probably be an honors candidate.

The ones I feel sorriest for are the plain girls: the under-endowed ones with stringy hair and sallow cheeks, or the pear-shaped ones whose bottoms dwarf their desk-chairs. Considering how much of Mississippi life resembles a combination beauty contest and political rally, appearances count for a lot. I noticed one particularly plump girl in the fifth row, her upper arms emerging broad, pink, and spongy from her tent of a T-shirt. She looked like an island unto herself, and when the class was over, she girded her heavy loins, picked up her books, and left without speaking to anyone. Her flesh seemed to move of its own powerful volition. I stood by the doorway, the host seeing off the last of his guests, and as she trudged by the stairwell, I saw Max emerge and glance at her. I waved.

"So? How'd it go?"

Max didn't hear me at first. He had stopped to jot down a note to himself, looking up only as the girl passed, slow as a barge. I waited till he had finished scribbling, then repeated my question.

"What? Oh, you mean the class." He shrugged. "Fine, I think. I mean, they didn't lob spitballs at me, and they didn't fall asleep."

"The novelty effect. Give 'em time."

"I give them more than time. I give them history. From 1648 to 1945, to be precise." He paused and pushed back the bridge of his nose, as if he had to shore it up occasionally. He did this an average of three or four times per conversation. "I have to keep them interested. Any way I can."

Since this is my own attitude, I nodded encouragingly. We were both headed out the door, so we turned a hall talk into an open-air discussion. "It's like acting," I suggested.

"Exactly." He made a histrionic gesture, a flourish with his cuff. "Except that actors give the same performance to different audiences every day, while we give different performances to the same audience every day."

This sounded good enough to be canned, but I didn't ask whether it was original. Instead, I filed it away to use on Susan that night. It was 2:20, the gap between classes, and students were milling about us in a sort of Brownian motion. Max seemed fascinated by all the bodies, letting his eyes rove even in the middle of our conversation. Some people might call that rude, but he did it in such a way, kid with nose pressed against candy store window, that you couldn't really feel annoyed. Here was someone, you felt, who—who what, exactly? Who had a thing about bodies? Which in particular was he looking at, anyway?

Just then, Marian showed up, smiling tightly. She was dressed for teaching, which for her meant a blue pleated skirt and a white blouse. Max's eyes darted back to the body beside him, and he pretended to survey her from top to bottom. He ended up crouching by her black pumps, feeling the leather and nodding approvingly.

"Oh, *stop*." Marian kicked like a startled mare. She had big strong calves, I noticed. They were alabaster, unconstrained by stockings. That's where Max's hands were when she cried, "Shoo!"

Max got up and bowed to her gallantly. "If madame will insist on maddening men's hearts. . . ."

This clearly annoyed her, but it also made her blush. In fact, it turned her face into a near-relative of the tomato family. Max took advantage of this temporary weakness to steer her forth by one Junoesque elbow in the direction of the exit doors. She seemed to be putting on weight, despite Max's assurances.

"C'mon, I'll walk you to your class. You can introduce me to your students as your unknown admirer." I couldn't tell Marian's expression from the back, but at least this time she didn't shake him off. Instead, Max was the one who wheeled around—his head, at any rate—and somehow mimed "sorry, resume conversation later." I mimed my acceptance (I nodded) and watched as they walked out of Bishop Hall together. When they reached the doorway, Max did not gallantly drop back. He pressed against her to make them the right width, cleaving right into her side, and they squeezed through together. The students had mostly dispersed, and when the door shut behind the toothsome twosome, I realized I was alone in the hall.

I saw Max fairly regularly the first month of the semester, which meant I also saw a lot of Marian, though it didn't always look as if the two of them were a couple, especially when they were together. Women with both strong views and strong calves don't really like being tickled in either area, and Max was no great respecter of persons or politics. They also argued constantly, about everything from the art of history (Max was usually right) to the history of art (Max was usually correct here, too, especially when it came to dates, and this annoyed Marian no end). They also contradicted each other on catfish and barbecue, two semi-sacred subjects in Mississippi. Lately, they had been arguing about their arguments, usually a sign of a degenerating relationship.

Some of this I gathered from Max, and some of this from Marian through Susan, who for some reason had become a semi-confidante. Max was fabulously irritating, Susan heard, but also sexy as hell. He was a frotteur who could also rub you the wrong way. In short, Max was provocative. You could see it in his eyes, which were always alert, occasionally kind, and usually roving. In crowds, this usually meant he was girl-watching.

Marian, for her part, was basically monogamous, and when she couldn't command his whole attention—for instance, when she was speaking to him—she grew understandably annoyed. I don't know what their private life was like, but somehow I got the impression that it fed on excess and abrasion. In any event, the night noises penetrating my study wall had become unpredictable, often indecipherable. I heard occasional slaps and odd, muffled intakes of breath. Also twangs of some sort, like the plucking of giant rubber bands. The creaks continued, but sometimes in a higher register.

You can get awfully tired of extrapolation without confirmation. Whenever I looked in that direction, all I saw was a Currier & Ives print of a sleigh, a gift from Susan last Christmas, hanging on the wall next to my overloaded bookshelf. I might have rigged up some sophisticated surveillance equipment if I'd had the knowledge. As it was, I had no access. Max's bedroom had only one window in back, with the shade always drawn all the way down. I couldn't see a damn thing.

That's not strictly true, I should add. Once—just once—I happened to be taking down some wash from the clothesline—no, that's not true, either. Susan always did that. All right: once when I happened to be wandering in the backyard, the shade flew up all the way, like an eye flickering open. And into that gaze stepped Marian, completely nude. She was full-thighed, with a luxuriant fleece. Also plump-breasted, with that delicate ivory hue that's even sexier than a tan because it spells concealment. The long brown hair cascading down her shoulders made her look like a Botticelli, except that her nipples were erect—shivery pink—and the Old Masters weren't quite that explicit.

She stood there for a moment, too dazzled by the sun, I think, to see the corner of me framing her view. Her face was flushed—post-coital afterglow, I figured. Max's arm soon snaked up to pull the shade, at an odd angle as if he were confined to bed. But when I got to my study a minute later, the sounds were louder than ever. So there was more going on than met the eye, or my eye, anyway. Call me myopic.

But I remained curious. Not just about the sex, though I realize that's how it comes across. Anyway, finally, I just decided to ask him.

Well, no. Not about those sounds. But one Tuesday afternoon, when he was pedaling back from one of his rides, I asked him how it was going with Marian. He coasted to a stop, but kept upright for a few seconds longer by shifting his balance—jockeying, I think it's called. His jersey was patched with sweat, his face was red, and his eyes were rimed with salt. September in Mississippi still has a few scorchers, and that day it was above ninety. My question about the relationship couldn't have chilled the temperature much.

"Okay, I guess." At which point, he lost his balance and had to jerk his foot out of the toe-clip before he fell over. "I mean," he temporized when he had both feet on the ground, "it has its ups and downs."

"You mean sexual or psychological?"

"Is there a third option?"

"Are you evading the question?"

"No, it's both of those, I guess, but not the way you think."

"How do you know what I think?"

"Well, I don't think the way you do."

"How do you know?"

"Because you married Susan, that's why." And he looked away. It was then that I saw how exhausted he was: his usually taut body was slumped at the angle of least resistance, and he wasn't even bothering to gesture. Or hold back things he might have otherwise.

"What about my wife?" I heard myself say, imitating every redneck within a radius of three states.

"Nothing, it's just—look, I have different tastes, let's just leave it at that. It has nothing to do with Susan. But it's a little hard to explain."

"I think you like arguing with Marian."

"Maybe. Maybe that's part of it, anyway. Look, I've got to get indoors—I'm dripping all over the place." He kicked open his apartment door, which he hadn't bothered to lock, and half-wheeled, half-walked himself inside. What about my wife? I wondered. The screen door, with its over-tight spring, shut with a bang.

"Because he's too touchy-feely, that's why," said Susan. We were having yesterday's dinner of pork chops and potatoes refried with onions and broccoli. It was actually better the second time around, which made it the culinary upset of the week, like the rare sequel that's better than the first book. Susan's cooking was excellent and abundant: no Barmecides at the Shapiro family table. It was such a change from my bachelor half-meals and sandwiches that as a newlywed I had gained twelve pounds before I realized what was happening. I was trying to cut back these days, but I found it difficult, especially with such seductive dishes. Susan kept thin, I think, by sheer force of will.

My prandial question brought out what Marian had told her, a lot more than what Max had let me know. Or at least more intimate, though Susan was probably withholding, too. Sometimes I think all women belong to a vast international union. You can marry into it, but you'll never have the privileges of a member.

I swallowed a last mouthful of potato. "Touchy-feely how? What parts?"

"That's another point. Not what you'd expect. He kisses her behind a lot, and sometimes he fondles her belly."

"And?"

"Well, he likes to go down on her a lot."

Nestling between those plump white thighs. Susan was looking at me, so I raised my eyebrows in mock astonishment. "No glove fetishes, no toe-sucking?"

"Yuk. I don't think so." She pushed her plate aside. "But here's something: he asked about her make-up. She thought that was strange."

"Asked about it how?"

"Oh, what kind of foundation she used, and how she applied eye-liner, that kind of thing."

"He was probably just curious." I could see Max adding to his store of arcana. "Would you show me how you do yours?"

"No."

"Why not?"

"Because. You ruin the illusion that way."

I'm married to you, for Christ's sake, is what I first thought of saying, but marriage is full of second thoughts. "C'mon—please?"

"Hmm. Maybe." She cleared the dishes waitress-style, stacking everything and marching over to the sink. She let the tap run for a while because our hot-water generator needs all the time it can get. Meanwhile the air conditioner hummed, and Susan hummed along with the air conditioner. I eased my waistband, pleasantly stuffed. With the evening light haloing the kitchen window, I suddenly saw my wife from behind in an attitude of love. These are the moments in a marriage when the sweetness returns, when you can adore the loved one because he or she is unconscious of you.

Sex reared its callipygian cheeks. As Susan bent over to start scouring, the rear of her jeans grew taut, outlining the sweet cleft between her buttocks. I thought briefly of planting a kiss on either side. I thought of wrapping my arms around her waist and rocking gently, moving slowly downward. Nuzzle her, rub my head against her thighs. But a minute passed, and I was still at the table. I'm not sure why I made no move. Inertia after a big meal, maybe, along with that slightly pregnant feeling. Or all the time it would take, from the first caress to the hand-in-hand walk to the bedroom. Or the image of Max preceding me, his arms groping fleshwards, a rapt expression on his hawklike features.

5

I soon had a chance to observe Max's relationship with Marian up close, at one of Vernon Knowles' get-togethers two Sundays later. The sheer tedium of Vernon's little gatherings may have precipitated matters—instant catatonia, as Ed Schamley once termed it, which may be why he wasn't on the guest-list any longer. Of course, to understand the boredom behind Vernon's Sunday afternoons, you had to understand something about Vernon, though I'm not sure that to understand all is to forgive all in this case.

Professor Vernon Knowles, emeritus, was a former member of our esteemed English department, from the days when an English professor was expected to be a cultured gentleman—there's your gentility again. He wore the emeritus label like a badge of honor, despite Ed Schamley's joke that *emeritus* in Vernon's case meant "without merit." Vernon had an appallingly large fund of eighteenth-century literary anecdotes with which he used to bore his classes: what Boswell said to Johnson, what Johnson replied, and so forth. Near the end of his tenure, he got kicked upstairs to administration, at which point he became a dean who told literary anecdotes. His deadliest quality was his habit of lecturing, developed over years at the front of a classroom. He didn't talk; he

pontificated, which is fine for a cathedral but ludicrous for a supermarket, or wherever you happened to meet him. His wife Iris
wisely became a lush some years ago.

It was touching, in a way: now that he was emeritus, he had no
one to lecture to. He started his Sunday afternoons several years
ago to recapture his audience. Over Bloody Marys and some crackers and cheese that Iris called canopies, a quorum of seven or so
guests listened to Southern neoclassical wit. When Vernon really
got going, he misquoted Pope's couplets. A sort of enforced dreari-
ness hung over the entire afternoon like a heavy, damp curtain;
you could slowly feel yourself smothered. As T.S. Eliot once said
of Lady Rothermere's garden parties, they're interesting "if you
concentrate on the essential horror of the thing."

Actually, it wasn't that easy to become a member of the Knowles
coterie. You had to be a good listener, also well-versed in the
weather and other staples of Southern conversation. A smattering
of eighteenth-century lore came in useful, though expertise was
unwise. Our current eighteenth-century specialist, a thorough type
named Elaine Dobson, corrected a reference to Swift and had to
listen to three smutty limericks as Vernon reasserted himself.

It also helped to have some affiliation with Ole Miss, since
Vernon had amassed myriad stories about old faculty members,
obscure, eccentric, and usually deceased. There was the one who
kept a horse in his boardinghouse, for instance, and the man who
went through three wives in one semester. Oddly, Vernon's off-
color stories were the most colorless I know, though some women
were offended by what Gina referred to as a verbal pinch on the
buttocks. Elaine went further, telling Gina (who told me), "When
he tells those jokes, I always feel as if he's masturbating in front
of me."

Given all this, why in God's name did we still go over there?
Susan insisted. She pitied him, or so she said. I privately thought
she enjoyed the social occasion: the genteel part of her showing its
rouged face. For all her lack of pretension, something in her wanted
the chance to wear a pretty dress (which Vernon would unfailingly
compliment her on), sip a watered-down drink, mingle with other
faculty wives, and munch on canopies. Maybe it took the place of
church—I'm a devout atheist, and Susan was a lapsed Presbyterian,
but people do backslide the other way.

So at around two o'clock, we got in the car and took a short
drive to the Knowles residence. Susan was wearing a peasant blouse

and dirndl that didn't quite gather the way it should, since Susan wasn't a peasant. She was fine-boned and trim. I know she had on light foundation with extra blusher because she'd let me watch her. Also eye-liner, mascara, and mauve lipstick: she explained it all, step by step. Thanks to Max's idea. It's amazing what women will put on their faces. At least it wasn't the formal make-up job I saw on Oxford ladies like Emma Spofford, with so many layers it looked like Troy before Schliemann decided to dig. My only concession in that direction was Brut after-shave, a gift from Susan. I wore the standard academic-at-leisure outfit, a shapeless jacket and a sports shirt. On Susan's lap was a tin box of pecan brownies, in return for the imminent hospitality.

Like most people in Oxford, the Knowleses lived in a ranch-style house, complete with its half-acre of manicured lawn. Parked in the driveway was Marian's red Camaro, its round double rear lights like bull's-eyes. Susan arched her eyebrows at me.

"Fresh blood," I shrugged. "Maybe Vernon needs a new infusion." It's true, our group got more interested in new faculty than the history department did, probably because they weren't history yet.

When we rang the bell, Vernon appeared at the door, imitating the literary creation known as The Genial Host. He was wearing a maroon smoking jacket with patched elbows, his middle buttoned down by a tartan vest. A few strands of gray hair were grown long and combed over the shell-pink scalp in a physical token of insincerity.

"Well, well, well! And who have we here!" he exclaimed, making me feel like a neighbor's child on Halloween. He pumped my hand and told me Susan was looking beautiful, as usual. She curtsied ever so slightly, I saw—I would argue with her about this later. We were led through an expansive gesture into the grand stuffiness of the living room, where dullness reigned upon a paunchy blue armchair. Iris was already seated in state, holding her drink as in a trance. Her face, I noted, was made up in the Trojan mold. She nodded vaguely at us as we entered.

I looked around the room, which held the familiar nondescript sofa and chairs—seating appurtenances, Vernon once called them—all subtly angled to point toward the armchair. Behind the throne were the crown jewels: an open latticework of a room-divider, all its levels crammed with souvenir ashtrays from county fairs, crystal snowflake paperweights, ornamental vases posing as Delft, framed photographs of men and women in old-style hats and coats, faded seashells, and brass figurines of obscure meaning. The weak light from behind the curtains did a poor job of illumination, but I'd had more than an ample opportunity to examine the array of bric-a-brac. Beyond the treasure-wall was the dining area, beyond that was a dingy kitchen, and beyond that the well-kept backyard beyond which lay all of northern Mississippi. I wondered how many other houses were hosting Sunday afternoons in the parlor, in this genteel time-warp of a state.

Susan had already begun greeting the assemblage: all known quantities, which is the price you pay for living in a small town. Sloping down in the high-backed chair was Benjamin Dalrymple, a courteous old ditherer who had served his time—also in our department, I'm afraid—and whose personality was slowly eroding like Delta soil. There was some story about him, that he had once been married to the former department chair's second wife, everyone involved either now retired or moribund. Dalrymple twitched a muscle in his right hand as greeting, and I waved back.

At the far corner of the room were Franklin and Jane Forster, separated by a distance of about twenty-five years. As his former student, she had settled into a cross between an acolyte, a wife, and an imitation of Franklin. Just then, for instance, she was literally seated at his feet. I also noticed Greg Pinelli there, too polite to decline an invitation even to a mausoleum opening. He was gamely trying to lead Dalrymple into the semblance of a conversation. Dalrymple looked puzzled that anyone should attempt such a thing.

But the centerpiece was formed by Max and Marian, squashed together in the orange loveseat that obliquely faced the throne. Maybe it was just the tan leanness of Max's frame, but Marian looked quite broad by comparison, her wide hips dwarfing his, her round white arms ending in a nest of fingers in her lap. Max's ropy forearms glowed bronze from bike-riding, though the color looked rubbed off at the wrists and elbows, as if someone had been chafing him. It wasn't immediately apparent, but you could see it whenever he reached for his drink. Marian acted both happy and nervous, a combination that Max seemed to inspire.

We were granted seats near the treasure-wall, and Vernon went for the pitcher of Bloody Marys. I waited for the usual joke—that a Bloody Mary without vodka was a Bloody Shame—and didn't have to wait long. It was delivered with the drinks. The canopies were passed. I struck up a conversation with Jane Forster, who soon deferred to her husband. Susan talked with Marian. Vernon sat back in his armchair and waited for an opportunity. I couldn't exactly hear what Greg was saying to Dalrymple, but I did catch a reference to the university library. He was still trying politely to draw out Dalrymple, who years ago had been instrumental in creating or changing or abolishing something at the library. Poor, accommodating Greg, well-intentioned—and doomed. I heard Vernon cough in a gentlemanly clearing of phlegm.

"The, ah, bibliographical matters of which you speak . . . I wonder if you're aware . . . this was some time ago, of course, but when Sutton was in charge of acquisition. . . ."

Dalrymple shifted his lower lip in recognition of a fallen colleague.

"Naturally, Sutton, who had a degree in biology, tended to favor requests from the sciences. I remember once trying to order a book on Sterne, only to receive, ah, a stern memo in return: 'What has this to do with scientific progress?'" Vernon patted the upholstered arm of his chair, warming to his subject. Max whipped out his wad of paper to take a note. In another moment, the pen and paper were retracted. There was a clink of ice as Iris raised her drink. "We seemed to have reached an impasse. However, I still wanted the book. So I prepared a memo of my own. . . ."

"You know, I had the same problem last week." Max separated himself ever so slightly from Marian as he spoke out. "Just who *is* in charge of acquisitions these days?"

"I really couldn't tell you," Vernon began testily.

"Bramwell," supplied Greg helpfully. "He's the one who always wears a brown suit."

"Is that who that is? He always gives me the creeps." This, from Jane in the corner, with an exaggerated shudder so that Franklin placed his fatherly hands on her shoulders. Greg, never one for character assassination, attempted to exonerate Bramwell, pointing out how complicated the process of acquisition could be. Max wanted to know more about the procedure, specifically as it concerned the book he'd requested, while Vernon dourly surveyed his deserters. He finally decided to fetch himself another drink. Iris rattled her glass as he passed, her signal that she was ready for another refill.

By the time Vernon got back, the subject had shifted to the topic that every faculty member has an opinion on: students. Franklin, stroking his thicket of a beard fiercely, was of the opinion that today's students were too rich.

"And the sororities," Jane chimed in. "The displays some of them put on! The dances, the dresses—"

"To lose her heart, or her necklace at the ball," Vernon quoted not quite relevantly, or accurately. "She stained her honor, or her new brocade." He cleared his throat. "You know, we had a co-ed here some years ago who—ahem—lost a good deal more than that. Peculiar story—peculiar girl, in fact—"

"That Pope quotation—syllepsis, isn't it?" The brightest student in the class, Max Finster, had his hand up again. The striped polo shirt he was wearing emphasized both his youth and those wiry arms.

"What?" The words "young man" hung in the air unspoken. Vernon was turning a lovely shade of carmine.

"The rhetorical device he's using—you know, heart and necklace, honor and brocade—abstract and concrete. It's syllepsis, isn't it—something with *syll* in it." He appealed to the rest of the group. I couldn't tell whether he knew the effect he was having on Vernon.

The word Max was looking for was indeed *syllepsis* (unless he was just looking to interrupt), and Greg corroborated it a second later, earning an undeserved dirty look from Vernon. Franklin pedagogically pointed out that it was really a subset of zeugma, thus earning an adoring look from Jane. Once again the podium had been wrested away from the armchair. To put it in syllepsis: Vernon sank back in his chair, along with his hopes for the conversation.

And that's the way the afternoon went. Every time Vernon began to discourse, Max would contrive some interruption to bring the lecture to a halt. Once it was the name of a Pope scholar Vernon didn't know; another time it was a reference to some vase in the treasure-wall. By the third or fourth instance, I realized that it was deliberate—I think even Iris eventually noticed that something was up. But what was he trying to accomplish? It was almost savage. As Vernon sank lower and lower into his armchair, I began feeling a bit sorry for the old windbag. After all, we were his invited guests.

As for the couple on the sofa, at first they shared the same face: the agreeable afternoon guest, innocently bland. But as Max's interruptions grew in scope and number, his blandness became a more and more obvious front, a forced cheeriness held in place by strong facial muscles. In contrast, Marian's whole demeanor was shifting toward anxiety. At first, the edginess showed itself physically. As Max built himself into a nuisance, she inched away from him, hitching up her broad navy skirt. Eventually, she had dissociated herself from him by over a foot of orange upholstery. But then, as Max showed no intention of stopping, her discomfort turned to irritation. Once or twice, she tried to intervene for Vernon, but had the same perverse results as poor Greg. When Max pretended unawareness, Marian's full lips compressed to a hard line. I saw her hand waver—if she were his mother, she would have given him a smack. I know that urge: to shut someone up by any means possible. I learned only later that they had come to the Knowleses' directly after a Sunday morning squabble.

By the time Max was asking rhetorically, "What *is* accuracy in biography, anyway?" Marian had shifted her leg next to his and gave him a fleshy nudge. He smiled at her and placed a hand on her thigh. She couldn't very well swat his hand away in front of all the others, so she gave him another nudge.

His hand crept deeper.

Marian bit her lip and put out an arm to steady herself. She could have moved away; she could at least have clamped her legs together. She did neither. For the life of me, I couldn't read her expression anymore. And as I said, the lighting was bad. The conversation had switched over to Franklin's side of the room, so at least no one was watching her.

Except for me. Marian's lips were slightly parted, her gaze unfocused. Max's hand, I saw, was rubbing the area where even slim women grow queenly, the soft smackwarm inner thigh. The hand seemed to know what it was doing independent of its owner, caressing and probing through the fabric of the skirt. Soon the other hand moved toward her supporting arm and began stroking up and down, lingering longest on the smooth vulnerable crook of the elbow.

She tried to reassert herself but failed, shivering instead of bristling. What she may have intended as a *tsk* of annoyance came out as a low moan. Her white padded shoulders drooped. I was witness to something that bordered on the unnatural. With a little legerdemain, Max was rendering her helpless. The damnedest part was that he wasn't even looking at her. Not directly, at any rate.

He gently pulled her against his side, her soft weight sloping into his shoulder. The hand sliding up and down her arm moved around to stroke the underside of her right breast and disappeared between the double wall of flesh beginning at her armpit. His arm went down, down, as if he were reaching for his wallet, but the angle was different. It's amazing how resilient those old sofa cushions are, how a hand can maneuver between the upholstery and the sitter. I imagined the smooth bulk of Marian's buttock, cupped and squeezed through her skirt, then deserted for the moister depths. I could almost feel the slick wetness. The two of them rocked gently back and forth, as if they were riding a buggy.

Susan, it happened, was helping Dalrymple to some crackers and cheese. Vernon was happily retelling the story about the Baptist minister and the English instructor. I took a quick gaze around at the other guests. Greg and the Forsters were feigning rapt attention to Vernon, and Iris was on her fourth or fifth drink. When I looked back, Max had withdrawn his hands. His face, like a mask, had reverted to his Look Of Utter Respectability. The familiar pall of the afternoon had returned, the audience back in place, except for one woman turned into a puddle. When Marian finally got up the strength to move at all, her palm reached over his and settled there. Someone, I felt, should offer her a cigarette.

After a steady half-hour at the seat of Mount Vernon, Greg began a prelude to an apology for an excuse to depart. Jane looked at Franklin's watch and announced brightly that it was later than she had thought. Amid the slow-motion flurry of goodbyes, Max helped Marian up from the sofa, with her leaning on him quite heavily. Susan, linking arms with me as we walked out to the car, was light and airy. In her blouse and dirndl, she barely felt like anything at all.

Next Sunday, I had to work. In fact, the whole weekend was given over to correcting a double set of papers from my two Introlit classes. I had asked them to rewrite an incident from one of the stories we read and then analyze how the plot was changed. Or do the same exercise by altering the tone in a passage of their choice. Or describe the story from a minor character's point of view. In order to carry out any of these assignments, of course, you need to have a good understanding of the story. I had come up with these three choices because I thought they gave a chance for both creativity and analysis. And since they were new assignments, they wouldn't be found in the fraternity files, which eventually catch up with any professor who doesn't change his tracks quickly enough.

Correcting papers over the weekend is like recovering from a long hangover. I started early Saturday morning with a coffee pot and a red-eyed pen. By noon, I had a headache, my vision was slightly blurred, and I had gone through about twenty papers. Most of them struck a false note, the students seeing it as their duty to reform the story-ending. The gun never went off, the conversation turned from bitter to forgiving, the skid-row bum worked hard and became an overnight success. Character consistency meant little—these students had been fed Christian stories of conversion, as well as large doses of adventure fiction for the males, while gender roles dictated Beagle romances for the females.

After the nth paper that ended happily ever after, I got tired of scratching "improbable" in the margins. Then I got one that subtly turned a Katherine Anne Porter story into a wife-beating, and another that altered the tone of Hemingway's "Hills Like White Elephants" into a joke-advertisement for Planned Parenthood. I decided I could live with my students for another six weeks.

When Sunday arrived, I was still plowing through the papers from my second section. I happen to be the kind who can't let a typo or grammatical solecism go without comment, and if that makes correcting papers a labor-intensive operation, so be it. One of the compensations is that I picked up wonderful bloopers, some of which I read to Susan if she were around. This crop of papers had some beauts: "She became a teacher and a secondhand mother." "Biting off her nose to spite her face." "We must learn to take the fall when it is thrown our way." And one I thought I would save for Max: "He knew animals ingeniously."

Then I got on a roll and didn't look up until it was two o'clock in the afternoon. Susan and I had discussed this—whether I let my work take me over—and come to a loose set of compromises. If I submerged myself for more than four hours at a stretch, for example, she was allowed to come in and lead me outdoors for a walk. Other compromises involved faculty meetings and household chores, or final grading and a night on the town. We usually celebrated the end of the semester by going to Darley's grocery and catfish restaurant, the place where Max—but I'm getting ahead of myself.

All that week, I'd been thinking intermittently about Max. Funny, I hadn't seen him from Monday on, though I knew he was around, in fact doing the same things I was doing: teaching, attending meetings, grading stacks of papers like mine. I wondered what his assignments were like and how he taught. I took for granted that he could be mesmerizing, even if you can't finger a class on a sofa. He had a certain presence, for lack of a better word. Sometimes I felt as if he practiced his presence the way other people worked on their elocution.

He could certainly be an irritant. The story of Max versus Vernon was circulated through the halls all that week, largely by Franklin, who I think grudgingly admired the feat. No one had mentioned the business with Marian. Had I imagined that? I don't think so. I still wasn't sure why Max had done it, other than for purely sadistic pleasure—I mean the business with Vernon. Then again, Max could act like a wall, and I don't mean my study wall. Here was a neighbor I'd known for—what? over four months?—and I still didn't really know him at all. Or rather, the more I knew him, the more uncertain I became. The day before, on a whim, I'd written to my friend Dorothy, still languishing in the English department at Columbia. In a postscript I asked her if she knew anything about a former history grad student named Maxwell Finster. I expected her to pull a blank, but you never knew.

Was The Problem of Max assuming undue proportions? It wasn't really my problem at all. I had no antagonistic relationship with my woman, who was glad we were still on the Knowleses' guest list. And I still had fifteen papers to grade. I took a sip of lukewarm coffee, mentally sharpened my pen, and went after another happy ending. After a moment, I looked up. The Currier & Ives print on the wall was trembling, ever so gently.

6

The foliage didn't change much around here in October, but my mood did. By Halloween, I turned somewhat elegiac, looking out windows more than usual and practicing what Susan called my Abstract Stare. Around campus, the football season was in full charge, with the rah-rah alumni and their families turning out in navy blazers and Laura Ashley dresses for every Rebel home game. The kids were dressed as scaled-down versions of mom and pop, though instead of lunching off fried chicken and bourbon in paper cups off a tailgate, they inhaled Cheez Whiz and chased each other around College Grove.

Two years earlier, when my parents paid a visit to Ole Miss, they happened to hit Homecoming weekend. After observing the whole scene, my father, the only person I knew who really thought before he spoke, said it was like being back in the Fifties. The girls in their cheerleader outfits, the men with well-maintained hair and badly maintained waistlines, the wives who with make-up accomplished more elaborate cover-ups than the Alger Hiss trial, the martial band music, the sea of smiles (nervous, genuine, blinding, drunk) that wafted everyone along to the Vaught Hemingway stadium, where the Rebel fans still waved the Confederate flag and yelled, "Hotty toddy!" as they spilled Tom Collins mix on the row in front of them—no matter how long I'd been here, I was always struck by this animated diorama, all of which could be summed up in one simple sentence: I lived in a foreign culture.

Foreign to me, at any rate, since I grew up in Philadelphia. In truth, I spent a lot of time on the living room couch, reading anything and everything that came my way, like some Tennysonian kraken reaching out for ambient nourishment. I took in stories from E. Nesbit to P.G. Wodehouse and knew the public library with an almost unhealthy intimacy. For a long time, I felt happier with literature than with reality—I suspect many future academics are like that. Even after you've stopped reading purely for escape, it leaves you with a preference for secondhand romance. And when I took a walk with Susan that Saturday through the diorama, holding hands with a native Georgian, I felt the pull of the Other. Indistinct but insistent, like a whisper through the magnolias, it urged me to put a lilt into my speech, buy a pickup truck, and learn to like grits.

I wasn't sure how to respond to this, and I'm not even sure how Susan felt about it. On the one hand, she encouraged me to fit in, to learn how to chat Southern style, to slow down and be more social. On the other hand, there were times when no one was more down on Southern culture than Susan. She hated the small-town provincialism and the big-time religion, the racism and the politeness that covered it all up. She'd made remarks about her hometown that offended even me. "But I can say those things and you can't," she told me, poking a finger into my chest. "You didn't grow up here and I did."

But at least one professor I knew, Bret Watson, went native. About five years ago, he came here from Cornell to teach sociology: a bright, new-minted Ph.D., scholarly but affable, not too money-dependent and willing to relocate almost anywhere. His first three years he lived in Northgate Apartments, which is how I got to know him. By the time I made his acquaintance, he was already showing signs of assimilation: a beer gut with a button-down tent over his jeans to accommodate it, and a slow, deliberate way of talking, or sometimes just a squint into the distance before replying. At some point, he had picked up a Dodge Ram and a Winchester .30-.30 to hang on its gun rack. The zeal of the convert always exceeds that of the flock, and Bret seemed well on the way to becoming the reddest neck around. From all accounts—Greg Pinelli's, Gina Pearson's—he had once been a rather thoughtful, solitary individual who liked to listen to bebop. But when he lived two doors down from me, all I ever heard was country and western with interludes of Paul Harvey.

He eventually moved to a house when he got married. His blushing bride was a local woman with bright red cheeks and a habit of nudging you in the ribs whenever anyone in the vicinity said something funny. The last time I talked to Bret had been just recently, when he asked me if I wanted to go hunting with him that weekend. I politely declined, then snapped at Susan that night when she asked, totally out of the blue, whether I liked venison.

An entire family moved into Bret's old apartment and became our new neighbors. They never had to assimilate; they were born here and never left. The wife did something clerical in the Lyceum, our main administration building. The husband I think was a plumber. Their daughter, seven years old, was an idiot. All she ever did was ride her tricycle around the premises and wrench the heads off dolls. She spoke, if that's the right word, mostly in disconnected verbs. Every weekend practically, the parents dressed her in junior ballerina costumes and drove her off in the pickup to another kiddie beauty contest. On the back of their pick-up was a bumper sticker: REBEL BY BIRTH, SOUTHERN BY THE GRACE OF GOD.

I smiled at them and said hello whenever I saw them. They did the same—and God knows what they thought of me. I figured I was immune to assimilation—I preferred observation—but it's something I was always a little wary about. It didn't have to creep up on you because it was all around you. To give you an example:

the 25-cent kids' ride outside the local Wal-Mart wasn't a horse or a sports car. It was a little red pickup truck.

So when Max started dropping in regularly at Ted & Larry's for a few beers, I began to wonder. True, Ted & Larry's wasn't the same as Flannagan's or the Factory, which were largely student hang-outs ("Thurs. Nite: Jell-O Shots! Bud Pitchers 1/2 Price"). As Ed Schamley had noted, Flannagan's was where the students started their fights, and the Factory was where they ended them. Ted & Larry's was more of an establishment than a joint, with a semblance of a restaurant downstairs and live music on the weekends. Whenever a group called the Hellbellies played there, for instance, Susan dragged me to hear an evening of country-southern-pop. And you could see other faculty there: John Finley, a Southern Studies specialist who had traced the influence of rock lyrics on Bobbie Ann Mason; or Elaine Dobson, who went there to forget what it's like to be an intellectual single woman in a mostly married community. Ed went from time to time, and had even held a few committee meetings in one of the booths.

But none of us was a regular. In fact, the only regular I could think of besides a few sliding grad students was Roy Bateson, the one celebrated Southern writer we had in our midst. Roy generally arrived at Ted & Larry's half-pickled and left totally stewed. If you caught him in the right mood, he was friendly enough, but you couldn't expect him to remember your name for longer than five minutes. Once he called me Joe all afternoon because, as he told me later, he'd confused me with his buddy killed in a logging accident. Roy told the kind of tales that branched out into three or four other stories before dovetailing back in. Roy would also tell you, especially if you were a woman, how he used to work in a logging camp handling the big ones. The sober truth was that Roy grew up in Chapel Hill and could saw only in his dreams. Even in his fiction he'd begun to repeat himself, as the critics repeatedly said these days. Still, if you wanted to hear the stories again, all you had to do was offer Roy a drink.

The afternoon darkness of a bar makes it look underwater, and that's the way Ted & Larry's felt at around four p.m. Once or twice after a class, I'd gone in there at that hour, but apart from Roving Roy the only other conversation was from a Korean War vet with an arm missing from his Hawaiian shirt. He asked how old you were, and shook his head sourly when he concluded you were too young to understand his Wound. I'm sure he got a lecture on the history of the war if he tried to pull his routine on Max.

The question, of course, was why Max was there at all. As far as I knew, Marian wasn't much for bars, though I'm sure Max could have persuaded her to go. In fact, the way I heard about this was through Marian. I was walking from Bondurant to Bishop Hall, enjoying the blue slice of outdoors between the two drab buildings, looking northward and filling my lungs with autumn air—and the next thing I knew, I had collided with a female body. It was Marian in a big red dress. Neither of us had been looking ahead.

It was a pleasantly soft collision, and for the briefest of moments I imagined what it would be like to run into Marian on a regular basis. We both apologized at the same time.

"Well, *I* bumped into *you*," I put in.

"They really should install a traffic light on these stairs."

A bit of Max was rubbing off on her. Or maybe she had been that way to begin with, and that's why he was attracted to her. We began a conversation about where I was headed. I had a date with the department Xerox machine. "Tell you the truth, I don't think there's much to do around here at four."

Her mouth tightened. "Do you ever go to Ted & Larry's?"

"Sometimes. Not usually at this hour. Why, is there some pre-Happy Hour special?"

"No."

"Have they remodeled the place?"

"Not likely." Half-smile turned to half-grimace. Then she looked troubled, or maybe just thoughtful. Her next question startled me. "Um, would you like a beer or something?"

It didn't sound like a come-on, more like a plea for support. And therefore, since I didn't want a drink but did want to help out Marian, I said sure. Her car was right down the street, so I mentally put aside my copying till tomorrow and got into her Camaro. It smelled vaguely of cinnamon, and where some people have a crucifix there was a perfect miniature of Rodin's *The Thinker*. It gave her dashboard a pensive air as we drove toward the Square.

Downtown Oxford was marked by the county courthouse in the center of the Square, with a statue of a Confederate soldier on a gray granite column. The soldier stood at attention, facing the South and Lowry's used-furniture Store. Most of the shops around the perimeter were genteel, including a pharmacy that charged far more than the local S & M, and a department store called Carlson's that high-hatted Susan when she tried to buy pants there once. Ted & Larry's was next door to an appliance emporium that rarely deigned to sell anything. Serendipity ordained that a parking space was open right in front, and Marian nosed expertly into the slot. She killed the engine, we got out, and we slammed the car doors in unison.

The place looked empty. But as we climbed the stairs to the second floor, I could hear voices from the bar. It took a moment for my eyes to get used to the shadows. First, I picked out the Korean vet in the corner, muttering to Roy. "Cha-nee. Ju-pan. 'N'all them other Ajun countries." Roy was writing, or at least scribbling something on a cocktail napkin. Neither looked up as we entered. But over at the bar, two heads bobbed around, and one was Max's. The other was a woman's. When my depth-perception slid into focus, I saw that she was behind the bar. This didn't make any sense to me until I realized that she was the bartender— bartendress? bartendrix? barmaid?—bartender.

She smiled professionally. "Can I get you something?" She had old-fashioned ruddy cheeks, with the kind of figure that used to be called pleasingly plump. Her bosom was big and friendly, and her round arms looked capable of both cossetting a baby and holding off the advances of a drunk. Blue jeans encased her thick thighs, growing breathtakingly tight over her hips. But she was quite agile, uncapping two Buds for us, swabbing the counter in front of us, and plucking two dollar bills from Marian's outstretched hand. Marian's arm looked childish next to hers.

For the past hour or so, I gathered, Max had been her main client. He watched her move about, attracted to her the way certain alcoholics will watch the silent television in the bar. Then, as if on cue, Max suddenly swiveled around.

"Hello, there!" His words came out sweetly, like too much sugar in a Manhattan. He also sounded well-lubricated.

"Hi." Marian and her red dress seemed dulled inside this place. She slid her bottom over a barstool and looked not quite at Max or me.

Max reached out an arm that might have gone around Marian's shoulders, but instead lay over the counter. His hand was palm-up in that lazy curl that looks like supplication.

"More peanuts?" The woman reached under the bar for a container to fill the bowl, by now reduced to a few leavings, crinkled skins, and nubbins. Peanut detritus.

"Don't you have anything else for patrons to munch on? Olives, pretzels, potato chips? C'mon, Holly, something *new* for our guests Don and Marian."

"Nope," she announced cheerfully, filling the peanut bowl to the brim. "Not at these prices. Here, eat up."

I, Don the peacemaker, reached for a handful. I offered the bowl to Marian, but she waved it away.

"Too salty," she said. "And anyway, I don't particularly like nuts."

"The peanut," announced Max pedantically, "is not a nut." Alcohol is a great loosener, but it seemed to do something slightly different to Max, to emphasize him somehow. Max to the max, as one of my students would say.

"It's not?" Holly pressed forward to look at the bowl, as if it had suddenly changed its contents. Her blouse strained its buttons, revealing a creamy bulge of breast. I wasn't particularly looking, but Max was, and I followed his gaze.

Marian played interception. "What do you mean? If it's not a nut, what is it?" She picked one up from the bowl and eyed it critically.

Max smirked. "It's a vegetable, an herb really. So is the chestnut." And he drew out his back-pocket pad to take a note. Holly was looking at him with the same raptness I saw in my students when I recited from memory.

Marian turned to me as arbiter—because I was male, maybe, and because the alternative was Roy or the Korean war vet. "Is that true?"

I thought about it. It had the ring of fact, the same "did you know?" quality I remember when someone first told me that the tomato was a fruit. The world was full of *lusus naturae*, and Max seemed to make a hobby of knowing about them. Where Max inevitably came up short was in diplomacy. "You could look it up," I said diplomatically.

"Maybe later," muttered Marian, clearly annoyed at Max, me, and probably male hegemony. She also glared at Holly.

Max shrugged. "Nuts to you," he offered. I think that was what did it. Marian's hand was only an inch or two away from the bowl, and with a catapult-flick, she sent the contents flying into Max's face.

Peanuts scattered everywhere, and at the far end of the bar the Korean war vet took cover. "We're bein' attacked!" he cried to Roy, trying to push him down with his good arm. "Hit the floor!" Roy seemed half to believe him.

Max was more surprised than hurt. "What," he got out first, pausing to brush himself off. "The hell did you do that for?"

Marian seemed hurt, confused, angry all at once. "I don't know—my hand slipped. I didn't realize. . . ."

Max exchanged a glance with Holly, blue-eyed complicity. I have seen these looks before and can sum them up in two sentences: "Look what I have to put up with," and "I sympathize with you."

Marian put her hand on my wrist. "Don, you want to drive me home?"

"But it's your—"

"I know, I know. Look, let's just get out of here, okay?" She reached for my support as she slid off her stool. But as we walked out of the bar, she called back to Max. "I'm sorry, Max, I'm *sorry*. I'll phone you tonight?"

Max nodded, or maybe it was to Holly, who had come around from the counter with a dustbin and broom. The last I saw as we descended the stairs was Holly bent at the waist, her behind positively blooming, as Max stood by, broom in hand. He looked knightly. With an armful of Marian, I felt more than a little chivalrous myself.

Marian was right: she was too distraught to drive. I got in the driver's seat and was about to start up, when I realized something was missing.

"Keys?"

"What about them?"

"Where are they?"

"Oh." She rummaged briefly through her purse but couldn't find them. "Oh, shit—God *damn* it." She looked through the windshield, up toward Ted & Larry's. "You know what?"

"You left them at the bar."

"Yup. I can't go back there now." There was a hopeless pause that somehow turned hopeful. "Um, Don—?"

"Sure. I'll be back in a minute." I got out and walked back to Ted & Larry's, taking the steps two at a time. Maybe I was too fast, because when I got upstairs I saw an unprepared tableau: in the background, Roy and the vet jabbing fingers at each other, arguing something about shrapnel; in the foreground, Holly bending over—to pick up one of the legumes, maybe—as Max came from behind and slid the broom between her legs. It didn't look as if there were any room between those fleshy thighs, but they just ate up the pole. She half-turned toward him.

"Silly."

"Thought you might want a ride." Max pulled gently back on the broom, and her hips rolled with the motion. Her buttocks pressed against his groin. I couldn't tell whether this was a prelude to an act or a recap from some previous act.

Max pulled the shaft out and pushed it back in again. When she came up against him a second time, all she said was, "Not here, not now," and affectionately nudged him away. They went back to playing Maid of the Dustbin and Knight of the Broom as he helped her sweep up. I pretended that I had just got to the top of the stairs and trod heavily on the floorboards. I strode right over to the bar, where Marian's keys lay in a dull gold heap. "Keys," I explained, when Max raised his bushy eyebrows. I jingled them. "Can't start the car without 'em."

"Always finish what you start," tossed in Roy from somewhere in left field. I nodded automatically—it was never a good idea to disagree with Roy; it took too much time—and vaulted downstairs again. On the way out, I noticed Eric Lasker, the resident Marxist in our department, pulling up to the curb. He had recently acquired a car and was capitalistically exploiting it by driving everywhere. Small town, Oxford. Now he would see me going home with Marian, but there wasn't much I could do about that. I waved to show I wasn't being covert, and he waved back. He also gave me a big, dirty wink.

7

Marian said nothing until we were driving away. She hadn't noticed the business with Eric at all. "So, what do you think?"

"Of Holly?" I knew whatever I said wouldn't help. "She's, uh, certainly well-rounded. Maybe not too intellectual."

"That's for sure." Marian nudged the dashboard with the heel of her hand. "I don't know why he's attracted to that—to her."

I looked at her curiously. Since the Knowles debacle some Sundays ago, I had looked up a few of the more esoteric rhetorical devices. The one Marian had just fallen into was called aposiopesis—breaking off in mid-sentence. Attracted to that what? That kind of bartender? "You mean, you think he likes . . . he, uh, goes after . . . "

"That kind of woman," muttered Marian in the smallest voice imaginable. It was odd how shrunken she looked, or maybe just in mental comparison to Holly, who was built along more generous lines.

Marian's breasts sagged against the front of her red dress, the nipples visible but weepy-eyed, pointing downward. I knew what those nipples looked like when excited; now they were depressed. I felt like patting each breast in turn and murmuring, "There, there." Instead, I mumbled, "*De gustibus*. . . ." I looked ahead at University Avenue, which is where we were traveling, and swerved just in time to avoid a road-kill in the right lane. It was an armadillo, orange-red entrails on display. It was armor plated like a miniature tank, but you can crush anything with enough weight. Muskrats, black squirrels, cottonmouth snakes, box turtles—the South had the most exotic squashed fauna I'd ever seen. Not to mention some extremely careless drivers. It occurred to me that I'd forgotten where Marian lived. "Um, where to?"

"Hell. Home, I mean. Just turn at the Baptist church."

I wasn't sure which one she meant, but sure enough, there was one on the corner. They were all over the South, like banks: Yellowleaf Baptist Church, Obeah Missionary Baptist Church, Second Free-Will Baptist Church of Oxford (I'd never seen the First), Baptist Church of Holy Deliverance, and on and on. This one had a white banner draped over the front, advertising a fried chicken dinner on Sunday. Women's Auxiliary Spaghetti Night, Young Christians' All U Can Eat Clam Bake—there's a direct association between the church and food. It was Christ, after all, who held the first bake sale. Though some of the three-tier cakes I've seen sold by the church ladies are positively sinful.

Two blocks past the church, we arrived at Villa Flats, a development whose location could have been anywhere in the South, the North, or certain parts of hell. The best description of Villa Flats is to call it an academic halfway house. It was for people who'd graduated from dorm life but didn't yet have enough money to move into real living quarters. The exteriors were lemon terra cotta with baby blue shutters under chocolate brown roofs. Three "villas" formed a unit, with every four units clustered around a purely ornamental quadrangle of turf.

"Don't say it." Marian was interpreting my gaze. "Max called it Villa of the Damned."

"I don't know, it's not that bad."

"Yes, it is, and that's why it's so cheap. I didn't get on the university housing list in time, so I had to settle for something like this." We stopped outside the unit she pointed at, #5, with the numeral in fuchsia. "I could have settled for something in more picturesque squalor, but they wouldn't show that to me. Wrong side of the color line."

Racism was an odd thing in the South. It usually wasn't ugly, the way it now was up North. It was controlled, which made it more livable and somehow worse. There weren't many middle-class black families in Oxford, for example, and there wasn't much encouragement in that area. In the end, it was just a gap, and gaps aren't as noticeable as presences. Some of this I said to Marian as we got out of the car, and she nodded. Most of the new faculty—that is, hired within the past five years—had noticed and commented on it. One day, ran the feeling, we might do something about it. With people like Eric Lasker as spearhead, we were far better at organizing rallies for social justice in Zimbabwe.

The pebbled path was lined by a double row of dwarf shrubbery. The grass on either side was manicured to putting-green tolerance, too cropped for the breeze to affect it at all. At the door to 5B, Marian took her keys back from me and unlocked the door. She swung it open and smiled wanly. "Would you care to come in?"

"Sure." Hesitation would have seemed an insult. Besides, what was she going to do, jump me in the hall?

The interior was far nicer than the outside let on, probably because Marian had fixed it up herself. A breakfront in the hall had a basket of dried lilacs and a faded mirror behind it that looked vaguely Spanish. A braided throw-rug covered the distance to a bedroom and a combination dining room and kitchen. Two sternly upright chairs sat in the second room, as if waiting for a servant to bring them coffee from the stove on the other side of the room. On a low table between the two chairs were a miniature folding screen and a French tricolor bungee cord. The last item I recognized as a touch of Max.

"This is it." She spread her arms, which stretched the material of her dress back into shape. "What you see is what you see."

"I see." What I couldn't see was the bedroom, not from my angle. All I could make out was a swatch of quilt on what looked like a standard bed. On the other hand, I told myself, so what? You are not on an inspection tour. You are not here to verify, instruct yourself, or inform curiosity or carry report. You are not here to quote T.S. Eliot. You are not looking for medieval torture equipment in the pantry closet, either. Though a hint of impropriety might be titillating.

"Cup of tea?" Marian crossed over to the kitchen part of the room and hefted a blue enamel kettle. "I have coffee, but it's instant."

"Tea is fine." As she bent over the sink to fill the kettle, I noticed how short she really was, about 5'2'', I'd say. You couldn't see it so much when she was facing you because then your attention was taken up with her amplitude.

After she put the kettle on, we sat down in the chairs and waited. I think we both were expecting the other to start first. Finally, she ventured a comment.

"Max can be a real pain in the ass sometimes." She didn't seem bitter, just matter of fact.

"I know what you mean."

"You do?" Her brown eyes widened.

"No—yes, I mean—no, not in the way you mean. I guess." Words will do you in every time. Polysemous perversity. I paused for a moment to get it right. "I think I understand how you feel."

But Marian wasn't letting me off easily. "Hmm . . . are you in love with Max, too?"

"He's my neighbor. I see a lot of him."

"Which parts?"

"Probably not the ones you see."

"I have no objection to those parts." She smiled and crossed her legs, rearranging her skirt over her thighs. For some reason, her skin looked sallow in that light. "I was talking about the way he treats others."

I thought of Max's abrasive humor. Then I recalled the broom in the bar and couldn't help myself. "I think he likes to ride people."

"That's the truth," she muttered, making me wonder if Marian hadn't ridden a besom with Max herself. Or maybe tried a few rope tricks. The whistle of the kettle got her up. Over her shoulder, she called out, "Do you take milk, sugar?"

"Nothing."

"Good, I don't think I have either left in the house. I'm trying to diet." She brought back two steaming mugs on a large plate with a bull's-eye design. We sipped a moment in silence. I wasn't sure why she was confiding in me, other than the principle of "any port in a storm." In any event, there was one question I wanted to ask her. So I did.

"What do you see in him, anyway?" It came out as a cliché because I didn't want to risk being misunderstood again.

Marian looked troubled. She licked her lower lip, then bit it. She made a noise in her throat like the beginning of an answer, then stopped. Eventually, she came up with a cliché of her own. "It's hard to explain."

"Try."

"Well, you know what he's like . . ."

"Only certain parts."

This time she blushed. "That's *not* what I meant. He's captivating. He can make you feel like you're the most important person in the room—like you're the *only* other person in the room. When he's not taking those damn notes."

"He does talk well, true."

"It's more than that. If you mention—I don't know—Caravaggio, he's seen *The Fortune Teller* and you can talk about it. Or Jasper John's flags. Or how much cumin to put in a pot of chili. You could talk about sanitary landfills, and he'd know the contents."

"Is that what you talk about?"

"Stop it! You know what I mean. Don't be like Max."

"Sorry. You're right. I know exactly what you mean." Since we were being so frank, I put in my own confession. "He fascinates me, too."

She rolled her eyes at me. More polysemous perversity.

"Um, except for certain parts."

"*Be serious.*"

So we were serious for about ten minutes, talking about how inconsiderate men could be, and how it was easier for men to meet women in Oxford than vice-versa. We didn't mention Max's sadism. I told her my joke that churches were better bets for getting acquainted than laundromats in this town. She asked if I knew any good-looking choir-boys. I said I'd keep a lookout, but that I got a finder's fee of ten percent. Ten per cent of what, she wanted to know. And back and forth and back and forth, without anything happening. That was mostly how I wanted it. Even if I were drawn to Marian, and I'll admit a certain attraction, it just wouldn't have been healthy. Not in my situation, and not in this small town. When I finally looked at my watch, it was almost six-thirty. I said I had to go, and brought the mugs into the kitchen area for her.

[59

At the door, she laid an arm on my shoulder, gave me a quick kiss, and propelled me through the door. I was halfway down the lawn when I realized I had no car. Marian was probably so used to Max, who bicycled everywhere, that she'd forgotten. And I didn't feel like going back; I didn't want to spoil the effect of the parting kiss. So I decided to walk the distance, which was just over a mile.

Halfway there, I was honked at by a passing car. It was Eric Lasker in his machine, a Chevy Nova, driving perilously close to the wrong side of the street. He rolled down his window. "Hello! Can I give you a lift?"

I considered the pros and cons. Riding with Eric would get me home quicker. On the other hand, I was sure to get snared in one of his political crusades. The last time I'd had a sustained conversation with him, I had found myself pledged to run ten miles for Greenpeace. It was always a sonorous pleasure talking with Eric—a true Oxonian, he sounded better reading the phone book than an American declaiming Shakespeare—but everything was political. Teaching was strictly politics, shopping involved informed economic choices, and sex of course was political (he had recently broken up with his girlfriend in a dispute over Amnesty International). When you ate with him, he could tell what parts of your meal were from oppressed Third-World countries.

So I waved him on. And he thought I meant for him to stop, which he did. He leaned out the window, his patched jacket-elbow meant to indicate proletarian sympathies. He gave another version of the enormous wink outside Ted & Larry's. "Trying to sneak home, are you? C'mon then, jump in."

Damn. I wondered whether it was worth explaining. "I just left Marian's . . . " I began.

"I'll bet you did. Bit of the old slap and tickle?"

"No, we were talking about a mutual friend, actually."

"Ah, the old mutual friend. Is that what you'll tell the wife?" He wore what Britishers call a silly-ass grin.

Walking away would have aroused even more suspicion, so I just got in. But I probably should have done something to remove the grin from his face. All I said was, "It's not what you think, Eric."

"Whatever you say." We zoomed off, since Eric had yet to get used to automatic transmissions. We almost collided with two Tri-Gam girls power-walking before dinner, and Eric honked amiably at them. They waved: they were former students. As the main Shakespeare teacher on campus, Eric had taught almost everyone in the three years he'd been here.

The problem was to defend myself without spreading gossip about Max. But before I could think of anything, Eric gestured at the back seat. "Here, flyers I've to distribute tomorrow. Take one."

"Thanks, I've got too much to read as it is."

"Don't be absurd. Take you two seconds. We're having a rally in the Square this Saturday for El Salvador."

"Oh." I wanted to attend about as much as I wanted five Fuller brush salesmen at my door. Once when I signed one of Eric's petitions, I got roped into donating funds for a revolution in Ethiopia. On the other hand, maybe accepting would shut him up about Marian. I also thought of opening the car door and walking away, though we were traveling around twenty miles an hour.

"Yes—I *do* hope people from the department show up. It's absolutely vital. God, the situation is dismal down there. In fact, I have some literature I can show you . . . now, where did it get to?" The car did a slow zig-zag as he reached under my seat, then under his, and finally found a white pamphlet wedged under the front floorboard mat. I glanced at it, and even read some to make him happy. Political prisoners, torture camps, military "peacekeeping" squads. I sighed, knowing I should be more committed. The worst part was that Eric's ethics were irreproachable, making all of us who taught literature feel guilty as hell for not rushing right out to help Honduran refugees.

I got out of the car having promised to attend the rally on Saturday with Susan. But I couldn't help adding, "And you might try Max Finster, too."

"Oh? Who's he?"

"New faculty in the history department. Very knowledgeable about these things. I'm surprised you haven't met him yet."

"Well, I'll certainly look him up." Eric's eyes lit up with the priestly glow of conversion. His father, I recalled his telling me, was a Salvation Army general.

I waved my thanks as he shot off again in his good cause. Susan had waited dinner for me, and though I'd had a late lunch, I was suddenly ravenous. I ate my way through half a pan of lasagna and went back to the kitchen for cheese and crackers an hour later. It surprised Susan but made her happy in a maternal way. She patted my head and called me "Donny boy."

When she asked why I was late, I told her that Eric had collared me to help hand out pamphlets. "And what's more," I added, "we've agreed to go to his rally tomorrow in the Square."

"We have?"

"It might be interesting."

"I think my highway beautification committee meets then." Susan had switched volunteer projects again. She was never sufficiently political for Eric, who had classed her as irredeemably bourgeois. She, in turn, had classed him as foreign.

"When is that?"

"When Eric's rally meets."

"But I haven't said what time it's meeting," I pointed out. I thought I had her.

"But it's got to be in the early afternoon—that's what time they always are. He never wakes up before noon."

It was true: Eric was like Greg in his nocturnal rhythm. If you wanted to see a disgruntled Marxist, all you had to do was knock on Eric's door at breakfast time. Mrs. Post, with the contempt of the early riser for the slugabed, used to phone him at nine about committee meetings, until he thought of leaving the receiver off the hook. On the other hand, nights when I couldn't sleep I'd look out across the backyard to see Eric's apartment. Two bright yellow rectangles, Eric's windows with the shades down, lent a cheery warmth to an otherwise ungodly hour.

"You just don't like Eric," I pointed out.

"Who does?"

"All right, but that's not the point. The cause is important, and people should show up for that."

"What is it this time?"

"Rebels in El Salvador."

Susan bit her lip, a sign that she was wavering. I could see her weighing highway litter against machete-waving revolutionaries. I could see her wondering what to wear. "All right," she said finally. "But you owe me one dinner out."

"You've got a deal." Going out usually meant fried catfish, which was one thing Susan wouldn't cook at home because of all the grease. We usually needed a catfish fix about once a month.

Soon after our discussion, Susan got on the phone to talk to her committee head, Mrs. Spofford, and I went into my study to work. Or at least I intended to. For a while I sat in front of my computer screen without touching a key. Then I picked up a collection of

Joycean criticism without reading it. No sounds came from behind the wall. I thought of silence. I thought of isolation. I thought of parts representing other parts. For some reason, I saw an image of caressing hands.

The hands were female, soft and white, and they comforted me. They came to rest on my shoulders, like a muse having a heart-to-heart talk with me. But then they worked their way downward, running lightly over my chest, and soon they were at my groin. They stroked and squeezed gently. Eventually, the hands became mine, and I did something I hadn't done in a long while, masturbating into a tissue I pulled from my desk. I wasn't even sure what I had masturbated to, though it certainly wasn't an image of my wife.

Susan was asleep by the time I finished trying to work for the night. I wanted to take a look at her hands, but they were curled under the sheets. I undressed quietly and got into bed. I lay with my arms at my sides, realizing that sleep would be slow in coming tonight. Idly, the way a vicarious traveler thinks of his friend's trip abroad, I wondered what Max was doing.

8

It was the hour of doldrums in Oxford Square, two in the afternoon on a November Saturday. Very little was stirring: most of the migrant birds had already left for the coast, and half the students were holed-up in the dorms or the library, studying for midterms. The other half were in Arkansas for the weekend football game, the Ole Miss Rebels versus the Razorbacks. Carlson's, the department store, was between its post-Halloween and pre-Christmas sales. Even the weather was in a sort of limbo, halfway between sunny and overcast. In the midst of all this indecision, Eric had hiked up the pedestal of the Confederate soldier statue with a megaphone in his hand, haranguing a crowd of ten.

Most of the people shared Eric's politics, including a few progressives from the law school. This wasn't entirely to Eric's liking, since it meant he was preaching to the converted. Somehow, the flyers he had placed all around the Student Union hadn't drawn well. He blamed student apathy, which was slightly unfair since it wasn't that the students didn't care about anything, but rather that they didn't care about what Eric did. He might as well have blamed friendship, for making those of us who didn't care show up under false pretenses. This is one reason I remain apolitical. Life is confusing enough without political allegiances crossing up personal affairs.

We were gathered outside the courthouse in the Square, a few more people slowly drifting in and making us look like more of a movement and less of an eddy. To the side of the pedestal was Nancy Crew, a young law professor who appeared at all of Eric's activities. They argued endlessly about socialism and respected each other intensely. The Kays were also there, a faculty couple from our department with five kids from various marriages. Mary Kay was an ex-hippie, only slightly disguised by the horn-rimmed glasses she wore these days. Her husband Joseph was a gray-bearded saint, the best-read man I've ever talked with, in everything from Homer to Pynchon. He wasn't quite aware of the El Salvadorian crisis—he hadn't read about it—but he was willing to learn.

Eric was feeling more righteous than usual, probably because of his recent break-up. He trumpeted into his megaphone, in a style that one student in his graduate seminar had characterized as ''relentlessly polysyllabic.'' From his vantage on the plinth of the pedestal, he kicked at the statue of the soldier, deriding it for its inactivity. At the same time, he deplored the invasion of U.S. troops into El Salvador. The figures he proceeded to unreel were appalling. He was just warming up to his statistics when Max showed up, Holly in tow.

I stood there with Susan, who wore the polite, unreadable expression she reserves for company. Still, we were doing something together, weren't we? I waved to Max, who squeezed between Nancy Crew and Joseph Kay to get to us. The crowd had grown to about twenty by this time, all focused on the pedestal. Both Max and Holly were wearing sweaters against the November chill, but hers was a good deal tighter than his. I don't know what it is, probably something fetishistic, maybe something bestial, but there's something about a woman in furry wool that's extremely sexy.

In Holly's case, it was more than just that. For one thing, there was more of Holly—those big, broad breasts stretching that poor soft sweater to its limits, and the same super-tight jeans I had seen her in at the bar, miraculously holding together as she walked. It was as if she were one large erogenous zone. In fact, the aperture Max squeezed through wasn't big enough for Holly, and her breasts pushed against Joseph while her protruding behind rubbed against Nancy. Nancy looked away; Joseph looked enchanted. Max briefly introduced Holly to Susan, who said she was charmed, which of course meant she wasn't. I assume she was annoyed because Holly wasn't Marian, though it occurred to me later—all right, I was told later—that I hadn't let Susan know about Holly. She was one of the parts I had left out from that afternoon at Ted & Larry's.

Eric had paused for a moment, as the augmented crowd re-grouped itself. All of a sudden, the Square had come to life. A few of the listeners even had signs: U.S. OUT OF EL SALVADOR in block capitals, a scrawled END POLICE STATES, and one in elegant purple lettering that was absolutely indecipherable. The purpose of the event, I recalled, was to march from the Square to the university Grove, but first Eric had to whip the crowd into a frenzied pitch, or whatever pitch he could manage. He could be quite eloquent, though more in the British parliamentary style than what people around here are used to, which is fire and brimstone preaching. If Eric were describing hell, he'd quote average temperatures and cite damning statistics.

Still, some of his talk was obviously having an effect, since the original crowd had tripled in size since he'd started. A lot of them had that rapt look, too, the kind most of America used to wear when watching *Dallas*. Maybe there was nothing good on the tube this Saturday afternoon. Max, I noticed, had his arm around Holly's comfortable waist. His hand was jammed into her back pocket, the fabric so tight it must have picked up his fingerprints. It didn't look as if she were wearing underwear. He was whispering something in her ear that made her laugh. I tried to think of something to murmur in Susan's shell-pink auricles, but couldn't come up with anything.

As if to compensate for his measured words, Eric was using more and more body English in his delivery. He pounded the statue's rifle and once, maybe accidentally, kneed the soldier in a sensitive area. He flung out his hand and almost lost his balance, saving himself at the last moment by holding on to the same eroge-nous zone. Out of the corner of my eye, I saw a few more people drift into the crowd. Men in blue.

I don't know what it is about cops in Oxford. Maybe it's an over-familiarity with frat boys more souped up than their cars on Saturday night. Then again, the one run-in I've had with the law happened when I was just walking around campus late at night and was stopped for questioning. They're a tad—how shall I put it?—overzealous. And they do like to intimidate. The way I see it, the South is big on authority figures, and your average Southern cop is your father, a judge, and a drill sergeant in one bulky body behind a mean pair of shades.

There were three of them right around the pedestal when one called out, "Now, hold it right there, son."

Eric paused in mid-invective. "I *beg* your pardon?"

The same voice, from a jowly type with his holster prominent, persisted. "You got a permit to be up there?"

"A permit? No, actually . . . this is public property, isn't it?"

"Sure is. And there's a law in this town against improper use of it. Now, why don't you just come down before I have to arrest you."

I could see Eric debating with himself. Would it be prudent to give in? Or would a martyr for El Salvador spur interest in the cause? Marxists nowadays aren't the proletariat, they're university intellectuals, and as a result they always smell faintly of chalk, of theory rather than practice. This bothers them a lot. For example, they hate being called armchair activists. As we all watched, Eric took a significant step toward activism. He spat on the bayonet of the Confederate soldier.

Instantly, a cop who had circled around behind the pedestal had him by the feet and was pulling him down. Eric's papers flew into the air, skittered sideways in the breeze, and settled right into Mary's hands as if she were an accomplice. When I glanced at them, I noticed what an elaborate outline Eric had made for such an impromptu speech: points to be stressed, figures inserted, quota-tions in full. This is what you learn from teaching: nothing sounds so sweetly spontaneous as something carefully prepared.

In the meantime, the cops had wrestled Eric against the base of the pedestal, which must have been annoying for them since Eric wasn't resisting. The jowly one was reciting to Eric his right to remain silent, though of course all Eric wanted to do was talk. And he did, exclaiming about suppression of free speech, and how this would never happen in England. If it had been a dark night with no one around, they probably would have slugged him, but in the midst of the crowd all they did was force his hands behind his back. Quickly they snapped on a pair of cuffs and led him to the squad car parked across the street. The car rolled out of the Square before anyone could react.

"Serves 'im right."

We swiveled our necks collectively. A boy in a ROTC uniform had been listening, along with his girlfriend. He had one arm around her slim waist, and he gestured with his other at the statue. "Spittin' on our boys in uniform, makin' fun of boys dyin' over there to support democracy." He himself spat on the ground eloquently. You could tell he knew how to do it several different ways. Then he turned on his heel (she turned as if hinged to him), and they walked up the street to his parked Jeep.

"The first amendment always protects the wrong people," muttered Nancy Crew. She had fished out a little black book from her bag and was jotting down notes in it.

"What's gonna happen?" asked a grad student wearing a peace-sign T-shirt with holes in it. Doug Robertson. I remembered him from one of my seminars the year before, in which he wrote a paper proving that Virginia Woolf was into Zen.

"That depends on how far they want to push it." Nancy sounded grim. "There's probably five stupid bylaws he violated just by being where he was." She continued taking notes furiously, looking up now and then as if to prompt herself. The sky was now definitely overcast, with the gray, unfocused air of imminent rain. The wind sprang up, whipping Eric's notes from Mary's hands and scudding them along the pavement. We were suddenly a group without a purpose, or at least a circle with the center pulled out.

"This is what my Czechoslovakian friends used to complain about," said Joseph, buttoning the top of his black vest against the wind.

"I wonder if they're coming back." This was from Mary, looking genuinely concerned, and it made us all wonder if we shouldn't be elsewhere. A few people at the fringes began to leave.

Just then, Nancy finished writing and snapped her notebook shut. "Listen, we're going to have to do something about this. Eric has no idea how the American legal system works, and no one down at the station is going to help him." A few more people walked away; it was clear that a lot of the crowd had been rubberneckers. The rest of us stayed, feeling all the more important as Nancy continued. "Now, we're all witnesses, which may be of some help, or maybe not. The important thing is to plan what happens next, not just leave it to chance. How about if we all meet at the Polka Dot in—what? Fifteen minutes?"

Murmurs of agreement. Holly whispered something in Max's ear, pressing herself against his shoulder, but he just shook his head slightly. He was jotting down something on a new wad of paper, though I doubt it corresponded at all to Nancy's notes. When Holly tried to see over his shoulder, he turned aside. She looked peeved but said nothing, another woman coming to terms with Max and his eccentricities. There was a moment of silence when all you could hear was the breeze in the courthouse oak trees. Then the crowd, as Dan Rather says, dispersed. And the Saturday afternoon doldrums came back to the Square.

9

"I don't think we should all go at once." We were seated around a scarred wooden table at the Polka Dot, and Nancy was outlining what to do and when to do it. In fact, it didn't look as if there was much to do. Holly had wanted to go to the police station with Max and a few others in protest, then she wanted to start a letter-writing campaign for Eric in jail. Nancy pointed out, in a pedagogical tone she must have used for her law students, that the first wouldn't be advisable and the second wouldn't be necessary. Basically, all one of us had to do was show up at the station to bail Eric out. Nancy intended to do that. But if it came to rebutting any trumped-up charges, we were all witnesses, and that was why we were meeting like this: to get our stories straight. We all felt involved and partici- patory in a smug, subversive sort of way.

Meeting at the Polka Dot was appropriate. Every white-bread town like Oxford has to have some kind of hang-out to balance the boutiques, churches, and social graces, and the Polka Dot was the local answer to it all. The sign on the screen door read, "NO SHOES, NO SHIRT, WHO CARES?" Inside, every inch of wall space was covered with graffiti, posters, bumper stickers, and visual art, a lot of it dating from the Sixties, much of it counter-culture, but some of it just plain weird. An anti-smoking sign warned about the effects of nicotine in the seventh dimension. A poster highlighting the crack epidemic in L.A. showed four bottoms in thong bikinis. One sign plainly asked, "Have you hugged a nuclear reactor today?" My favorite was a bumper sticker above the coffee machine: "Throw me something, Mister."

Most of the food came with bean sprouts, with the exception of the cheesecake, which had no right to be so good this far south of the Mason-Dixon line. The proprietor Andy Hillman claimed he stole it from a Brooklyn bakery where he once dated the pastry chef. The service was friendly and inefficient, and I often used to nurse a cup of herbal tea at a table near the door before I met Susan. In fact, the café was only half of a tin-roofed warehouse, the other half of which Andy had turned into a theater showing real films instead of the homogenized schlock that came to the Cinema 3 in the mall. The ticket-taker was an autistic stutterer named Earl, with an idiot savant talent for film lore. Anyway, Andy and the Polka Dot had been there for over ten years, and if some Oxford citizens would have liked to ride him out of town on a rail, there were others who wanted to elect him mayor.

Andy still had his ponytail from the Sixties, as well as a beard that always looked a bit chewed. He didn't talk all that much, but he was extremely savvy about the American political scene. Some of this came from always being on the wrong side of the election results, but he wasn't too bitter about it. He did have more than a passing acquaintance with protest movements and jail cells.

On the other hand, this was no longer the Sixties, and Nancy made it quite clear that expediency was the watchword. "I admire Eric," she said, etching a new scar in the table with one red fingernail, "and I share most of his politics. But I wouldn't have spit on that statue."

"Maybe we should go back and wipe it off?" Again, it was well-meant, and again it was Holly, but Max pointed out brusquely that the spitting wasn't open to question. He squeezed her arm affectionately as he said it. This was confusing because his tone betrayed irritation. But Max's actions often seemed to belie his words, I'd noticed. Not that he was a hypocrite exactly, rather that there was a gap or disjunction between what he said and did. Susan said she thought of him as a dangerously absent-minded professor, but Max had none of the fuzziness associated with the species. I noticed that his hand left a red mark on Holly's fair skin.

We spent the next half-hour hammering out a coherent testimony, which was surprisingly difficult, considering we'd all seen the same event. Mary thought that the policeman who grabbed Eric had hold of him before Eric spat, and Holly thought the second cop had used undue force to restrain him. Joseph for some reason thought there had been four cops. Max volunteered the license-plate number of the patrol car as a joke. For some reason, he had memorized it. We eventually wrote down all our phone numbers on seven polka-dotted napkins, just in case one of us had to get hold of the others in a hurry. This seems absurd in retrospect, but you have to understand how dull this weekend had been only two hours earlier.

Nancy went off to the bank machine to get the bail money, and the rest of us drove home. The football game was being broadcast over the university station, but neither of us turned on the car radio. I know it's unpatriotic, but I don't really care for football, and I think Susan liked it only because her father used to feed her pretzels when they watched it on the tube together.

We drove through five blocks of silence. I swerved to avoid a dead cat in the road. There seemed to be a lot of them lately. Halfway home, Susan spoke. "You know, that's not the way things get done around here."

"What do you mean?"

"I mean abusing the courthouse statue and pissing off the cops. One of these days, Eric's going to get himself into real trouble."

"He already is."

"Oh, Donald, it could have been so much worse." Whenever she called me Donald, I felt all of ten years old. But she also seemed to be brooding about something else, and as we stopped in front of our apartment block, she let it out. "And why didn't you tell me about Max and Holly?"

I shrugged my shoulders, which is hard to show in a car seat, so I got out and shrugged them again for her. I had no good answer.

"Where did she come from? What's she doing with Max?"

"She came from another solar system. Her mission is to destroy him."

"I mean it. How did they meet? And what happened to Marian?"

"I think they met at Ted & Larry's. She works there." And I told her somewhat less than what little I knew, I'm not sure why. I'd begun keeping things from her without realizing it. Or maybe that's just my habit, on the assumption that it's always good to keep something in reserve. I teach my classes the same way. I admit I'm a slightly unreliable narrator.

Susan was annoyed at Holly for Marian's sake. "She's not his type, you can see that. And she really should go on a diet. They look like a pole bean and a pear together."

"She seems kind." And wears a lovely sweater, I thought.

"Yes, but not too bright. I didn't think he went after that kind. I almost feel sorry for her. Someone should straighten Max out."

She blamed Max, I noticed. I wasn't sure I did, despite what I'd seen. He seemed to repel all charges against him, or maybe just deflect them onto others.

In about an hour, the phone rang. I picked it up at once. "Hello?"

"Jamie? That you?"

"Sorry, wrong number." I replaced the receiver. After a moment, the phone rang again. I answered it warily.

"Jamie?"

"No. *You've got the wrong number.*"

A pause. "Is this 555-1057?"

"Yes, but there's no Jamie here. Maybe we got his old number."

"Well, then, would you pass this on?" the voice pursued illogically. "Tell him he's got to call John. *Soon.*" And he hung up.

I sighed. This had happened before. When we'd moved in the year before, we'd had a rash of wrong-number calls, all asking for Jamie. Apparently, Jamie owed a lot of people a lot of money; it wasn't clear why. After a month, the calls had dropped off, but now for some reason they were back again. The worst case was an old woman who insisted we were lying. "If you're not Jamie," she asked me craftily, "then what have you done with him?" We were thinking of having our number changed but didn't want to go through the hassle.

The phone rang once more. I ignored it. On the fifth ring, I figured what the hell and picked it up. It was Nancy. She'd arrived at the police station with five hundred dollars, but apparently for minor crimes like this it was only a hundred and thirty.

"So what's the problem?"

"Don, he doesn't want to come out."

"What do you mean?"

"He wants to be a jailed revolutionary. So he's not leaving until the hearing."

I rolled my eyes for Susan's benefit, then realized she didn't know what was going on. "When's the hearing?"

"It hasn't been set yet." Nancy sighed in disgust. "Tell me, you think we should let him rot in there?"

"What's the alternative?"

"Well, we could bring some pressure to drop the charges. Maybe someone higher up at the university, someone who could intercede."

"What *are* the charges, anyway?" At this point, Susan was practically kissing my earlobe, not out of sexual passion but just to hear the other side of the conversation. We have no second phone.

"Sort of what you'd expect. Abuse of public property. Spitting in public. Maybe trespassing."

"Too bad he didn't drop his pants."

"Yeah. Sorry, I'm kind of losing my sense of humor over this thing. Anyway, I thought I'd tell you what was going on. I've been calling everyone, just to let them know."

"Thanks. Look, if we go by later to visit him, is there anything we should bring?"

"A lot of attention. That's what he wants." And she rang off.

In about an hour, we went to see Eric. We went then because an hour is how long it took Susan to make a batch of pecan brownies for the jailed revolutionary. Considering how she felt about the whole business, this was an act of Southern heroism, if that's a word, and it ought to be. Something like "I disagree with your means of expression, but I'll feed you anyway." My contribution was to scrape the bowl. There was no file baked inside the pan, since breaking out was the last thing Eric wanted to do.

The Oxford police station was situated near a garbage-collection center, which might be metonymic or pure coincidence. The station was a lot of brick, steel, and glass planes, topped off by what looked like a church steeple. Always parked outside was an ancient black-and-white Dynaflo, with a new paint job to look like this year's model cop car, and maybe that indicated something, too. When we got there, a man in shirt-sleeves was polishing the paint job.

As I've mentioned, Oxford was a genteel community, and its police station had a receptionist instead of a gruff desk-sergeant out front. She sat there in a lavender dress, clacking away on an IBM Selectric while maintaining a painfully erect posture and a coathanger smile. When we asked about Eric, the smile faded a bit. She nodded toward the rear of the station and said, in a lilting Mississippi accent, that we'd have to speak to Sergeant Pumpernickel. She gestured us to an inner office. The man inside the office didn't know any Pumpernickel. When Sergeant Poppernick finally appeared, the message was brief: Eric had already been taken to the county jail.

Since Oxford was the county seat of Lafayette, we had the honor of housing the county jail. Note: to avoid confusing our county with a deceased French general, local residents pronounced "Lafayette" to rhyme with "pay it." The jail was a short drive away from the university (to avoid confusing the prison with the school), right next to the Jitney Jungle supermarket. The outside door, in surprisingly gaudy gold lettering, read "LAFAYETTE COUNTY SHERIFF DEPARTMENT." Inside was an authentic-looking police desk, but with the police station receptionist's twin sister at another IBM Selectric. We asked to see Eric Lasker, and in a few minutes we were face to face with him. Separated by some healthy-looking iron bars.

"Hell-*o*, Don—and Susan, too! How d'ye like my new quarters?" He leaned against one whitewashed wall, as his cellmate studiously avoided our gaze. He was a large black man with such broad, overarching shoulders that his head was half-buried. He sat on his cot, saying nothing, bent low in painful scrutiny of something in his hand. At first I thought it might be something from Jehovah's Witness, but it looked suspiciously like one of Eric's leaflets.

Susan held forth the foil-wrapped brownies, which had already been inspected (and sampled) by a police officer. "Since you won't come out, we thought we'd bring something in." The cellmate looked up with a flicker of interest, though I noticed he had an identical foil package by his side. From what I learned later, the prisoners were given two meals a day, with a constant flow from relatives making up any shortages.

"Well, how thoughtful! Mind if I share 'em?" He gestured graciously toward the cellmate. "Don, Susan, this is Nathaniel."

Nathaniel performed a hat-doffing motion without any hat. "Howdy. Please meecha." He went back to his leaflet.

The formalities over, I began asking Eric what the hell he thought he was doing. In the meantime, Susan took out a brownie for Nathaniel and started talking with him at the far end of the bars. With all her volunteer work, she had more acquaintance with this place than Eric or I had. When I asked what had gone on, Eric muttered something about barbaric Yankees. It took a moment to realize what he was talking about: from the vantage of Oxford, England, we were all Yankees.

They had booked him on three counts, the ones Nancy had guessed at. It was a travesty of justice, a sham of legal process, a mockery of something or other—as he said this, he began to pace like Rilke's panther. It was a real performance: Eric was the only person I knew who could beat his breast with his hands behind his back. To make a short visit even shorter: I found the only thing resolved was Eric. He was staying in as a protest, but he would fight his case in city court.

"Got a lawyer?"

"You mean a barrister?"

"Yes. Someone to make sure you don't make a fool of yourself in court."

"Well, Nancy said she might have a go at it." He paused reflectively. "She sounded a bit upset a while ago."

"She was."

"Hmm . . . funny."

We left it at that. And we left Eric like that. Sunday we begged off an invitation to the Knowleses' and drove to Memphis, just to get out of Oxford for a day. We never did hear how Saturday's football game turned out—not until Monday, when our student newspaper, *The Daily Mississippian*, featured an item actually worth reading.

10

"REBEL PLAYER INJURED IN GAME," read the headline in *The Daily Mississippian*. "Wilson 'Willy' Tucker, defensive back for the Rebels, performed like a hero this past Saturday. Always one to give 100%, Tucker was attempting to intercept a touchdown pass in the third quarter of the game when he was caught in the scrimmage and fractured two cervical vertebrae. Tucker was immediately taken to the Baptist Central Hospital in Memphis, where doctors examined him''—and here I stopped reading for a moment. I didn't know who Tucker was, but I know what that kind of fracture means, and I could have written the headline myself: "TUCKER BREAKS NECK; PARALYZED FOR LIFE." Jesus.

The rest of the article talked around the facts. For what it's worth, the Rebels won the game 22-17. Tucker was now in intensive care, unable to move. The prognosis wasn't good. He appeared to be paralyzed from the neck down and was in critical condition. But he wasn't giving up, fans, no, not a true-blue Rebel like Willy. And he's going to need all the help he can get to triumph over this accident, so please pray for our—and here I put the paper down again, too disgusted to continue. It wasn't just the waste of a life— what football players do best is sports, and when they can't do sports, they can't do much else. Tucker was black, and that didn't help his chances in life any. It was this business of false hope, something I can't help associating with organized religion. Yes, I may be club-footed, but Jesus can heal me! God will stop the bank from foreclosing on the mortgage. If I just pray for that test score, it can happen.

Hope, that's what people feed on, and when it's a baseless hope, it's just a pernicious illusion. No one ever gets well after a broken neck. A heap of prayers doesn't pile up to anything. You know what? When Pandora opened her box and let forth all the evils into the world, and the one consolation was hope at the bottom of the box—well, that's a misreading of the myth. The true meaning is that the worst evil was at the bottom of the box, and that was hope. Hope leads men on, makes them gamble instead of trying the hard way, feeds them lies in place of reality. My father used to quote a saying from Kazantzakis, the author of *Zorba the Greek*: "I have no hopes, I have no fears, I am free."

Kazantzakis was a brave man.

I don't know why I got so worked up, but when I looked down at the paper again, I realized I was crying. And not so much over the unmendable broken neck as over the ceaseless hope that would be expended on the poor son of a bitch. Even if he survived. Especially if he survived.

On Wednesday, the paper announced that Tucker had been operated on to realign the damaged vertebrae. "If anyone can take the pressure of something like this,'' said one of his fellow players in an interview, ''it's Willy.'' A prayer vigil was scheduled for Thursday night. That made me flinch. A special Willy Tucker fund had already been set up to cover medical expenses. Now *that* made good sense: not hope, but charity, and the only one of the trinity of virtues that I believe in. As a matter of fact, $30,000 had already been sent in.

On Thursday, Willy had a tracheotomy to help him breathe, and was placed on a respirator. And I had my first suffocation dream in years.

When I was young, my father and I used to visit a friend of the family, a man in an iron lung, paralyzed by polio when he was in his early twenties. His name was Lennie Segal, and he was an absolute whiz at any kind of mental game like Ghost, Geography, or Who Am I? And I used to read to him: he particularly liked the adventures of Sherlock Holmes. At first, the wheezing of Lennie's iron lung made me uneasy, but eventually I got inured to it. If he could get used to it, I figured, so could I. And he acted as if it weren't there at all, as if he were reclining because he was too lazy to get up. But the one thing I never got used to was his laugh, which was a series of evenly-spaced monosyllables in one tone: ''Ha . . . ha . . . ha . . . ha . . . ha. . . .''

Lennie died from pulmonary complications when I was in junior high, but I think of him from time to time, particularly when I'm trying to visualize mind without body. And also in occasional dreams. Lennie came back to me that week when I thought about Tucker. A few of the football players wandering around the halls wore red armbands, which was supposed to lend support like some magical thread. I myself sent in fifty dollars toward the Help Willy Tucker Fund. The money wasn't much, it wouldn't pay for even a day's intensive care, but it helped me sleep better.

It was right after my morning class that Thursday, and I was headed toward the department office to pick up my mail, when I saw Max in the hall. He wasn't moving, which looked odd. When classes let out at 10:45, the whole hall becomes alive with bodies streaming toward the outdoors. If you're not caught in that swarm, you look a little peculiar, and also people tend to bump into you. Max had solved that second problem by finding a recessed area where the corridor abruptly broadened. He was watching the student body, or maybe I should say students' bodies.

I watched him watch, but it's always hard to tell what someone else is looking at from any distance. Was he fastening on the blonde Delta Gamma girl, who seemed to be all legs and hair, or the hourglass houri on her left, whose mother must have laced her into a bustle every day until it shaped her permanently? Maybe he was looking at the raven-haired girl from my class, who had skin so pale it looked like fresh-poured milk. Now he was jotting something down on the wad of paper he always shoved into his back pocket. As he wrote, a broad bullet-headed jock waved a friendly paw in Max's face. Max smiled briefly and nodded, though you could tell he didn't like being interrupted. Just then, the big girl from my class podged by, and I lost my view of Max against a vast wall of flesh. She was wearing a white sweatshirt large even by her measurements and moved as smoothly and slowly as a draped float at a parade.

When I regained my view, Max was gone.

I took the elevator up to the department office, got my mail, and schmoozed a bit. Gina was talking with Greg about a discovery she'd made on the Faulkner suicide trail. Apparently, Faulkner had been taking sleeping pills under prescription for a while when he fell from his horse. "And the examining doctor never made any mention of pills at the scene. Don't you think that's odd?" Gina's eyes were bright and sleuthlike.

Greg, ever the apostle of reason, offered another possibility. "Maybe he left them at home."

"No. The reason they weren't found is that Faulkner had swallowed them all. I'm sure of it."

Greg and Gina looked in my direction as the deciding vote. "Um, what about the doctor?" I offered. "Did you ever track him down?"

"That's just it. He retired a few years ago, but he's still living in Lafayette county. So I invited him to speak to my class."

"And?"

"Well, I don't know. He said it's okay with him, but his daughter seems to think it would be bad for his health. I think it's an excuse."

"Maybe his health isn't so good." Greg-on-the-spot.

I drifted out of the argument at this point. Gina was a friend of mine, bright, warm, obsessive. She moved around Faulkner's novels like a person who'd lived in the same boardinghouse for thirty years, with the Snopeses as neighbors. Every summer, she put in a back-breaking amount of work for the annual Faulkner and Yoknapatawpha Conference. When I first came here, for my faculty interview, Gina took me around in her old Plymouth to show me where Jason Compson did something hideous, or where he would have if Jason had been real and not a word-mass Faulkner put into *The Sound and the Fury*. The weird part about it was that Gina didn't care for Mississippi much—hated the rednecks, couldn't eat the local food, and frankly would have been much happier in California. But this was Faulkner country, so this was where she lived. Greg could probably have been happy teaching modern poetry at Antarctic U, and this was the fundamental difference between them.

After a minute, Ed Schamley poked his head out of his office. With his loosened tie, mussed hair, and bags under his eyes, he looked like a newspaperman who'd just worked around the clock to file a story. But if you asked him, he'd say full-time at *Newsday* was a hell of a lot easier than department chair at Ole Miss. He was up against the usual academic hurdles: incompetent administrators, insufficient funding, and overcrowded classes. But he managed to keep a sense of humor. And he hated red tape, so he cut through it wherever possible. All our faculty meetings were guaranteed one hour maximum. I pitied Max, having to work under Spofford, who had a fondness for long-winded theatrics.

Ed looked at me and waggled his eyebrows. "You're not Melvin Kent."

"Do I look like a gnome?"

"You're right. Sorry." He turned to Mrs. Post. "Would you send in Professor Kent when he comes by? He has an appointment with me at eleven."

"I believe he was here a few minutes ago."

Ed squinted up at the big office clock, which read 11:03.

As if on cue, Melvin appeared in the doorway. He always wore his hair in a monk's tonsure, maybe because he was a medievalist, but since he didn't wear a robe and sandals, it never looked right. "I was here at eleven, and your office door was closed," he told Ed. "I thought I would come back later." Then he noticed me. "Ah, Don. A piece of your mail got dropped into my box. Inadvertently, I'm sure." He reached into his briefcase. "Here it is."

This was Travis' fault, of course, but I didn't say anything. I took the envelope, hoping it was a letter from my friend Dorothy, my friend at Columbia. I probably could have reached her by phone, but ours was an epistolary friendship, at its best on the page. This was the first time she'd taken more than a few weeks to respond. Anyway, the item in question was just a promotional flyer from an academic press. Why Melvin couldn't simply have dropped it into my box is beyond me. He was a literalist, I suppose. Or as Ed put it, Melvin was a literal pain in the ass. He was also rude. When I first met him, I wasn't sure whether it was intentional or simply sheer obliviousness to others. I still hadn't decided, but at that point I didn't care; I just avoided him.

On my way out, I bumped into Travis, eavesdropping as usual. He pretended to be reading the bulletin board, where nothing new had been pinned up in weeks. "Would you do me a favor?" I asked.

"Sure, what?"

"Slip an envelope for Professor Kent into my box next time, okay? Just to even things out."

When I got home, I saw Max talking with Susan on the steps. He was leaning on his brown bomber bicycle, or his bicycle was leaning on him—the relationship always looked vaguely symbiotic. At first, I thought Susan must be lecturing him on his new girlfriend. Then I figured they were talking about Tucker because I heard the phrase "can't even go for a walk." But it turned out they were discussing Eric, whom Max had visited the day before with Holly.

"Oh, I'm sure he was happy enough to see us," said Max in that tone he reserved for pronouncements. He hooked and unhooked a long purple bungee cord on the bike rack. "But you know, I think he likes being unable to move."

"What do you mean?" The question was Susan's, but it could have been from me.

"No decisions, no hassle about where to go or what to eat for dinner. He's trapped, but he's taken care of. A womb with a lock on it."

"The men in there don't think of it that way, I'm sure."

"Maybe not consciously, no. But why do you think they keep getting imprisoned?" Max left his bike to fend for itself in order to gesture. "Moving around gets them in trouble."

"Max—"

"Immobility is freedom."

I couldn't stand it any longer. "So? Is that football player Willy Tucker free now? Does it help that the poor son of a bitch can't even breathe on his own?"

Max wore the same enchanted look as when I'd seen him in the corridor. He looked as if he were going to say something straight out but swerved at the last minute. "That—that's different. All Tucker probably wanted to do was play ball."

Susan cut in. "Well, it's more than that. I mean—"

"I know, it's a tragedy. 'A tragedy of human dimension'—that's what *The Daily Mississippian* called it yesterday—whatever that means." He shook his head. He seemed more aggrieved at the reporting than the injury. The conversation ended after that. Max wheeled his bike into his apartment, holding it by the scruff of the handlebars like some miscreant pet. I wondered if he fed it, and if so, what.

Susan took me back to our kitchen and cooked me a hot lunch: fried ham steaks and apples, along with some leftover greens. Usually we had sandwiches, but occasionally Susan liked making a platter. It may be old-fashioned up North, but down here the meat & 2 veg lunch is still going strong. The main item is usually beef stew or a pork chop or chicken leg. The so-called vegetables range from overcooked squash and field peas to macaroni and cheese and peach cobbler. I obediently eat it all. About the only one I can't get my mouth around is stewed okra and tomatoes, also known as train wreck. In fact, the only way I can eat okra is fried, which is how it appears on a lot of meat & 2 veg menus. Southerners fry everything—fried fish, fried chicken, fried pies. Betty's on the Square even offers fried dill pickles, a Delta specialty that tastes exactly the way you think.

When I was single, I used to buy a cheap meat & 2 veg lunch at the Jitney Jungle, mostly to foster the illusion that someone was cooking for me. It was filling, but that was the only thing it had in common with Susan's cooking. Susan knew how to fry ham steaks with a fine salt edge, the apples caramelized, the cornbread hot and buttery. That day I didn't think I'd be able to eat much, not with images of Eric eating swill, and Willy unable to eat at all. But somehow the scenes of adversity made me all the hungrier, and I polished my plate twice. I had to loosen my belt afterwards.

As we were finishing with coffee in the living room, we saw Max roll out of his apartment in a winter jersey and tights. Lately, he had been taking lunch-time rides on days when his schedule was tight. Always active. I wondered how he would look immobilized. As he pedalled down the sidewalk, our neighbor's little girl came from the opposite direction on her tricycle. I saw the girl's mother poke her head out the door. "Sheila, you watch out for that man." This was Southern manners: she was really talking to Max.

Max didn't even swerve, but flashed by Sheila with an inch to spare. At the edge of the sidewalk he hopped the curb, cut between two parked cars, and merged into the lane as a mini-van came the other way. I bit my lip. Susan said what was on my mind, though not the way I'd have put it. "I hope," she murmured, "he doesn't break his goddamn neck."

11

Eric's trial was set for Friday, so he was due to come out on Saturday. Nancy had already planned a party right after his release, inviting mostly the people who had been at the original demonstration. In the meantime, Eric was handling his courses through the mail, correcting batches of essays in his cell. He had given a Shakespeare reading to the other prisoners that proved immensely popular, mostly because he was savvy enough to choose Edmund's bastard speech from *King Lear*. Probably all the guys in with him were illegitimate, one way or another. When I'd dropped by on Wednesday, Nathaniel was hunched in the same shoulder-heavy posture as before, but this time peering at an Arden edition of *Macbeth*. "He said he liked murder mysteries," said Eric cheerfully, "so I had one of my students bring this."

Not all of this went unnoticed. The good old *Daily Mississippian* had run a brief article on the case, with some headline like "PROF JAILED." That wasn't telling the whole story, and the article was slanted precisely because it was so sketchy on facts, but then that was the *Mississippian*. As Ed Schamley, with his years at *Newsday*, once said, "You know you've been here too long when you read the *Mississippian* and don't see anything funny about it."

Inside was Dear Abby and a page of comics with the easiest crossword in the world. Sports were big, of course, along with frat and sorority news. The student-written columns were typically about school pride, waving the rebel flag at football games, and virginity. But the most noteworthy were the letters to the editor, which were pure ditziness in all different directions. It was Ed who one day showed how they could all be reduced to a formula:

> To the Editor:
> Rhetorical opening.
> Irrelevant anecdote.
> Misstatement of facts.
> Nostalgic comment about tradition.
> Grim prediction for the future.
> Signed, Concerned Alumnus.

I should point out that I read *The Daily Mississippian* every day and got annoyed whenever it ceased publication during vacation or finals week. For one thing, the *Mississippian* relied heavily on AP stories when campus news was slack, items listing twenty new uses for cotton, studies showing that fat people were happier, and recent messes celebrities had gotten into. I won't attempt to justify myself. Anyone addicted to scanning *The National Enquirer* on checkout lines knows how I felt. Eric had several copies of the *Mississippian* lying around when I visited him, with the political columns annotated in red pen. He also appeared to be working on a new speech.

I didn't think much about that—Eric was always writing some screed or other, and it seemed particularly apt in prison, since he wasn't the Madame Defarge type and couldn't knit. Max was at least partly right: prison seemed to suit Eric. Still, we were looking forward to having him out.

Friday afternoon I got a call from Nancy. This was when the old woman with her wrong number usually called. "Jamie isn't here," I told the receiver.

"What? Who is this?"

"Don Shapiro. Who's this?"

"Don, it's Nancy. Who's Jamie?"

I sighed. "Never mind, it's a long story."

"Well, get this . . . "

"Is it about the trial?"

"Uh-huh. Happened this morning. Open and shut, abuse of public property, fine of a hundred dollars."

"He paid?"

"Not exactly."

"Did *you* pay? You know, I don't think that's right. Eric was the one who caused the trouble—"

"There's more trouble."

"No one paid?"

"Eric disrupted the proceedings. He started speaking out of turn, giving a speech. Mostly about fascism in the American justice system. They warned him, and he still wouldn't shut up. Contempt of court—two days."

"Two days, just for giving a speech?"

"Don, he stood on the *table*."

"Oh."

"It wasn't a very strong table, and it broke."

"Hm."

"And now they've added the cost of the table to everything else."

"I see." I thought for a moment of the implications. "Uh, does that mean the party on Saturday is off?"

"Actually, that's what I wanted to ask you about. Would you let a self-righteous guest, no matter how well-intentioned, ruin a special occasion?"

"Um, no?"

"Right, I didn't think so. So the party's still on as planned, only Eric won't be there. Hell, let him hold his own party. If he ever gets out." Nancy was beginning to snort, sounding oddly equine over the phone.

"If you say so."

"I do. Around nine o'clock Saturday night at my place, okay?"

"Um, sure. Is there anything we can bring?"

"I hear Susan bakes great pecan brownies."

"You do? Oh, right. She'll be happy to. See you on Saturday."

I hung up in a bit of a daze. I remember wandering into the kitchen to tell Susan about the brownies, then backtracking to tell her what had happened. I usually act perfectly respectable at parties, but tomorrow I thought I just might get stinking. Whether in honor of Eric or in spite of him, I honestly couldn't say.

One of the nice things about Mississippi is that you can leave any town and within five minutes be on a dirt road to the middle of nowhere. Literally the middle sometimes, since some of those turn-offs end half a mile into the woods or at the edge of a field. Nancy lived at the end of one of those roads, in a renovated log cabin with all its former chinks filled. Unlike the pinched log cabins of New England, this one was large and roomy, with a huge fireplace and a living room where you could roll up the carpet and dance. It even had a second story, though it must have been designed for children or a tenantry of dwarves, since the roof-beams loomed three feet over the floor. John Finley, who's tall and angular, once cracked his head on a rafter up there and bled profusely, though that may just show what a good time everyone has at Nancy's parties. Nancy's three wire-haired terriers all ran around the place, making footing more difficult than in most houses.

We showed up at nine-fifteen, a compromise between Susan's wish to be on time and my idea of being fashionably late. Thanks to Susan, I always caught my train; I never missed an appointment. Telling her that lateness for social occasions was almost expected up North didn't help matters. She said lateness was a form of rudeness, and maybe she was right. I suppose around here punctuality was still equated with courtesy—though there were exceptions. For example, Jerome Hill used it as a form of hostility. And Max's punctuality was different still: an inner exactitude, another instance of his precision.

In any event, we weren't the first guests to arrive. Max and Holly were already there, mingling with the hors d'oeuvres. Nancy is an extravagant cook, and her parties always have real food laid out, rather than chips 'n' dip. That night, she had made tortellini salad, salmon mousse, two kinds of pâté, and a giant pastry log filled with raspberry jam and whipped cream. To the side were small trays of sausage in phylo dough and something Scandinavian and fishy-looking on brown bread. Calamata olives and feta cheese were at the far end. Susan held out her brownies almost apologetically, but Nancy gave them a place of honor near the fireplace, next to a large bowl of walnuts and raisins.

Max was informing Holly about log cabins, how they each had their individual tilt, or something. She nodded attentively as she bit into one of the sausage appetizers. She had nice teeth, I noticed, big and white and sharp-looking. I helloed them both and took one of the sausage appetizers myself. And then, since I was married, I gave it to Susan, who had just materialized by my side.

"What are we protesting tonight?" Max grinned slightly as he said this, making his sympathies unclear. Holly gave him a broad dig in the ribs. I noted Max's plaid work-shirt and cowboy jeans; i.e., the kind of clothes worn by someone who gets dug in the ribs. Max could always play his part. Tonight he looked like the kind of guy who would go out with someone like Holly.

"Protesting the absence of Eric." Nancy had just set out a huge bucket of ice by a forest of bottles in the corner. "There ought to be more lenient laws for crazy Brits in the South."

Holly had a piece of feta ready, but she interrupted her loading process to interject. "I think it's mean."

"I think it's the law." Max took a quick bite of her feta.

"Well, the law is mean—that's my cheese!"

"Ingestion is nine-tenths of possession."

She slapped at him, but playfully. I got the feeling she did this a lot. Max bent over to take a note.

Nancy told us to help ourselves to drinks and went to answer the door. We struck up a four-cornered conversation about political dissent in America as we moved in on the tortellini salad. Susan said that these weren't the Sixties anymore. Max said that the Sixties were a mass-hallucination in the minds of Americans. Holly nudged him and said he couldn't mean that. I asked him to define *hallucination*.

"Something that people only think they're experiencing. It looks like reality, but it isn't."

I felt like picking. "How about a strong point of view?"

"No one would claim that's objective."

"You've never talked with my father," put in Susan. I knew what she meant: Susan's father doesn't have opinions; he has certainties. He's still sure, somewhere in his cerebrum, that the South will rise again. Or maybe Max is right, and he and his kind are victims of a cultural hallucination. But from there we went on to talk about family, including Holly's kid brother in Memphis, who worked at a Kentucky Fried Chicken franchise. I should have asked Max to define *reality*, a far trickier construct. Instead, we headed into a digression on Colonel Sanders' Extra Crispy.

By nine-thirty, about fifteen more guests had shown up, including Robert Weston, who ran the Bookworm, a local bookstore *cum* café, and a source of support for local authors. He was always helping out some writer or other, including Roy Bateson, who had tapped him for several large loans. I liked Robert: he seemed altogether honorable, which is not to be confused with humorless. His wife Laura was a California import, though now firmly entrenched in Oxford. The one sign of her past was her earrings, which tonight were little globes of the world. The last time I had seen her, they had been tiny Calder mobiles. Once they were crossed knives and forks, stolen, she solemnly told me, from a Michelin Guide. Laura taught some form of art at the university, so she knew Marian—whom I hadn't seen lately.

The Kays were there, with Mary hailing a drink and Joseph wandering off to check out Nancy's bookshelves. Most of the others I knew vaguely as Nancy's law crowd, including one woman law student, pale and fidgety and gorgeous, whose ambition seemed to be to bed down every faculty member at Ole Miss. This I had heard from two victims and one hold-out.

The conversation with Max was getting slightly annoying. I knew his style by now: he was being deliberately right wing because so many of us there were leftish. Of the original four interlocutors, Max was still holding forth, coming up with historical precedents to prove I've forgotten what. Something about how left-wingers always chose dark meat at Colonel Sanders'. Holly was confused with the liberal to conservative transformation. She was still unused to Max's switches, and must have felt as if she had entered with a different partner. Susan tried gamely to interject from time to time, and Max always built up her points only to demolish them artfully in between bites of salad. Me, I had remembered my resolution and was acting on it. I was on my third gin and tonic, halfway to my goal of oblivion.

Holly, I noticed, kept on munching fretfully, as if she were eating her own words. Every time it looked as if she were about to say anything, she put something in her mouth instead: celery sticks with wine-cheddar, pâté spread thickly on zwieback, or some of the salmon mousse over raw vegetables. Eventually, Max noticed, or chose to say something. He patted her stomach affectionately.

"Where *does* it all go?"

"Her hips," muttered Laura Weston in my ear as she glided by. I made a mental note to track down Laura later in the evening.

Max repeated his question, stroking Holly's broad midsection. She was blushing, but made no move to take away his arm. "The food enters here"—Max passed a hand over her still-chewing mouth, down her throat—"and passes down this way. . . ." He cut a smooth path between her breasts and settled in the region of her belly. Then he started to massage her there, kneading her plumpness through the taut fabric below.

Susan looked pointedly away, and soon she actually was away, over with Mary Kay. I felt a pleasant numbness from the G & T's and decided not to move. Holly was wearing a navy blue blouse with tight little buttons. Max soon insinuated himself between two of the buttons like Napoleon's hand. I could see his hardened fingers rhythmically palpating smooth white belly-flesh. "And this is where the pâté goes," he was saying, "and over here is the salmon. . . ."

Holly smiled nervously, unsure how to react, or maybe just uncertain how to act with me around. All I could do was watch with glazed eyeballs. "Maybe I shouldn't eat that much," she finally announced bravely, "but it's delicious."

"Then have some more! I'll nibble a little myself." He chewed on her ear, and this time she nudged him, her familiar response returning. He pushed her over to the buffet, one hand around her comfortable waist, his other hand planted firmly against her rear. Holly's buttocks curved hugely, but there was something vaguely facial about their aspect, almost cherubic. And that, I thought as I went for some more gin, is why they're called cheeks. It seemed clever as hell to me at the time.

David Bowie was playing in the background. The music got louder, and someone started rolling up the carpet. The fireplace was going—it does get cold enough in Mississippi for that—and someone was in front of it trying to toast a piece of cheese on a long fork. The law student was lounging lazily on Nancy's overstuffed sofa in extreme proximity to Joseph Kay. It looked as if she were doing something to his beard—removing burrs, maybe—though one slender arm was around his shoulders. Joseph looked both troubled and entranced. Mary was in the kitchen, probably still talking with my wife. Out of a felt solidarity with Susan, I helped myself to a brownie. It tasted of gin. One of Nancy's dogs nudged me with its damp nose, so I gave the rest of it to him. I freshened up my drink and retraced some unsteady steps.

At the buffet table, I bumped into a local architect named Chet something, along with his sidekick, a contractor in the area. They were sipping something from a flask, shaking their heads like dogs after every swallow. Whatever it was smelled like cleaning fluid. Figuring it would get me drunk faster, I asked Chet if I could have a swig.

"This isn't legal stuff, it's moonshine," he said, looking me up and down. His short ponytail wagged, making him look like an intelligent horse. "It's damn near pure grain alcohol. Strong stuff."

"It'll knock your dick in the dirt," added his friend, nodding. His arms hung down in front of him, veined red and blue as a road map.

I'd never had any, though I'd certainly read enough about it. This was the stuff they distilled through a carburetor coil, the kind that might accidentally explode in the back shed one night. "If it's that strong," I said, "why don't they mix it with grape juice or something?"

They both looked at me as if I'd suggested diluting Châteauneuf-du-Pape with soda pop. It was too late to kick myself.

"Did you hear what I heard?" asked Chet.

"Hell, he just don't know any better," said the contractor. They were about to walk away. Given the circles I travel in, I might not get this chance again.

"Wait—can I just try it? Straight?"

Chet looked at the contractor. The contractor looked at Chet. They shrugged. Chet reached into a roomy side pocket and brought out the flask again. "Go easy on it."

I tilted it back the way I'd seen them do and gulped down a mouthful. It was like a dozen Olympians running down my esophagus with torches. I couldn't even feel liquid, just fire.

"Aah!" I spat out what I could on Chet.

"Hey, that's my coat."

"Aaaahhh! Aaaaaahhhhhh!" My mouth and throat were still burning, so I grabbed the nearest bottle and began to chug straight bourbon. It soothed a bit. The contractor handed me a lime slice to suck, and that helped. Chet took back the flask, they regarded me for a moment, and then they walked away.

I took a few steps in the opposite direction, but tripped on the rolled-up carpet and sat down heavily on top of it. It was comfortable enough, and someone had left a fresh drink a few feet away. With a full glass and a decent view, I decided to stay put. Mostly I saw people's legs, though it wasn't easy to see anything since someone had dimmed the lights. There had been some recent arrivals, including John Finley's legs and his wife's. John was one of the faculty members to the law student's credit, but she only raised a hand briefly to wave hello. You could tell she was a professional at this, and not easily distracted. She was smoothing back Joseph's hair from his brow, occasionally touching his cheek. There was a kiss coming, but would it be just lip-contact or a smooch? It was neither: a clear case of tonguing, and I was thinking of crying foul.

"Christ, that makes five this semester." Laura made a little place for herself on the carpet beside me and sat down. She gestured toward the record-breaker. "I don't know how she does it—I mean I know how she does it, but I don't know why she does it."

Laura is a funny woman, so I laughed. Her globular earrings revolved lazily. I raised my glass to her and found it almost empty. "I need another drink," I remarked wittily.

"Here, you can switch with me. I've drunk too much already." She sniffed my breath. "So have you."

"It's only temporary. I mean, it's just tonight."

"Uh-huh. Where's Susan?"

"She's around." I looked around, but she wasn't.

"Don't dance, huh, Don?"

I was about to reply when I got kicked in the shin by a dancing fool. It was Laura's husband Robert, hustling his long legs around the floor. Robert happens to be 6'6". The Rolling Stones were on, and through Robert's legs, I could see Nancy trying to follow his impossible lead.

"Son of a bitch."

"Sorry, did I hit you?" Robert called back over his shoulder.

"No, just a very sensitive carpet." I took a deep sip of Laura's drink, vodka and something.

"Let's move back some," said Laura, so we did. Pretty soon, we spotted Max and Holly on the dance floor, gyrating irresponsibly. I will say, for a plump woman, Holly could shake and shimmy with the best of them. Max, on the other hand, demonstrated what I have always known: that there is a dance gene, and it is distributed unequally across the sexes. He was better coordinated than a dancing fool like Robert, but he was too determined, too tight in his movements. Even during "Angie," which is slow, she softly swayed, while he tensed back and forth. He seemed capable of only two opposed positions: holding her and being held by her. For the briefest of moments, I imagined him nude and still dancing.

I tried to get up for another drink, but my feet had somehow become jammed under the carpet roll. Magically, Laura had acquired another glass, and she passed this one on to me, too. Her hands free, she pointed to Holly. "That's Marian's successor."

"I know."

"I like Marian."

"So do I." I tried to be diplomatic. "But I think Max likes Holly a lot."

"There's a lot of Holly." Laura reached back for her drink. "Max ought to have his head examined."

"I don't know about that."

"What do you mean?"

I tried to think what I meant, but it was difficult. That last drink had closed off a certain area of the brain where I do most of my thinking. I tried to tell her anyway. Funny how alcohol never seems to close off the speech center.

"Never mind, Don." She looked out onto the dance floor as Max entered his holding pattern, squeezing Holly around her middle. One of Nancy's terriers skirted clumsily around them. "I don't know Max that well, anyway."

"It's hard," I agreed, leaning back on the carpet, which made me dizzy, so I stopped. My limbs weren't very well attached to the rest of my body, and I somehow got the idea that dancing would get me back together. "Wanna dance?"

Laura put down her drink (where it would get stomped on by Finley) and flexed her Californian legs. "Why not?" And she graciously helped me to my feet, all two of them.

The rest of that evening is kind of foggy. We bumped into a few couples, though I don't think I ever managed to repay Robert for that kick. The music played louder and faster. Through a gap between couples I thought I saw Andy Hillman, the owner of the Polka Dot, in a white tux with a rainbow bow tie. He was dancing with Earl, his idiot factotum, indulgently following every misstep. I blinked and he was gone. When I tried blinking out Robert, it didn't work. I remember whirling Laura around, or trying to, as she shouted at me to get with it. At that point, I think I must have let go and spun off by centripetal force. My last memory is whirling with arms thrust back, head down through the dancing couples, on a direct collision course with Holly's broad behind.

12

I woke up Sunday morning to a distinctly Southern aroma: the fused fragrant molecules of fried eggs, sausage, biscuits, and coffee. Luckily, my nose was working because all my other senses were on the fritz. My eyes were encrusted with sleep dust, and my ears felt as waxy as a dummy at Madame Tussaud's. My fingers were stiff—but oddly not my penis—and my mouth felt as if someone had just pulled an old boot out of it. There's an old W.C. Fields film where he wakes up in bed and says he feels as if he has a manhole cover resting on his head. And since it's a W.C. Fields film, he actually does. I couldn't find the manhole cover resting right over my eyelids, but I knew it was there.

All that was left of Susan was a 5'5" depression on the other side of the bed. The rest of her was in the kitchen, sizzling away. I assume this meant we made love the night before, since this is Susan's traditional way of thanking her man. The smell was so overpowering that it actually lured me out of my hospital bed, where I barked my shin on the doorframe to remind me that my sense of balance hadn't quite returned. I limped into the kitchen in my saggy underwear and saw Susan with a spatula in her hand, an apron tied around her peach panties. I could see only the back of her head, but I knew she was smiling to herself.

"Ghumpph."

"What's that, dear?"

I made another attempt at conversation, despite a rising ball of phlegm in my throat. My grandfather used to start every day by leaning out the window and hawking into the bushes, which is what I did now. Something that looked like an oyster flew onto the nearest azalea bush and clung there, slowly elongating. I rubbed my eyes blearily, but it was still there and so was I, with an awful taste in my mouth. Over at the stove, Susan was expertly flipping sausage patties onto biscuit halves. She put one onto a plate. "Go ahead, nibble."

"Mgnn takasha fst."

"What?"

I made an effort. "I'm going. To take a shower first. So I feel halfway human. Then. You can tell me what I did last night." I stumbled gracefully toward the bathroom, blessed source of morning comfort. I didn't offer to help—that was her domain. Gender arguments were no use. Once, when I'd tried to cook breakfast for her the morning after, she stayed angry all day.

Ten minutes later, I was seated at the kitchen table, being served over my shoulder. The coffee was strong, cut with chicory to give it an edge. I took a large swig and sighed, feeling it flow through me, brown ichor, replacing the blood in my veins. The sausage patty had oozed onto the white pith of the biscuit, and I could feel it doing me harm as I swallowed my first bite. The limpid yolk of the egg broke at the first touch of the fork, coating the tines. A purely Southern diet is deadly, but it's irresistible at times. Susan watched as if supervising the care and feeding of some large land animal. I wondered fleetingly if this was how Holly felt.

"You were funny last night," Susan said.

"Funny ha-ha or funny peculiar?"

"Just funny. Nancy thought so, too."

"Damn. What'd I say?"

"Oh, just . . . things."

I scratched my forehead, trying to recall some of the things I had said last night, but there was too much cotton up there. The one memory I recalled vividly was flying head-on into Holly's derriere. "Was Holly angry after, uh, what happened?"

"Angry at what?" Susan paused, fork midway to mouth.

"Didn't I slam into her?—I think while I was dancing."

Susan shook her head uncertainly. "I think you were dancing in your mind. Anyway, Holly was mostly over by the buffet. And Max was disgusting."

I nodded wearily. But I remembered that Susan had been in the kitchen for a lot of the evening. She must have come out at a later stage of my inebriation than I could recall. Maybe I could ask Max. Maybe I should just forget the whole thing.

Susan placed a warm arm around my neck and gave me an eggy kiss. "I like it when you're befuddled. You're not so academic. It's cute. You were cute in bed last night, too."

I didn't ask for details this time. I took another sip of coffee, trying to look sly, basking in the warmth from the window, from the yellow center of the egg, and from Susan nuzzling my unshaven neck. I was enjoying another Southern tradition, that Sundays spent in repentance are also for convalescence.

Monday returned me to a semblance of normalcy. *The Daily Mississippian* chose not to report on the wild weekend event at law professor Nancy Crew's house. Instead, it offered an update on Willy's situation. Volunteers were now soliciting contributions at every football game. Ole Miss had beaten LSU this weekend. The fund now topped $130,000. Willy's guardian—to add to his other problems, Willy was an orphan—reported to the paper that his ward was in good spirits. "Where the spirit is strong, the Lord will prevail," he pronounced.

Buried on page six was a squib about Eric: English prof returns to jail. Contempt of court cited. Long sound-bite from Eric: "I will remain a prisoner of the system until such time as the system is reformed." I wondered what his cellmate Nathaniel was reading by now—*Das Kapital*?—or maybe Nathaniel had already been sprung.

Thanksgiving was next week. That meant preaching to half-empty classes on Monday and Tuesday. Some teachers had already unofficially canceled classes. I resented such caving in under pressure, but I did make sure to keep lessons on those days light. Elaine Dobson, sure that she was being taken advantage of because she was a woman, fought back by giving an exam that week. It didn't help much. All it did was give her an armful of tests to correct over the holiday, and a batch of make-ups to hand out to the students who hadn't shown up anyway.

Ole Miss students were a slippery bunch. If you pressed them, most wouldn't admit they'd skipped out early. They'd invent a pressing need to have been elsewhere, usually a dying grand-mother. I had one student two years ago who went through three grandmothers in one semester. Then again, you have to be careful: I had another student who gave me medical excuses until finally I called her into my office, and that's when I found out she had leukemia.

Considering how many young people were at the university, it's odd how Old Mortality hovered over the campus. Three years ago, five Kappa Theta sorority members were walkathoning from Bates-ville when a trailer truck ran right through them. The memorial crosses were still there alongside Route 6. Every month or so, there was a fatality of some kind, usually a DUI accident. Then there were the mysterious tumors, the quiet cancers that always claimed some honors student, whose parents set up a scholarship fund when properly approached by the university chancellor. The tanning sa-lons—UNLIMITED TANNING! LOW MEMBERSHIP FEE!—

produced a bizarre incident when a girl overdid it and almost cooked her liver. I thought about these ends sometimes when I was walking near the old Confederate graveyard just beyond the campus. The Civil War is also a testament to early deaths.

The graveyard wasn't much; it didn't even have gravestones. It was right past the Tad Smith Memorial Coliseum, at the end of a chained-off road marked by two stone gateposts. A slate stepping-stone path led into the middle of a clipped expanse of lawn, with an obelisk at the center. The obelisk had a brass plaque gone green with age, and that was the commemoration for seven hundred dead—not those killed in battle but those who died in the hospital, which is what they turned the university buildings into during the war. Most of them, the plaque noted, were wounded at Shiloh, though there was a bit of a mix, including a few of Grant's men. Then there was a list of eighty or so names, the rest "KNOWN BUT TO GOD."

Roy Bateson swore he'd seen spirits out there, but they probably came from the bottle he was holding. I myself liked going out there every once in a while because it was so peaceful. The lawn was springy and soft, not like the wiry grass on most of the campus. The yard was surrounded by a low wall that somehow kept in the atmosphere of the past, and large, overhanging oak trees penned it in further. Shadows gathered at the edges and shifted in the breeze.

I had just finished my pre-Thanksgiving afternoon class, an audience of twelve students more concerned with plane tickets than with *Moll Flanders*, and I was looking for moral justification. I decided on a trip to the graveyard. It was the right time of day for it, with the light just beginning to fade behind the trees, and the oncoming stillness of dusk. The word *gloaming* suggested itself. It would prepare me for *Wuthering Heights*, which was next on the syllabus. I left my papers in my office and walked toward the edge of the universe, or at least the edge of the university.

At a school with over ten thousand students, there was almost always someone around, but not when they all had relatives expecting them for Thanksgiving. I saw no one. The parking lot held a lone Ford pickup truck, its front fender caked with mud, like a bedraggled, overgrown dog waiting for its owner to return. I rounded the curve of the coliseum, towards the lane to the graveyard. The trees whispered something indecipherable. When I passed between the stone posts, I thought I heard a muffled cry.

I am not superstitious. I don't believe in ghosts, reincarnation, or the daily horoscope. But that doesn't mean I'm fearless. Or a fool. I stopped at the posts and peered around. At first I couldn't see much, since the corners of the graveyard were already dissolved in green-black shadow. Then I heard the cry again, coming from somewhere around the far-left interior. I didn't move any closer, but now I knew where to focus.

It looked like two people sharing one torso. When I looked a little harder, I could make out two figures, one bigger and broader than the other, descending again and again onto the one below. It looked heavy and hurtful. Like a pile driver. But the one on top was definitely female, and I realized with a slight flush that I'd stumbled on what Southern gentility would call a tryst. They were making love in the high grass, on the border where the mower never reached. I crept closer.

The one on the top was Holly, who looked in the flesh exactly as I thought she would: big round breasts riding high over her plump white belly, her broad bottom rising and falling like a big pink sex machine. To relieve some of the pressure from her weight, she was squatting over the body in question. Which had to be Max, though all I could see was a pair of legs jutting out from between her fleshy thighs, like some jokey anatomical add-on. As my eyes adjusted to the shadow, I could see Max's dark sinewy hands clutching at Holly's flanks, sinking into her soft, heavy abundance. The rest of him was obscured by her wide back, a moving swath of skin against the silent sward of green.

I stayed there for longer than I thought. I know because the light began to change. Holly had made climaxing noises more than once. After each throbbing pause and throaty cry she would reach down as if reinserting, though somehow it looked as if she were dismembering and rearranging limbs. Max made no sound that I could hear. Finally, I couldn't stand myself any longer and tiptoed away. When I looked back, the entire graveyard was cloaked in darkness, as if the trees had spread all their branches to the ground.

Yet another incident I didn't pass on to Susan. The list was growing. Well, she didn't ask, so I didn't say anything. Besides, how would I describe it—what would it mean to her, anyway? Susan was no prude, but we didn't talk much about sex. This was something I wanted to share with myself. That night, I masturbated with a particular image in mind: Max and Holly.

The Knowleses had invited us for Thanksgiving dinner, but we tendered regrets. Susan and I left the next morning for her parents' place in Macon. This was also what we'd done for Thanksgiving the year before, because we had to visit one family or the other, and it was too expensive to travel to Philadelphia for a few days. Never mind that some of my students were flying home to Texas; they lived in a higher tax bracket. As for Max, Susan worried about him for a few days until Spofford, his department chair, invited him over with a few other faculty at liberty. Better bored than lonely—if this isn't a Southern maxim, it should be.

As for myself, I already knew what to expect. Susan's father, a retired high-school teacher, would uncork the same old jokes about civil rights, while my mother-in-law would fill us in on all the local gossip as if we lived in the same town. Susan obliged them for a while by turning back into a Georgia belle. They tended to treat me as one of the family, which was both heartwarming and tedious, since I refused to turn into anything. Susan's brother Steve, a lawyer in Atlanta, would arrive with his pink-cheeked wife and kids, and at some point in the evening I'd be expected to dandle at least one of them on my knee. The Thanksgiving meal itself was predictably huge, with both a ham and a turkey and everything from creamed onions to pecan pie. What we didn't eat the first night returned to haunt us until we left on Sunday.

I'm probably making it sound worse than it was. As family occasions go, this one was far more innocuous than others I've heard of. At least Susan's family talked and kept me busy. And even if it wasn't my idea of a dream vacation, this time I was glad just to be away. I'd been having more disturbing dreams, which I thought could somehow be escaped by driving to Georgia. I was wrong. There may be certain things you can't return to—home, childhood—but there are others you just can't leave.

13

We came back on Sunday after the pleasantly boring experience I'd predicted. Susan's father had told us that when he was young there were three water fountains in the town park: one for blacks, one for whites, and one for mulattoes. Susan's mother told Susan that Ellen Wheeler had just had a baby boy, and when were we going to start in that direction? Steve's kids were as cute as last year, though the three-year-old already knew the word *damnyankee*. The sweet-potato casserole and pecan pie were delicious. By Sunday, Susan had indigestion and I had a touch of a hangover from Susan's father's bourbon.

We brought back more than just memories: we had several large aluminum-foil food packages in a shopping bag in the back seat. The driving was dull. It always seems a shorter drive from Oxford to Macon than back again. This isn't just my imagination. Route 20 was clogged with returning families, just as overstuffed and tired as we were, probably with the same leftovers in the back seat.

Around Birmingham we got stuck in some serious traffic, and Susan fell asleep against my side. Her mouth was slightly open, and her auburn tresses splayed helplessly over my jacket made me feel protective. There's nothing heavier on your shoulder than the head of a woman who has faith in you. She gives you her whole weight, trusting you to take it all. It feels particularly heavy when you feel lightly suspect yourself.

I hadn't told Susan anything on my mind the past few days. First, I wasn't sure how she would take any of it. Second, I wasn't sure what to tell her. It wasn't that Susan and I were one of those couples who Can't Communicate. We often traded news about people we knew. This was different. I couldn't tell just why. I couldn't tell Susan, either.

I wasn't sharing what I knew about Max. Or what I thought about it. In retaliation for my close-mouthed attitude, my mind spilled forth at night. Lately I'd been having a series of cafeteria dreams, for lack of a better phrase. Whatever the sequence of events—which ranged from missing trains to getting lost in hotels—I'd invariably end up in some large dining hall, where everyone was getting served but me. Vast arrays of meats, vegetables, and desserts were all on display, but I couldn't seem to fill my tray. It wasn't even so much that I went hungry, but that everyone else was eating and having a good time.

I also had some real nightmares: graveyards that rose in the air and flew, bodies that turned into coffins with limbs sticking out. The night of Thanksgiving, I watched a Confederate marble statue eating an endless jelly doughnut, though my face was the one that got all red and sticky. I woke from that one in the middle of the night, clawing at my oversoft pillow. Susan woke up then and reached out her hand, which I felt guilty clutching. She murmured that it must be indigestion, and I didn't contradict her.

I wanted to talk to Max. I hadn't had these visions before I met him.

The dreams didn't stop. They repeated and multiplied. The more I clamped down on what I said, the more these images burgeoned forth, the less I could talk freely—a circle from which I couldn't break free. In the Renaissance circles were symbols of wholeness and return, but nowadays they're vicious circles, never-ending. Go blame Beckett. Of course, it's also a mistake to think that you and your suffering alone are all the world. As I looked at the traffic ahead on the highway, stealing occasional glances at Susan asleep, I wondered what was running through her psyche. Just then, she swallowed reflexively and started a bit. The autonomic nervous system making itself felt? The scene of a feast? Had she been in the body of a fish, snapping after a fly on the blue ceiling of the lake? I had no answers. I put my arm half around her and steered us as straight as I could, homeward.

Monday morning found me in the department office, picking up morning mail and ambient news. Everything was post-holiday, subdued. The students roamed the hallways like rats in a maze. Mrs. Post fiddled with envelopes and rubber bands on her desk, not even volunteering the false smile reserved for strangers. Thanksgiving seemed to provoke a massive postprandial depression in everyone. Elaine walked in, dressed in a severe skirt and a grim face, clutching a batch of tests. "Never again," she muttered.

"No more tests right before the break?"

"No, no more flying back to New Jersey to visit a lot of relatives I can't stand." She thought about it a moment and qualified her statement. "The tests didn't help."

Finley slouched in wearing jeans and a faded workshirt, picked up his mail without a word to anyone, and walked out.

I nudged a thumb toward the door. "What's with him?"

Elaine pressed her lips together. "You don't know?"

"What's to know?"

"Weren't you at Nancy Crew's party?"

"Sort of. I mean, yes, I was. What about it?"

"Uh, John got kind of cozy upstairs with a law student, someone who's been making the rounds. It hasn't gotten back to his wife yet, but most people are pissed off at him. I think he's afraid even to open his mouth."

"John?"

"Uh-huh."

I performed a mental dredging operation. I got an image of a woman's hand stroking a beard. "You're sure you don't mean Joseph?"

Elaine shrugged. "I don't know, I wasn't there. This is just what I heard."

I nodded as if in agreement. Maybe the law student had been more active that night than I knew. Or maybe I had been drunker than I thought. It did make me realize how gossip traveled in a small town like Oxford. Like osmosis in a small cell, like electricity in a limited length of wire. And here I was with this fantastic graveyard incident that I hadn't told anyone. Maybe I'd imagined that, too.

Like hell I had.

I decided to see Max sometime in the next day or two and just sort of broach the topic, nothing specific, just an exploratory question or two. As I walked down the hall, Mary came out of her office. She had on blue love-beads, a relic from younger, freer days. "Hey, did you hear?" she said. "Eric's been sprung."

"Really?" Apparently, the re-trial had also gone badly, but this time the judge just sentenced him to fifty hours of community service. When I asked what kind of service, Mary said she thought it meant working in the local schools. I tried to visualize it. Fifty hours was a lot of time. They'd adore his British accent. Maybe Eric could produce a new Marxist intelligentsia among the fifth graders.

I walked over to the Student Union, killing time before lunch and a planned afternoon bout with my essay. Picking up my mail, I scanned the envelopes and picked out one immediately: a letter from Dorothy Trauble, my Columbia contact. But the return address was new—I clumsily tore it open and read it standing up:

> Dear Don,
>   Sorry to be so long in getting back to you. In case you didn't know, I've dropped out of the Ph.D. program at Columbia. The slouch-faced professors, that grim secretary in Philosophy Hall—for a while I just couldn't go back there at all. When I finally did, I found your letter, which no one bothered to forward, of course. One more strike against an institution that gives new meaning to the word "Kafkaesque". . . .

I read on, enthralled as I always am by morbid detail. Poor Dorothy had been evicted from her student housing, and was now waitressing and living with a roommate on 23rd Street. More pay dirt came near the end of the letter. "About this Maxwell Finster," she wrote. "I'm not sure if it's the same name, but someone in the history department got into a lot of trouble last year. Sexual harassment of female undergraduates—business as usual around here— only this was kind of kinky, I hear. It never surfaced in the newspaper, but the students knew about it. Anyway, he got his degree and disappeared. God knows where he ended up."

As I got to the bottom of the letter, I realized I'd been nodding to myself. It could have been someone else described, but it probably wasn't. That explained his hegira to the South: he'd wanted to put a lot of distance between himself and his situation. And so Max had ended up at Ole Miss. Except that people tend to bring their situations with them; either that, or the circumstances catch up with them somehow. I bit my lip and thought a while. Was it fair to judge someone on such hearsay evidence? No, unless it fit so well it was hard to resist. But even then, suppose he'd cleaned up his act? From what I'd seen and heard, Max was painfully correct around his students. Of course, that fit, too, the way a reformed alcoholic won't touch a drink.

Call it a callous disregard for public safety, but I decided it was none of my business. To interfere, I mean—I had no intention of breaking off my friendship on that basis. I simply put it out of my mind. My reply to Dorothy would contain only sympathy. Slipping the letter in my coat pocket, I stepped away from the mailboxes and got caught in the usual swirl of bodies at the Union: a pair of football hunks in jeans grabbing a snack, several nearsighted faculty members intent on using the cash machine, twenty identical fashion plates from the same sorority getting their mail at the same time, a few anxious-faced Asian students scanning the bulletin board for cheap appliances, and so on. Maybe it was Max's influence, but I was increasingly aware of body shapes: the delicate, birdlike paunch of an elderly professor in the classics department, the doll-limbs of a Psi Mu pledge.

A young man with a Gomer Pyle body waved at me.

"Hey, there, Doctor Shapiro!"

I nodded benignly, groping onomastically as usual. I often see former students of mine at the Union and, though I've forgotten their names, I remember their faces, and sometimes even what they wrote for me. This was a student who had nearly drowned in my British literature survey last year. I noticed he was putting up a flyer on the bulletin board: the Sigma Delta bike race to benefit whatchamacallit. Next Saturday. This was news—usually, the fraternities' idea of a fund-raiser was a barbecue, a merchandise-promotion, or a party. Of course, most students around here didn't ride bicycles. Some even car-pooled to classes from their fraternity house, a distance all of three blocks.

"What kind of turn-out are you expecting?"

If his hands hadn't been occupied with masking tape, he would have scratched his head, but instead he put on a head-scratching expression. "Don't really know. Never been done before." Then his natural optimism (the same problem he'd had in my class) reasserted itself. He smiled confidently. "But we're expectin' a real big crowd. You ride, Doctor Shapiro?"

"No. I gave away my bike years ago. But I know someone who rides a lot."

"Well, hey, tell 'em about our race! We got some good prizes."

I nodded again, and walked on. I figured Max was a sure bet for first place, if he was interested. Maybe he could win a Sigma Delta gold-plated hood ornament. But the competition would draw him. When I saw him, I'd pass on the news. In the meantime, I had done a successful job of stretching out my errands and it was almost time for lunch. I was headed out the left entrance when Marian walked in the right. I waved.

"Don!"

She sounded so urgent that I came right back through her entrance into the Union again. I was still a little early for home, and this would fill a few more minutes. Also, I hadn't seen her since that disastrous afternoon at Ted & Larry's. Had I been avoiding her, the way you avoid half a divorced couple? Somehow, you always feel like an accomplice to the other half. I had talked to Holly; therefore I was a traitor.

But Marian didn't seem to think so, or at least she didn't mention it. She wanted to know how I'd been, and what I was doing for lunch.

"Going home. But I'll buy you a cup of coffee." Don Shapiro's male gallantry.

"No, I'll buy you one. I never paid you back for those drinks in the bar." Her smile was crooked. As we walked to the cafeteria, I noticed that she'd changed somewhat. More subdued. Her face looked narrower, and I realized with a start that she'd lost a lot of weight. Her skirt, which used to buoy out, hung slacker, and her bosom had diminished. Her arms were definitely thinner, more angular, as if she'd been scraping them away on something sharp. She was wearing a green blouse bagging loosely around her. I couldn't help comparing her to the far more pneumatic Holly.

I had my coffee with cream. I liked the taste. I suspected Marian did, too, but she had hers black, stirring it anyway. "So what's with you?" she finally asked, in a voice that begged, "So what's with me?"

"Oh, nothing much." I patted my stomach, snug against my belt. "Finished recovering from Thanksgiving. You?"

"Still recovering." She took hold of her arm and pinched the flesh, twisting it about.

I knew we were talking about two different kinds of recovery, but I didn't know how to address the second type, so I sipped my coffee instead. I added half a packet of sugar. A group of students at the next table pushed their chairs back noisily and left.

"I'm sorry if it seems like I've been avoiding you and Susan."

"Not at all." This saved me the trouble of apologizing for the same behavior.

She touched my arm. "Don, are you still friends with Max?"

"Um, I think so. He's kind of hard to be bosom buddies with."

"You don't know the half of it." Marian rolled her eyes and took her first swallow of coffee. She grimaced. "He's like some animal that puts up defenses whenever people come too near." I had a vision of Max raising hackles, or maybe quills. "Still, there's something about him that pulls me in . . . I can't describe it. He . . . *matters* a great deal. He makes me matter, too."

I nodded. I might have used those words myself.

"There's only one Max." She drank her coffee as if it were some alcoholic anodyne. "And I can't stop thinking about him."

"You're better off not."

"I can't do that. I know he's going out with that fat fool Molly—"

"Holly."

"Whatever. Anyone can see she's not right for him. What does he see in her?"

A flesh goddess. Since I couldn't say that, I shrugged diplomatically. There are times when I feel like a British university don, or maybe this is just one of my defenses. Don the don.

"It's got to be sex. You know, most people have fantasies, but Max—." She shifted uncomfortably. "You wouldn't believe it."

I thought of the letter in my pocket. "Really?"

"I can't believe it myself." She looked away, taking a noisy sip of coffee to cover her embarrassment. We endured a moment's silence, and I began to make departure noises, moving back my chair. She reached out for my arm again. "Ask him, the next time you see him. Ask him if he still thinks about me occasionally. I know it's stupid. I know I should be put in a home for romantics. But ask him, okay?"

I promised I would and got up to go. She smiled crookedly at me once again—had her smile always been that way?—and I left her there, in the middle of a vast sea of cafeteria tables and chairs, sipping at her black coffee.

That night, Susan passed me the car keys instead of a plate. "We're going out tonight," she announced, going to get changed. "You promised, remember? Because of Eric's rally."

"But we still have the Thanksgiving leftovers."

"I froze them. We'll have them for Christmas."

"All right." I hadn't exactly been looking forward to warmed-over stuffing, either. "What would you like to eat?"

Susan rubbed her flat stomach. "Catfish. The craving came over me just this afternoon."

So we headed out to Darley's, a grocery store about seven miles out from Oxford. If this seems peculiar, you should know that some of the best Southern cooking is done in the backs of grocery stores: Doc's Eat Place in Greenville, where you can get a T-bone as big as a doormat; or Deb 'n' Ronnie's in Abbeville, where you pass right by the soap flakes and live-bait bucket to order your meat & 2 veg. Darley's store was right next door to the post office, and that, along with a stop sign fifty feet away, was all of downtown Taylor. The store itself was a ramshackle structure with a couple of cats lounging on the front porch. "EAT OR WE BOTH STARVE," read a red-and-white sign tacked up on a post.

Darley's offered the best catfish around, which in Mississippi is saying something. And though they didn't allow any beer because a few beery Ole Miss football players tore up the place a while back, they did let you brown-bag a bottle of wine, on the assumption that anyone who drank wine was cultured and wouldn't cause a ruckus. We had a bottle of chardonnay rolling around under the front seat. We both wore jeans. Greg, who was fastidious, always cautioned any guests he brought not to wear good clothing there: the smell of fried fish got in your hair and your shirt and even your socks and underwear. The catfish, served with hush puppies and fries and slaw, was rich in grease, also known as vitamin G. But the fish was fresh, firm-fleshed, and sweet to the bone. Nothing else like it.

Driving down Old Taylor Road, I asked Susan how her afternoon had gone. She was off the highway beautification project for missing too many meetings, something I felt personally responsible for. But not too guilty. These days she was volunteering at the local hospital, acting as a candy-striper without the uniform. She said it went okay, but the doctors seemed snobbish. I said she needed to give it more time. She agreed. Then there was a pause because we'd run out of things to say.

A mile passed before I broke the silence. "I saw Marian at the Student Union today."

"And?"

"She's kind of depressed."

"Still keeping the porch-light burning?" This was what I liked about Susan, when she could have said "carrying the torch." Sometimes she came up with expressions like "six-sided snake-eating scoundrel" that left me in admiration.

"Something's still burning. She wants me to see Max and pump him for his true feelings."

"I'm not sure that's a good idea."

"I thought you liked him."

"Not any more. Oh, I think he's interesting. But he can't be trusted."

I bridled at that. It implied she had privileged knowledge. If I'd asked what made her think that, I'm sure she would have said "women's intuition," so I didn't ask. It didn't seem fair that she grasped Max without half the exposure I'd had. But intuition isn't the same as knowledge, and neither is infallible, not with all the other things going on in your mind at the same time. When we got to Darley's, all the windows were dark and the store was shut up.

"I forgot," said Susan in a small voice. "Darley's isn't open Monday nights."

"I should have remembered," I said. "Sorry."

"No, it was my fault." She reached out to hold my hand, and we stayed like that for a minute or two. Eventually, we turned around and drove to Sterne's, a catfish place in Abbeville with red plastic booths and a larger menu, and which some people thought was even better than Darley's. But it wasn't the same. When we got back home, the phone was ringing, and I knew even before I answered that it was for Jamie.

14

How do you feel about the people you work with? Are they friends, colleagues, salt or scum of the earth? How about those who work below you, if there happen to be any? If you're a teacher, do your students count as subordinates? I was thinking about these questions, which Max had posed during one of our odd interludes, as I entered class to finish off Emily Brontë.

"Some days all the students are working for me," Max had said, "as if I were the captain of the ship. Other days I sense mutiny in the air." What he omitted, for whatever motive, was the vast middle ground of apathy. From the lectern at the front of the room, the teacher can see every single seat: the vacant look, the covertly placed newspaper, eyes shut from torpor—each expression, each gesture. This is something most students didn't realize until I told them. I did this not to let them know that Big Brother was watching but to show them that I cared. I believe in motivation, which is always a combination of self-interest and fear. Anyone who believes in an innate desire to learn has spent too much time with Rousseau and not enough hours in the classroom.

Having made these pronouncements, let me say that I genuinely liked my students. Some of them were bright, some were funny, others were puzzled, but most of them were trying to do well. There was Lisa Jenkins, who always scored 100 on the quizzes; Tim Bradford, whose brow furrowed like a plowed field every time he answered a question; Charlene Dodd, who seemed to feel that her smile should count in her written work; Dan Malone, who had ideas in class that astonished even himself; and a whole raft of others whom I thought about during the course of the semester. My favorite students were the ones I was teaching at the moment. I'm not sure I could define the relationship any better than "teacher-student." And I *cared*. Some of them even called me up at home, which I'd told them to do if it was at all important.

But I wasn't prepared for Cheryl Matt's call that Thursday afternoon. First of all, Cheryl hadn't shown up for class. That in itself was unusual, since Cheryl was one of those students whose main virtue was tenacity: not overly bright, but she had perfect attendance and always did the reading. Shy smile, quiet voice.

The voice I heard at the other end of the line sounded as if it had been dragged through something thick and jagged. At first I thought it was a wrong number. Then I realized who it was.

"Cheryl, is that you?"

"Uh . . . huh. Can—can you help me? I'm sorry I wasn't in class today."

"Never mind the class. What happened?"

"I got a . . . into a . . . I mean I tried . . . oh, *God*. . . ."

"It's okay. It's all right. Now see if you can tell me what happened." I listened, offering a word here and there, but I hardly knew what to say. She broke down a few times, all the while acting as if she had committed some awful crime, as if she were begging forgiveness. In a way, that was the worst part.

It started with the offer of a ride from her father's friend. She had to go back to her apartment before school, and he happened to be going her way. "Hop in," he said, and I could hear him saying it, just as I could hear her broken voice repeating it. She hopped in. He started making obscene suggestions. She pretended not to hear. When they got to her place, he followed her inside and raped her.

Maybe *rape* isn't quite right. He couldn't get inside her. Cheryl was a virgin and weighed about ninety pounds. "What the hell's the matter with you?" he demanded. "You're a college girl—I should be able to drive a truck through you!" He punched her around some. When he failed a second time, he picked her up and threw her against the wall. Twice. Then he left. She'd been lying there for an hour and finally decided to call me.

Me. Her teacher. The one who told his students to call in case of an emergency. God. I told her I'd call back in a minute and not to move until then. I phoned for an ambulance. Then I called her back and said I'd be right over. I drove over to her apartment, the ground floor of a sepia house on College Hill Road. When I knocked gently, the front door sagged open, as if someone had pulled the hinges half off. I looked closer at the door, and saw that someone had.

Cheryl was in the bedroom, worse off than I'd thought. He'd bashed in two of her teeth, kicked her around, and maybe broken a rib or two. There was blood all over the place, and she was covered with it. A pair of yellow shorts lay nearby, torn down the middle, and her white cotton blouse was down around her waist. Even so, she managed to look modest somehow. Mostly she moaned quietly until the ambulance arrived, with two guys wearing identical green jackets and caps.

"We'll take her," said one of them, as if they were considering not to.

"Look like she busted a rib," said the other. They were from the Baptist Memorial Hospital, a mile down on South Lamar Road. I told her they'd take good care of her there, hoping this was true. But when they loaded her onto a stretcher, she reached out for my hand and asked me not to leave her.

"I'm afraid," she mouthed.

"Why?" I said. "That bastard won't come back, you can be sure of that." But she kept shaking her head. Then she told me. Here's someone beaten almost senseless in a rape attempt, and what is she worried about? She was afraid of what her parents might say. I told her I'd handle them, and she finally let go. After the ambulance drove off, I went back into the apartment to phone them. This was not going to be what Susan called a social call.

The Matts lived in Tupelo, which happens to be Elvis' birthplace, as well as the home of Citizens for a Decent America. This was an organization devoted to exactly what you suspect. I had no way of knowing what to expect from the Matts, but I had an idea. It was around five-thirty when I called, and the father had just come home. In the background, I could hear something sizzling on the stove, which meant his wife was home, too.

"Mr. Matt, this is Don Shapiro. I'm Cheryl's English professor." A clunky opening, but situations like this don't bring out finesse.

"That littachur class she talks about? What's the matter, she done something wrong?"

"No! Um, no. Not at all. In fact, someone did something wrong to her." I cleared my throat. I explained the situation in a few terse sentences.

"Where is that son of a bitch?" cried Mr. Matt. "I'll kill him if I find him!" He sure as hell wanted to kill someone. He shouted something offstage to his wife, who got on the extension. I had to explain all over again, with livid interpolations from Big Daddy.

"How could this happen to Cheryl?" I could almost see Mrs. Matt wringing her hands. "She's always been such a good girl." She paused significantly. "What was she wearing? Did she lead him on?"

"Tell me the name of that son of a bitch and I'll murder him!"

It was a full five minutes before they asked how Cheryl was. I was so disgusted I almost hung up. Instead, I said something to make myself unpopular. "She needs your sympathy, not your anger."

"She's *my* child, thank you," Mrs. Matt sniffed.

"I don't need a man telling me what to think about my daughter. How come you're in on this, anyway?"

"Because she was frightened to call you." I let that sink in. Then I told them her condition and gave them the name of the hospital. After I hung up, I started to clean some, swabbing futilely at dried blood, but I soon stopped. I tried to picture Cheryl's attacker: some big red-faced guy with a beer belly and a pickup truck, but I knew it wasn't true. Cheryl had said he was a lawyer who drove a red BMW. So much for sexual stereotypes. I went home annoyed at Tupelo because I was tired of getting angry at individuals.

Anyway, I met my match at home. Susan was obviously in a bad mood because whenever she got that way she cleaned the apartment. Armed with a rag and a canister of polish, she was buffing what few items of furniture we had. Her hair was done up in a towel-turban, her bare arms flailing, like some many-limbed cleaning goddess. Our upright vacuum cleaner stood by the door, a crocodile with its head planted in the ground. The linoleum had been wet-mopped, and I practically skidded all the way down the hall. "Watch out, it's still slippery!" called out Susan superfluously.

I made my way into the bedroom. It was almost time for dinner, but I wasn't hungry. "Gonna lie down for a bit!" I shouted back—I don't know why. We were about ten feet from each other.

"All right! Dinner'll be about an hour!"

I closed the door behind me and embraced the broad bulk of the bed. When I shut my eyes, the image of Cheryl splatting against the wall kept coming back to me, even though I hadn't seen it. She was such a fragile thing, and so petite. Would the man have tried it with the hefty girl I taught in that same class? How would he have addressed those thighs that dwarfed his own? I saw him reach around her and lose his grip against her slick paunch. When he fumbled for her panties, which were vast and bulging, she squashed him between her stevedore arms, stifling his outcry with one plump palm pressed against his face. Her face changed to Holly's, then to Susan's, telling me plainly and reasonably that dinner was ready. I got up groggily.

My appetite hadn't really recovered, but then Susan didn't seem too interested in food tonight, either. Both of us just pushed around the rib eye steak and peas on our plates. I thought I might as well tell her what had happened. "One of my students got hurt today."

"Like Jim McAlpin? It isn't even water-skiing season."

"No. Not like Jim." A student of mine the year before, Jim had broken his leg hotdogging over a water ramp at Sardis Lake. He had called excitedly to tell me all about it and got Susan instead. I dismissed Jim from my mind and swallowed whatever I was chewing. "This was a rape."

"Son of a bitch."

"Friend of her father's."

Susan nodded slowly as if confirming the relationship. "How is she?"

"Not so good. She lost some teeth and probably broke a rib or two. I don't know what else. I think I'm going to visit her in the hospital tomorrow." I had just decided that as I spoke.

"Wait. Is she at Baptist Memorial?"

"That's where they took her, yeah."

"She must have been the one I saw this afternoon. Just before I left." Susan clutched my arm. "Oh, Don—she looked awful."

"I know. I'm the one who called the ambulance. About an hour after he finished with her."

"What condition is *he* in? Where is he?"

"I don't know. He's probably suffering a bruised ego. He couldn't get in—she was too tight, a virgin."

"Pig. I hope they cut his balls off."

"Well, her father might take care of that."

"Might. But I'll bet her father's a pig, too. Do you know how many times I heard stories like this when I was growing up? Sometimes from the men involved." Susan began to clear the table, even though neither of us had finished. She carried the dishes to the sink and began to scrape perfectly good food into the garbage disposal. Now I understood why she'd been cleaning when I got home. It was a domestic exorcism. She turned back to face me, her chest heaving. "And you know something else about those men? Sometimes, you know, I could have sworn they were boasting."

We stopped talking about it then. She was clearly as furious as I was, maybe more. But gut reactions must have something to do with sexuality. Go figure—Stanley Pearson could probably have explained the connection. All I can tell you is that night we made love for the first time in weeks.

Cheryl was with her parents when we dropped by the hospital the next day. She wore a cast and her jaw was wired, but they were going to take her home to care for her there. Mr. Matt, a pale ectomorph instead of the beefy type I'd imagined, was polishing his horn-rimmed glasses with his handkerchief. He did this five times in the few minutes we spoke. Mrs. Matt looked like a chicken, pacing nervously about the barnyard. Both were studiously ignoring the sight of their daughter, who sat immobile in a white plastic chair.

I said hello to Cheryl, who replied by mumbling non-syllables and batting her brown eyes. Her face was badly bruised and would probably need plastic surgery. I introduced Susan and myself to the parents, and Mr. Matt sidled over as if he were offering me something under the counter.

"Just want to thank you," he muttered, "for helping out my daughter."

I nodded absently, as if I routinely took care of rape victims.

110]

Mrs. Matt invited us to come over to Tupelo sometime to visit. "Cheryl will need company during her recovery."

I had to ask: "What about the guy who did it?"

Mr. Matt's lips set in a cement line. "We'll take care of that. Don't want any publicity, you understand."

I understood. It was just as Susan said. This was a locally prominent figure. They were quietly going to blackball him from the Kiwanis Club. I squeezed Cheryl's hand and told her I'd see how she was doing in a few weeks. She squeezed back with a surprisingly strong grip. I took that as a good sign. On the way back, Susan said dully, "I wonder how many years it'll take."

"For what?"

"For her to get over it."

"Try not to think about it."

"I try." Susan had confessed last night that this same thing had happened to her best friend from high school, who had wandered in and out of three marriages and was now in a detox program in Memphis. We'd spent a long time talking about it, though it obviously hurt a lot. But pain has its uses: it brought us closer again.

I'm not sure why I told Max about the incident, but by that point I was telling him so many other things, why shouldn't I mention the rape? We usually picked up our mail together at the Student Union, when we were both in the mood to talk. Against a faceless wall of post office boxes, we had discussed tan-lines and summer vacations, teaching methods and cold sweats and connubial bliss, the shape of women's breasts and kudzu, all in looping associations where bike-riding led to buttocks, or laundry led to undergarments.

It's been said that Max sometimes talked like a rapist, but that's not true. Yes, I knew all about his supposed past, but that was another place and time, and anyway a different category. Yes, some of our conversational paths led to the landscape of women's bodies, but with Max this didn't seem exploitive. It was *interesting*. I recall one discussion about the elastic in women's panties and the ribbed mark it leaves below the waist. Max was right: it looks like a tire track in a soft clay road. Now whenever I saw a panty line, that image came to mind. Did that make me guilty of depersonalization? On the contrary, Max made me see things I hadn't noticed before.

He also had the most attentive manner, adding just the right interjection to keep you going. He built your trivial anecdote into something more compelling. It was curious how he made you feel both spellbinding and spellbound. His eyes would blink less, growing larger and rounder until they seemed to swallow yours. I had no trouble understanding how Max got his women; I occasionally felt half-seduced myself. In fact, I often saved snippets of the day— a funny mistake on a student paper, Gina's latest Faulkner revelation—to offer to him. And Max would make one of his bizarre associations, and we'd be off and running. But most of these conversations broke off just when they seemed most provocative: time to go teach, or go for a ride, or run errands. Every talk was *in medias res* because he wasn't around long enough for anything else. Sometimes I thought he just liked to tease me. I hadn't even seen the inside of his apartment since he'd moved in.

Maybe I wanted to lead him on. See how much he'd reveal. Anyway, it seemed natural to tell him about Cheryl. We met by Max's office in Bondurant Hall, where I had just finished teaching my Introlit class. Today had been the last session on Brontë, and I still felt a little wuthering. Heathcliff had dominated the discussion, with half the class cheering him on. No one liked Edgar much (they identified him with the weak Edgar in the first half of *King Lear* from three weeks ago). "He's a wuss," explained our resident jock Tom Fallon, who clearly saw the Earnshaws and the Lintons as two opposing football squads. I felt obliged to defend Edgar, though the only student on my side was a tall, stooped-over boy in back whose first name happened to be Ed.

"Still disturbing those unquiet graves at the heath?" asked Max. He was what they used to call nattily attired, with a striped vest under his jacket and the kind of silk necktie that bunches into a bouquet at the base of the collar. Lately he'd taken to lampooning Spofford's sartorial style, though he wore blue jeans around the apartment for Holly's sake. Just now he stared at me with his Look Of Utter Respectability. "Necrophilia's a felony down here, you know."

"They should do more to protect the living." I stepped halfway into his office. "One of my students got raped on Thursday."

His eyebrows shot upwards. Was it shock, concern, prurient interest? He moved back toward his swivel-chair, gesturing me in. He'd been working on something at his desk, the flat middle drawer half open. He shoved it home with a bang. "And you have an alibi, I hope?"

"Cut it out, Max." I might have been angry at him if I hadn't known Max. That's been my contention all along, that not enough people knew what he was about.

"Sorry. What happened?"

I told him.

"Poor girl. Did she bleed a lot?"

"All over. You should have seen the room."

"How about her clothing?" Max's eyes narrowed. "Was it torn?"

"Practically in half. She was wearing this pair of yellow shorts, or she had been. . . ."

Max nodded alertly. He wanted as many details as I could supply: the contusions, her expression, the angle her body made with the floor. It was as if he were filing it all away, or rather projecting it onto a screen in some back booth of his mind. It seemed slightly ludicrous, the two of us talking this way in Max's office, amid a few rows of scholarly tomes, a gray filing cabinet, and a poster of Rasputin. This wasn't about a failed exam or a semester project but about battered flesh flung against sheetrock. Maybe the decor was partly appropriate: the drawing of Rasputin was done after they chopped his head off.

We ended up talking about the guy who did it. His motive baffled me: lust, rage, misogyny? The third, I pointed out, was often a combination of the first two. Max pointed out that, from the guy's viewpoint, he was probably just out to have some fun. We tasted this unpalatable truth for a moment, as the afternoon light from his window shifted its angle ever so slightly. I noticed he had an excellent view, not of the trees or the sweep of the campus, but of the stream of bodies outside on the sidewalk. Potential victims, I couldn't help thinking.

"I guess," said Max slowly, "he'll never have done to him what he did to her." He dug his ballpoint pen absently into the fleshy part of his thumb. I noticed that several of his fingers were pockmarked in this way.

"Not likely," I said. "At most, divorced and abandoned. I'm assuming he's married."

"Well, then, maybe have his sex drive surgically removed."

"Do they still do that in Mississippi?"

"I meant have his gonads chewed on by a pit bull." Max jabbed the pen into his thumb again.

"Lashed to the underside of a Cadillac going down a dirt road."

"Sodomized by three huge dykes with dildos." Max elaborated on this with pleasure, having found the punishment he was looking for. "First they engage in tribadism, then force those rubber nightsticks down every orifice he's got, and maybe some he hasn't got."

He emphasized the maneuver with his pen. "That's it. I like poetic justice."

I hadn't been in the mood for joking, but Max's flippancy always had a serious edge to it, or maybe I mean the other way around. We were making things fit. Cheryl, we decided, should receive a memory erasure and five days of guaranteed happiness a year. Then we debated what to do with the parents. And the town of Tupelo. And humankind in general. I quoted Hobbes on the solitary, poor, nasty, brutish, and short aspects of life. He cited Machiavelli on how to get ahead. I referred to Freud on how to replace neurotic misery with ordinary misery. He brought up Jung on how to escape the ordinary. We walked out of the building half an hour later adjusting our neckties, tired but righteous, having once again conquered all the problems of Western civilization.

15

When I got up Monday morning, it was pouring, in the kind of relentless drive you could tell was going to continue all day. The sky was iron-gray, an inverted soup cauldron. It was a little after seven, the time at which all good Mississippians have been up for at least an hour, feeding the livestock or the children. I was supposed to be teaching *Heart of Darkness* at nine-thirty. I rolled over onto Susan, who put her arm around me without fully waking up, and I dozed fitfully until around eight.

More poisonous dreams recently: falling down holes, boarding trains that flew into stygian darkness and ended up in swampy suburbs, walking an increasingly menacing corridor to the bathroom. The cafeteria dream had returned, too, the food on the trays often turned to disgusting writhings. I would wake up with a vile taste in my mouth, as if I had tongued each foul vision through my mind's eye. But the worst dreams seemed mostly about extremely ordinary situations, such as teaching or writing. I couldn't make much of them, but I think it was their sheer banality that made them so terrifying. My class would run overtime, or I would type away at a paragraph without apparent end, or I'd be in front of the room unprepared for class.

When I woke up that morning for good, I knew I'd had a bad episode. I couldn't recall much, but for half an hour in the kitchen, I moved around as if I were underwater. The dampness made it worse: real Southern humidity always makes my head feel like a door swollen two sizes too large for the jamb. Finally, I thought of switching on the air conditioner, and that helped. So did a cup of coffee and a look at my lesson plan.

Last semester, I had foisted Dickens on my students. If you want evidence of changing reading patterns, consider that Dickens was at one time England's greatest crowd-pleaser, real mass-entertainment. And now here were college students tripping up on the language and getting lost in the convolutions of the plot. As for Conrad, I had a feeling Marlow would lose them somewhere up the Congo. So I prepared a brief life of Conrad—can't see the show without a program—emphasizing the parallels between his own life and that of his protagonist. It always helps the class to think what they're reading is real; that's why movies always add, "Based on a true incident." I sketched out a life of gambling, shipping out from Marseilles, South Sea islands, and storms at sea. Then I shifted to *Heart of Darkness*, paddling back to the world's beginning in a steamship in jungular darkness. It struck me halfway through that I was leading a vicarious life.

Maybe that's what literature's all about. Take a character like Max: would I prefer to know him or just read about him? The choice was no longer mine: if Max were Kurtz, I was Marlow. And did that make the students savages in the jungle?

Susan came into the kitchen at this point and kissed my scholarly forehead. It was getting on toward nine, and I was still in my underwear. Susan looked uxorial in her nightgown, and I realized I'd omitted Jessie, Conrad's wife, from my brief biography. I left Susan the rest of the coffee and walked back into the bedroom to change. It was still raining, so I selected a yellow tie to go against the gray day. The rain was probably causing five homesteads to wash away in the next county. Five minutes later, armed with umbrella, rubbers, and briefcase, I plunged heroically into the Mississippi mud. I was on a mission that would carry me back to the beginnings of civilization: I was going to teach.

Surprisingly, the class liked Conrad. Or some of the students did. Those who didn't were at least bothered by him, and that's just as good. One of the farmer types in the back, chewing his phantom hayseed, wanted to know why Marlow had done such a fool thing as take on the job he did. For the adventure, argued a guy who had ridden his motorcycle in the rain to get here.

"But it's not real. It's a journey of the mind," said the girl with the nose-pinching glasses. I noticed the empty seat next to her, where Cheryl used to sit.

"Okay, but can't real things happen in the mind?" I threw this out for discussion, getting slightly further into the jungle, as we began to talk about the story. We were going to spend two more sessions on Conrad, and this was a good start. At the end of the class, the plump girl in the fifth row extricated herself from her desk-chair and moved slowly toward me. She had on a pair of huge tight jeans today, emphasizing the broad lines of a ship hull. She wore a white blouse that outlined the tilt of her breasts, her belly reined in smartly by a wide beaded ceinture. Her flesh was remarkably smooth and full-hued, the kind of white that contains hints of gold and ivory.

I might not have noticed any of this if it hadn't been for Max. Two weeks ago, we'd had a talk about skin: its color and texture. There's white the pallor of moonshine, in close-pored breasts with a latticework of blue veins; brown arms with the shine of liquid chocolate; the ageless bronze back of the lifeguard, hairless and without blemish; a woman's milk-white thighs, looking as if you could sink your thumb into the flesh; blue-black sprinter's legs like an arid plain in the shade. Susan's flesh was basic pink and white all over, like denatured roses; Max's was a deep tan, glowing from within. The miracle of flesh is how it's made up of all those tiny scales, yet it remains supple, sleek, sexy. Mine, Max joked, was fluorescent from the amount of time I spent indoors under artificial light.

So I was gazing at my student with new interest. "You know, I like this book," she said. I asked her why. "Because it takes me out of myself," she told me. And that was all she'd say.

I watched her move down the hall, slow and heavy, and it occurred to me that some people need to be taken out of themselves a lot more than others do. I thought of what it must be like to have so much flesh around me, to be so weighed down. I found it hard to visualize, though I was getting thicker around the middle than I cared to admit. I unbuttoned my shirt and fingered the gentle loll of flesh over my waistband. It felt curiously soothing. But then I didn't have the kind of belly that preceded me into a room. What was it like to be hugely padded all over? Was it comfortable or oppressive? How did it feel to sit down in a movie seat and find your hips clamped fast? What was it like when you bought a half gallon of ice cream at the supermarket and met a disapproving glance from the lady in front of you? Or did all that extra flesh insulate you from the world?

"I felt ugly before I met Max," Holly had told me once. "Don't you know, all big women feel that way." But whose fault was that? Everyone's, I suppose. Or almost everyone.

Most literary heroines after Moll Flanders were svelte. Madame Bovary never dieted. Brontë's heroines were conveniently tubercular. Literature was unfair, but then so was life. I packed up my books, flicked off the lights, and left the empty classroom. The sky was still gray, the rain unrelenting.

That afternoon, I was pecking moodily at the keyboard of my word processor, trying to circumvent a critical problem by typing around it. I was still working on Joycean synecdoche, but had gotten bogged down on the whole notion of part for whole. The point was to take a literary device and analyze it for motive. What was the purpose of referring to a person or object piecemeal? Well, the opposite of personification, for one—I typed that out. A braggart swain claims seven maidenheads; a crime boss surveys his hired guns. On an epic scale, a part was used because it emphasized how grand the whole must be: forty prows cresting the high seas. At that point, I bumped into metonymy again, one part leading to its connecting part. I thought of Molly Bloom's parts—now there was a fleshy heroine. The plump arm linked to the generous breast. Good for Joyce.

I got up to get another cup of coffee. Was the question "Would you like another cup?" synecdoche or metonymy? It was the coffee I wanted, not the cup. Susan would have said I was being too academic. I took a sip of coffee, stared at the screen again, and decided I needed a break. It was still raining, getting on toward three in the afternoon, and I suddenly wondered what Max was doing for exercise. Riding between the raindrops?

Max had been our neighbor for months, but somehow I had never had the occasion to visit. He hadn't extended an invitation, and he seemed like the type who might regard it as trespassing. But there was no law against knocking on his door. I would tell him about the bike race, that would be my excuse. Was he even home at this time? I listened at my diaphragm of a study wall: no sounds of habitation, except for a dull whirring, like a giant spinning top locked in a closet. Maybe it was some appliance he had left on. Maybe it was space aliens from the planet Vrogg.

The whirring sound increased as the floor began to vibrate. Suddenly my Currier & Ives print fell to the ground. Glass from the frame flew everywhere, and I ran to get a dustbin and broom. The whirring had stopped, but by the time I got back to my study, it had started up again, subdued or removed somehow. As I was sweeping up the mess, taking great care not to cut myself on the glass splinters, the nail that had held up the frame slid out of its hole and fell into the dustbin. It was like a neat, pointed comment a minute after the conversation has ended.

I reached up absently to stick the nail back into the hole. I'd just duck out and take the sleigh scene to the frame shop. And if the print was irreparably damaged—was that a paper-white slash across the snow-white expanse?—I'd find something else to hang up in its place. But the nail, a three-inch wire brad, slid in past its head. That was odd. Purely as an experiment, I unbent a paper clip from my desk and pushed it in after the nail.

It disappeared into the hole like the White Rabbit in *Alice in Wonderland*. Well, well. Given, say, a six-inch hole. . . . I stepped back and calculated. I admit I'm not much of a fix-it man, but I did inherit my grandfather's carpentry skills, along with a set of woodworking tools when he died some years ago. They included an old-fashioned hand drill. I went to fetch the tools from the hall closet. First I pulled out the paperclip and brad with a magnetized screwdriver. Then I bored an elegant peephole all of one eighth-inch thick. I broke through with a slight give of the drill. Compared to the whirring behind the wall, it made no noise at all.

It was only after I'd done the job that I began to panic. There I was, staring into Max's bedroom, with a privileged if rather limited view of half the bed, some floor space, and the beginning of the door—a sort of pinhole-camera effect. The door was shut, the whirring noise obviously from the other side. But what would the aperture look like from Max's vantage? I eyed my side of the hole. Nothing too obtrusive. With a little putty and spackling compound, I could easily block it up. Or camouflage it. A stiff wire with a spackled plug at the end. Only somehow I had to get over to the other side to ensure a proper fit.

Thought is father to the deed, as someone excluded from *Bartlett's Familiar Quotations* once said. In five minutes, I had fashioned my wire and putty plug, slid it home, and left my study to check my handiwork on the other side. Telling him about the upcoming bike race, that would be my *raison de venir*. Then somehow I'd have to occupy the bedroom alone for a moment. Sorry, I feel dizzy. Mind if I lie down for a minute?

I crossed from our porch to his, a distance of five feet, and knocked on the door. The whirring sound came through louder, but there was no reply. I knocked again, harder. This time I thought I heard a muffled voice, but it subsided into the whir. So I drew back for one final thump, only this time I slipped and smashed my fist through the front pane of Max's door.

"Come on in, damn it!"

My hand was bleeding, and there was broken glass where the door swung open. It hadn't been locked, just stubborn. I crunched over the glass into a sort of anteroom, with a Japanese screen blocking off the foyer from the living room. The screen folded along a scene of cranes among lily pads, a neatly demarcated zone of tranquility. I would have looked longer, but my right hand was starting to bleed little red droplets on Max's linoleum. And I'd been so careful handling the shards of the glass frame. Situational irony is better read about than experienced, like so many other things in literature.

I looked around for a box of tissues, or anything soft and absorbent. I still couldn't see where Max was, so I figured he couldn't see me and pressed my hand against the undercushion of a ratty throw rug. It left a ruby-red knuckle-shaped stain. And my hand immediately welled up again in blood. I needed attention of some kind.

"Where the hell are you?" I shouted. The whirring filled my ears.

"In the hall! I can't turn around—you'll have to walk past me."

Had he strained a ligament? And why should I pass him? When I got to the hall connecting the living room with the rest of the apartment, I saw Max, half-naked, his back turned to me. He was riding his bicycle on top of what looked like supermarket rollers. The faster he pedaled, the faster the rollers underneath him spun backwards, so that he never moved forward an inch. But the whirring noise increased, the bike swayed from side to side, and the beaded sweat on his body was jumping around. It looked as if he were racing furiously to get to the bathroom at the end of the hall, and getting nowhere.

"Max!"

"Yeah!"

"Are you going to be through soon?"

"What!"

"I said, are you going to be through soon!"

"Huh? No—wait, I'll be through in a minute." He reached down to shift gears and really began pedaling hard. I stepped around him—there wasn't much clearance—to watch him from the bathroom door. His quadriceps bulged from the strain, the muscles grouping and regrouping under the skin as if he had no flesh at all. It looked as if he were pedaling through sludge, except that the rollers underneath were really whipping around. Their speed blurred the motion, blurred everything—even the whirring smoothed into a light hum. He could have been going forty miles an hour easily, a few inches away from the wall. He kept up the pace for half a minute, then slowed down, shifted gears, and descended back into an easier cadence. After another half minute or so, he stopped pedaling. As his bike rolled to a stop, it began to tilt, and he put his hand against the wall to steady himself. He had fastened himself to the bike, with only his speed to hold him upright.

He bent over to loosen the straps of his toe-clips. The black Lycra shorts he was wearing were soaked. He wasn't breathing too hard, but his face was scarlet. Sweat puddled the floor below the rollers.

"What if you fall off at that speed?"

He shrugged. "It happens every once in a while. The wheels stop as soon as they hit the floor."

"How come you sweat that much?"

"It's indoors, and I'm not moving—no breeze. Could you hand me that towel?" He gestured toward the rack in the bathroom.

"Sure." Then I remembered about my hand. "Uh, maybe I better not. I might get it all bloody." I held up my cut knuckles.

His eyes flickered with interest. "What happened?"

"I just put my fist through your front doorpane. Don't worry, I'll pay for the glass."

"Screw the glass, how about your hand? Wait, I've got some bandages and stuff." He pushed past me into the bathroom and opened the medicine cabinet. He rummaged around for what he wanted, a package of gauze and a huge roll of sturdy-looking surgical tape. I noticed among the Band-Aids and pill vials a jumble of rubber tubing and an old-fashioned straight razor with not one but several leather strops. They all appeared chewed, as if some animal had been gnawing at them. Below, on the floor, was a bathroom scale that looked well used. "Here, bring your hand over to the sink."

He took over my whole arm, dabbing delicately at the wound with iodine to clean it, then wrapping a compress around my hand and commanding me to hold it upright for a while. He finished up with the gauze and surgical tape, winding it tight, patted me, and said, "There." He beamed at me. "Did it hurt?"

"No, not really." The cut wasn't nearly so large as the blood had made it look, and I was slightly disappointed. Max looked let down, too. And I hadn't yet explained why I had crashed in. "There was something I wanted to tell you, but I forget what it was."

"Hmm." Max looked unconvinced, or maybe just preoccupied. He was still pumped up from his workout, and his thighs were ridged, his calves jutted fiercely. His upper body wasn't nearly so built up, but flat, almost pressed in, and a thin rivulet of sweat had run down into the waistband of his cycling shorts. The groin bulged squashily—hard to tell dimensions. He looked kind of menacing, or kind of vulnerable, depending on your angle of reflection. I thought of him on top of Holly, riding her, or no, vice-versa. Riding . . . I remembered my ostensible reason for coming over.

I snapped my fingers on my good hand. "I got it. I wanted to tell you about a bike race."

"Where?"

"On campus. I saw a student putting up signs for it just yesterday."

"Oh, that. Sigma Delta."

"I think that's the one. How do these fraternities get their names, anyway?"

"They're the letters that begin the first words of famous Greek maxims. That's why each club is supposed to have its own personality."

"Really?" I collect these curios, and Max was a fund for them. I had practically doubled my store since he had moved here, just from casual conversation. "Anyway . . . so you know about the race?"

"Yup. I must have seen the same posters you did."

"Well, you should be a cinch to win it." My upright bandaged arm looked like a show of solidarity.

"Maybe. I've heard there's competition."

"But you're going to enter, right?"

"I guess so. Holly wants me to."

"How's that going?"

"With us? Okay." His muscles tensed involuntarily, but nothing stirred in the priapic region.

"I saw Marian yesterday." The sentence slipped out like a clumsy puck of soap in the shower. I had squeezed it inward, only to have it shoot in the opposite direction.

"Huh." A one-beat pause. "How's she doing?"

"Not great." I had an image of Marian dwindling down, down. Leaning over her black coffee, she fell into the cup with a soundless splash. "I think she misses you."

"Sorry to hear that." He spread his hands. "You know, it wasn't a question of personality. We just didn't get along in bed. We talked about it. My vampire tastes. It's my problem, not hers."

Doesn't dig the graveyard scene? Won't go around the world? Objects to strange appliances? To Max, I said, "I understand." Whatever else figured in his sexual preferences, I didn't think I'd get too far asking him outright. I looked toward the rest of the apartment: know the person through his dwelling-place. Metonymy. "You know, I've never really seen your apartment. Mind if I look around a bit?"

"Go ahead. But I'm going to take a shower, or these shorts are going to corrode on me. Stay as long as you like. Just be careful of the trap door and the body behind the sofa."

He went back into the bathroom and shut the door. In a moment came the sound of running water. How convenient. My footfalls echoed as if it were still a new apartment, since there was very little on the white walls. One sign in giant black Oriental calligraphy hung just outside the bedroom, and I made a mental note to ask for a translation at some point. The bedroom was more or less how I'd visualized it: the giant box-spring mattress in its wooden frame, pressed up against my study wall. A floppy button-down shirt embraced a Wal-Mart chair. Above a plain pine dresser hung a glass-framed Magritte painting, entitled *The Rape*, but it wasn't at all what you might guess. It showed a fair face upon a slender neck, with auburn hair. But the eyes were breasts, the nose was a navel, and the mouth was a pubic triangle. The neck started just below the perineum. On my side of the wall, just about that spot, in fact, had been my Currier & Ives sleigh scene. I looked more closely at the Magritte. A hair's breadth away from the left side was the hole I'd drilled. It certainly wasn't immediately apparent unless you looked closely at the wall rather than at the painting. I jiggled the plug until I got the white spackling flush with the white wall. The only reason I still noticed at all, I argued with myself, was that I knew about the hole. Yet I tiptoed away as if I'd set a bomb ticking.

The shower was still running. Now was my chance to find out at least three guilty secrets, but I'm a damned poor detective. I'm a literary sleuth, at best. I follow up descriptions and thumbnail sketches, not actual objects and people. There weren't too many objects around the apartment, anyway, which I suppose said something in itself. The Japanese screen was a neat touch, creating a separation where there hadn't been one before. I circumvented the boundary. The throw rug was a dingy green and beige, undistinguished. In the corner of the living room was the flattop desk where his computer was parked, but he kept covers over the monitor and keyboard, like shrouds over the dead. The desk drawers were locked, an odd precaution for someone who lived alone. Instead of chairs, there were several cushions on the floor, looking oddly squashed, or maybe just misshapen without the confines of a chairframe. The only other furniture to speak of was a massive bookshelf against the far wall. It held a lot of history, as well as an orderly row of reference works, including some oddities like a Chinese encyclopedia and two yellow-bound volumes on the etiology of disease and pain. On a higher shelf were some of the tools of my trade: Joyce, Mann, Nabokov, Burgess—all the polymathic authors. There was a twin of that bookshelf in the corridor, with a lot more history volumes.

I didn't have time to check closets, except for the giant walk-in closet right off the living room, where the door happened to be ajar. His brown bomber stood inside like a banished pet, with a double bungee cord strapped around the rack. On the wall hung jerseys and tights and a few tires. A huge box in the middle was filled with bicycle equipment, including a light, an extra seat, and a lot more bungee cords, most of which looked twisted and spent. A few had been stretched so hard that their hooks had come off, leaving decapitated knobs of fabric and elastic. One of them looked flecked with blood, but on closer examination it seemed to be part of the weave.

No handcuffs, no vibrators. Maybe Max was just a specialist in verbal abuse. Or maybe I wasn't looking in any of the right places. I found two normal chairs and a table in the kitchen, with a radio sitting in the corner. The statue of Priapus was on the table—why the kitchen?—but someone had taped a magnolia leaf over the most prominent part. The stove looked clean but well-used, and ranged along the counter were mason jars of dried beans, barley, and rice. I turned away, a bit disappointed not to have found a skeleton. It was a bachelor's apartment of the non-sumptuous variety. Deliberately Spartan, in fact. If someone's been living in the same place for half a year and hasn't yet bought proper chairs, it's not from laziness. Under the sink, I found a dustbin and broom, Wal-Mart duplicates of those in our apartment, and before leaving I swept up the broken glass at the entrance.

I shouted goodbye to Max, who was out of the shower but still in the bathroom. I wanted to linger, but there are limits to living vicariously. Susan was working at the hospital; it was only three-thirty; I was on my own. Earlier, I would have regarded this as a depressingly large hole of time to fill before dinner. Now it seemed as if the hole had shrunk—well, to more manageable dimensions. Back in my study, I measured exactly how far the wire protruded when the plug was in place and clipped it flush with the wall. Next, I picked up the Currier & Ives print where I'd leaned it against the bookshelf. I glued down the flaps of the one slight rip and squinted at it. It still looked fairly respectable and would provide excellent cover. I got an umbrella from the hall closet, slid the print into a plastic bag, and walked to the frame shop in town. An hour and a half later, the print was on my study wall again, hanging slightly above its former resting place.

That night after dinner, I went into my study and shut the door. I pulled out the plug oh-so-carefully. The putty was hardening, and so was I. But when I looked through my peephole, all I saw was a tightly made bed. He was probably over at Holly's, who was renting ten miles out in Tula. The next evening, I waited till after midnight, but all I got was darkness and the measured breaths of Max asleep.

If that's not sexual frustration, what is? I decided to wait for the weekend and the bright promise of a Saturday night.

16

The bicycle race wasn't a big draw. Out of ten thousand students, fifteen was a small showing for anything. Even the foreign film series (at Ole Miss, foreign meant arty meant boring) did better than that. And this was supposed to be a charity drive. Still, I'd never seen a bicycle race before, and I don't think the people who came to watch had, either. Of the fifteen entrants, only one was a woman, who should have automatically won first prize in the female division. But they decided to make her race with the men, who were cycling around the Grove, warming up before the start.

The event could have been planned better. December is not the likeliest month for a bike race. It must have been forty degrees and damp, as well. Also, people have other things to do when December hits, like making up for everything they didn't study for during the semester. The publicity had been lousy, apart from a few signs. They hadn't even announced the event in the newspaper. And the organization was sloppy. Apparently, the person running it wanted to try something different from the usual Fun Run, and Sigma Delta figured why not, and left him on his own. He'd gotten a flock of flashy trophies—he knew that much—but a few other items were missing. I talked with him briefly, a red-haired boy with matching-colored acne. His name was Dwight. He meant well, but he was a transfer student from Rhode Island, and he didn't know how things should be run in the South.

Even I could have given him a few pointers. First of all, there was no Cycling Queen Pageant, with the winner ridden aloft through campus; second, there was no drink-fest promised after the event; third, no SigDelt First Annual Bike Race T-shirts—I could go on. Instead, there was just a race, attended by the contestants and a few friends. Not even the members of Sigma Delta swelled the ranks much. I didn't see my former student who'd been advertising the race in the Union, for example. It was a Saturday morning, and probably too early for the hangover crowd.

But I was curious, so I was there, stamping my feet with the cold, alone. Susan had said she wanted to go but then fell asleep again, and I hadn't the heart to wake her. I think the truth was that she didn't want to go see Max. A few law students were there—

anything to break the monotony of cramming, and the race went right by the law library. I heard there were even a few law students racing, including one in a candy-striped jersey earnestly discussing liability with a worried-looking Dwight. I also noticed that the law student who had made out with both John and Joseph was present, looking quite athletic herself in a pair of skintight black jeans. She blew a kiss to one of the would-be lawyers riding around the Grove. Then she winked at me. I gave her a goofy grin.

Holly was also on the sidelines, not looking bad herself. She was definitely a sweater girl, and the powder-blue one she was wearing emphasized her wide curves. Having seen her nude once, even obscured by high grass, I felt friendlier toward her, or at least more intimate. I waved at her with my bandaged hand, and she ambled over.

She looked at my hand admiringly. "Ooh, what happened to you?" Really, Max had taped it up far too well for such a minor injury.

"Went through some glass. Max's front door, actually." I hid it behind my back coyly. "It's not as bad as it looks."

"You've got to be careful with Max," she said obscurely. "You know he's racing today?"

"Yup. That's why I'm here."

"Me, too." She gave herself a little hug. "I hope he beats the tar out of the other riders."

"Uh-huh." There was something I'd been meaning to ask her, about Nancy Crew's party and my late-night collision, but it was already a few weeks ago. Still, better late than later, as Susan's mother always said. "Um, Holly? That party at Nancy's. I got kind of drunk that evening. . . ."

She giggled, not so demurely. "You sure did."

"Well, I'm sorry if I knocked you over or anything, on the dance floor, I mean."

"Well, hey. You were weaving a lot, but you didn't run into me. Not that I can recall. Besides," she grinned, "it would take more than that to knock me over. I do a mean bump myself." And she nudged me with one hefty haunch, almost bouncing me off my feet. "I'm going to the start-finish line. Remember, root for Max!"

I nodded, only half relieved. Maybe Holly had swerved at the last minute, in which case whom did I hit? Nancy's gate-leg table? Best to forget the whole business. I looked around. The only other

126]

person I knew at the race was the absent guest at Nancy's party: Eric. He was wearing his usual tweedy jacket and tennis shoes, with a sheaf of leaflets under his arm, probably intending to use the starting line as a soapbox. Standing right by him was a big black man with a sullen, vaguely familiar face, half-hidden under an old-fashioned checkered cap. I looked closer: it was Nathaniel, Eric's former cellmate, with his own sheaf of leaflets. Eric's propensity for picking up acolytes was wondrous. As a precaution against receiving a leaflet, I crossed to the other side of the road.

The racers were still riding around, warming up. They tooled around the curve, shot down the straightaway, then turned around and did it again. None of them looked too professional, though some of the bicycles looked magnificent. Most had sleek paint jobs and clean racing lines, with pedals that snapped right into the soles of the riders' shoes. The wheels flashed in the winter morning light, the profiles of the tires thin as two black lines. They had about as much in common with your average kickabout bike as a Maserati has with an old Chevy. They also looked harder to handle. Curiously, the point where the riders exhibited least control was when they were going slowest: then they tended to wobble, and one even lost his balance when the woman law student blew him another kiss.

I noticed that our work-study assistant Travis had joined the group, riding a beat-up Schwinn with fenders. So much for the English department. But I didn't see Max, and it was already 8:25. The race was due to go off at 8:30. Dwight was already stretching duct tape across the starting line. Standing by the line he had just made, he announced the course. The riders would take off from the journalism building, swing past the sororities, and then swoop down a long hill past the Crosby women's dorm. Then they would pay for all that downhill with a long rise towards the athletic dorms, where no one ever went much, unless you were an athlete or a trainer. Everyone knew the residents were kept segregated from the rest of the student body and had raw horse meat thrown at them for breakfast. What they would make of a bike race was anybody's guess.

Halfway to the dorms, the rise turned into a vicious climb that lasted for a quarter of a mile, until the riders curved around the ROTC building. Then came a long flat backstretch to return to the Grove and the journalism building. The whole loop was about two miles, and the riders were to complete five circuits. A few of the best riders had already ridden it several times to get the feel of it, according to Holly. She suddenly seemed a fund of cycling information; she'd obviously been instructed. Max himself was still somewhere on the course, riding one last lap. "If he doesn't get back in time," she grumbled, "I'm just going to have to lay across the starting line."

At 8:27, Max rode up from the backstretch in black tights and a white and blue jersey that read MIYATA. A white paper #2 was pinned flat on his left hip. He was pumping hard, but it was Holly who looked flushed from his effort. To see him arrive was to realize what made a bike racer, when any fool could ride a bike. He rode smoothly around the last corner and glided the final hundred yards. His posture made it look as if he were born on two wheels: the slick yellow bike responded perfectly to his every move. There was no stress, no wasted motion. He waved at Holly and stopped his front wheel right on the duct tape. Out of the corner of my eye, I thought I saw another rider coming up from the engineering building, but Dwight had raised his bullhorn, and my attention was elsewhere.

One of Dwight's frat brothers handed him a starting gun, but he looked startled and handed it right back. "Five laps. On the last lap, we'll ring a bell. Ready, riders . . . on your mark, get set, *go!*" On the "*go!*" he jumped a foot in the air—not because he was carried away by excitement, but because his frat brother had shot off the pistol anyway, right behind his back. Anyone could tell Dwight didn't have the proper Sigma Delta spirit.

Most of the riders straggled forward, but a few immediately separated themselves from the rest of the pack. By the time they hit the first turn, I could see Max out in front, with three or four other riders right on his tail. The gap between them and the rest was only about twenty feet, but it grew as Max pumped downhill, receding into a patch of white and blue.

They were back in under eight minutes. Or four of them were: Max, a gangly law student, one ROTC cadet, and the rider who had shown up just after Max. They rode along in a smooth line, with Max coming off the front just as the second rider pedaled through to become the next front rider. The law student was gasping; the ROTC cadet just looked scornful, as if breathing were unmilitary. Max nodded briefly to Holly, implying that he was working but not dying. The other biker, #9, watched the road.

I didn't realize how fast they were going until someone did a quick calculation and came up with almost 25 m.p.h. I wish I could have seen the climb, but I was afraid I'd miss the finish. It took over a minute for the rest of the pack to ride by, and they looked beat. They also looked gloomy: one of the frat riders, I knew, had been predicting easy victory to his girlfriend just before the race. The woman rider had two bike lengths on him. In back, Travis was barely hanging on, his rear fender having worked loose and sending up sparks from the pavement. It looked like an army in retreat. Like so many other things around here, it reminded me of the Civil War.

By the second lap, the gasper was off the back of the lead group, but he managed to close it up by the time they rode over the duct tape. He was to repeat that pattern every lap. The ROTC rider remained adamantly in the middle. This time, the unidentified rider #9 was leading, though Holly whispered to me that position meant nothing on the second lap. Her full lips were an inch from my ear, and she seemed to have turned her breath into honeysuckle for the occasion. I thought of varieties of flesh: Holly's was smooth but dimpled. Her breasts were about to nudge me softly in the chest. I turned away, finally, to see the woman law student eyeing us narrowly.

"I hope he doesn't have an accident," murmured Holly. That hadn't occurred to me—I don't know why, since I always think of accidents. All the riders wore helmets, but I'm sure that falling off a bicycle at that speed can break your neck. Especially if you smash into an oncoming vehicle. The police had sealed off all the nearby intersections, but there were parked cars all along the route. I thought of Willy Tucker and then tried not to think of him.

The third time around, the ROTC student had opened up a small gap. He had prodigious thighs, and with his head lowered like a bull he pounded away. Max and #9, spinning their pedals faster but with seemingly far less effort, soon caught up with him, and the gasper again managed to hang on. The pack came by two minutes later. As they were rounding the turn, a lipstick-red BMW pulled out of the journalism parking lot.

There was a shout and an instant squeal of bicycle-brakes. Luckily, the group was all strung out, so it swerved like a snake. The driver, realizing her mistake, stopped halfway into the road. But one hapless rider couldn't brake in time and for some reason couldn't turn. The accident looked like a stunt scene perfectly executed: the front wheel hit the car's left fender, stopping the bike instantly. The rider shot from the saddle and slid gracefully across the hood, one hand outstretched as if presenting a bouquet. The driver, an anorexic blonde in a pink sweater and scarf, just stared at him. She was heavily made-up, and her lips formed a perfectly round red O.

Dwight dog-trotted over to see if the rider was okay, which he was. He seemed almost sheepish about it. Yet another instance of Southern gentility. Any New Yorker would have been screaming at her, or at least taking down her insurance data. Instead, he climbed off her hood and said, loud enough for all of us to hear, "Sorry, ma'am, if I got your car mussed up." He patted the fender as if it were a skittish filly.

The woman was still mortified, but managed to make her neck move and nod her head. When her speech center freed up, the Southern lilt on her sentences was so slick you could skate down it. "Well, I'm so *sorry*? I just had no idea? You sure y'all right?" Dwight looked at the rider; the rider shrugged at Dwight. So Dwight waved her on, and she just drove away. The rider knelt down to look at his front wheel, which was all bent out of shape. His knee had started to bleed, but he waved away Dwight's offer of a handkerchief. He shook his head softly, walked the bike to the sidelines, and remained a spectator for the rest of the race.

The rest of the race finished up quickly. At the start of the last lap, Dwight rang the bell, then asked a few of us to be spotters for the finish. I had nothing else to do, so I volunteered. In a while, the front four showed up coming around the backstretch. The funny thing was, they looked as if they were dragging their wheels. Holly nudged me, explaining that no one wanted to lead out. Or almost no one: the ROTC rider got in front, head down as usual. "Watch this," Holly whispered. About a hundred yards from the finish line, Max made his move, coming around the gasper and the ROTC rider and accelerating fast. He stomped on the pedals, leaning hard out of the saddle. The ROTC rider didn't even look up; the gasper had fallen behind. Already ten feet in front, Max must have been doing about 35 m.p.h., his bike twitching back and forth with the force of his legs. About 100 yards left, that was all.

That's when #9 came around Max. It didn't even look that difficult, the way it happened. The rider did just what Max had done, only so fast it looked as if Max had slowed down for him. #9's bike just shot forward, and in a few seconds the race was over. He crossed the duct tape with his hands upraised, a professional touch. Max came in second, exhausted and angry. In a last-moment burst of energy, the law came in third, and the army brought up the rear.

They all coasted an extra block or two, then rode slowly back. Everyone wanted to see the winner up close. When #9 removed his helmet, he reminded me of an old physics teacher of mine. It turned out he was in the acoustical physics program at the university, so I wasn't far off. There's something about people who deal all the time with physical laws that marks them somehow: a set look, a knowledge of limits etched into their faces. Fred Piggot—Dwight announced his name, saying it wrong, of course. One of Susan's cousins has that name, which Southerners pronounce "Pie-gut."

Max rode around us, slowing to a stop. Holly looked troubled, and I knew why. Should she congratulate him on his second-place win, or should she commiserate with him because he didn't get first place? Max had a temper. She compromised by walking up to him still on his bike and hugging him hard.

It's curious how a buxom woman's curves fit against another body. The bulges flatten out and accommodate the other person, even if the other is on a bicycle. Max put out a gloved hand to steady himself, but there was no stationary object except Holly, so he held onto her. Her broad body enveloped his. For a moment they merged into a creature with two legs and two wheels. Unable to smooth his brow, she ran her hand over his helmet. I couldn't hear what she murmured to him, but he nodded in frustration and pointed to #9.

The other riders finished in a ragged pack, most too tired to sprint. I recorded the numbers of fourth and fifth place. The woman entrant had dropped out somewhere along the course and was nowhere to be seen. One lone rider came by a few minutes later, his face etched with pain. It was Travis, going about as fast as the sorority girls' morning power-walks. "Least I finished!" he announced to anyone who would pay attention. It was clear what we'd have to listen to in the office next week.

Once the race was over, Eric began to hand out his leaflets, particularly to riders now off their bikes and too tired to refuse. Nathaniel took the other side of the road. He talked far less than Eric, but he looked a good deal more menacing and handed out far more leaflets. I took one myself. The text started with a bold headline: "NO FAIR TRIALS IN OXFORD." I hoped for Eric's sake that one of the cops patrolling the bike race didn't swing too close by. They'd probably pick him up again for disturbing something or other.

Max was alone, having weaned himself away from Holly for a moment. He was staring hard at the rider who had stolen his prize. He bit his lip so hard it bled and sucked at it for a moment. He took a deep breath and held it, letting out the air, and maybe his anger, by degrees. Then, to his credit, he rode up alongside Fred Piggot and introduced himself. I learned later from Max that Fred rode for a Mississippi team, sponsored by some gas company down in Jackson. He was of slight build, but had clefts in his thighs and calves that I'd never seen on anyone before. From that day on, Max trained at least once a week with him. I'd see them set out together occasionally from the acoustical physics lab. I have no idea what they discussed for twenty or thirty miles. I could have been jealous, but I gather they didn't have much breath to talk.

After about fifteen minutes, Dwight handed out the trophies, cast metal cups with a golden image of a cyclist on the front. Holly hugged Max again, but I could tell he was getting annoyed. He told her to hold onto his bike while he got his trophy, clopping to the table in his cleated cycling shoes. Dwight congratulated him, after Fred Pig-it, of course, and mispronounced Max's last name as Funster. Since only the top three counted, the law got its share and the army got none. Max brought back his trophy to where Holly had been.

But Holly was no longer there. She was riding around on Max's bicycle, steering badly, her legs too short, her bottom swallowing the saddle as she pedaled slowly and precariously in the opposite direction. I could understand the urge, especially when Max had looked so slick warming up. Max obviously wasn't impressed. She hadn't been able to put her shoes into the toe-clips, which scraped the pavement on every pedal stroke. Max couldn't run after her in his cleats, so he bent down and started picking at his double-knotted cycling shoes.

"Yoo-hoo, Max!" Holly attempted a wave, but the effort made her swerve off the road.

"Hey, get off the bike! It's not built for you!" Max had one shoe off and was working frantically at the other one.

Holly was back on the road, but now that the race was over, the course was open to cars again. Holly was teetering on the double yellow line when a familiar red BMW came by. The driver tried to speed past her, but Holly swerved right into the car. There was a sharp crash of metal on pavement. Dwight muttered something and ran to the scene. Fred, who had never bothered to dismount, simply rode over. Max was still trying to undo his last knot, but he began hopping in that general direction. I followed Max.

"Oh! My gosh! And I thought it was *safe* to come back now?" It was the same stick-figure blonde with the same stunned look as last time.

"Lady, you're bad luck," said the guy she'd collided with earlier, coming alongside. He shook his head knowingly.

"But the *police*man said—I asked him? And he said—"

"Never mind what the hell he said. How about getting out of your car, for starters?" Max had arrived on the scene.

The blonde looked offended but did as she was told. Holly lay a few feet from the bike, facing the sky, her plump limbs splayed out awkwardly. Her head was bleeding, and there was a big rip down the side of her jeans. Her sweater had hiked upwards, baring her soft white belly like the cream filling in a sandwich cookie. Her lips were slightly parted as if to bestow a French kiss. Exposed that way, her flesh looked both vulnerable and unrestrained, even slightly obscene. But she made no move to cover herself: she was unconscious.

For the second time in two weeks, I called the ambulance.

17

Holly had a minor concussion and ended up with three stitches in her head. The woman in the red BMW, who must have had the brains of a half-starved chicken, got off scot-free—you don't punish a chicken. Max's bike needed some new parts, but the frame was okay. This became a sore point between him and Holly, who accused him of being more concerned for his bicycle than for his sweetheart who might have died. Max did in fact make a trip to the local bike shop after the hospital. She said he didn't care about what happened to her. She was wrong there. I was right behind Max, and I saw how he looked when Holly lay ripped and bleeding, her girth overflowing her clothes.

He looked enraptured.

Maybe I'm making too much of this. No one else noticed, and anyway it was soon replaced with a look of great concern. That's why I was the one deputized to call the ambulance: Max was busy being concerned, and Dwight was wishing he'd never had the bright idea of running a bicycle race. When I got back from using the phone in the journalism building, a whole crowd had gathered. Eric and Nathaniel were handing out leaflets to the rubberneckers. I went back home and told Susan an edited account of the story, as usual. In this way, I felt that I was protecting Max. I didn't realize what effect it was having on Susan. Not realizing was part of the problem, but then, that seems to be in my character. Anyway, at the time, I was busy.

The end of the semester promised nothing much except the end of the semester itself, a period of rest. But to get past the final two weeks you had to survive an obstacle course of paper assignments, final exams, and foul weather both literally and figuratively. It rained a lot, or at least it felt that way. It's also a perverse phenomenon of autumn that as the days get shorter the workday lengthens. By the second week of December, I was staring at eighty final exams and a hefty research paper from each of the fifteen graduate students in my Modernism seminar. My grades were due, as always, several days before I could possibly hand them in.

I took a look at the first research paper in the stack, a fifteen-pager entitled "The Eyes Have It: Optic Imagery in Conrad." This was the opus of Brad Sewell, who meant well but always produced the most obvious interpretation of a given work. "Eyes are, first and foremost, devices to see with," he began winningly. "Where would we be without them?" He would offer up these observations like a dog yielding a particularly tasty bone to its master, hoping for a reward. I wasn't in a dog-kicking mood. I put aside his paper and dug at random for another.

This one was a twenty-page tract entitled "Political Empowerment in Yeats' 'Leda and the Swan.' " It was by Laura Reynolds, a serious-minded undergraduate who had special permission to take my class. Apparently, she had long ago decided that everything in life was political, from eating breakfast to having sex. Which is how some noted feminist critics view the world, so I didn't complain. The essay opened like this: "The most notable aspect of Yeats' sonnet 'Leda and the Swan' is its phallic mastery of the subject matter." True enough: it's a poem about rape. I scanned farther down the page: "Swanherding itself is a politically oppressed activity, combining as it does enforced isolation from the social group and a particularly unfulfilling form of interspecies caretaking. The Mother becomes Other (see Chodorow 59)."

The hell of it was that Laura was the closest to a budding professional critic in the seminar. Open the pages of any current lit crit journal, and you'll see what I mean. So I would be fair-minded in reading the essay. In grading it, I would suppress my suspicion that she had no idea of what sexual mastery was really like. But not now. I wasn't in the proper frame of mind. I walked over to my wall-hanging, unhung it, and futilely checked my peephole. Nothing—it was only mid-afternoon. Damn. I'd rigged up my device over a week ago, suffered all the guilt, but had yet to surprise anyone in the act of anything. Since I hadn't seen Max around much lately, I gathered he was spending more and more time with Holly in Tula. I took another look at his room, the bed representing Max, but I was tired of metonymy. I replaced the plug, rehung the print, and sat down at my desk again. I swiveled away from the seminar papers to where the bluebooks, piled precariously high, loomed like a corrupt piece of architecture. I got up abruptly from my chair and left the room. I needed air.

This sudden claustrophobia is part of academia: the recurrent idea that you'd be better off driving a big rig down Route 55. John Finley, the Southern culture specialist, had acute attacks of this nature. When the smell of chalk dust and musty tomes became overpowering, he zoomed off to New Orleans at eighty miles an hour, a bolt-rattling speed for his old Chevy. I don't know what his wife told the kids, maybe "Daddy's on another business trip." Not surprisingly, John was a Kerouac fan and taught *On the Road* in a Beat literature section. But you can't always live vicariously through others' fiction. It's like pressing your nose against a window—you get your nose out of joint.

Normally, Susan was supposed to be around to help me through this. She would point out the gauzy sac the moths had hung from the scrub pine, or the lone black man fishing in a ditch five minutes away from the campus. But Susan was gone for the afternoon, doing more volunteer work. The hospital job had proved too disturbing, so now she was helping out at the local animal shelter. I was on my own. I thought of driving to Tupelo to visit Cheryl. She was slowly healing, though she still didn't understand why it had happened to her. Or why she was being punished: in some perverse line of reasoning, her parents had forbidden her to leave the house. Now on top of everything else she was suffering extreme boredom, which her parents probably mistook for morality. She needed the company of other people. But I had seen her this past weekend, and I didn't want to push things. I also thought of going to the Bookworm to browse, but for once I was tired of text. If I'd been Max, I might have gone for a killing bike ride. But I was Don, and I was pedestrian. I decided to take a walk.

There are times when I'm in a peripatetic mood, and other occasions when I need a definite destination. Today I felt purposeful, so I stuck to the campus paths, which are mostly concrete sidewalk around the buildings, in the hopes of arriving somewhere. But I would trust in serendipity and hunches. First I passed the Barnard Observatory, an old brick mansion with a round tower, long co-opted by the Center for the Study of Southern Culture. The only contact I had with those people was during the annual Faulkner convention, when I would go in there to pick up my free meal tickets. I passed the Grove, an overgrown traffic circle of trees and grass criss-crossed by picnic tables and walks. At night it became a hangout for couples performing a variety of covert acts, some of which were illegal in Mississippi.

Along University Avenue were some buildings I had never been inside before. Gray reinforced concrete, sciences and engineering, mostly. I moved on, past the administration building known as the Lyceum, a dominant piece of architecture with six white columns on opposite sides, somewhat like an ante-bellum Parthenon. It was there that I renewed my job contract every year; it was there that I would have to hand in my grades. I walked quickly by, circling around the John Davis Williams Library.

Not too far from the library was a doppelgänger of the library, with the same beige brick façade, steps, and windows. My first year here, I occasionally used to come here and realize only halfway up the steps that I was in the wrong place to take out books. Eventually, in my hazy way, I realized that this building differed somewhat from the library. Among other details, the letters "GEORGE PEABODY BUILDING" were chiseled across the beige stone pediment. After noticing that, I could spot my mistake from across the street, but I never did find out the purpose of the building—geology, I thought, for no good reason.

Now, as I passed the Peabody building, my shoes turned leftward, and I found myself walking up the gray stone steps. It was still exam period, and there weren't many students visible. That is, they were either immured in classrooms trying to figure out the answer to question 5, or they'd finished and had already driven home for the Christian holiday. I could hear the scuffle of my shoes on the stone.

Entering the double doors of this enigma, I was immediately enlightened. I don't know why I'd never done it before. "PSYCHOLOGY DIRECTORY," read the sign in white snap-on letters on black ridged backing, under glass. The letters looked as if they'd been moved around a lot lately: the spacing was off in spots. The third line down, I read: STANLE Y PEA SON, DEPT. C HAIR 310D. Well, now, how about that?

I felt as if I'd just made a discovery worthy of Balboa in this vast beige continent. Stanley, I knew from Gina's frequent complaints, was always at the lab—so this was where he worked. On the spur of my enthusiasm, I decided to pay him a visit. As I punched the elevator button, I thought of suitable openers. I was just in the neighborhood. Is this where you experiment? Could I borrow a cup of steroids?

The elevator had no floor indicators and felt as if it were barely moving. When the doors slid open to the same dull beige, I figured I hadn't pushed the button right and stabbed at *3* once more. When the door immediately opened again, I realized that the third floor looked just like the ground floor and got off. I found 310 at the end of the hall, the door half ajar. Inside was a warren of interior offices, A through E. All the doors were firmly shut, but I decided to knock on 310D anyway.

A scrabbling sound came from behind the door, like animal paws on newspaper. "Just a minute," announced Stanley. "Who's there?"

The steroids line wouldn't go over, I knew. Not with a literalist like Stanley—he'd give me a look. Either that, or he'd say he didn't have any and shut the door. Ten minutes later, maybe he'd realize who it had been.

"It's Don Shapiro. I was in the building and thought I'd take a look around."

The door opened abruptly outward, missing my head by inches. "Don, what are you doing here?"

"Nothing in particular." His expression reminded me of the half-ajar door, so I amplified. "I've never been in this building before. I thought I'd take a look."

"Most of the doors are locked around here. Security." He checked his watch, a large imitation Rolex. "Not too many people here at this time, either. Want me to show you around?"

"Um, sure. Thanks. I don't think I've ever seen . . . the facilities." Stanley, I remembered Gina telling me, was doing research on peptides injected into rats' brains, though she'd neglected to tell me why.

"All right, then, hold on a second. Let me just finish up here." He retreated into his office for a moment, pressed a few computer keys and waited for a response. When he emerged, he locked his office door behind him. "Can't be too careful these days. Animal-rights activists are after me."

I nodded, remembering a recent column in *The Daily Mississippian* about our poor canine brethren, "the Christian martyrs of today's world." Considering how popular hunting was around here, I was surprised to see the article appear at all. "I take it you didn't like that column last week."

Stanley shook his head. "The column was nothing. Did you see the activities listing on Friday?" He took out his wallet and extracted a clipping, which he handed to me. "RAAR Meeting," read the notice. "Researchers Against Animal Rights, 1st annual Marquis de Sade Film Festival in Peabody Hall. Crippled mice, starved pigeons, guillotined cats . . . if you're into animal-torture, don't pass this up!" The location listed was third floor, Peabody Hall.

I handed him back the announcement, unamused. When satire gets too vicious, I find it tends to backfire on the perpetrator. Still, not the kind of humor I'd care to read if it were about me. "They put this in the activities listing?"

"The page-editor's too dumb to know when someone's playing a joke. And the notice was unsigned, so they don't know who did it." He shook his head again. "Probably never even seen the inside of a lab."

Now I understood why Stanley had offered the tour. He had to show someone he was innocent. Actually, I was more on Stanley's side than not. I liked animals, but in the end I preferred my own species. I'd applaud a vaccine developed through animal research, even if it meant sacrificing hundreds of what P.G. Wodehouse used to call "our dumb chums." Also, I couldn't help noticing that many animal-rights activists hated people. Years ago, when I still lived up North, my neighbors stuck a bumper-sticker on their car reading "CAUTION: I BRAKE FOR ANIMALS." The neighbors on the other side slapped a rebuttal on the back of their VW: "CAUTION: I BRAKE FOR HUMANS." And that's sort of the way I felt.

Was I for cosmetics companies blinding hundreds of rabbits to test out new mascara? No, I didn't think any life should be wasted frivolously. But if it'd help cure cancer or even just help us live longer, then sure, I was all for it. I found myself rehearsing these arguments as I accompanied Stanley downstairs, even though I'd hardly have to defend this position to him. But I often prepared lectures and anti-lectures in my mind, whole speeches with rhetorical force and flourish that never reached the dais. I suppose it was part of being a mumbly-minded academic. Or maybe it was just me.

"Here's where we house most of the lab animals." Stanley unlocked a door in the basement to reveal tier upon tier of wire cages, each housing a furry white rat with pink tail and robot red eyes. The cages themselves looked as if someone had gutted a lot of space heaters, leaving only the grills and the backing. A large water bottle hung like an appendage outside each cage. The room smelled bestial, though Stanley assured me the air was regularly purified. "Otherwise, we couldn't get our grad students to work in here." Stanley had a strong smile, with a broad row of teeth white as paint.

"What do they eat?"

Stanley rummaged around in a cabinet and came up with what looked like dog biscuits in the shape of wine corks. "These. One of the lab technicians passed these around to his party guests last year for a joke. Want to try one?"

I should have. Byron said you should try everything—once. But Romantic wasn't my period. And Byron lived to age thirty-six. I was a timid soul who'd last to retirement, if they'd tenure me.

I parried the offer with another question. "How often do they eat?"

"Just once a day. Some animals, like dogs, it's better for them that way. Regulates them." Stanley replaced the rat food in the cabinet.

The rats rustled about in their cages. To tell the truth, they all looked fairly well regulated, fairly content. If you'd polled them, they'd probably have shown a satisfaction-rating higher than most academics. The one nearest me, I noticed, was staring at me as if I were the experiment.

Stanley poked the rat gently with his pen. "This one doesn't miss many meals. Of course, you can stop them eating altogether if you destroy cells in the lateral hypothalamus. Aphagia."

Dimly, I remembered an illustration from my old Psych 101 textbook, a picture of a hugely obese rat. "Isn't there some other procedure with the opposite effect?"

"That's the ventromedial hypothalamus. Mess around with that and you get hyperphagia. They'll keep eating till they can't even move. Quadruple their weight." He frowned. "One of the experiments I'm running is to get that under measured control."

I couldn't help smiling. "I know a lot of human beings who'd like that done for them."

"Don't I know it. You know, there's just as much bulimia on this campus as there is obesity. But I can't use human subjects."

"Can I see where you do the actual experiments?" I had visions of a rodent-sized cafeteria. Or would it be all electrodes and restraints?

Stanley eyed me briefly, sizing me up. I must have passed. "C'mon, I'll show you some of the apparatus." Which was right across the hall and turned out to be no Frankenstein lab but simply what looked like a row of gray refrigerators. When he opened the door to one, you could see it housed two Skinner boxes, hooked up to a complex of wires that trailed through a hole in the far wall. "The other room is where the computers are. They monitor the studies."

"How long do the rats stay in here?"

He shrugged. "That depends. For the appetite studies, usually just a few months. But if you're running a behavior-based experiment, it can take up to a year."

"Doesn't a weight-gain affect behavior?"

Stanley scratched his head. "That's a good question. It might increase their sexual drive." He wiped a speck of dust from the lucite front of one of the boxes. "We might try that one of these days if we get some more lab help. When you're studying behavior, you need a lot of time for observation."

I thought of asking whether the rats got any time off for good behavior, but I knew I'd get a quizzical smile. I thought of the Lafayette county jail, and Nathaniel poring over one of Eric's books. But of course they weren't there anymore; they had finished with society's experiment. Whether it had worked was another question. Recidivism seems to be a physical principle, like entropy.

In a room down the hall, Stanley showed me the enhanced-environment cage, a huge wire tank with hanging baskets, exercise wheels, and what looked like rodent jungle gyms. Two normal-looking rats were clinging to a piece of chicken wire. "They climb all over this stuff—rats have a great sense of balance. But you know, if they don't get a chance to do this at an early age, they're helpless. They just crouch down among all the equipment and look frightened."

I realized I had my hand at the back of my scalp. When I was five years old, I fell off a swing. They had to stitch up my head. The scar is now almost invisible underneath my thatch of hair. The first night I slept with Susan, she found it, stroking my head.

Stanley nodded vaguely. "I'd show you the machine where we wash out the cages, but it's just like a giant autoclave."

I suddenly had an odd desire. "Any chance of seeing a fat rat?"

He shook his head. "I told you, we don't do that here. We're trying to regulate growth, not let it get out of hand. We've had a few cases where the peptide has spurred gross obesity, but those rats are sacrificed." He frowned again. "Anything else you want to see?"

"Hmm? Oh, no, thanks. But thanks for your time." I tried to think compassionately of the sacrificed rats, but the truth is that I was getting hungry. It was nearing dinner time. We walked back upstairs in silence, and I left him at the door of his office.

For the rest of my peregrinations, I walked around the Turner Recreation Center and Bondurant Hall. In Bondurant, I heard the sounds of a typewriter from an empty classroom and saw Roy Bateson in the back row, tapping away. He must have been sober, hunched over with a styrofoam cup of coffee by his side. Tap-tap. Tappety-tap. Bing. He looked like a wayward student hustling to finish his term paper. So this was how he got his writing done: by interning himself back at school. Self-regulation. I tiptoed out.

I was trying to articulate something to myself, but I couldn't get it clear. The cold December wind blew all the thoughts from my head. When I got home, Susan was back, seated at the kitchen table. I asked if she wanted to go for a short walk.

"No, I don't think so."

I put my hands on her shoulders and began to work downward. "How about something indoors?"

We hadn't made love recently—we hadn't even touched much in a while—but she shrugged me off. "I have to go make dinner," she announced. I came back half an hour later to an awful meal, the aluminum-foil Thanksgiving packages tasting of freezer-burn, and a wilted salad. We barely talked. The seminar papers were waiting for me after dinner. I managed to get through about five of them. Brad Sewell had simply proved that vision in literature is important for seeing things. Laura Reynolds had complexly argued that Yeats' main poetic failing was his masculinity, though she acknowledged that socioeconomic forces beyond his control had dictated thus. In between these poles was the usual range of interpretive exegeses, including one perceptive paper on Thomas Hardy and the relation of landscape to mood. The only problem was that we hadn't read Hardy this semester. I remembered the student, a young woman named Elizabeth Hart who'd contributed little to the seminar except for nervous smiles. On second reading, the paper looked store-bought, grounds for automatic failure. But I don't like snap-judgments. I made a note to call Elizabeth to hear what she had to say.

Eventually, I began thinking of all these papers as a host of bodies—padded, strong, awkward, shapely—pressing and jostling for my attention. I inserted my pen: palpated, stroked, and corrected. My study wall looked on, unconcerned. There was nothing doing on either side. At ten, I took a break to snatch some cheese from the fridge. Why had dinner been so bad? At eleven, I staggered out of my study, eyed myself in the bathroom, and crawled into bed. Stanley's rats had it a lot easier. Susan was facing away from me, asleep in a pool of shadow. I snuggled up against her, sliding my shoulder under her head. Something didn't feel right, but I couldn't think what it was. After a minute or so, I realized that Susan's head wasn't at all heavy on my shoulder. No trust. She wouldn't yield her weight to me.

"Susan."

No response. I thought of our cold dinner.

"Susan, what's the matter?"

"Nothing."

I sighed. "Come on, what is it?"

"I don't want to talk about it now." She rolled away from me.

"Don't want to talk about *what* right now?"

"Your affair with Marian."

"What?" I snapped on the bedside light. "An affair with Marian? Who told you that?"

"Someone at the animal shelter, never mind who."

"Said that I was having an affair with Marian?" I seemed to be afflicted with echolalia.

"Well? Is it true?"

"Susan! Are you crazy?"

"Please answer the question." In the thin shaft of light from the bedside lamp, I saw that she was trembling.

"No. I am not having, nor have I ever had, an affair with Marian Hardwick."

"What about that afternoon at her place?"

So that was it. Eric must have told someone who told someone else, and my private life ended up in the dog pound. Great. Wonderful. "Listen to me," I said. And I explained what had happened, omitting only a few details about Max. Not exactly pillow talk. "That was all. Call Marian if you don't believe me."

"All right, but sometimes you just disappear. Last Saturday—"

"Last Saturday, I went to see Cheryl—remember her? You'll be happy to know her jaw is healing nicely. I didn't mention it because I thought you'd be upset."

"Oh."

"Susan, I'm not the philandering type." I realized as soon as I said this how true it was. Not so much through lack of imagination as failure of nerve. I found this knowledge irksome. But it was what Susan needed to hear. At least I thought it was. After a moment, she snuggled up to me.

Then she said: "Sometimes I feel you're not here at all."

"But I spend a lot of time at home."

"That's not what I mean."

"I'll try to be more responsive."

She sighed. Maybe I should have said "passionate." I lay my head against her breast, still bothered by my non-affair. It was like an itchy spot somewhere on the top of my scalp. I kissed her breasts; I nuzzled against her neck. Eventually, she did what I wanted without my having to ask, holding me tight, breathing gently into my ear, running her long white fingers over and over again through my hair.

18

"But what's the point if it's all hypothetical? And what's your sprained wrist got to do with her cleavage?"

"It's a mind-game. It makes you realize your priorities, see?"

Max and I were seated in desk-chairs, the kind with molded backs that don't fit human spines. The kind that make you feel like a Puritan: upright, plain, and uncomfortable. It didn't matter at this point: we were both hunched forward, ignoring the crowd around us, which had gathered to hear the Longest lecture. So had we, mostly out of duty to our dear old liberal arts college. The faculty should set an example to its students: attending endowed lectures, for instance, when staying home would have been more comfortable. Susan was home watching television. Max said Holly was working that night.

"But suppose it's not an equal trade? What was that one you used earlier—about getting your thumb jammed in a closing door? And fingering Molly McIver's snatch?"

"Right."

In fact, the university had several endowed lecture series, talks on the changing image of gold in the Renaissance, or Christianity and culture, or the role of physics in the twentieth century, or whatever the featured pundit wanted to speak about. This year we had attracted an English professor from Harvard, known for her work on Renaissance drama. Tonight she was slated to talk on bestiality in Shakespeare's *Tempest*.

"Doesn't it depend on what Molly's like?"

"Sure, but I know that. And I can always imagine the rest."

Max took a note at this juncture.

There's nothing unusual about a lecture series like this. Most universities have them. But only the University of Mississippi would come up with such an unfortuitous name: the Longest lecture series, named after a classics professor named Christopher Longest. The alternate series during the spring semester, so help me, is the Savage lecture, named after a deceased English professor. Touches like these, presented without a trace of humor, make Ole Miss a minefield of potential ironies.

"Okay, I get the idea. But why is it always some physical injury matched up with sex?"

"Isn't that the way it usually works out?"

I was there because the talk was in the field of English literature, and Max was there because he was curious. I also saw a lot of my colleagues. Gina was there, seemingly focused on the podium but with an "I'm really thinking about Faulkner" look. Greg had told me she was currently on the trail of another lead, an old retired pharmacist who had supplied Faulkner with drugs. Stanley was there beside her, examining his watch with more than scientific curiosity. The Kays were seated in the front row *sans* enfants (I heard they'd lately been exploiting grad students in Mary's class as sitters). John Finley, I saw with a slight shock, was seated right in front of me with the perilous law student leaning against him. Her dark red hair, a recent tint that must have come from a bottle, was bonding to his wool sweater in a compromising way. Even the Westons were there, with Robert blocking the view of at least three people in back with his height, and Laura distracting them with her catfish-scale earrings. It wasn't until after the lecture that I noticed Marian just three rows behind us. I hoped to hell she hadn't heard Max and me.

"Haven't you ever heard of no-fault intercourse?"

"That's no fun. Where's your sense of danger?"

"Why all this risk? What's the matter with some good, clean sex?"

"If it's not dirty, it's not exciting." Max made this last pronouncement quietly but emphatically, as if capping a proof Q.E.D. I got his point. I just wasn't sure I agreed with it.

The whole thing had started when we walked over to the auditorium together. I had an area above my upper lip bandaged, having cut it rather badly shaving with the straight razor. Max, never one for tact, asked if Susan had closed her legs too fast. He meant it as a joke, but then he launched into one of his patented monologues. When he was just a sweaty-palmed adolescent, he used to play Trade-Offs. He talked about it as we reached Farley Hall, climbed the stairs, and found two seats. He continued the description until I started interjecting, just before the chancellor introduced the speaker. This is as best as I can reconstruct it:

Imagine you're a sweaty-palmed adolescent. Okay? Good, now there you are lying in bed, thinking about Celia's tits—Celia's the one in your algebra class who must be about a 38D. And she wears those sheer blouses that show her bra straps straining the limit. When her nipples are erect, they look like noses pressing against the fabric. What wouldn't you give for a chance to cop a feel? What's it worth to you? How about if it meant your hand squeezed accidentally in a vise? Maybe. Let's up the ante. What about Celia plunging your whole head into her cleavage? What do you say—a broken nose? How far are you willing to go? A concussion?

If you want pleasure, you've got to pay for it with pain. The price for Marjorie wrapping her cheerleader thighs around your face: a dislocated jaw? Temporary paralysis? Some of the punishments didn't even link up anatomically with the pleasures, but that, Max explained, wasn't the point. The point was to decide what you were willing to undergo, what you could take.

It was at this point that I began to fire questions at Max. He actually answered a few.

"I take it you weren't going out with many girls then."

"Nope. Wanna see a picture?" He took out his wallet and extracted a cheap plasticized ID, yellow with age. The face staring out was round-cheeked, almost moon-faced, with a mixing-bowl haircut that looked frankly silly.

"Who's that?"

"Me."

"When was this?"

"High school. I was a chunky teenager. I hated high school."

Come to think of it, so had I. I thought about it later, and it explains a lot. In fact, I'll venture a generalization: most academics were dogs in high school, late bloomers who got their revenge in college and afterwards. I have friends and colleagues who have spent the bulk of their professional careers making up for high school. Otiose adolescents, we take up jogging in our twenties. Our dull nerdy conversation becomes political and suddenly relevant in college. And those of us who may have once been shapeless and acne-scarred gradually become almost attractive. Max and I were just warming to the subject when the chancellor harrumphed from the podium.

Aaron Tanner, the chancellor at Ole Miss, was the university's answer to the modern college president. With a boyish complexion and well-dyed hair, Tanner combined the elocutionary style of a Fundamentalist preacher and a Georgia auctioneer. In another era, he might have sold snake oil in a Chautauqua tent, but at Ole Miss he sold public relations and was damned good at it. Most of us on the faculty were of two minds about him: God, could he go on, but God, was he effective in making the alumni cough up money.

His introduction to the night's speaker, Beatrice Vendome, was predictable: half about her accomplishments, half about the emolument that made it possible to have her with us here tonight. You could almost feel an invisible collection-plate making the rounds. As he wound down to a closing, Max and I tabled the rest of our high-school discussion for later.

When Professor Vendome came out on stage, I recognized her face from the back of a book-jacket. But those head-shots never do justice to the whole person, and the whole of Beatrice Vendome was quite substantial. Dressed in a roomy blue jacket and skirt, she still seemed to overflow her boundaries, with a comfortable waist and a significant behind. She looked hale and cheerful, with plump cheeks above which two intelligent brown eyes had been dropped like raisins in a pudding. Her skin was slightly flushed. I tried to catch Max's gaze, but it was fixed onstage.

I won't go into much detail on her talk, except to say that it was well-delivered and intelligent. It even had shape, a quality you don't find much these days in Post-structuralism. Her basic point was that *The Tempest* was really all about Caliban, Prospero's servant, the dumb flesh, the walking appetite, but also the loyal work force—until betrayed. Eric, who was seated in front of us and who had somehow managed to convince Nathaniel to attend, was eagerly jotting down notes on the program. Nathaniel was staring sideways at his row rather than up at the stage. He seemed to be thumb-wrestling himself.

The applause at the end was led by Ed Schamley, whose idea it had been to ask Vendome to speak. The reception afterwards was mobbed, the coffee strong, the praline cookies snapped up by all the hungry graduate students there. My budding literary critic Laura Reynolds, I noticed, stowed a stack of them in her purse. Beatrice Vendome was in the center of it all, like a queen bee attended by drones. Yes, she found Oxford quite pleasant; no, the fleshly focus as she conceived it was multivalent; yes, another cookie would be fine, thank you. Max, the sapient sutler, went and fetched it for her. Doug Robertson, our grad student *cum* Woolf-Zen specialist, had just taken the last one, but Max convinced him that Beatrice Vendome's need was greater than Doug's.

By the time Max got back, Eric had muscled his way through the crowd, largely with the help of Nathaniel's shoulders. I knew that Beatrice Vendome's fatal mistake was in not invoking the Marxist perspective, and that someone would pay for it. Eric's questions were generally non-questions, the kind that always began "Don't you think—?" They were always eloquent, ultra-polite, and magnificently irrelevant.

"Don't you think," Eric began winningly, "that the dialectical interplay between Caliban and Ariel prefigures a Marxist concern with the perils of humanism? I mean, when one examines the notion of proletariat and sprite, it does seem, after all—"

"The last cookie." Max ceremoniously transferred the gem from his napkin to Beatrice Vendome's.

She accepted with a slow smile, the kind that begins somewhere around the belly and works its way upwards. For a moment, she and Max were in perfect communion. Then she turned back to Eric. "I'm sorry—you were saying?"

Eric repeated his question verbatim.

She frowned as she bit into her cookie. She was what they used to call big-boned, and her sheer physical presence seemed to dwarf both Eric and his argument. Nathaniel had faded away somewhere. "Well, yes, Shakespeare *is* concerned with the marriage of body and soul," she admitted after chewing a bit. "But the class-level is only one possible aspect of the struggle."

"But don't you agree. . . ." Eric had shifted to his second rhetorical ploy, slightly more insistent. The third was "But don't you see," usually accompanied by an emphatic gesture. For a socialist, he was a master at private monopoly. What he really needed was a soapbox in a quiet corner of Hyde Park. At the last public lecture, Eric had so rattled the speaker that Ed Schamley had to whisk the man away for a few drinks at Ted & Larry's.

She did in fact answer one of his points, but that led to two objections on Eric's part. With Eric, things never got ugly, just interminable. She had reached the bottom of her coffee cup when Max bent forward to whisper in Eric's ear.

Eric suddenly looked worried. "Are you sure?"

Max gave him one of those "it's your life, pal" shrugs. Then he began his own conversation with Beatrice, about Thomas Kyd. He had read her first book. So had I, but that's because Renaissance was one of my minors in graduate school; it wasn't even remotely Max's field. Max, the controversial polymath. Or a very great faker.

Meanwhile Eric scuttled off like a man with a tetchy bladder. The last I saw of him was his tweed coat and sneakers disappearing out the side entrance of Farley Hall, into the dark. I turned my attention back to Max, who was doing quite well with Beatrice. They shared some acquaintances in Cambridge and were busy dissecting one of them. It was an equal conversation in all ways but one: Beatrice, I noticed, looked mostly into Max's eyes, while Max tended to focus more on her body. The distance between them was narrowing, but I couldn't tell who was closing the gap. I stood by their side like a chaperone and nodded occasionally.

After about five more minutes, her husband showed up. He was a portly man in a rumpled business suit, with graying hair and rueful features. He had been delayed in his flight, some foul-up in Atlanta, sorry he'd missed the talk. He squeezed his wife's hand. She introduced him to Max and me, but there were other people who wanted to talk to her, and soon we found ourselves at the periphery of the crowd from the refreshments table. It was as if Max had held back the others for as long as he could, then opened the dam.

I couldn't help asking. "You disappointed?"

"Disappointed? No." He stared hard at the spot where Beatrice was standing. "Chagrined is more like it." We walked out together into the expectant night. As soon as we were away from the hall, he muttered, "A hand slammed in a car door—no, a broken arm for a chance to fondle that plumpness." He turned back as if to embrace the hall. "Think of all the meals that went into that waist!"

Max was back at his game, only now I thought of another objection. "Yeah, but what does she get out of it?"

"Her?" He turned toward me, surprised. He slammed one fist into his other hand, which was how he cracked his knuckles, which he did often. "She gets me. She gets my pain."

Was he talking about sadism or masochism? Max was the type I could see making a deliberate incision with a penknife, but all of a sudden I wasn't sure whose flesh it would be. Would I never catch him in the act, preferably a front-on view? He walked on just ahead of me, sloping forward and shoving his hands around as if he were bushwhacking through the darkness.

"Max?"

"Uh-huh."

"Have you ever had a stable relationship?"

"A stable relationship." He mimicked my tone. "Now there's a contradiction in terms. A relationship's got to have instability or where's the danger, the pleasure?"

I couldn't think of an answer for a moment. All sorts of responses came to me later: security, mutual respect, sharing the same trustworthy bed. But they obviously weren't what he was getting at. The way Max stated his terms, they sounded inalterable. I shrugged, a gesture he probably didn't see in the dark, behind him. I don't think he expected an answer, anyway. Eventually he slowed down, and we walked abreast in silence.

We were approaching Northgate Apartments when we heard a prolonged British wail. "Bloody hell! Shit-sticks! You bastard—where *are* you?" The next moment, a wiry tweed body rounded the corner and hurtled into Max, knocking them both to the ground. There was no scuffle. Max got up first, nimble as a quadruped. The other person, who turned out to be Eric, wasn't as successful in rising. "Blast it! I think I've twisted my ankle—*ahhh!*"

The two of us bent down to help him to his feet, but when he put pressure on his left leg, he winced dreadfully. Max immediately took charge. "You need ice on that, the sooner the better. It's probably swelling up right now."

"D'ye really think—"

"Yes." Max was firm. "Your apartment's right around here, isn't it?"

"Yes—what's left of it. Do you know what that bastard Nathaniel's done?"

"No, but you can tell us later. Don, you want to give me a hand? Two of them. This way. Okay, now sit down."

We made one of those human seats, composed of four interlocking hands, something I hadn't done since summer camp. Max's grip on my wrists was amazingly tight, and I tried to grip harder in return, but it hurt my fingers. Eric sat oblivious as a traveling raj as we transported him down the pathway to his apartment, B-4. Every single light in the apartment had been left on, looking as if the place were on fire. Max pushed open the front door with his foot, and we trooped in.

I'd never been inside Eric's apartment before, so I didn't at first realize what was wrong. The small foyer had twin posters of Marx and Engels from some London exhibition, staring sternly at the viewer. The rest of the apartment was friendlier, with a stereo opposite a comfortable-looking couch, and two wooden floor-lamps like elderly guardians on either side. Records and tapes were all over, and a lot of books were tumbled onto an upset chair. We settled Eric on the couch, and I rubbed my wrists in relief. Max went into the kitchen to look for some ice.

"Got any plastic bags?" he called back.

"Check in the cupboard . . . below the sink." Eric clamped his head between his hands. "God, what a hell of a night. The bedroom is the worst."

I took a peek through the half-open door. The mattress had been slashed and flung into a corner, and the bureau drawers were all open. Clothing and papers were strewn everywhere. The most touching sight was Eric's old manual typewriter, toppled and help-less-looking as a bug on its back.

"You think Nathaniel did this?"

Eric nodded his head miserably. "It's partly my own fault. I wasn't supposed to let him out of my sight. He was so good for a while. Now he's violated parole *and* wrecked my flat."

Max came back with a plastic bag full of ice. "Here, put this on your ankle. Which is it, the left?"

"No, the right." Of course, Eric was always plagued by the Right. He hiked up his pants leg to reveal an ankle already swollen to the size of his calf. "*Ow*—okay. Thanks."

"Keep that on for a while. If you can't put any weight on it tomorrow, better see a doctor." Eric didn't think of contradicting Max, and neither did I. He had assumed that air of absolute com-mand shared by generals and surgeons. He cleared off the books from the chair, righted it, and sat down. "So what happened? What'd he do?"

"I'm not sure, actually. When I think—!" He cursed, then sighed. "Thanks for letting me know he'd gone, though. He must have shoved off when I started talking to that Vendome woman."

I looked at Max but couldn't catch his eye. So that was what had pulled Eric away. I had thought it was some kind of threat.

"He'd been restless as hell all during the lecture. So was I, come to think of it—that woman's analysis of Shakespeare—"

"Never mind that," put in Max brusquely. "So he came back here and tore up everything. What was he looking for, do you know?"

Eric threw up his hands, which somehow agitated his ankle. "Who knows—*oww!* I mean," he continued, the Marxist reassert-ing himself, "money of course, but I don't have any."

"None?"

"Well, none to speak of. You know how this place pays us. It's all I can do to keep my car in petrol."

It was true, the apartment didn't seem too opulent. It looked like what it was, cheap bachelor digs, as Eric put it. To Nathaniel, it was probably luxurious.

Max bent over Eric's hunched-over figure, having finished with the physician act and now impersonating an officer. "What'd he take? Any idea?"

"Oh, everything." Eric waved his hands about, but guardedly, so as not to jostle his ankle. "I mean, he didn't take everything, but he went through it all. I get the feeling he's experienced."

"What was he in for?"

"I beg your pardon?"

"His jail sentence. What crime did he commit?"

"Oh. Burglary, I think."

"Uh-huh. Well, that answers my questions." Max stepped back, his arms folded over his chest.

I felt as if something were missing. I felt dumbly practical as I suggested, "Shouldn't you call the police?"

Both Max and Eric looked at me as if I were Saint John with a revelation. The Apostle of Common Sense. I went over to the phone book, spread-eagled on the floor next to one of the lamps, and checked the number. Then I made my way to the telephone, propped against a table-leg with the receiver off the hook, and dialed. Why was it always me?

19

Of course, a simple phone call didn't solve matters. Nor did the passage of time, though it helped with Eric's sprained ankle. By the time we were all back from Christmas break, several things had happened—or not happened, depending on how you looked at it. One thing that hadn't occurred was Nathaniel's arrest. The police had put out a dragnet, or an all-points bulletin, or maybe just called the sheriff in the next county and asked him to keep an eye out—I don't know how the police work. In Oxford, they seemed to operate mostly by patrolling up and down the local stretch of bars on Saturday night and checking for DUI's. Weekdays around lunchtime, you could see their patrol cars parked outside Top's Diner, where the men in blue stuffed themselves with fried food. If I wanted to commit a crime, I'd do it at noon.

Add all this to the fact that the local police weren't too crazy about Eric anyway, and I wasn't surprised that the robber of Eric's apartment hadn't been apprehended. In the meantime, Eric had a security lock put on his door, which was against university housing regulations, so they made him remove it.

Nothing had also happened to Willy Tucker, still languishing in almost total paralysis as his trust fund surged to impressive heights. By January, it had reached well over half a million dollars, and the university was planning to build him a special home for the disabled in Oxford. His jersey number was worn by the number-one passer on the Ole Miss team, and he had been elected Colonel Reb, the team figurehead, *in absentia*. *The Daily Mississippian* printed a poem he had written in the hospital, from which I recall four lines: "Here I lie, on the bed, / Water dripping to my head. / To all the girls I give a kiss, / God bless my teammates and Ole Miss." It turned out later that his Baptist minister had written it for him, but, added the man of the cloth, "The *feelings* were Willy's. All I did was act as his instrument."

Max particularly appreciated this phrasing. "His *instrument*, that's good." He smacked the paper. "And this paper is an *organ*— I love that kind of phrasing."

He and I were in the Student Union, both picking up our mail. It was January, it was cold—it can sink below 20° here—and I was in no hurry to leave for the library. Max, for his part, had just returned from a long harsh ride with Fred Piggot, the two of them bundled up on their bikes like snowmen on rails. Max's thighs ached enough for him to complain about the pain, which was unusual for him. He said he didn't feel like moving much at all that afternoon. He had no teaching that day, anyway.

That's one of the main problems with academia: apart from classes and occasional committee meetings, you don't have to be anywhere at any particular time, so you tend not to be. In this instance, it was sometime in the early afternoon, and I was somewhere other than the library. I had to do some research on Huxley's *Brave New World* for a course I was teaching next semester, and I knew I'd get to it eventually. In the meantime, I was talking with

Max, as usual. We seemed to have our best discussions within the huge anonymity of the Student Union. Yesterday had been furniture and female nesting behavior. Holly was pressing him to move in. "Trying to domesticate me," he complained. Today, we had shifted from bike-riding to exercise to lack of exercise, obesity, and immobility.

Something about the Tucker accident had possessed him. Me, too: the waste of a life, the public money and effort piled upon personal tragedy. Also, I couldn't get the image of Lennie Segal's iron lung out of my mind. It still haunted some of my nastier dreams. Maybe Max's, too. But as I listened to him perorate, I realized that he had different visions.

"Imagine it," he said, staring at the newspaper. "Here's this stud of a football player, his business is to break through others' bodies, and then he breaks up his own body. He's used to running, hurtling through the air. Suddenly he can't even shrug his shoulders."

I shook my head. "I know, it's awful. It's absurd, in a way."

"Flat immobilized, staring at the ceiling." Max tilted back his head. "Has to depend on the nurse to feed him, clean him, take away his shit. Think of that."

"I try not to."

"Wipe away his drool, swab the bedsores—the nurses probably know certain parts of him better than he does anymore. And half the favors they do him are life-saving maneuvers. How does he maintain any sense of self-respect? He's probably half-filled with tears of gratitude, half-filled with some kind of hate."

"This doesn't have anything to do with Willy's being black?" I asked.

"Why not?" said Max. "Just one more form of disempowerment."

"But he's rich enough." I was just kidding. I didn't like the path the conversation was taking.

"Money, sure, but what can it buy for him? A more expensive wheelchair? A mobile breathing unit? Think about it. You can slap him and he can't hit back. You're his ex-girlfriend and he's just a doll now. A living doll. You can slide your hand anywhere you want." Max's tongue darted out to moisten his lips. "Hell, take *his* hand and rub it around yourself. Or get the head of an ex-jock between your legs. If he doesn't like it, punish him."

This is embarrassing to confess, but I was getting slightly aroused. Max had this tone he could sink into, slow and sensual.

In news broadcast classes, they call it putting you in the picture, but Max's technique was far more seductive. I was lying on the hospital bed, and I was staring at the naked space between two smooth thighs bearing down on me.

"He's absolutely trapped," whispered Max. "A kid could take advantage of him—a chubby six-year-old girl could come by and sit on him. Plump her fat ass right down on him, play patty-cake on his chest."

But someone might come by, I couldn't help thinking, and someone did. Just as Max was describing the feel of smooth girlflesh on his sternum, Stanley walked right past us. He looked abstracted, as if his mind were in a cage with the rats. I waved involuntarily.

He caught my wave, returned it, and swung around to say hello. My guess is that he also was in no hurry to get to wherever he thought he should be. Max was just finishing up his description, and Stanley caught the tail-end. So to speak.

Stanley nodded briefly. "Discussing aggressive behavior in females, huh? Happens in rats under certain conditions."

"I like praying mantises." Max spoke slowly, dreamily. "They eat their mates after copulation."

"They're not the only ones. Scorpions sometimes do it, too." Stanley warmed to his topic. "But it's not dominant behavior—there's no thought involved. It's just biological reflex."

"How can you tell?" I asked, more to join the conversation than for anything else.

"Well, the number of synapses involved to execute the action. It's minimal."

"How about rats?" Max's tone had hardened.

"They've got neurons working up there. Generally, the females are more submissive. But for something like defending their young—I've seen some pretty vicious behavior."

Max leaned forward. "So what makes a woman a sadist?"

"Synapses firing in the wrong sequence." Stanley grinned uncertainly. "I don't know, they won't let us put them in cages."

I felt a sudden draft. At the entrance to the Union, a husky football player was gallantly holding open the door for two blonde specimens wearing Delta Gamma parkas. They rewarded him with sexy smiles. The door banged shut just as the hefty girl from last semester's Introlit class reached the same spot. She shrugged and heaved the door open herself. Or was that a scowl on her moon-face? The lame, the halt, and the fat are generally given shabby treatment in this world. She looked like Holly stretched sideways. Suddenly I wished very hard that I had been at the door to open it for her. Max, I noticed, had followed my gaze.

Stanley was still talking, explaining what he could do if he had a big enough NSF grant. Of course, the figures he was talking about would support ten academics in liberal arts for ten years, but then, we don't handle rats. I suddenly realized that I should have been at the library a while ago—internal prodding, academic reflex, I don't know—so I waved goodbye and made for the door.

The cold breeze hit me the moment I was outside, a parade of leaves swirling about my feet. Up ahead, my former student was making her way along the walk, her broad haunches hardly slowed by the wind. She was wearing a heavy parka, but her real defense against the weather seemed to be sheer bulk. I couldn't imagine a tornado knocking her down. I wished I were traveling right behind her, but I stayed about fifty feet in back until our paths diverged. It occurred to me I'd forgotten her name. And that seemed a merciful escape somehow.

Passing through the Lyceum circle, I saw the university policewoman I knew driving around without enough cars to spot for violations. We exchanged brief but friendly nods: she had once waived a ticket for me. When she stopped at the curb, she got out stiffly. She still had a slight limp, I noticed, from an incident two years ago: her ex-husband chasing her across the Grove with a .22. He managed to wing her in the hip before someone called the real cops. From what I'd read, she didn't even press charges—afraid to, especially since she had a kid. That thin Ole Miss police jacket didn't offer much protection, against the wind or anything else. And the damp cold around here penetrated everything.

The overheated library was a welcome relief. The two volumes I was returning I fed into the maw of the book deposit slot. I smiled at the blonde girl at the circulation desk, and she smiled back. The South runs on smiles, and neither of us meant ours. I was vaguely irritated at her for always taking forever to check out my books, and she, if she remembered me at all, probably thought of me as the bookworm who checked out far more volumes than a body could want to read in two lifetimes.

I went over to the reference area, where Rita Pointz was on duty, trim and efficient, just the way reference librarians are supposed to look. She was helping a large, untidy student with the *New York Times* index, probably pointing out how it was alphabetical—that's the kind of help some of our students needed. What I liked about Rita, whom I met my second day here, was that she knew where everything was. She was the one who found an obscure magazine index to locate the obscure magazine I needed; she knew when to check the *DNB* as opposed to *Who's Who*. And she handled all her queries with the same polite deference, even when someone was asking her for the tenth time that day where the men's room was. She'd always struck me as somewhat sexless, but that seemed to go with the job.

I had no queries for Rita today, but I needed to check something in *Books in Print*, which happened to be shelved right near Rita's desk. So I was standing nearby, thumbing through a heavy hardback, when Roy Bateson rolled up to the reference card catalogue and yanked out a drawer. Roy's motions tended to be a combination of jerky and fluid: jerky because he was a nervous individual, and fluid because he drank to calm his nerves. After half a minute of card-searching, he cursed and shoved the drawer back into its slot. Or rather, tried to shove it back in, but he got the angle wrong or something. When he tried to force it, at first it wouldn't go—then it slammed home, right on his thumb.

"Son of a *bitch!*" He hopped around as if it were his foot he'd hurt. Then his eyes lit on Rita, erect and proper in her chair. "How come no one can find a damn thing in this library?"

Rita attempted a courteous smile. "What were you looking for?"

"What the hell's it to you?" Roy examined his thumb fiercely. Gina, endlessly pursuing her Freudian work on Faulkner, would have noted castration symbolism. I lost my place in the A-G volume and had to start again.

Rita said nothing.

Roy came over to her desk and leaned on the side. "Hey, I don't mean that. I just got a lotta pain right now. I don't mean my thumb"—he shoved it into his pocket. "I mean personal stuff." He tapped his head tiredly. Rita nodded ever so slightly, and Roy was encouraged to continue. "Sometimes I think if I don't let it all out I'm gonna explode."

It's a good thing Roy doesn't copy down his own dialogue, I thought.

"You know, you look like an understanding woman," Roy moved on. "Pretty woman like you, sitting at a desk all alone like this. . . ." He left the sentence unfinished as he hovered closer, his beer-gut hanging over the top of the desk.

I lost my place again.

"How about you and me go out for a drink later on? I know a real nice spot." He breathed heavily on her.

"I don't think so."

"Aw, c'mon—" he reached out for her shoulder, but she swiveled away.

When he circled around the desk, she stood up and placed her hands on her trim hips. "Roy Bateson," she said in a perfectly even tone, "if you don't stop bothering me, I'm going to kick your balls off." She put one foot forward in a punting stance. I noticed something I hadn't before: Rita had terrific legs.

Roy backed away slowly. He tried to grin, but it didn't come off. "Sorry if I offended you, Miss Rita." His troubled gaze widened to include me. "Didn't mean nothing by it." Tipping an imaginary hat, he rolled away.

Rita stood there, leg flexed, until he was gone. Then she sat down again and resumed her librarian's pose.

I snapped my volume closed. "Maybe I should have said something," I offered. Apologies for my sex were in order. "Roy can get kind of crude sometimes."

"Roy?" Rita dismissed him with a wave of her hand. "He tries that every week." She smiled, and though I regard myself as an adept reader of smiles, I couldn't read this one. It didn't last long, in any event. She shifted back into her professional mode. "Is there something I can help you with, Dr. Shapiro?"

I smiled, said I didn't think so, and went to find a book. Later I wondered how Rita would do in one of Stanley's hypothetical studies, or the policewoman, but Stanley wasn't around for me to tell him the cases, so I told Susan instead. You know what Susan said? She offered her own solution, showing that my wife was more practical and hardheaded than I gave her credit for. She said something about a bannister and a razor blade that even now makes me want to cross my legs.

20

They caught Nathaniel a month later. He'd been hiding out at a friend's house, but cabin fever finally got to him, and the cops picked him up as he was walking down the road. Why he didn't go to Memphis isn't clear. Then again, why don't half the blacks in the South move up North?—half of them have; I mean the other half. I guess this is home to them. And Nathaniel didn't want to leave his hometown.

Eric visited Nathaniel in jail, not out of grim satisfaction but to ask a question that had been preying on his mind. He wanted to know why Nathaniel had done what he'd done. Here Eric had gone out of his way to be nice, helped him out of jail, and then—. Nathaniel gave him no answer. When Eric grew insistent, Nathaniel opened up a book and started to read. Eric wasn't sure whether to be angry or pleased with the book Nathaniel had with him in the cell. It was Marx and Engels, and it was stolen from Eric's apartment. When the police asked Eric what charges he was going to press, Eric, after a moment's pained pause, said none.

"Beg pardon?" said the sergeant, fully a head taller than Eric. He looked like a father watching his son lose the crucial cricket match. Or so Eric told me later.

Eric repeated his gaffe, and the sergeant rolled his eyes to the audience of the clerk and a patrolman. See what these professor-types are like, he shrugged. Book-learning does something to your head.

"Then we're going to set him loose," he told Eric. "No sense in keeping around a man who hasn't committed any crime."

That stopped Eric for a moment. The idea of Nathaniel at the mercy of socioeconomic forces he was just beginning to understand bothered Eric. But so did the thought of Nathaniel at large. "In the end, I had to let him off," Eric told me. "If I've created a monster, at least it's a Marxist monster."

On the other side of town, the university was halfway through building that special home for our paralyzed hero Willy Tucker. The town of Oxford had donated the land, which I thought was quite decent of them until Ed Schamley pointed out where it was: just beyond the railroad tracks, right in the middle of the black project housing. Well, he wouldn't feel comfortable anywhere else, I could hear concerned voices saying. Frankly, the whole situation made me uncomfortable.

The capper came in early February, just after the new semester had started. I was home putting the finishing touches on my Joyce essay when the phone rang. I let it ring a while, but Susan must have been out at the animal shelter. Lately we'd managed to see each other very little, even though we slept in the same bed. I made a mad dash to the kitchen to catch the phone on the seventh ring.

"Is Jamie there?" inquired a fussy masculine voice.

"No. Jamie hasn't been at this number for some time now."

"Really?" The voice sniggered unpleasantly. "If you see him, tell him he still owes me two hundred dollars." The connection ended with a click. I was halfway back to the computer when the phone rang. Hopefully, I picked up the receiver. Somehow, just once, it might be Jamie himself.

"Is Dr. Shapiro there?" a woman asked.

"Speaking."

"Dr. Shapiro, this is Mrs. Matt, Cheryl's mother. You don't happen to have seen her recently, have you?"

"Um, no. Why?" My last visit had been over a month ago, when Cheryl had asked me wistfully why there wasn't an operation that could restore virginity. Her parents persisted in treating her as fallen.

"Well, she's run away. We don't know where she's got to. My husband thought—he thought she might have come to you . . . "

"I'm sorry, Mrs. Matt. I can understand your concern, but I have no information." My tone was public and firm, though privately I wasn't sure I'd tell her parents even if she were sleeping in the next room. I hung up glad that Cheryl had escaped from Tupelo. I also hoped she wouldn't get maimed in Memphis, or wherever she was by now.

To complicate matters, the spring semester had started up. Spring comes early in the South, and it tends to be a rather heady experience. While people are contending with slushy driveways and crocus bulbs up North, the magnolia trees are beginning to bud here, and the nippy breeze plays about the bare legs of the sorority girls. Sap rises in the vegetable kingdom, and hormone levels rise in all the saps around campus. You could see it in the face of an Ole Miss freshman itching to lose his innocence, or a pack of Tri-Gam girls cruising around in a red Cabriolet with the roof down.

I always got heightened attention in my classes in the spring, though not always for my teaching. Spring pulls at you, makes you horny in the morning, puts a bounce in the most lackluster step. If you're already randy, it may make you slightly insane.

I'd had a close encounter with temptation myself, when Elizabeth Hart had come to my office to discuss her paper. She was all made up and wore a svelte off-the-shoulder dress that kept slipping more and more off her shoulder during the discussion. She had skin so unblemished it looked almost out of focus, and a salon tan all the way up to her lace panties, which she made sure I could see when she crossed her tapered legs. Every year, one or two students sort of flirt with me, but no one had ever been this blatant. It would have been even more enticing if the whole thing weren't so hokey. Maybe it's from reading too much literature, but I have a strong aversion to clichés, except for humorous purposes.

I wheeled around in my desk-chair so as not to face her directly. "It's about your paper, Elizabeth."

"Yes, Dr. Shapiro?" She batted her baby-blue eyes at me, repeatedly.

"Well. . . ." I took out the offending document, splotched with emissions from my pen. "It just doesn't seem like the rest of your work."

"It *doesn't?*" She scooted her chair closer to mine. Her Chanel No. 5 tickled my nostrils.

"No. For one thing, we didn't even read Hardy this semester."

"No . . . but I read him for another course last year."

"But why for this seminar?" I pointed at the third page. "Also, you've got some quotations here from sources that I don't see how—"

"Oh, a friend of mine helped me out there." She smiled, her capped white teeth parted slightly to reveal carmine depths.

"You know you're not supposed to get outside help for this."

"But he just helped me get books. That's okay, isn't it?" Her left breast accidentally rubbed against my shoulder, her head bent attentively toward the paper in my lap. I got another infusion of Chanel No. 5 rising from her cleavage. I tried to prop myself up on the arm of the chair, but her arm was there already. I felt half seduced and half irked at her predictability. I tried to think of Susan, but all that accomplished was to transplant Elizabeth's breasts onto Susan's chest.

I was saved by *Max ex machina*. He knocked on the door. "Don, you in there? Or is that a tape recorder?"

Elizabeth drew back as if she'd been stung on some tender part of her anatomy. The spell was broken. The interview, if you could call it that, was clearly over. I sighed my professional sigh. "Hold on, Max, I'm with a student." Now it was easy to withdraw. Since I had no concrete evidence, I decided to give Elizabeth a break. "Look, you know as well as I do that this isn't acceptable. I could give you an F. Tell you what, why don't you try again, *all your own work this time*, okay?"

"You won't penalize me?"

"No." Why? For whom? I thought. What'd you have in mind? thought a nastier part of me, but I suppressed that voice. "For the moment, you've got an 'Incomplete.' Just get it to me before the next semester starts."

"Dr. Shapiro, you're a sweetheart!" She jumped up and kissed me on the cheek.

Max observed her exit a moment later with quiet amusement. "Grading dispute?"

I looked sheepish. "Sort of." I pushed back the chair just vacated. "Have a seat. What's up?"

Max just wanted to talk. This was happening more and more, and it was flattering in a way. As for the subject, the pollen in the air had gotten to Max, as well. Except that his spring offensive was to ditch Holly. This was inevitable, I suppose, but it still seemed callous. I still thought of her as a soft, vulnerable body, supine in the middle of the road. The split had been made easier since Holly had gotten a new job as a waitress in Jackson. The distance was a good excuse for breaking off, though that wasn't what he told her.

"I told her we weren't compatible. Women always buy that cliché talk. They learn it from magazines."

"Why *did* you break it off?"

"It got old. Time to move on." He shrugged. I noticed he had dressed down today, in jeans and a faded sports jacket out at the elbows.

I didn't think the Kerouac pose suited someone as bright as Max. "What about marriage? After a few years—'time to move on'?"

Max got up from his chair. "First of all, not with someone like Holly. Ever tried having a sustained conversation with her? I'm telling you: irony bounces off her. Subtlety sinks without a trace." He paced a little. "And marriage—marriage may be fine for most people. I'm not like most people. In case you hadn't noticed."

I would have been annoyed if another person had made that statement. So many people, particularly in New York, are sure they're markedly divergent from everyone else. Or they cultivate eccentricities, train their neuroses in attempts to bring forth a truly exotic bloom. The unbearable truth is that they're just the average of their species, revealed when all the grafts fall off, leaving a homely stem. But there *was* something about Max, an eccentricity and intensity that was no fake. Of course, in a conformist region like the Bible Belt, it's awfully easy to be a maverick. I was thought somewhat odd and Northern myself. Until Max came along. "So what are you looking for these days?" I asked.

Max assumed a predatory grin. He reached out his arms as he tilted his head forward. "Someone I can sink my teeth into."

When I relayed this to Susan, omitting the body language, she said she was glad that Max had dropped Holly, who hadn't been at all suitable. "But neither is Max," she added, and though I knew what she meant, that kind of talk annoyed me. We were reading in bed, after a mostly conversationless evening. After dinner, I'd retreated to my study, and Susan had gone out to see a movie whose title she'd already forgotten. Anyway, it wasn't so much the time we spent away from each other as the time we spent together but apart. We just didn't seem to have that much to talk about anymore, except maybe about Max, and even there I was withholding a lot. That made me feel guilty and hold back even more.

Sex had also become a non-event. That afternoon, I'd masturbated again in my study, thinking of certain members of the young nubility. The peephole would have to remain dormant until next-door showed some more action. I wondered afterwards if Max could hear me, not that one body made much noise. Did Susan ever do that when I wasn't around, and if I asked, would that incriminate me?

If you understand my character at all by now, you know I didn't ask. And though Susan was wearing her flimsiest nightgown, with one shapely thin shoulder bare, I didn't make a move. Over the past few months, I had noticeably increased my girth, and now I felt fat and foolish in a pair of boxer shorts that no longer fit. In the back of my mind, I was sort of wondering whether Susan would reach out and grab me, but that wasn't going to happen. So I mentioned Max as an item of titillation, but all that did was put her off.

"Thank God you're not like Max." Susan readjusted her night-gown upward.

This was my cue. "Well. How's your Holly imitation?" I reached out to pull down her nightgown.

Susan drew back, so I pinched her, and then she did something to my boxer shorts that demanded retaliation to her nightgown, though I had to apologize for tearing it. We were on our way to something, but at the crucial moment I couldn't get it up. What it looked like—like something under the neck of a turkey—didn't help matters. I felt lousy, and Susan said it didn't matter, which only made me feel lousier.

After we turned out the light, it took me over an hour to fall asleep. And when I did, I dreamed that I was being introduced to a kick-line of women who all narrowly missed punting my balls. The stage manager, a hugely obese statue of Priapus with a stogie in his mouth, stood by and criticized.

Susan flatly refused to come up with any more names for Max. But this time Max didn't wait for any introductions. The next woman he took up with was a hefty singer named Helen Klaus from the music department. Helen, who sang soprano for the Memphis Opera Company, had the stoutness Germans call *Bleibtheit*. (The French, who always have such elegant terms for bodies, have two in this case: *avoirdupois* and *embonpoint*.) She was a thick column of a woman who wouldn't have looked out of place holding up the roof of some antebellum mansion. Her manner was imperious, but Max cut right through that. He told her he'd been waiting for someone to introduce them for months, and finally he'd decided to take matters into his own hands. She liked the idea of being worshipped from afar. Max was a great scenario-builder.

He was also a chameleon. To Marian, he had been an intellectual, an artist *manqué* with sensual urges. He flattered her sense of self-worth—until he dropped her. For Holly, he changed entirely into a blunt manly type, quick with a joke, who just happened to be an academic. That was when he started wearing lumberjack shirts. With Helen, he was a patron of music, polished *ad unguem*. The tweed jacket came back. And since Max really was a polymath, he knew a fair amount about opera and lieder.

I was in my study the night that an aria hit the air. Max's sound system, a pair of Aiwa speakers balanced on milk crates, wasn't all that powerful. When the notes shifted from Verdi to Wagner, I realized it was live. A few minutes later, I heard the bedroom door open.

"I'm sorry," I heard Max apologize, "I just can't get enough of your voice."

"Would you like to hear something from *Tristan und Isolde*?"

"After the intermission."

A throaty giggle came back, probably because Max was accompanying the words with appropriate—or inappropriate—gestures. Was he caressing her throat, smoothing her hand over his? "Tickle them," Max had told me when he was still going out with Holly. "It's the easiest way to get physical, and if they draw back, it's just a joke."

The tail-end of the giggle segued into a sonorous sigh. This was what I'd been waiting for. I moved impatiently to my peephole but paused as I grasped the wire plug. Would they notice anything? Would I be exposed? Would I ever forgive myself if I passed up this opportunity? Slowly, soundlessly, I twisted the plug from its smooth bore. The sounds behind the wall were going up and down, as if Max were practicing scales on her.

I put my eye to the hole. Helen, who wore high calf-leather boots to hide her ungainly calves, was still wearing them. But Max was generously helping her out of her blue silk blouse. With the utmost fastidiousness, he folded it and laid it on the chair. His hands came back to linger on her broad shoulders, below which rose two snow-capped promontories, with blue veins descending like mountain paths. Yet all was soft and quivery, as if the Memphis Opera Company had molded a soprano from aspic. Her breasts would slide into the sea of her belly if her great, girding bra came off. Maybe that was why, when Max's hands paused suggestively behind her back, she guided him instead to the placket at the top of her black velvet skirt. Is there any sound so seductive as a women's zipper coming down? Helen's thighs were of the same mold as the rest of her body, plump, pale, and helpless-looking when unconfined. They were two billowy curves reined in cruelly by the elastic of her mauve panties.

"Don't," she said as Max edged his hand around the waistband of her panties. "You shouldn't," she urged as his hand disappeared under the mauve expanse. "A little lower," she told him after a moment. "Yes, *there*. Mmm. . . ."

As he stroked, he inched down her panty-level till it reached mid-thigh. Her luxuriant blue-black bush emerged, a curiosity since Helen advertised herself to the world as a blonde. But Max acted as if he'd uncovered a marvel, petting and crooning over it. He'd already taken off his shirt one-handedly. Now he shucked off his pants in one fluid move, so that they looked like discarded legs for a second before they flattened out. Max's muscles moved under his skin like serpents. Suddenly he twisted under and up and emerged with his head between her legs. Thigh-flesh wreathed his face as he turned to the matter at hand.

"But I haven't—I mean—"

"'S'okay," said Max, somewhat muffled. "Just want to show you how I appreciate great art."

His tongue seemed prehensile as it flicked around, and the top half of Helen sunk from my sight. I was getting a crick in my neck keeping my eye at the right level, not to mention a hard-on that demanded attention. Max bobbed up and down, tonguing till my own jaw ached just from watching. He had wedged himself between her legs, his suntanned hands gripping her flanks. Head encircled, he looked like a drowning sailor, with Helen as either the life raft or the threatening depths. Finally, a wave passed through her body and she announced, in a strangely Teutonic voice, "I *must* have you."

So I got to watch Max unroll a condom over his penis. It was long, with a prominent vein on the underside, but so pale in comparison to the rest of his body that it looked prosthetic. The beige condom only accentuated that look. Still, it was obviously responsive: all it took was the touch of Helen's well-padded hand to make it hard and upthrusting as a coat hook. Then Helen's bra came off like a bridge collapsing, her gelatinous breasts sliding overboard. Max sucked hard on one fat nipple till Helen moaned and buried his face in her cleavage. You could see where her vocal projection came from. Or maybe, as a singer told me once, it comes from the belly, in which case Helen was still a star performer. When he mounted her, he sank into her flesh as if he were being half-absorbed, his buttocks taut with the strain of heaving upwards. By this time my hand was in my fly, pumping along, and I think I came about the same time Max did—what Elaine Dobson would have called male bonding.

It was a wonderful introduction to the Memphis Opera Company. Over the next week, I saw two more shows, with Max managing to get into every nook and cranny that woman had: nose up armpit, tongue in ear, finger up asshole, you name it. She never went down on him, I noticed; in fact, she didn't move much at all. She certainly did quiver a lot, though, and there was a lot of her to quiver.

Max brought her to a faculty party right before spring vacation. Not having any truck with the music department on campus, I hadn't really seen Helen except in the flesh, through a wall. So it was startling to see her clothed, and in a way more salacious since I knew what lay beneath. And she did look good. Max had a knack for bringing out the sexy qualities in a woman, or making her feel sexy, which amounts to the same thing. At the party, which was really just Greg Pinelli's mass pay-off for the semester's accumulated social obligations, Helen appeared in a tight-fitting diva's red gown with her cleavage artfully exposed. She also wore black calfskin boots, her shoulders were bared, and so help me she had a tiara in her golden hair. She caused something of a sensation, especially since most of us were in slacks or the equivalent, helping ourselves to kielbasa on toothpicks.

Helen scanned the room as if counting the house. It had been my idea to invite Max, whom Greg didn't know all that well. It had been Max's idea to bring along Helen, whom Greg didn't know at all. But Greg's sensitivity was big enough to encompass any occasion, and he hurriedly acquired her name and began making introductions. The embellishments accumulated as she made the rounds, from music teacher to semi-professional singer to *artiste*. She nodded to the other guests, a satisfied expression settling on her wide face like a cat curling up on the sofa.

Max acted proprietorial, a showman exhibiting his star. I don't think Helen noticed this. If she had, she might have been annoyed. There's a difference between a manager and an impresario, and it has to do with the value of the art and the deference paid to it. Max was clearly in the impresario role, except when he got near to her and the allure of her body did something to him. That inflated bosom, those huge bare arms—the presence of so much flesh was slightly menacing. Her calves were like piano legs, somehow inserted into boots absurdly dainty for her size. After she gave the nod to Susan and me, she turned and exhibited a rump that flounced the entire back of the gown. "They must have laced her into that with pliers," whispered Susan.

"Shh." I admit I was slightly in awe of her. But there was also something in me that wanted to ridicule her, to poke that wide belly, or watch a seam split down her dress. I suppose it's the emotion felt when beholding any monument: some people bow their heads respectfully; others have to resist the temptation to throw a stone. Still others, possessed of an incurable sense of dislocation and irony, have the urge to do both. What is it about a fat woman that says "KICK ME" when she bends over?

Greg rushed about, putting out more toothpicks, refilling drinks, keeping up a soothing patter of conversation. There were half a dozen people he hadn't invited directly, and he felt he had to chat up all of them. At one point, the phone rang, and Greg went into the kitchen to answer it. He came out a moment later, looking slightly confused. "Is someone named Jamie here tonight?" he asked.

There are some things about the South and the telephone system I will never understand. Somehow our wrong-number problem was passed on to Greg that night, and we weren't bothered again.

Near the end of the evening, Helen consented to sing. It didn't take too much urging—in fact, I think it was a set-up. Max consulted with Greg, and a small space was cleared by the stereo. A little later, Max circulated about the living room, starting a whispering campaign. He had parked Helen on the couch with a glass of red wine in her hand, and since I happened to be seated on the cushion next to hers, we got to talking. We were closer than the normal interlocutory distance: Helen's weight had created a crevasse in the contours of the couch, and I slid helplessly down the other side of the ravine to meet her in the middle.

At first, she acknowledged my presence with a gracious nod but said nothing. Since our thighs were pressed together, I felt I should say something. But since I had introduced myself earlier, I couldn't now extend a hand. I felt on embarrassingly intimate terms with a woman I'd never even talked to. I groped for some phatic comment: the weather (changeable), the time of year (early March), the university and its vagaries (risky to mention without knowing that person's politics). I don't know why I had such trouble coming up with a suitable aside. I'd been in the South for over three years, where everyone learns to talk charmingly about nothing at all. But when I glanced over at her, seated like a Roman regina, any trivial remarks about the early spring froze on my lips. In the meantime, the one attempt I made to shift away from her only made me slide down farther, to the point where my ribs were pressing against her warmly padded side. She was so *soft*. I had the frantic idea that she felt nothing, that I could slide half under her before she noticed anything out of the ordinary.

"Greg's couch certainly is well-cushioned, isn't it?" Hardly inspired, I'll admit, but give me credit for being slightly less than obvious. Besides, my mind was becoming obsessed with the notion of resiliency.

"The couch?" The words had depth and lilt, as if Greg's upholstered furniture were the lead-in to an aria. Her eyebrows arched magnificently.

"I feel as if I could sink down here forever—so comfortable, I mean"—me scrabbling for purchase on the back of the couch and slipping back against her plump thigh.

And so we began to discuss cushion stuffings, a subject about which she seemed peculiarly well informed. In Japan, she told me, they filled their pillows with dried beans; in India, the charpoys had wooden blocks at their heads. The only salient contribution I made was something I had learned from Max, that they use human hair for some kinds of pillows. Helen favored goose-down herself: it yielded so luxuriously to pressure. Here she shrugged her milk-white shoulders, further exposing a cleavage that looked like the couch-cushion abyss. It heaved breathily over the massive diaphragm below, like fleshy white clouds over a mountainscape. The view was dizzying.

Mercifully, she was called on to sing at that point. As she got up, the couch reasserted its former shape, and I was back on even ground. Susan, who had been jawing with Elaine Dobson in the corner, came over to claim the seat as soon as the recital was announced. Susan's demure bottom hardly altered the contour at all. She leaned forward ever so slightly with her hands folded over her knees—"sitting pretty," you could call it—with a healthy six inches between me and her. It was time for the concert to start.

Helen's performance punctuated the evening. As they say, it ain't over till the fat lady sings. Actually, her voice wasn't so accomplished as compelling, as powerful as her figure promised. She had chosen to sing *"Un bel di"* from *Madame Butterfly*, a dramatic, ringing piece. At times it almost sounded as if several smaller women were contained inside her, captive beneath several layers of flesh. Actually, Marian had told me she felt that way, which was probably why she was still stubbornly dieting.

I scanned the room. Franklin Forster was absently attending, alternating between stroking his beard and the hair of his wife, who was seated as usual at his feet. If there's a fine line between adoration and abasement, Jane was arrested at the border like a suspect immigrant. Seeing one of Max's women always put me in a prurient frame of mind, and now I wondered idly what the Forsters' sex-life was like. Did Jane perform all the manual labor, or would

[169

Franklin condescend to lend a hand? Did she ride him to spare his bad back, or was that too undignified? And did his patrician beard somehow figure into the proceedings, or would that run counter to Mississippi's anti-sodomy statute?

John Finley sat rigidly in a cane-backed chair, his wife Carol equally stiff in a matching chair beside his, like *American Gothic* in a seated position without the pitchfork. By this point, Carol had to know about John's infidelities; there was no other explanation for the glacial air between them. They looked about as far apart as a couple can be and still be next to each other. John's expression reminded me of an old Stephen Leacock line, about being in a state of profound subtraction. I don't know where his mind actually was—probably in the studio apartment of the nympho law student, which Forster & Co. were already calling "love nest." Carol's mood was easier to read: grim. Helen sang on.

"Music hath charms to soothe the savage breast," wrote Pope. From all accounts, Pope never had a sex-life.

Oblivious to all fleshly currents, Benjamin Dalrymple sat like a cadaverous Buddha directly opposite Helen. His gnarled hands reposed in his lap, his eyes shut against the world, taking in only the pure sound of Puccini—or so it seemed until Helen paused after a particularly high crescendo and I heard a gentle snore punctuate the pause. I exchanged glances with Susan, who bit her lip in order not to laugh. I wish she could have bitten mine.

Trouper that she was, Helen continued despite the poor acoustics of a shag rug and a row of potted plants, despite a large volume of Wordsworth falling from the bookshelf behind her halfway through the aria, and in the face of Dalrymple catching some shut-eye and contributing some nose-music of his own. She finished to a scattering—or smattering, or spattering—of applause, and nodded icily. She then resumed her seat, or rather returned to the sofa to find that Susan had taken it.

I instantly got up and offered my portion of the sofa. As Helen sat down with a *whumpf*, I could see Susan start to slide across the divide. But Southern women are magnificently equipped to handle any social embarrassment, and she promptly hunched forward while gripping the edge of the couch with her knees. She even arranged her hands over her legs to look graceful and proper. She began to praise Helen for her fine voice. I stole away, looking for other diversions, looking for Max. We had a discussion in the kitchen as to why divas ran so heavily to the flesh. We both agreed it had something to do with resonance, and Max said he would ask Fred Piggot about the acoustics of it on his next training ride.

But Helen didn't last long. I suppose from another point of view Max didn't last long, but he was the one who left her: Max the nomad lover, Max the Don Juan of Oxford. Franklin, that old gossip, took pains to inform me that Helen Klaus would *not* forgive Max Finster for that dreadful, demeaning party at Greg Pinelli's. But that was to salvage her pride. Marian, with whom I had coffee once more at the Union, said something about demeaning sexual practices, "and I hear he's getting worse," she added but wouldn't elaborate. She also made me swear not to let Max know what she'd said. So I didn't—her tone almost scared me. The next time Max and I picked up our mail together at the Union, all I asked about was the aftermath of the party. His response was brief.

"I could have fixed that. Wasn't worth it."

"I thought you liked Helen."

"*Like* doesn't enter into it." He slit open a large manila envelope with his thumbnail. All I found in my box was a flyer from Wal-Mart, which I'd tucked under my arm until I could find a suitable receptacle. As usual when talking to Max, I felt a bit envious, slightly inadequate, yet hoped that some of his brio would rub off on me.

"So what are you looking for?" I asked.

"A mail-order catalogue that should have come by now."

"No, I mean in a relationship. Why'd you go after Helen, for instance?"

"Because she was there."

"No, really."

Max looked away—at the far wall, at a spot just to the right of my neck, at a hefty girl in shorts bisecting the horizon. Her belly hung over her waistband at a weirdly vertiginous angle. Her breasts warped the design of her T-shirt like twin Mercator projections. Her fat face grinned hopefully at something ahead neither of us could see. When Max finally spoke, his voice was almost pleading. "Because I go after that type of woman. Is that okay?"

"Sure—but you don't seem to like them that much."

"That's only half true." He looked as if he wished he were elsewhere. In a moment, I knew, he would look as if he *were* elsewhere, and in another moment he'd be gone. I'd experienced Max's disappearing act before. But this time he just stood there as the girl with the poke-belly podged by again, her arms unable to hang straight because of her sheer girth. "Actually, I think maybe I like them too much."

"Too much for what?"

"For my own good."

I thought of poor Marian and how he had dumped her, how he had used Holly for his own ends—or for her big end, those beach-ball buttocks that attracted him like a fleshly beacon. I thought of Bloom in *Ulysses*, following the servant girl with the wide skirt. I thought of Arabella in *Jude the Obscure*, of Huxley's pneumatic women in *Brave New World*. Why?—because I'm a professor of literature, after all, and my associations tend to be literary. Literature is supposed to evoke reality, I know, but for me reality always reminds me of books.

Is this a digression? It all has to do with Max. But these were my own associations, and since I'm not telepathic I didn't transmit them to Max. All I said was "Oh" after a long pause, and that wasn't enough to get him back into the confessional mode. The heavy girl had walked away. Our mail had all been opened. The days were lengthening again, and I was teaching only two classes, which made the days stretch even longer. I ate more, which had a predictable effect. The courses I was teaching were repeats from previous years, so the drudgery of preparation was minimal. I was trying to step up my research. My marriage was becoming theoretical. Max and I nodded at each other and parted company, me to the library and Max to his private campaigns, plans for personal conquests, and his heroic one-man ascent of the Mount of Venus.

21

Academic life—as opposed to normal life elsewhere—took several odd turns in the following weeks. First of all, Elaine Dobson got a man. Given her interests, eighteenth-century literature and feminism, no one expected much for her in Oxford. At one point, she had considered Eric Lasker, but Marxism was his true love. She had thought about the only other bachelor in the department, Greg, but had decided he was gay; i.e., he wasn't interested in her. She had even considered me, I think—largely on the basis of a misunderstanding at a cocktail party. I liked Elaine well enough, but I was married. Besides, I wouldn't be attracted to someone like me, bookish and slightly myopic. I needed someone to take me out of myself occasionally, which may be why I found a contrasting type.

Elaine found Nathaniel.

Found is the right word: a week or so after his release, she saw him by the side of the road, half-unconscious in a ditch. She stopped her Toyota and got out, which not every woman would do. (Gina thought she was crazy.) He could have been dangerous; he could have taken a swing at her. All Nathaniel did was throw up on her shoes. Then he stumbled through an incoherent apology. He said he wasn't himself today. He offered to buy her a new pair of shoes, but his wallet was missing. (Eric told Elaine that Nathaniel had never owned a wallet.) In fact, he was missing most everything but a mud-caked pair of overalls and one left boot—half the pair that Eric had bought him when they got out of jail. He looked up at her—she was still standing over him in the ditch—with brown, beseeching eyes. His wiry black hair hung over his stained brow, making him look like an intelligent child of uncertain parents. (Franklin, the genteel racist in our department, said Nathaniel was a different species altogether.) He also looked beat up, as if someone had worked him over with a tire jack.

Elaine bit her lip. She gave him a hand up from the ditch, almost getting pulled down with him. She offered him a ride. When she found out he had no place to ride to, she drove him back to her house to get him cleaned up. What happened after that is anybody's guess, though it isn't hard to conjecture. Within a week, word got round that Professor Dobson had taken in a lodger. Women like reclamation jobs; it's the Salvation Army instinct in them. When Eric heard who it was, he tried to argue Elaine out of it, but he couldn't sway her. "History goes in cycles," he quoted gloomily. "First time tragedy, second time farce."

Despite the dire predictions, they seemed to get along well. Nathaniel got some kind of lawn maintenance job and rode home on the back of a pickup truck in the afternoons. They didn't seem to go out much, but from time to time, I heard Elaine humming in the corridor outside the department office. Susan and I finally met the happy couple a few weeks later as they were walking out of Wal-Mart with a ton of merchandise between them. Nathaniel had on an extra-large pair of overalls over a work-shirt and a complete set of boots. Elaine had on, I swear, a frilly blouse and a skirt.

"Well, hello there!" Susan waved sunnily. I nodded. In the dividing up of our social duties, Susan still did the greetings. They put down their bags, and Nathaniel shook hands firmly with me while Elaine smiled as if someone had slipped a coat-hanger into her mouth. I'd forgotten how sizable Nathaniel was, his forearm a solid wedge of muscle joined to a hand that felt like lumber.

Since no one could think of anything to say after that, Susan covered the pause with chat. "Isn't it a lovely day today? I see y'all been shopping."

Elaine waved away her three full bags. "Oh, just a few items."

Susan turned to Nathaniel. "Getting settled in?"

Nathaniel nudged one of the bags with his foot. "Manner a speakin'."

"Well, isn't that nice?"

Elaine agreed it was nice. While she and Susan chatted some more, I asked Nathaniel what he was reading these days. He reached into a giant side-pocket and pulled out a tattered copy of the Bible. "Mos'ly New Testament," he rumbled. Eric would have labeled this backsliding.

I couldn't resist. "No more Marx?" I asked.

"'Bout the same. Firs' thing Christ did, clear out all the money-changers from the temple."

I found myself nodding. So he had a mind of his own. He certainly hadn't gotten that line from Eric. And whereas Eric spoke in high-pitched polysyllables, Nathaniel had the low, magnetic tone of a born preacher. We had a short talk about what the apostle Marx meant by "the last shall be first," and then it was time for them to go. When they got to Elaine's Toyota, we saw him bend down to open the door for her.

It must be like making love to a tree, I thought. Hard mahogany.

"Sure is a hunk," Susan said. "I hope it lasts."

That was in early March. The rest of the month was equally unpredictable. Here are some of the events, in no particular order:

Bateson went on a three-day drunk during which he exposed himself to his creative writing workshop. No disciplinary action was planned because no one in administration officially knew about it. In the meantime, one of Roy's female students had written a short story about big Southern writers and small Southern pricks. My Joyce essay came back double-quick from *Twentieth Century Literature*, with a reader's note saying the analysis wasn't sufficiently genderized. I filed the note in my trash basket and sent the essay out again.

Missing-person posters with Cheryl Matt's photo began appearing around campus, with a reward of $500 and a number to call in Tupelo. In mid-March, the reward climbed to $750.

Gina met a professor of Southern literature from Knoxville who believed that Faulkner had not died a natural death. They started a correspondence, ceasing abruptly when the Knoxville professor insisted that Faulkner had been murdered.

Susan quit her job at the animal shelter after three rednecks in a pickup adopted two Dobermans, bet money on them in a staged dogfight, then dumped them back half-dead on the doorstep of the shelter. She had started investigating the possibility of a desk-job somewhere.

Vernon Knowles suffered a severe stroke, from which he was slowly recovering. He had regained the use of most of his muscles, but he still couldn't speak. During one March Sunday at his house, he interjected as best as he could with semaphores.

Someone broke into Stanley's lab and set free half the rats. Luckily, said Stanley, most had been in the pre-experimental stage, but it was still a large inconvenience. From then on, pink-tailed white rats could occasionally be seen nosing around the Student Union, looking for food.

Elizabeth Hart handed in her revised paper, this time on landscape in D.H. Lawrence. It was clearly her own work—it was dismal—and I gave it a C-. She didn't protest the grade.

Franklin surprised John Finley and his law-student lover in Finley's office through the simple expedient of not knocking. "They were *en flagrante*," he told everyone. Finley's wife Carol took the children to visit their grandmother in North Carolina.

And Max inevitably, ineluctably, found himself another partner. Her name was Bibi Bibber, showing that onomatopoeia is not a lost art. She was a new clerk in the bursar's office, and she was the one who serviced him, or however you want to put it, when he went to pay his monthly rent. Only the top half of her was visible over the counter, but that was enough. She was almost spherical, with a pair of fat red cheeks, agate eyes, and chestnut hair to top off the composition. The line he used on her was something about how sticklike modern women were. Bibi murmured something about being an old-fashioned girl. I assume he waited until he was leaning over the counter and then gave her the full treatment with those true-blue eyes. Freud explicitly compares the eyes with the testicles, so maybe that has something to do with it. And that gaze. I knew the force of that gaze; it transfixed even me at times.

I don't know how he wooed her because I was out of town for a few days, attending a literary conference. By the time I got back, the acquaintanceship had already moved from something in the air to a *fait accompli*. Yet the same was true of Marian, where I had obviously missed some crucial stage in my own living room. Spying on him and Helen had been inculcatory, but how did he get them to accompany him in the first place? Or did he just commandeer their cars? Bibi, by the way, drove a Ford Escort that listed noticeably on the driver's side. Did he just flatter shamelessly, and if so, how? "You know, there aren't many women I've ever cared about." "The sway of your bottom drives me insane with desire." Was it his touch? That warm, hard hand tracing a crooked line down your bare arm. That gentle squeeze.

The simple answer, if it's an answer at all, is that it was simply Max. Max and his overpowering desire. That look in his eyes made it perfectly clear that he was after her, but just as clearly hinted that he would abase himself, act outrageously, do anything to win her. Once she was his, he tended to treat her proprietorially.

He squeezed Bibi in public. I don't mean hugged or caressed, I mean pinched and pawed. When I first saw them, they were walking by the Student Union and he had his arm casually sloped about her plump shoulders. I was awed. It was as if Max had blown her up with his bike pump. It was hard to tell where her bust ended and her belly began, she was so round, her inflated arms hanging wide. Her waist was like some monumental equator, which old-time navigators might take months to cross. Her paunch blended seamlessly into her hips and upper thighs. And she was under five feet tall, which made the whole feat more impressive. But she didn't jiggle when she walked; she was pneumatic. You got the feeling that if you jumped on her belly, it would be like a trampoline.

As I stood there gaping, I saw him reach down and snap the wide elastic waistband of her skirt. She slapped pleasantly at him, so he squeezed one globular buttock.

176]

"Stop that!" She sounded half-annoyed. He tickled her under her armpit, so she clamped down on his hand, imprisoning it against the fleshy swell of her upper arm. They walked on like that for a few steps until she released him, at which point he reached halfway around her waist and settled there. Her hand crept hopefully into his. They were in that position when they saw me around the corner.

Max didn't harrumph or disengage his hand. "Don," he said, "this is Bibi."

Bibi extracted her hand from Max's to shake mine. It was soft and pink, but she had a tight grip. "Pleasure to meet you," she announced. Her face was all made-up, with enough blusher to make her look like an apple. Her lipstick was the shade my mother used to wear, in the days when all lipstick was brick-red.

"Bibi," continued Max, as if he were speaking about someone in another room, "works in the bursar's office, stealing money from the endowment."

"Don't you wish," murmured Bibi. "Fact is, I barely get enough money to eat on."

I suppressed the obvious comment.

"I feed her." Max stroked the crook of her dimpled elbow. "I found this poor waif with almost no lunch on her tray at the Union, so I invited her for a home-cooked meal."

"That's a lie, Maxie."

"All right. There was a line of men waiting for Bibi, all offering her money. When it was my turn, I asked her out to lunch."

"Now that's the truth, but I don't like the way you put it." She nudged him with one wide hip. She turned to me in appeal. "I'm trying to make him into an honest man. What do you think my chances are?"

I liked Bibi, I decided. She was substantial, and I don't mean just physically. I got the feeling she could handle Max, even if she did call him Maxie. And I suspected playful kindness behind her actions. She reminded me of someone I had known, though I couldn't place this someone at first. The association wouldn't go away but also wouldn't resolve. Only after they had walked on did I remember, as if Bibi's bigness had blocked my recall.

When I was very young, I had an obese relative named Aunt Clara. All I remember is her tickling me when she lay down with her shoes off. She had extraordinarily dainty feet for a woman of her size, and they hurt her a lot, which is why she was often horizontal. Then her mountain of a belly became a great lake, her generous triple-chinned face propped up against two or three pillows. Framing me between her huge knees, she would creep around my chest with her pudgy hands, like two pink five-footed animals finding their way about. If I squealed, she would squeeze me with her legs. After a minute, she would open a drawer from her nighttable and pull out two pieces of candy, one for me and one for her. That's what she was to me, the candy lady, only I never got to know her well because she died of a heart attack when I was only three.

I hadn't thought of Aunt Clara in twenty-five years or more. It took Bibi, with the same fat cheekiness, to bring her back. Not that there weren't a lot of hefty women around Oxford. They called them big or full-figured, but everyone knew that was a euphemism. You could see them shopping at Kroger's, their vast buttocks swaddled in sweatpants, unintentionally blocking the aisle. They were on display at the Oxford Mall, complete with husband and sullen child; or you'd spot one driving around, great arms billowing around the wheel. Had they always been fat, or did they become that way after they married? How had Bibi gotten that way? What was it like to put on pound after pound, helplessly growing bigger and bigger? Was it glandular? Stanley Pearson had ridiculed this idea, claiming that the vast majority of people—or the majority of vast people—were that way because they ate too much and didn't exercise enough.

That was the kind of statistical information Stanley was great for, but what about other factors? Was it just the Great American Laziness? Maybe some women want to be big—feel more comfortable that way, feel more *powerful*. And isn't power supposed to be sexy? Did Kinsey ever run a questionnaire on poundage? Some people like their mates with a little extra heft. The way Susan kept feeding me, I should have been worrying about it myself. But this was a matter of extremes, as well as a different sex. I can often put myself in the woman's place—Susan once said it was my asset— but here I could only guess. What does it feel like to outweigh your man by fifty pounds or more? To stick out behind and poke forward in front—melon breasts, plump pudenda, beachball buttocks—to have your erogenous zones so prominent that a swimsuit just can't contain you?

These thoughts pulled at me that spring the way my dreams tugged at me in bed with Susan. One night with the moon barging through our fake-lace curtains, I lay in a spent post-coital posture, belly up, legs extended frogwise, arms under my head. Only we hadn't had sex, we'd just tried—and Susan was getting tired of extending sympathy. When she asked what I was thinking about, I said—I don't know, something about her hair, something appropriately flattering. But that's not what was going through my mind.

Before coming to bed, I had been in my study half-working, half-listening to the sounds my study wall was making. In Max's apartment were a lot of things that went bump in the night, and those funny twangs, but there's no mistaking the sound of flesh slapping against flesh. Then came noises like a vacuum cleaner, and finally I couldn't bear it anymore and went over to the peephole. I wanted to see Bibi in the nude, but she was fully clothed when I looked through. Max was worrying at her short-sleeved blouse, meanwhile smothering her with kisses up and down her plump tanned arms—with a sucking sound, as if he were trying to draw her flesh into his mouth and nostrils.

"Stop it, Maxie, that tickles!"

"Does it tickle you pink? Let's see." He unbuttoned the top of her blouse with a flick of his fingers. She didn't exactly resist but twitched her shoulders forward. When his hand began to massage her breast, she strong-armed him using her weight as leverage. Rather than fight against her heaving bulk, he withdrew.

She straightened her bra. "Not now," she told him.

"No time like the present." He draped his hand around her shoulder. "I just love the *feel* of you."

"Hmph." That was all she said, but when he let his hand stray again, this time she let him. Bibi's girth was vast, and so deep that I lost sight of his forearm as Bibi let him fondle her. His other hand encircled her belly, his lean torso pushing against her overflowing side.

Would he take longer strokes to penetrate such plumpness? I never found out. Just as he glided downward to her thigh, she smacked his hand away.

"C'mon, we're not in high school," Max complained.

"I don't care. You're not going all the way until—"

"Until what? Until death do us part?" The sarcasm was visible through the peephole, and the conversation had the ring of repetition.

"You know what . . . " she said. The scent of marriage hung in the air. She buttoned up her blouse daintily.

Max said nothing, his face turned away from my purview. I felt his annoyance—hell, *I* was frustrated, too. My fingers trembling, I closed up the hole and lay down on the carpet. Then I masturbated to the memory of Helen and her soft white body, palpating my own plump belly as I stroked myself ever harder. What was Susan compared to my monstrous imaginings?

Now in bed, I saw in my mind's eye a view of Bibi in all her roundness. I heard the full, throaty sob of a woman being plumbed to her depths, though Max, the silent predatory male, made little or no sound. I imagined he made love the way he worked out: deliberately, efficiently, extracting maximum effect. Totally in charge. Working up to the final sprint.

I was wrong, as it turned out. But how could I have known that then?

22

Max the wanderer seemed to have found contentment in Bibi. The consensus agreed on that. I knew better. Max was itchier than he'd been with any other woman, only everyone else took it for amorousness. Henry Clay Spofford saw the new couple in the corridor of Bishop Hall, got off his white horse, and invited them to dinner. Nancy Crew asked them over to one of her parties *cum* smorgasbords. The Pearsons wanted to meet them for lunch. Even Vernon Knowles heard about them and was curious enough to issue an RSVP through his wife Iris, though Max told me he declined. "I need conversation to keep me going," he told me, avoiding my eye.

Marian curled her lip when I met her in Oxford Square and asked her if she'd seen Bibi, but then, she was desperately trying to be what Bibi was not. By now she had dropped well over forty pounds. The irony was that the more flesh she lost, the less central she appeared in the social scene. Her face had become sharp and pinched, as if she were honing her chin on the wind. She hadn't bothered to buy any new clothes as she shrank, and she practically swam in her old wardrobe. Her arms looked puny whenever she wore short sleeves. Her personality was becoming thinner and sharper, as well. One day she would become an emaciated cat-woman, a furtive shadow seen only around Kroger's at midnight, adding to her hoard of no-cal food. No one dared ask her over for coffee, afraid of how she might react to cookies or cake.

"Do you want to go for a bite to eat?" I asked her one noontime.

She shook her head. "I already ate this morning," she explained.

Bibi, on the other hand, seemed to bring out everyone's feeding instincts. She was the extreme of a type everyone recognized, Southern Rotund, plump and saucy. "Now, Don, I can't believe you've *read* all these books," she told me when they came over for dinner one evening. It had taken me two weeks to persuade Susan to have them over. Seeing Bibi now, she was thoroughly convinced of Max's boorishness. Bibi gestured at the professional bookshelf in my study, which ran from Albee to Woolf. "Window-dressing, right?" The shelves in our hall went from Douglas Adams to Roger Zelazny. My vicarious lives.

I made a few modest sounds. "Well, it *is* my job . . . "

She snatched my copy of *Pilgrim's Progress*. "How about this one?"

"It's about sin and error. Religious allegory."

She wrinkled her nose attractively. "How about that one, then?" She slid out Lawrence's *Women in Love*. "Is it as racy as it sounds?" She gave me one of her hip-nudges.

"Yes," I admitted. "I teach it every other semester."

Her agate eyes grew wide. "To your students? Why, Professor Shapiro, I'm surprised at you."

Damn. I'd misread the signs and offended her, something a Northerner always worries about in the South. I harrumphed and began concocting the standard academic apology for literature—and she gave an explosive snort, like a miniature bomb going off in that deep cleavage.

"You don't have to pull that professor stuff with me. Just testing."

"Did I pass?"

"You'll do."

I grinned in relief, feeling both teased and flattered. Susan occasionally had this effect on me, too. Let me make an observation here: Northern women know how to cope with men; Southern women know how to handle them. Bibi could have been a hump-backed dwarf and she'd still have had that saucy manner. She could have had me cleaning out her cesspool by joking me into the job. No wonder she had led Max along this far without losing out. In another minute, she skipped over to where Max was perched on our couch and pretended to sit down on him. She missed him by inches, but I couldn't help thinking how her big round bottom would look on top of his tautly muscled shanks. Like a cage-ball on a balance beam, except that a cage-ball is mostly rubberized canvas and air. Bibi was all warm flesh. How much did she weigh, anyway? I'm never good at estimating weights, but I guessed at least two hundred thirty pounds. The average Ole Miss woman student probably weighed about one hundred fifteen, I figured, and Bibi looked like two of them put together.

For all the poundage she carried, she was amazingly agile on those small feet. She looked as if she could have waltzed around a dime. She also didn't have the anxiety most heavy women have about their size, the weight of others' opinions that causes stoop-shoulders and belly-creases. Bibi was sleek and buoyant; her integument looked perfect. Max looked like a small boy given a huge gift, which he hadn't quite figured out how to unwrap.

Greg Pinelli and Elaine Dobson were over, as well, to make a dinner party out of it. For some reason Bibi made Greg nervous: he skirted her as if he were a mariner and she an iceberg, as if she might reach out and pull him against her lower depths. I don't think he felt too easy about Max, either, not after Helen's semi-debacle in his living room. This was a shame, especially since we had invited Greg for his most useful trait, mediation. In the right situation, he could probably have been middleman between the Klan and the NAACP. Anyone could see he always meant well.

He decided to use his consoling powers on Elaine, who had arrived without Nathaniel. She didn't explain except to say that he couldn't make it, but the way she said it didn't sound promising. Franklin Forster claimed he had heard the two of them last week arguing heatedly in the parking lot at Kroger's—I sometimes thought Franklin had the entire town of Oxford wired for sound. That night, Elaine acted tired and moody, and she sported a pur-plish bruise on her neck. I might have said something, but Max also had some sort of neck abrasion that night, and that seemed to normalize it all. Max was always getting into scrapes. And Elaine is fine-boned, with skin so delicate it's almost translucent. In any event, she quickly downed two gin and tonics and barely touched her food. She seemed annoyed at all couples, especially the one on prominent display that night.

Bibi was in fine form. During dinner, she took second helpings of everything, including the sweet-potato soufflé. The recipe includes two sticks of butter, a cup of brown sugar, a bag of pecan halves, and a cup of Amaretto. I knew: I'd watched Susan make it before. All afternoon, I'd been working in my study against the smell of it in the oven. The aroma entered my computer through the fan vent and seduced the circuits. Around six-thirty, when I could no longer resist, I stormed the kitchen in a daring raid. I made off with a tiny piece of ham, one lima bean, and a patch of soufflé that burned my fingers.

They say the only part of Southern culture not based on a myth is Southern cooking. Despite her disapproval of Max and Bibi, Susan was determined to feed everyone well. Greg ate everything on his plate, praising the food while regretting the calories. Max took two helpings of the soufflé, saying it renewed his faith in tubers. He came from the old shovel and pickaxe school of eating— but Bibi took small fast bites and finished before him. The usual question to ask, in a mock-despairing tone, is "Where do you put it all?" With Bibi the answer was obvious. She was wearing a purple dress with straps that showed off the roundest, creamiest shoulders I've ever seen. The surface of the table ridged her belly into two generous shelves.

"The soufflé is a trifle rich," Susan said. "I can never think whether to serve it with the ham or for dessert."

"We'll have to try it both ways." Max took hold of the ham platter for the third time. "Bibi, you want some more? Or did you already have some?"

Bibi nodded to the first question and shook her head to the second. She reached for the platter, quoting, "For whosoever hath, to him shall be given, and he shall have more abundance." She looked around the table confidently. "Matthew 13:12."

"Uh-huh," grunted Max. He finished chewing. "And ye shall eat fat till ye be full. Ezekiel 39:19." Bibi looked slightly hurt but helped herself to more anyway. Max put his hand on her plump shoulder, a gesture somehow making it all right at the same time it was terribly wrong. What's acceptable in the boudoir is not necessarily what you want to see around a dining room table. Perhaps in defense, Max put on his Look Of Utter Respectability. Elaine bit her lip, visibly. No one said anything. No one even raised a fork.

Susan broke the silence. "Are you interested in scripture?" She ignored Max, whom she knew was interested in everything.

Bibi shrugged so that Max's hand slid away. "I grew up reading a lot of it. My uncle was a Missionary Baptist preacher."

"Really!" Greg's eyebrows shot up to their full surprise-quotient. "And he taught you?"

"Yep. Until they put him in jail for income-tax evasion." Bibi giggled, a pleasing sight. "Now we consider him the black sheep of the family."

Susan had also been raised on scripture, and she can still fake piety. At one point, her father even sent her to a Bible camp, but she rebelled and came home after only a week. Me, I've taught the Bible as literature, but like Max and the devil I quote scripture for my own purposes. I don't see it as the revealed word of an omnipotent writer, though I like the poetry. I do think it reveals a lot of things—mostly about the frailty of humankind and the people who wrote it.

When scripture petered out as a subject, the topic shifted to the break-up of John Finley's marriage. Speculations were unnecessary at this point. This past Monday, John had clinched matters by moving into the law student's apartment. The law student's name was Dorothy, though most of us knew her as "that woman." This wasn't quite fair—it takes two—but then most of Dorothy's friends probably knew John as "that man." By now, it was all over but the divorce settlement, which was bound to be substantial, especially the child-support.

"I hope Carol takes him for everything he's got." Elaine pronounced her words with vehement care.

"What's he got?" Bibi sounded half-joking.

Greg frowned conscientiously. "Not much, from what I hear. The whole thing is a mess, just a mess."

Elaine turned toward him like mobile artillery. "He brought it on himself. He's a pig."

This wasn't quite fair either. John may have been a lot of things, but he wasn't porcine. "He wasn't like that before he met—that woman," I said.

"Stop blaming the woman, for God's sake. It was his decision, right?" Elaine placed her hands on the table as if to shove us all away. "You're acting like he's some martyr. He's more like Martin Bormann. Or Judas."

"Maybe he *was* Judas—in an earlier life, I mean." Bibi leaned forward so far that it looked as if the table-top were cutting her in half.

"What do you mean?" said Max flatly.

"Reincarnation, you know. With some people I just have a feeling."

"Don't you believe it." Max shook his head. "I'm sure John has enough problems without people making him into a mythical figure."

"It's no myth!"

Max was about to reply when Greg the mediator broke in. "Well, after all, who really knows about these things, anyway—I mean, I don't believe in it myself—"

"Greg—"

"—but everyone's entitled to their own beliefs. This world would be a boring place if we all thought the same—let a hundred flowers bloom, I always say—"

"*Greg*—"

"—especially when we can't even agree on certain of the basics—at that faculty meeting last week, for instance, when we were going to vote on the curriculum committee's report, I thought for sure that everyone was behind it, that we all—"

"Greg!"

It was no use. A poet would say Greg lacked caesurae. Prompted by the threat of disharmony at the dinner table, he plunged ahead selflessly, continuously, without regard for personal safety—even as I saw Max's hands whiten with tension. Elaine was annoyed, too: her point had been swept away into the maelstrom of Greg's logorrhea. We never did decide what or who John was, and Greg finished his excursus a minute later and several miles away from the original topic.

We finished the meal with chicory coffee and praline cookies. Elaine reduced one of the cookies to crumbs without eating much of it. When Bibi worried about drinking strong coffee before going to bed, Greg launched into a thorough explanation of chicory. Max interrupted him only to point out that the greens were used for salad. Bibi smiled admiringly at him, all forgiven. She seemed resilient in more ways than one.

What happened two weeks later was unfortunate and slightly mysterious. Maybe even numinous. Some might say it was God's plan, since it had to do with one of his minions. His name was Brother Jim.

The word *phenomenon* is pressed into service these days to describe everything from coincidences to quarterbacks. That's a shame, because it bankrupts a word that ought to be reserved for true, inexplicable exotica. Like cosmic rays. Or the Grand Canyon. Or an itinerant suspender-snapping preacher who draws in both faithful and faithless alike, and everyone else in between. The first time I encountered Brother Jim, all I could see at first was a huge swarm of students and faculty on the plaza outside the Student Union. A juggler, I figured, or a mime—they've brought a mime to the South, and these people have never seen one before. I was on my way to my afternoon class, so I skirted the crowd. I'm not wild about mimes, anyway.

Suddenly, a powerful voice sounded from inside the gathering, like an articulate thunderclap. *"Do you know,"* it rumbled and then paused, "that sorority women are instruments of the devil?"

A ragged fringe hooted and clapped. Two girls standing nearby me blushed down to their ankles.

"Tell it like it is, Brother Jim!" shouted a loud male voice on the far right.

"You're full of it!" cried an androgynous rejoinder.

"And that makes . . . all fraternity brothers . . . whoremongers."

Louder hooting this time, including some well-aimed profanity. I stopped by a parked car to listen further. By climbing onto the bumper, I could see the star attraction gathering momentum for another roll. He was short but reedy, with a thatch of blond hair over a well-scrubbed face. He wore a button-down white shirt and stovepipe black trousers, held up by old-style gaiters, which he snapped like banjo strings from time to time. Mostly he kept his hands behind his back, bending over slightly so that he always looked as if he were preaching from the mount. In one hand he held a big black Bible, which he brought forward and thumped when he wanted to emphasize a point.

"There are *four* things that I want to warn you against," he intoned, with a grand pause.

"SEX AND ALCOHOL, DRUGS AND *ROCK 'N' ROLL!*" This time, the audience shouted it out with him, like a well-rehearsed refrain. Brother Jim nodded deeply, then launched into a sermon on the evils of drink. His text came mostly from his own early days, before he had seen the light.

"In my high-school days, I was a real . . . *hell-raiser.*"

"Raise some hell, Brother Jim!" A frat boy wearing a "WASTED AT SIGMA PSI" T-shirt vaulted on top of a concrete embankment.

Brother Jim shook his blond head smilingly, pityingly. "I was once like you . . . I'd get up late in the morning, and on my way to school, I'd gulp down a whole pint of vodka!" He tilted his head back, his hand clutched around an imaginary bottle. I even saw his Adam's apple bob as he swallowed.

"SHAME!" cried an entire segment of Chi Mu girls, as if on cue.

"Chug it, Jim!"—this from a sniper on the Union steps.

Brother Jim took it all in, good, bad, but never indifferent. He himself was unstoppable, in any event. "And just before I got to class, I'd stop and fire up some . . . "

"MARI-*JUANA!*" Nearly everyone joined in this last refrain, which seemed to crop up a lot in the rest of the sermon.

"That's right! And one day they caught me, and they were going to throw me in the darkest cell of the county jail . . . "

"SHAME!" cried you-know-who.

"But luckily I knew the mayor's son . . . "

"IT'S NOT *WHAT* YOU KNOW, IT'S *WHO* YOU KNOW!" A competing group of five Alpha Chi girls came in on cue, in perfect unison. Brother Jim took up right where he had left off, continuing his sorry tale of sin. Redemption was just around the corner, but not yet. This was old-time preaching with a Bones and Tambo dialogue to get everyone involved. There were pauses for citing scripture, gaps for audience participation, and stops to deal with hecklers. Mostly, it was good-natured, but one boy was deeply offended at Brother Jim's slurs on Southern womanhood and had to be restrained by his frat brothers.

Brother Jim finished his attack on high-school indecency and began to assault rock music. Only a reformed sinner could know so much of the devil's tongue—the man's memory for old lyrics was amazing. He had, someone informed me later, been saved at a Van Halen concert. I asked the woman in front of me how often he did this here, and she whispered back, "Twice a year." When I finally looked at my watch, I realized I was already ten minutes late and I ran all the way to the classroom. Luckily, half the class straggled in after me. They had also been in the crowd. I had to resist the temptation, as I launched into an exposition of Milton, of intoning like Brother Jim.

[187

From then on, I made it a point to attend Brother Jim's appearances. Opinion was divided as to how to label these events: some people called Brother Jim a sign from above, while others called him a pain in the ass (I thought both might be correct). Others said he was an entertainer. I'd also heard that he was paid a stipend by some ecumenical council to preach to colleges across the country. I didn't bother about terminology and just went to hear the phenomenon.

Of course, not everyone was so pleased when Brother Jim's black van appeared on campus every six months or so. After one particularly offensive sermon, four guys from Eta Pi took hold of Brother Jim and hoisted him into a green trash dumpster, but Brother Jim took it like a martyr. It's that strange combination of meekness and power that pulled them in. "Like Christ," offered Susan sourly, the one time she accompanied me to a Brother Jim sermon. It was her first and last time: I think it reawakened unpleasant evangelical memories.

It was half past noon on a Friday when Brother Jim rolled up in his van. He liked to start just after lunchtime, which Gina Pearson claimed was because a well-fed crowd feels guiltier than a hungry mob. I was surprised to hear that, not because I thought she was wrong, but because that meant she'd listened to him—add one more notch to Brother Jim's belt. I didn't see her there that day, but Greg Pinelli was just emerging from the Union with a cafeteria tray of food, and I waved. I mentioned Gina's theory to him.

"I don't know about guilt—our students don't seem to suffer much from that." He waved his plastic fork dismissively. "Maybe they're just more inclined to stay in one place on a full stomach." On his tray was a styrofoam divider-plate of black-eyed peas, turnip greens, and cornbread. The student cafeteria charts an uncertain course between gastronomic heaven and hell, but your best route is the Southern food they serve. "Want some?" he offered.

I did—I suddenly realized how hungry I was—but Greg's generosity always provokes me to refuse it. I'm not sure why. Maybe because it's so innocent, so disarming that I feel the need to arm myself. So I thanked him and said I was just about to eat, too. I'd buy my own. Why not? Susan wasn't around that day, anyway. She had finally quit volunteer work, much to the disgust of Emma Spofford, and had just started a new job typing for a local attorney.

Inside the Union was a smaller crowd, ranged around a black student in a motorized wheelchair. At first I didn't know who it was. Then I realized it was Willy Tucker, out for an airing. I knew that his special home had been finished just recently in a ribbon-cutting ceremony, reported on by *The Daily Mississippian*. To see him now was a humbling experience. The pictures of him on the Tucker Fund posters showed a big jock in football uniform, but six months of muscle atrophy had reduced him to a cross between a frail old man and a little boy. His arms and legs were like dry kindling, the type you can snap across your knee. A padded strut supported his scrawny back and neck, and his head was kept upright by a chin rest. His flesh was the color of ash. What did he do with himself now that he couldn't run for passes? What did he do when he needed to feel masterful? What did he find to do with himself every waking hour? Still, there he was smiling, or at least showing his teeth.

I joined the line at the cafeteria. When I came out again with exactly what Greg had gotten, Max and Bibi were sitting in two metal-mesh chairs on the plaza. They looked like Jack Spratt and his wife catching some sun. I waved and walked over to them, having mislaid Greg somewhere.

Bibi nudged Max, "Now, *that* smells wonderful," as if they had just been talking about something malodorous.

I held out my tray like a cigarette girl. "Would you like some?"

"You bet I would!" Bibi rose from her chair like an overgrown Venus. "May I?"

"Sure." I said this slightly reluctantly: it was my lunch, after all. But I could always go back for more, and besides, there was something appealing about feeding Bibi. It was like abetting some pleasurable crime.

She took healthy bites from all three portions and rubbed her mammoth stomach. "My, that's good." She looked deliberately away from Max.

"All right, all right" said Max after a moment. He stood up with a wallet-searching motion. "Lunch for two?"

"Why, thank you, Maxie, yes. That'd be just fine." She batted her eyelashes, which most men find seductive and some find off-putting, but which works anyway. Max bowed elaborately and shambled off.

Brother Jim got out of his van and began setting up.

Not much preparation was involved. He didn't use a microphone or elaborate props. He looked the same as last year and the year before that, stoop-shouldered but fresh-faced and ready to carry on

God's work. Stepping to the center of the plaza, he assumed his stance and called out, "Citizens!"

A group of students had been gathering on the plaza steps, but now more came, some of them running. Brother Jim was here! Time to listen up!

Bibi looked around, slightly anxious. "What is this? A rally?"

"Sort of." I told her about Brother Jim and his drawing power.

She got up from her chair. "Let's walk over there. I want to hear this."

"What about Max?"

She waved her hand negligently. "Oh, he'll find us."

The first few layers of the circle had already formed, and we had to walk around to find an opening. I noticed Travis, our departmental work-study student neither working nor studying; also Roy Bateson, who certainly couldn't be there for the temperance sermon. On the far periphery I spotted Elaine and Nathaniel, holding hands grimly. This time, Elaine's upper right arm sported a gorgeous ripe bruise, as if someone had squeezed her too hard. Nathaniel looked slightly hungover, sort of chewed at the edges. Bibi and I said hello, but they didn't seem to want to talk.

We had just found a spot in the inner circle when Brother Jim revved up.

"*Now hear me!* The problem with you students is that you've fallen upon sinful ways!" Brother Jim's eyes opened wide as the sky to take them all in.

"Who're you calling a sinner?" A basketball player who looked like a pituitary accident was lounging along the steps, cradling his ball.

"We are all sinners, brother." Jim lowered his voice in penitence. It rose slowly, sorrowfully. "But some of us have yet to make amends."

"Hey, why don't you pack up and get gone?"

Jim spread his arms and hung his head as if he'd been crucified. He stuck out his tongue like a corpse. That got a laugh. He began again. "The problem that I want to talk about today has to do with the *s*-word."

"*SSSSSSSS* . . . "

"That's right, *sex!* The urge that makes man into an animal, the lust that turns a woman into a tramp!" Cheers and hisses accompanied this, as well as some boos. One student rolled on the ground in a credible imitation of a snake, until someone stepped on him.

At this juncture, Max arrived with two fried-chicken specials, which started where Greg and I had left off, with helpings twice as high and two thick wedges of pecan pie. "What's going on out here? A magic show?"

"Sort of." I told him essentially what I'd told Bibi, but in more caustic terms. Max, I knew, wasn't burdened by faith. He nodded as he settled down to his chicken, grasping a breast. Bibi seemed to be listening with her whole body and didn't touch hers. When Max draped his arm around her in a comradely fashion, she shook it off.

Brother Jim paced back and forth in a tight loop. "Adam and Eve had it made! Freedom from pain, freedom from death! And what ruined them?"

"SSSEX!"

"Yup, original sin! That's why we're born into this world of pain and suffering—because someone didn't know when to hold off!" Brother Jim crossed his arms in a referee's foul sign.

"That's not what original sin means," muttered Max. Bibi wasn't listening to him, so he spoke a little louder. "Original sin was going after knowledge—read your damn Bible." Maybe he was talking to me. Out of the corner of my eye I saw Willy Tucker in back, taking in the message. Was he hoping for a miracle cure? Not even Brother Jim, I thought, would try that. At the farthest edge of the crowd I saw a man circling around as smoothly as if he were skating. It turned out to be Fred Piggot on his bicycle, the sun reflecting off his steel-rimmed glasses.

Now Brother Jim was on a roll, hunching and roaring, timing the refrains. People tilted back and forth along with him and shouted their amens. Bibi's wide body, perched on a low stone parapet, was rocking like a boat. Crouched behind, Max fastidiously wiped his fingers on a paper napkin and reached out for her, around the waist. She took no notice. The spirit was with her.

"It's a clear violation!" Jim made the referee sign again, mimicked by a squad of students. "The body is a temple!"

"Garbage." Max put down his lunch. One of his hands was already engaged, and with his other hand he completed the circle around Bibi's waist. Bibi tried to push away his arms, then let her hands settle on his. They rocked gently together. Anyone could see she wasn't in the mood, but that seemed only to spur him on. From the nearby bushes, a white rat crept up to forage in Max's lunch tray. It looked cute, almost tame, and moved as if it were still within the confines of an invisible cage. Obviously one of Stanley's minions. A frat boy's hiking boot sent it scurrying away.

"*Mensanitation incorporate sane!* A clean mind in a healthy body! And Christ—you know what he was?"

"CHRIST WAS A VIRGIN!" contributed the sorority bleachers. Bibi swallowed hard.

Max gently nosed the curve of Bibi's buttocks with his knee, almost causing her to lose her balance. She twisted against him, but that just had the effect of pulling him in closer. His hands sunk lower on her belly, toward the fertile delta. Once again, I had the fate of watching when no one else was. Everyone else was held fast by Brother Jim. He had opened his Bible to quote something, though it was probably a deliberate pause. He knew by heart what he wanted to say.

Max's hands rose and fell as the two of them swayed in tandem. Bibi was making small groans, even as she struggled unsuccessfully against his grip. Brother Jim had completed one of his circumscribed walks and was coming back this way. The argus-eyes of the crowd followed. Bibi grew frantic, but it was like watching a helpless fat child harnessed in place on a joyride.

"Maxie!" Bibi tried to twist away, but he hung on. She looked absolutely horrified. "*Max*, let go! *Please.*"

Should I have tapped him on the shoulder? Hauled him away? Told him to unhand Bibi, or at least stop fingering her? I did nothing.

Brother Jim arrived at the limit of his circle, five feet away from the merge of Max and Bibi. He hunched forward, his black suspenders thrumming with tension. Bibi looked beseechingly at him in true religious terror. Her huge bosom, which had been heaving tumultuously, was suddenly still.

Brother Jim eyed them for just a moment. It was a long moment. "Know ye not that ye are the temple of God and that the Spirit of God dwelleth in you? Corinthians 3:16!" He wheeled around and started off for the center again. Halfway there he turned and shouted, "ROT IN HELL!" His eyes, so help me, flamed red.

And Bibi fell backwards, as if pushed by the hand of Providence, right on top of her seducer. "And they shall fall one upon another." Leviticus 26:37.

23

Max broke his left wrist in the fall. And Bibi broke up with Max that day, after driving him to the hospital. I understood her grounds: she felt publicly violated. Probably only a few people in the crowd realized what had led up to her fall, but then, how many birds and beasts in the garden knew what Adam and Eve were up to? The point is that Bibi felt betrayed spiritually as well as physically. She had a strong sense of sin and needed to purge herself. Even if her preacher-uncle had turned out to be a crook, even if she long ago left the Baptist faith, she obviously believed on some level. Max's creed, if he had one, was alien to all that, though I think it also fed on the illusion of omnipotence. Max believed in himself.

Bibi shook that belief. Max simply wasn't used to being led on. He wasn't used to being dumped. To add injury to insult, she had also broken his wrist. Indirectly. When Bibi fell back on him, he shot out his hand to brace himself. He snapped his wrist in what's known as a Colle's fracture, a break in the distal end of the radius, as Max reported to us later. It's the kind of fracture people get when they try to break their fall on the pavement. It might have worked had he been alone, but not carrying over two hundred extra pounds of flesh. When I saw Max the next day, he had his forearm in a half-cast.

"It's a clean break," he told me, "but it's still going to take four to six weeks to heal."

I couldn't ask how long it would take his ego to heal, so I asked about Bibi instead. She had quit her job at the bursar's and left Oxford altogether. It was curious how all Max's women fled when it was over, as if mortified. Even Helen had given notice to leave at the end of the semester. Only Marian was still around, and she looked as if it were killing her.

"Bibi was a mistake, I admit. Religion . . . !" He smacked his fist against his open hand for emphasis, and winced. He wasn't supposed to jar the splinting. He'd already been out riding that morning against the doctor's instructions, resting the cast on the handlebars. "I don't need that kind of obsession. It conflicts with my own." He paused, as if examining what he had just said.

"You could slow down, you know."

"Slow down, hell. I'm not going to let this stop me." He waved his cast in the air and winced again. He couldn't get used to the fact that he'd broken something. Naturally, he had to over-compensate. He started putting in even longer miles than Piggot, and his face grew gaunt. He also went out and bought a second-hand Mazda, just like that, and began driving regularly to Memphis. The first time I saw him behind the wheel I almost didn't recognize him: it couldn't be Max, looking so inconsequential inside a ton of metal parts. That didn't mean he cut down on his training—not Max—but we became used to the sight of a bright red Mazda 323 parked alongside our staid Honda Civic.

I don't know what he did in Memphis, but I can guess. The peephole showed an empty bed some nights, and his Mazda began looking lived-in. We were going over *Lycidas* in my English lit survey class just then, and the line "Tomorrow, to fresh woods, and pastures new" stuck in my mind. He bought the Mazda, he told me with a straight face, because of its roomy back seat. What was I to say? I think I just sort of nodded. By this stage, Max was losing all discretion. Though at least all undergraduates seemed to be off-limits. Burnt once, twice shy. His experience in New York, whatever it had been, must have taught him a lesson. But Bibi marked the last of the kind of women that Susan wouldn't mind having over for dinner. I don't recall any invitations extended during this period. But then, I don't think he wanted any graciousness. He wanted to wallow. It was as if the muscles he used to hold himself in were abruptly reversed for letting it all out. Same Max, opposite impulse.

I can't tell you that much about Harriet or Maggie or any of Max's women during this period, since they all came and went as if Max's apartment were a bus depot. I heard flatulent backfires in the night and creaks that rose louder daily. And damn it, my peephole was suddenly blocked! The plug slid out easily enough, but all I could see was blackness. Hell, the painting must have slewed sideways with all that ruckus. I was left in the dark, literally and figuratively. My inferences were stretched to their limit. Groans and slaps and the sharp rips of something adhesive like surgical tape. At one point, I joked to Susan that Max should install a revolving door to his apartment (though some of the women might not have fit through). At the very least, he could turn the vacant apartment next door into a waiting room. Max's other neighbor, a computer type who was never around much, had left over a month previously.

I thought about breaking into his apartment and adjusting that painting. I even contemplated drilling through the damned thing. I kept trying the peephole, just in case. Then one night it was suddenly clear viewing. I saw a powerfully muscled woman, completely nude, step on the bed as if she were trying to tame it.

"More," she said.

"I'll give you another twenty," said Max, out of the angle of my vision.

"Fifty." She placed an arm on one thick thigh.

Max's hand put down forty, but she grunted okay. He entered my circle brandishing a set of bungee cords. The woman lay down heavily, spread-eagled and supine. Her pudenda looked overgrown, ferocious. An expression of delight or terror crossed and recrossed Max's face like a train over tracks. The sight of the bungee cords threw me for a moment, like seeing an ordinary kitchen utensil turned into something demonic. I looked away for a moment. When I turned back to watch, Max was fastening both their ankles to the footboard. Then came the wrists, his on top of hers. When the woman arched her back, Max was borne aloft, stretched on a human rack.

I clawed the wall and almost crushed the wire plug in my hand. She bent him and squeezed him and finally pulled him inside her with a strong flex of her pelvis. The bungee cords stretched just enough to make it interesting. The next day, the hole was dark again. Three days later, an open view again—and I got to see Max licking at a giant shaved armpit as his victim squirmed and scissored him between her round knees. She was pink all over and had an appealing squeal. Then I suffered a blank for almost a week. It was maddening, this on-again off-again business. But the women kept coming steadily. I assume they were paid. Some of them, anyway. Susan had threatened to complain to the police, only I wouldn't have it.

"Goddamn it, leave him alone." I was surprised at my own vehemence.

Susan looked at me peculiarly. "You really care for him, don't you?"

"What do you mean? I care about his privacy, sure."

"Sometimes I think you care about that bastard more than you care about me."

I should have denied it immediately, but I couldn't think of anything to say. And in that moment of silence, Susan turned away. After that, she just didn't talk about it anymore, so I assumed the incident was passed over. I know I talk too much, and I've never gotten used to the idea that silence is a response, too.

In the meantime, I had my hands full with Max. Once I consoled a large "friend" of his who was cursing outside his doorstep for no apparent reason. She wouldn't go back inside; all she wanted was a ride to the bus depot. Another time, when Susan was out typing, I actually invited one of his women into the kitchen for a cup of coffee. This was Maggie or Hattie or Harriet, I forget which. She sat at the kitchen table and didn't say much, looking mostly at her big feet, visible in open-toed sandals, her toenails painted grass-green. I had waylaid her on the porch and told her Max was out. I knew he was with someone else just then, and I figured I'd save him the embarrassment. My mistake—he *had* been tied up with another woman, and was waiting for someone that evening, and Maggie or Hattie was to fill the gap. Or make a third? And how did he mean, "tied up with someone"? The hole was blocked that day. I masturbated to memories and imagined scenes, my own flesh slapping gently against the floor.

I didn't think the women were in any real danger. Occasionally, Max showed a few strawberry marks himself. His explanations grew vague and improbable. "Early and constant exercise of fingers insisted upon," he recited, quoting the orthopedist he saw— was that how he jammed two fingers on his other hand? After that, I tried not to get involved, and for the most part I didn't. But I did live next door. You can't keep your blinds shut all day, or you get no light. And Susan was away for most of each day, typing away at the attorney's office. With the peephole out of commission, I still got some breathtaking cameos.

First, I think, came Alexandria, an amiable pudgy black woman whom Max somehow enticed into his lair. She was the kind of woman in her mid-twenties who still hadn't lost her baby fat, whose clothes looked as if she had just outgrown them last year. I saw Max and this woman dissected thirty times through the Venetian blinds in my study. When I raised the window to get some air, I was introduced. Rather cursorily—it looked as if Max were interested in getting this woman in and out of his apartment before the lunch hour was up. For a moment, I rebelled against the corruption of the innocent: Alexandria really did look an overgrown thirteen-year-old, with a fat brown tummy-bulge where her pants failed to meet her T-shirt, and chunky thighs. Even her voice was baby-cute, which I thought was an affectation until later I heard her say in the same sugary tone, "Fuck that shit!" Maybe she took him for a ride on her belly, which I never saw in its entirety. Maybe he paid her off in pink bubble gum. I don't think she came back.

Then there was Sylvia, who looked like the proverbial housewife from Wichita, Kansas, multiplied by 1.5. She wore severe jumpers stretched to their limit and sensible shoes. She had plump marble calves and no ankles to speak of. She looked like what my father used to call a capable woman, the kind who can darn a sock or bandage your cut finger, cook you dinner or give you a backrub with liniment. She shook my hand warmly, and for a moment I felt encased in warm, coarse-grained flesh. I wondered what it would be like to feel that way down to my toes. When Max winked at me, I felt snared in complicity. I did get a rare peephole view of Sylvia in a lacy apron skimpy as a napkin, the apron ties biting into her broad hips. Max was force-feeding her something soft and spongy, the inside of a loaf of bread, I think. Several loaves, it looked like: you could see her stomach expand over the course of the feeding. At the last bite she pulled him down and chewed on him. Or at least nibbled him some—I figured that was how he got a scab on his chin. "I disagreed with something that ate me," he mentioned when I asked him about it.

He was hard to gauge at this point. Sometimes he was secretive; other times he wanted to show off. The women he courted, if that's the right word, were naturally salient, anyway. Marjorie was a perfectly proportioned woman except for her rear end, which deepened like a coastal shelf. It was the most amazing thing and probably required special attention. Marjorie I actually got a good look at in broad daylight: she just thundered out of Max's apartment one afternoon with no clothes on at all. She sported so much flesh that she looked twice as naked as most women. Her buttocks jiggled enormously, her thighs short and powerful to take the strain. Surplus flesh collected in front, obscuring her pubes with a sleek armor of flab. Placing her hands on her wide hips, she looked like some enchanted swamp creature.

I don't think she had any idea of where she was going; she just wanted out, so out she went. A moment later, a sinewy nude Max grabbed her by the arm. His biker's tan was growing ever darker, deep cocoa up to mid-arm and thigh, loins dead-white except for his engorged red penis, rudely veined and purple-capped. It looked even longer than usual but not as thick, as if it had somehow been stretched. His rib cage showed, and the hair on his head had somehow gotten so kinky it looked like the hair down below.

Marjorie was scared about something, and it was a job getting her back inside. Maybe I should have called someone—good old responsible Don—but I didn't. Max slapped her vast cheeks a few times, and when that didn't work, he planted himself in front of her and slowly backed her inside like a tug moving a barge. He was limping slightly, one ankle raw. They were both sweating heavily. The screen door banged shut after the two bodies, leaving no evidence whatsoever. I saw Marjorie only once after that, in a pair of riveted jeans that must have been a bitch to pull on. Steatopygous, Max termed her—you can look that up yourself.

Some of this must have been so painful it was funny, or vice-versa. One woman named Donna with a particularly capacious bosom used a scent between her breasts that Max called eau de hell with it. I think she was the one who broke Max's statue of Priapus, though I'm not sure how. Max glued the parts back together again— I lent him my Epoxy. Another woman with arms like a longshoreman insisted Max take her to a crawfish boil at Flannagan's in town. Bateson was there that night, and he was telling the story the next day in the faculty lounge. "I swear, she beat two football guys in an arm-wrestling match! Max Finster, he was holding her around that big wide belly of hers, like he wanted to feel her expanding. She threw crawfish down that gorge of hers like Cajun popcorn." He shook his head. "That guy Finster, you know what I think? He's got a thing for trash."

The most poignant scene came one afternoon when I looked out the window and saw Holly advancing up the hill. She had put on some weight, I noticed, mostly in her beam, what Susan and her mother called "sitting flesh." She knocked on Max's door. Max happened to be in, and alone. He let her in. The season for remorse, I figured, and reconciliation. I ran to my peephole, which was clear, but the bedroom remained empty, the door closed. I heard voices rising and falling and possibly the sound of something physical; mostly, the cessation of talk. Ten minutes after she entered, the screen door *screeed* open, and Holly walked out with an angry hunch in her shoulders. After a few steps, she swiveled around. "You," she addressed the screen door, "are *insatiable!*" The door flapped in reply. A minute later, as she drove away, she sideswiped Max's Mazda.

At around this time, someone broke into Greg Pinelli's house. There wasn't much physical damage, but the place was turned inside-out like a sock, and the stereo and television were taken. Greg dutifully informed the police, who took a report and said they'd keep an eye out for his stolen property. He seemed more hurt than angry, shaking his head sadly over the incident. "I can't understand why anyone would do such a thing," he murmured repeatedly to anyone in the department office who would listen.

"Because some people are mean and nasty," said Elaine, picking up her mail and leaving. She had raccoon rings under her eyes and was often short-tempered these days. Naturally everyone blamed Nathaniel, though naturally no one had talked to him. He didn't seem too visible these days, anyway.

"Yes, but why would anyone do this to me?" reiterated Greg.

"Money," Ed Schamley finally replied, leaning out of his office for a moment and tilting back in again.

This brightened up Greg. "At least it wasn't out of malice," he concluded.

Then the Spoffords' home got hit. What galled Emma Spofford was how unappreciative the burglar had been. "He didn't touch the Waterford crystal," she sniffed. Or Henry's precious collection of silk ties, apparently. The Spoffords were out one TV and VCR, and that was it. The police said they'd keep an eye out, et cetera.

The end of the semester was approaching again. Not the crash-bang of December; more like a slow train winding along the pass, heard in the distance. Three weeks, two weeks left. Max's wrist was healing slower than expected, but then the doctor had no idea of Max's active life. For a while, I worried that Max's private life would interfere, bulge somehow, protrude into his classes. But in what way would it affect his teaching, and what was his teaching like, anyway? I was thinking about this one afternoon in April when I passed a Bishop Hall classroom door slightly ajar. I heard Max's stentorian tone and took a peek inside. I listened. He was talking about British suffragism in the early 1900's, chalking something on the blackboard I couldn't see. Thirty captive students sat in various degrees of attention.

"Society on the whole has always been somewhat misogynistic," Max told them. He paused. "Now what's a misogynist?"

One woman in front volunteered. "A hater of women?"

"Yes, literally. Now—"

"You mean a *queer?*" cried a guy in a backwards baseball cap from the rear of the room.

There was a sharp intake of breath. Maybe it was mine. This is the kind of issue that should be discussed in the classroom, but hardly ever is. For one thing, the class usually mistakes you for whatever you're trying to explain. I didn't envy Max just then.

"No, it's not the same thing," Max replied. "A homosexual loves other men. But a misogynist may love women."

"But you just said—"

"Let me explain." Max loosened his tie. "Take an average guy with a wife and kids. He comes home late after a few drinks with the guys. He wants dinner on the table, maybe a beer and the sports section. He walks in the door. His kids are watching some stupid program on TV. His wife's got her hair up in curlers, and she starts to nag at him."

All eyes were up front. Max had clearly been spying on their family life.

"She tells him he should have been home an hour ago, the dinner's already burnt, and why can't he call if he's going to be late? Maybe he gives her some lip back, calls her a dumb broad. Or maybe *he slaps her around a little*, you know what I mean?" Max smacked his fist against his palm and grimaced. The cast was off, but his wrist hadn't yet completely healed. "Then maybe he'll get restless one night and go sleep with someone else. You ask him whether he's a woman-hater, he'll say hell no, he loves women. Loves 'em so much it hurts sometimes."

The boy in the back bit his lip and nodded. A few students wrote in their notebooks; I would like to have read what. I tiptoed away as Max pulled back for the historical view. I might have stayed longer, but I was afraid of being seen. I walked to the elevator, wondering whether Max loved women, and by whose definition. In the elevator, someone had posted a new Cheryl Matt poster. It featured a picture that must have been Cheryl's high-school graduation photo. "MISSING SINCE FEBRUARY," read the caption. "PLEASE CALL THE NUMBER BELOW WITH ANY INFORMATION. $1,000 REWARD OFFERED."

In the English office, I talked with Mrs. Post for a while. Mrs. Post knows how to chat, a soothing, non-directed activity. It was a genteel Mississippi conversation, except that I'm from up North and Mrs. Post once confessed to me that she's originally from Texas. So much for typecasting, which Southerners are just as guilty of as Northerners. Some days, I'm convinced there are no United States. I knew Travis the Confederate was listening from the next room, but the only secrets we divulged had to do with the weather and food prices at Kroger's.

Just as we had reached the concluding pleasantries, Franklin came by. He plucked a student paper from his mailbox and scrutinized it, frowning into his beard. Since he held it in front of him like a newspaper, I couldn't help reading the name on the first page: Elizabeth Hart. Well, well, *well*, as Franklin often murmured.

"I had Elizabeth in a class last semester," I said. "How's she doing?"

Franklin was startled. He hurriedly stuffed the paper into the maw of his bulging briefcase without reading further. "Oh, she's coming *along*, coming along just *fine*."

"Really? I wasn't too impressed with her performance in my seminar."

"Hmm, yes. She's been to my office a *few* times for help. But she's *quite* open to suggestion."

I bet she was. Franklin exited whistling vigorously. Coming along just fine. I wondered whether Franklin loved his students. From all accounts, he was such a tyrannical teacher that this would seem a peculiar accusation. It all has to do, I concluded as I walked back to my own office, with the phrasing.

The scene in Max's classroom stayed with me. I imagined Max's students wouldn't soon forget it, either. Was Max a misogynist, did he believe what he was saying, and what does it matter? I don't really have answers to these questions. In my literature classes, I try to teach by raising troublesome points. I tend not to give a simple plot summary (the class can get that on its own), to dictate the meaning of an incident (I believe in multiple interpretations), or to go through lists of names and dates (we have better things to discuss). So I won't bother with further details of Max's springtime spree. You can just extrapolate until we reach Maxine, who came into the story when we were all exhausted, having just reached the end of the spring semester.

By then, we were all used to seeing Max in the company of a woman wider than he was. We had grown accustomed to plump cheeks and thick ankles, big busts and bottoms. Though he had once managed to squeeze through the Bishop Hall entrance alongside Marian, he would never have managed it with Maggie, or was it Hattie? Broad-buttocked Marjorie might have had to edge sideways. These were women who gave full weight to the meaning of *fodgel* or *pyknic* (Max had a cache of these words). But none of them could even begin to measure up to Maxine. They just weren't in her class.

It's hard to describe Maxine without resorting to epic similes. She was nearly four cubits high. Her belly was as wide as a rich fallow field, her bottom a promontory that cast its own shadow, supported by two vast tree-trunks for legs. Her watermelon breasts were held by a bra that must have used the same underwire as in suspension bridges. Her upper arms were the circumference of most women's thighs, dimpling at the elbow, swelling again at the forearm, and ending in small but beautifully shaped hands. Her neck was thick and columnar, half obscured by several chins. Her skin was pale and fair, her chestnut hair long and silky, like Rapunzel with a henna job. Her smile was several yards wide.

She wasn't Southern. She was an import from Wisconsin, here to do graduate work in Southern Studies, starting in the summer. I didn't know what Max's reaction would be when he saw her lumbering through the hallway, but I figured it would be worth seeing. Here was a woman from the land of milk and honey, or a land unto herself, a bulky Brunhilda who must have stepped right from the depths of Max's fantasies, unretouched.

Actually, I was the one who introduced them.

24

I was talking to Gina outside her office, or rather listening to the latest results of her Faulkner post-mortem. Wright's sanatorium, where Faulkner did his final drying out, was no longer around. It had been turned into a cancer ward and then razed in the late '60's. Of the two attending doctors, Wright was dead, and McClarty wasn't saying anything about Mr. Bill. But Gina had managed to track down an old woman, Mrs. Gar, now in her nineties, who used to live next to the sanatorium. It hadn't been a good residential spot: apparently, the patients used to leave the grounds to hunt for alcohol, often breaking into the surrounding houses.

"She told me," said Gina darkly, "that Faulkner's body was found in the woods. All I had to do was ask, and she answered as if it were yesterday."

"Maybe her faculties aren't all there," I suggested unwisely. "Anyway, what does that prove?"

"*It proves he did himself in.* Don't you see? He went out there to die." Gina's usually soft eyes looked bright and hard, focused on certainty.

"Why couldn't he have gone out to find some alcohol?"

"In the middle of the woods?"

"Well, didn't he have to cross them to get to the other side?"

We kept circumventing the woods until Gina said she was going to find out more from Mrs. Gar. And then, because I was running late for a final exam I had to give, I ran down the hallway, straight into Maxine Conklin.

It was like bumping into Marian all those months ago, only ever so much more so. Have you ever collided with an enormous woman? Forget how the animationists show it—you don't bounce off. You get a yielding, resilient sensation that's like nothing else in this world. It's like a cross between embracing an air mattress and a waterbed, but beds aren't living, and even the most responsive mattress doesn't move the way flesh does. I rammed right into Maxine's stupendous belly and breasts, and must have sunk in a foot or more. She barely budged. For one brief moment, our flesh was one. It was a few seconds before I extricated myself and recovered sufficiently to speak.

"I—I'm sorry. Excuse me. I couldn't see you around the corner," I said, forgetting that there hadn't been any corner.

"No problem." She didn't look offended. I hadn't even made much of an impression. Natural padding has its advantages. She smiled tentatively.

"Well, it was nice—um, meeting you. . . ." I'd almost said "running into you" but had stopped just before the abyss.

"Maxine Conklin." She looked inquiringly at me.

"Oh. Don. Don Shapiro. Are you new here?"

She nodded, her third chin briefly disappearing into her neck. Her huge plaid blouse was missing a button, I noticed, and the shirttails hung over the wide waistband of her jeans like pennants.

"I'm in the Southern Studies program. Thought I'd get an early start this summer."

"Good, good. I'm in modern British, actually, but we're always glad to get promising students." I was launched into my hearty professor role and could have kept at it for a while, but suddenly I remembered why I'd been running down the hall. I ostentatiously checked my watch. "Listen, I'm sorry, but I have to give an exam right now. I'm sure we'll bump—um, see each other again."

"People bump into me all the time." She laughed, rather daintily for her size. Then she turned sideways so I could pass. At the elevator, I couldn't resist turning my head to see her retreating figure. It was like the back of a school bus done in denim, and I'd never seen that before. In a moment the elevator doors swallowed me up, and I began to descend.

I paced nervously around the room after passing out the test, as my students calmly started their essays. Susan always found this amusing, that I got more worked up over the final exam than those taking it. I even felt a kind of separation anxiety for my class, these thirty or so individuals whom I might never see again. For a while, I tried to read the Eudora Welty collection I'd brought with me, but I couldn't concentrate with all those pens scribbling away. I took a circuit of the room to glance at their cacography. One of the women in front dropped a coin that rolled all the way to my desk as she scampered after it. "My lucky quarter," she explained as she took her seat again. One guy in back stared fixedly at the ceiling for so long I looked up myself, but there was only the white acoustic tiling matching the white linoleum floor. So I looked at my student bodies, taking an inventory of sizes and shapes. They were pretty much the same as last semester's group, though this time there was no woman I'd even call big. Too bad. I read some more. The exam seemed to stretch on forever, and I was glad when it was over.

I walked home with a sloppy bundle of bluebooks and dumped them onto my desk. "I think I found someone today for Max," I told Susan over lamb chops and peas.

She rolled her eyes. "What's the matter, is he running out of prospects? Did you see that last one, the one with the tattoo?"

I had. The tattoo in question was a large spotted butterfly on her large spotted upper arm. She had hinted that she had other tattoos in more private places, and had simpered outrageously. I never got to see how outrageously she behaved indoors, since the picture on the wall had slid again. Obviously I couldn't tell Susan any of this. There seemed very little I could tell her these days. Our marriage seemed increasingly like a bad phone connection.

"At least she was better than the one who had a fit on the sidewalk," I answered Susan. "I think that was Jane."

"I missed that." Despite herself, she wanted to hear something outrageous. "What was it about?"

"I don't know—she just turned and began throwing things from her pocketbook at him." This, or something like it, happened more frequently than I let on. Knowing how to pick up women isn't the same as knowing how to get rid of them. Anyway, there had been scenes.

"He ought to take out accident insurance." Susan pronounced that last word with an emphasis on *in*, and I pronounced it by accenting *sur*, a difference that once was endearing. "So what's this one like?"

"Big." I held my hands apart like the fisherman showing the one that got away, but sheer length didn't convey the full image. "You've got to see her. She's like some natural phenomenon—the Grand Canyon, or Mount Rushmore."

"Mount Rushmore isn't a natural phenomenon."

"Nit-picker." I pinched Susan's skinny arm. "Anyway, Mount Rushmore's a mountain carved in human form. That's how I think of this woman."

"Does she have a name, this woman-mountain?"

"Maxine. I've forgotten her last name."

Susan snorted in disgust. "Max and Maxine, you're kidding! That's the limit."

I shrugged. It didn't really make any difference how Susan felt about them. I spent the rest of dinner making elaborate plans for their conjunction. A costume ball, a luncheon *à deux*, an arranged crossing of paths. I calculated that by now Max owed me a tidy bundle in finder's fees and chaperoned dinners. I thought about Maggie and Hattie and Jane and Bertha as if they were already has-beens, wiped out by the latest competition.

We actually had a good time in bed that night, aping Max and Maxine, with Susan wiggling her buttocks as if they were breasts. I wasn't sure how to imitate Max, so I pedaled in bed. Then we switched, with me playing Maxine's part and Susan manhandling me like Max. She knew that part, at least. She rode me and squeezed me unmercifully until I managed to flip her over and pin her by sheer weight. She thrust upward, and the smooth hardness of her knees against my belly felt wonderful. Her hands roamed all over me, stroking and kneading and even pummeling. No ejaculation—I'd already taken care of that twice earlier in the day—but

I tongued her clitoris up and down and around, burying my head in her groin. She made some appropriate noises, anyway.

While Susan was enjoying her afterglow, I got up to splash water on my face. The bathroom scale told me I weighed 170 pounds, but I had clearly leveled off. Something about the scale of Maxine frightened me. Or maybe it was Max and what he might do that was scary. That night I dreamed I had posted Maxine along Max's regular bike route to derail him with a bungee cord, but when he saw it he rode right through her. The scene replayed itself in the second half of the dream, only now it was terrifying and I woke in a sweat.

As it turned out, none of my elaborate preparations for Max were necessary. The next day, I saw Maxine outside the department office, frowning at a poster for a poetry-writing competition. She was wearing an overgrown T-shirt and a pair of elephant-gray sweatpants. The elastic in the waistband alone would have been enough to make five girdles. When she saw me, she pointed at the poster. "You know anything about this?"

At first, I didn't realize she was talking to me. So many of our Mississippi-bred students called me "sir" and "professor" that I'd gotten used to that form of address. I suppose this showed how far I'd come since my teaching-assistant days in grad school, when I used to look over my shoulder if someone called me that. But there wasn't anyone else in the hallway, and she was looking right at me. I looked closer. The poster advertised one of those small-press contests—you know the type—sponsored by some magazine named *Hibiscus*, *Purple Goldfish*, or *The Five-Dimensional Review*. This one was called *Yellowcat*, and they were offering $100 for the best poem sent in. Second prize was $50, third was $25, all entries to be typed on one side postmarked by June 1st becoming the property of the magazine. At least they didn't charge a reading fee.

"We get these announcements from time to time," I said cautiously. "This one looks legitimate enough. Why, are you thinking of entering?"

"I don't know." And the frown came back, as if her face had turned upside-down. "I'm kind of defensive about what I write. I don't show it to too many people."

Was this a veiled invitation? I sighed inwardly. Academia is riddled with closet writers and poets. Most of them are sensitive and suffering; a few are actually talented. I used to write short stories myself but long ago suppressed the urge. I found I was better at criticism, a fitting revenge on my former self and others like me.

Out of the corner of my eye, I saw Max headed toward the lounge from the opposite direction. I had a nefarious inspiration. "Tell you what. I don't think I can be of much help to you, but I know someone who can. He's in the history department, but he knows an awful lot about poetry." Or can work it up, I privately amended.

"I don't really—"

"You should try to meet the faculty here, anyway. Some of them are surprisingly human. I'll introduce you." I led the way to the lounge. She looked doubtful, but I was the professor and she was the student, and that carried some weight. There was certainly no other way I could have outweighed her.

"This is where we drink coffee and gossip about our students." Odd how I'd suddenly found the courage to lead this woman on. Odd how I suddenly sounded like Max.

Max was helping himself to what we call home brew when we walked in. One of these days, when the budget allows, we should buy a new coffee machine. In the meantime—that is to say, for eternity—we have something that makes sounds like a percolator and dispenses a brown fluid that we all loyally mistake for coffee. Max was taking his first sip when he saw Maxine.

He didn't quite fall all over himself. But he must have inhaled powerfully, causing him to suck up a mouthful of hot coffee. I give him credit for not spraying it all over the floor, though it must have been scalding. You could see strong throat muscles in action as he forced himself to swallow it all.

I slapped him unnecessarily on the back. "Maxine, this is Max Finster. Max, this is Maxine. Maxine—"

"Conklin." It was an assertion rather than a question, unlike the Southern women who say "My name is Ella Sue?" as if it weren't too polite to insist on it.

"Maxine is a new student in our department. I told her you might be able to talk to her about poetry." I stood back, watching Max's eyes. He betrayed no surprise. He nodded—of course everyone came to see Finster, poet in residence at Northgate Apartments. Shaking her hand with his patented vise-grip (I saw her wince), he smiled poetically.

"So what have you been telling her about us?" he asked.

"The facts, just the facts."

"You'll never find where the bodies are buried, you know."

Certainly not all the ones you've gone through this month, I was thinking. Better call Hattie or Maggie this afternoon and tell her not to bother. We talked on, saying nothing really, with Maxine growing more uncomfortable, moodily shifting her weight back and forth. I tried to swing the conversation around to poetry, but Max had started talking about some faculty matter, which of course Maxine knew nothing about. I remember listening to these professorial discussions when I was a graduate student, and I know that the student tends to feel both privileged and left out. It's easy to think a large woman is large in all respects, but often the opposite is true, and Maxine had only a small sense of self-esteem. What was she doing standing here, anyway? Or maybe it was all calculated by Max, who interrupted himself in mid-sentence and looked with renewed interest at Maxine.

"Sorry, this doesn't have much to do with poetry, does it?" He checked his watch, which by some magic read noon exactly. "I'm going to grab some lunch at the Union—how about you, Maxine? Like a bite to eat?"

Maxine was ritually protesting that she wasn't hungry when we heard a sound like a gravel truck issuing from her stomach. The Greeks called it borborygmus, pure onomatopoeia. Maxine's reaction was pure embarrassment. A bright pink blush spread from her cheeks to her ears, then to her neck and arms. I wondered if her vast breasts and belly had also turned roseate.

Max waited a beat, then interjected into the perfect silence, "Poor Maxine. You sound starved. Come with me."

She smiled gratefully at him. She nodded. She said that would be fine. For a moment, I thought he was going to extend his arm to her, but instead he gallantly drew back to let her precede him. The invitation clearly didn't include me. Maxine listed heavily down the corridor, an ocean liner with the tugboat Max in tow. I would have waved a handkerchief if I'd had one.

"I'm working on it," was all Max would say when I asked him about Maxine a week later. He did look like a man at work, and irritated because he'd been interrupted at it. Did Maxine eat seven fried chicken platters at the Student Union, did you get her phone number, did she end up in your lap—or vice-versa? How did you get rid of Hattie *cum* Maggie? These were questions I wanted to ask, but refrained. There would always be time later, I thought. Meanwhile the procession of women at Max's residence had disappeared. Concomitantly, the campus cleared out as students drove away for the summer.

The commencement ceremony was that Saturday. The graduating seniors suddenly looked spruced up wherever they went, having traded in jeans for slacks, and slacks for skirts and summer-weight trousers. Students of mine who'd gone through the entire semester in shorts and torn T-shirts sprouted blue blazers and white dresses. Laura Reynolds, my vanguard of social awareness, the student who'd written on the sexual politics of swanherding in Yeats, appeared on the Student Union plaza in a flame-red gown and high-heels, holding on to the arm of a ROTC cadet in full uniform. When I waved, she pretended she didn't see me. It must be embarrassing when one half of your life meets the other half.

This week, the lives students had left at home were coming to visit them. Around Thursday, parents started arriving in everything from beat-up station wagons to BMW's and Winnebagos. They packed the local Holiday Inn, the University Inn, Johnson's Motor Inn, the Ole Miss Motel, and every other hostelry in the vicinity. Trying to get a meal in town was a disaster, with people lined up five deep at all the major watering holes, even the Polka Dot. Of course, every college town has at least one formal restaurant for the well-heeled crowd, so there was a nightly mob at the Oxford Grill, with extra waiters and waitresses hired specially not to spill things on you.

By the abandoned railroad tracks, the kudzu was blooming, filling the gully under the bridge and reaching out creepers to the roadside. A few miles out toward Taylor, entire valleys of kudzu began reclaiming their summer acreage, wrapping around trees, boulders, maybe even a few slow-moving cows. The fact that kudzu was introduced in the South to stop soil erosion is typical of so much of what goes on around here: starting out respectably and getting out of hand. Whenever I needed a metaphor in class for creeping paralysis, I pointed to kudzu. Students from way out of state pointed it out to awe-struck parents.

Another venerable metaphor was Rowan Oak, Faulkner's house. The university had bought it and turned it into a museum, with an eccentric character named Henry Burns as caretaker. Henry was one of ours, an English graduate student, a former Vietnam war pilot, and a confirmed bachelor. He might never finish his dissertation on aviation in Faulkner's novels, but no one pressed him about it anymore. In fact, as caretaker of Rowan Oak, he'd become part of the house himself. When you saw Faulkner's tie draped carelessly over the dressing-table mirror, that was Henry's touch, and so was the half-empty bottle of horse liniment on the far table, and the assortment of books in Faulkner's living room. Tourists came from as far away as Tokyo to see it.

All of Oxford was on display during graduation, I suppose. Certainly the faculty was. I got out my academic gown from the closet and as usual scrutinized the dark blue velvet bars of Philosophy. Hmmph. They should add a stripe for every graduation attended. This was the one time all year that I actually entered the Tad Smith Memorial Coliseum, that great tribute to university overspending. The coliseum could probably have housed a small city if the residents agreed not to use the sanitary facilities all at the same time. As it was, the place came to life for basketball games and rock concerts; otherwise, it usually lay dormant. On Commencement Day, the place became a skirling parade of academic gowns, mostly black rentals, but some from recognizable seats of higher learning, proudly owned and displayed. All faculty were required to attend, which guaranteed around thirty per cent. The ceremony lasted for hours, and those attendees with any sense brought books to be read surreptitiously under the wide sleeves of the gowns. Last year, Franklin Forster read an entire Victorian pornographic novel under cover of velvet. The parents and students took it all in patiently: in the South, most people expect to be bored, or it's not a proper ceremony.

I saw Max at the coliseum, wearing his Columbia slate-blue. He stood to the side of the history department crowd, scribbling something on a scrap of paper. Something on the commencement ceremony, on how ridiculous most of his colleagues looked in gowns, or on some private pleasure of his own? "I write down what occurs to me," he told me, once when I asked. So many notes. But then Max had more to write about than most academics.

My own department was sadly (or happily) diminished. Ed, our department chair, had bethought himself out of town. Greg had delayed to the last minute renting a gown and then, finding that none were left, used that as an excuse not to come. Gina was probably out somewhere in the wilds of Mississippi tracking down Mrs. Gar. But Elaine Dobson was there, with her own fuchsia gown that Harvard insists is scarlet. Eric Lasker wore real white ermine stripes on his robe from the real Oxford. The medievalist Melvin Kent managed to look like the monk he was in some sort of cowling, and Franklin showed up in an ample robe which concealed his ample form.

There were several other faculty members, absent and present, who just don't figure into the story. For example, Milton Flint was present, and if I haven't mentioned him before it's only because he was so unassuming and mild-mannered that he almost didn't exist. Under the guise of teaching Spenser, he droned quietly about his wife and his dog. That year he was retiring, in fact—or maybe it had been the year before, I can't recall. His robe, made of some fustian material from Fustian University, practically enveloped him in its folds.

I wondered what Maxine looked like in a flowing robe—there was no one of her magnitude in sight. I'd seen Baptist women in the local choirs, women of impressive girth whose robes made them look like parade floats. But Maxine was more than impressive. I think Max was a little scared by that, the way a mountaineer feels about Everest. This is a more exact analogy than you know.

Anyway, there we all were, or there some of us were, waiting for the commencement to begin, or for the beginning to commence. This year's speaker was an anti-attraction, a politician so non-representative of education and higher purpose that his choice remained a bit of a mystery. Or maybe a travesty. Still, I suppose it was a coup of sorts to be addressed by the Vice President of the United States. Danforth Quayle would be an event. Many of us even had high hopes of entertainment, the way you expect laughs from a malaprop. The Secret Service men were already in place, wiry bodies hidden under gentlemanly dress like a snake in a suit, heads tilted slightly leftwards to catch the whispers from the electronic ear-bug. The dais was already crowded with *eminences grises*. There was a brief diversion as one of Stanley's overfed rats was discovered near the stand. It exited in haste, chased by a Secret Service man.

We filed in according to our departments, with English sitting just in front of History. The wooden-backed seats were all jammed together, and I was ensconced between Elaine and Eric. Even before we sat down, Elaine had opened a P.D. James mystery. I had brought a book myself, an Anita Brookner novel, but Eric was flipping through *The Dan Quayle Joke Book*, and I looked on.

[211

For someone reading a humor book, Eric didn't look too amused. "Ghastly," he muttered as he flipped each page, and once or twice "Atrocious." He looked like an Oxford don disgusted with the latest batch of tutorial papers.

Max sat right in back of us, scanning the crowd. He had brought a pair of antique opera glasses that looked like a cross between binoculars and a lorgnette. They hung from an elegant black silk strap and were marked by the initials D.E.F. Dorothy Elmira Finster? David Evans? Max was such a self-wrapped enigma, it had never occurred to me that he had relatives. I wondered just then what his mother was like. Was she enormous? Had she used these glasses to attend *Die Fledermaus*? The funny thing was that Max wasn't pointing them toward the speakers' platform but at the audience.

I tried, as I had so many times before, to follow his gaze. The array of humanity settled in the coliseum seats would have heartened any early Christian martyr hoping for an audience. The place was filled with mothers and fathers who had made sacrifices; also little sisters, brothers and cousins and second aunts, girlfriends and wives and others bound by consanguinity, marriage, or social obligation. Max, I figured, was checking out likely women.

The opera glasses traveled in a slow arc and then stopped right around thirty degrees. I nudged his shoulder. "How big is she? Who is she, Max?"

"How should I know?" he snapped. I had jostled his view. "Damn it, now I've lost her."

"You'll find another, don't worry." You always do, I thought. He was still with Maxine, but that wouldn't stop him. I had a sudden vision of Max at eighty, chasing after women with his cane. Sometimes just watching Max made me feel like somebody's ancient uncle. 'Forever panting, and forever young'—but what did Keats know about middle age? I guess some people are never intended to get there.

I turned back toward the front, where Chancellor Tanner was about to begin his speech. "This is an auspicious occasion," he began inauspiciously. Why are all commencement addresses reminiscent of after-dinner speeches at the local Elks Club? Then again, I suppose that's what the crowd has assembled to hear. I looked to the left of me: Elaine turning a page of her mystery. To the right of me: Eric grimacing over a particularly pungent anti-Quayle reference. He seemed to be growing more and more agitated, not at all the kind of response you expect from a joke book. I opened my Brookner novel and tried to link my fate with that of an unhappy woman protagonist who had an ambivalent relationship to food.

The introduction segued into another speech delivered by a balding, rubicund man who blessed us repeatedly. I looked down at the program underneath my book: "Invocation by university chaplain"—I hadn't even known we had one. Then he stood down, and Quayle ascended to the podium as the Secret Service men subtly closed their ranks. I saw Elaine turn her page; I heard Eric grind his teeth. "As I look out among you," Quayle started, with all the spontaneity of someone reading off cue-cards, "I see faces of promise."

The whole speech was like that: strive to excel, shapers of destiny, overcoming the odds—this last phrase a reference to the few physically challenged students graduating. We used to call them handicapped. Before that, we called them crippled. There was a young man from Yazoo City born without arms, and a local woman with multiple sclerosis, and a girl from a Georgia sharecropping family of twelve. This last reference was impressive: the first admission from this political administration that poverty could be a crippling condition. Eric muttered something politely obscene. There was also a passing reference to Willy Tucker, who intended to return to classes next autumn. I registered Max in back of me, his opera glasses now down, scribbling a note on his pad.

Near the end of his speech, Quayle shifted to the Mars shot, a fifty-billion dollar boondoggle the President had proclaimed just a few days before. Once again, the theme was strive to excel, but this time to the stars. If the Vice-President had known any Latin, he could have intoned, "*Ad astra per aspera*," but as he didn't, he said something about how difficult the stars were. A decorous torpor now held most of the audience.

Then it happened.

Eric turned the last page of his book and smacked it down in disgust. Standing up in his full academic regalia, he pointed his hand pistol-fashion at Quayle, and shouted "Bang!"

One of the Secret Service men by the side of the stage leaped to the dais and forced a panicked Quayle under the podium. Another came from nowhere, crashing through three rows of seated academics and wrestling Eric to the ground. The only way to do this in the tight space was to smash him over the seat-back, right into Max, who went over sideways. Two more agents broke through our ranks and spirited away Eric with amazing speed. The whole thing was over so fast that no one even realized that Max had been hurt until he spoke. "Son of a bitch," he said.

Elaine and I tried to help him to his feet, but when she pulled his hand, he told her not to do that. "I think—*shit*—I think I broke my wrist again." He got to his feet unsteadily as two medics appeared at the end of Max's row. "No, that's okay, I can walk," he told everybody in a pained but determined tone. He walked hesitantly toward the waiting men in white as if he'd arranged a blind date with them. A wave goodbye to us with his good arm, and he was gone.

The worst part was yet to come: Quayle got up cautiously from his crouch and decided to take up where he had left off. The whole stadium cheered, making me feel depressed and alone. "What you have witnessed here, my friends, just goes to show . . . that in this great land of ours. . . ." Elaine stoically took up her mystery novel again. I looked down and noticed, among the wreckage of two chairs, an item that neither side had collected on the way out. Taking cover from the amplified bombast all around me, I picked up *The Dan Quayle Jokebook* and began to read.

25

So Max's wrist was broken again, this time by agents of the United States government. X-rays from the Baptist Memorial Hospital showed a dislocation of the original fracture, and the orthopedist put Max into a new cast. No hard exercise or sudden contortion for six weeks, which must have been torture, though not the kind Max enjoyed. As it was, he got the doctor to arrange a sort of rigid sling that he could ride with. The tricky part was mounting and dismounting, Max told me—at least I think he was talking about bicycles. Certainly he got a lot of sympathy from Maxine. I don't think they'd had sex yet. Maxine was easily 400 pounds, and I hadn't heard that kind of groan from the bed. My peephole seemed permanently out of commission this time. I'd tried to nudge the Magritte from behind with a thin metal rod, but now the painting seemed fixed in place, as if Max had glued it there.

The incident at the coliseum was a worse break for Eric. For two days, no one heard any news. Then it all came out at once: charges leveled, the I.N.S. looking into his background and deciding he was politically undesirable, green card revoked, job contract not renewed. The charges themselves were trivial. Disturbing the peace was all they could hang on him. But Chancellor Tanner was livid. He had personally invited Vice-President Quayle to speak, and he took the disgrace personally, too.

"Tanner told me I had besmirched the good name of Ole Miss. I like that: besmirched. Tell me, why do Americans always employ the fanciest diction when defending the lowest of their institutions?"

It was the day after the news from On High, and Eric was protesting at the Polka Dot, a mug of herbal tea steaming in front of him. Around the table were Susan and me, the Kays, Nancy Crew, and a few graduate students, including Doug Robertson. It seemed like déjà vu defending Eric against charges, but is it déjà vu when it really has happened before? Or was Eric paranoid because he thought that most of the school was now against him? A moot point. This whole meeting had started out as a strategy session, but Nancy had put the damper on that by saying there wasn't a chance of a reprieve. "Hell, Eric, you're lucky they didn't lynch you." This was said with a fine Southern relish, despite Nancy's being from California.

Elaine wasn't there, although she had said she wanted to come. She was probably at the county jail. During the commencement ceremonies, Nathaniel had wandered through the paradise of parked cars and helped himself to whatever was available. He might have gotten away with it if it hadn't started raining. One of the traffic cops noticed a trail of muddy footprints all from the same boots and followed them to the source. He caught Nathaniel trying to force an Audi lock with a stick of sheet metal. The suspect tried to evade arrest—at least that was what the cops said. They must have handled him roughly, since his jaw was swollen and he was nursing his left arm when Elaine visited him. Most of us felt sorry for Elaine, but no one cared to defend Nathaniel. By some weird coincidence, those were the two areas where he had bruised her before she finally kicked him out of her house. Two days later he was caught in the parking lot.

Nathaniel didn't seem to care to defend himself, either. He confessed to breaking into the Spoffords' house and Greg's place. It wasn't clear where he'd fenced the items. "Redistribution of wealth," was all he'd say. Elaine didn't swear out any complaint against him. She even cried a bit, something Susan said I wouldn't understand. The sentencing was quick. The day we met at the Polka Dot, Elaine was saying goodbye to Nathaniel before he was carted off to Parchman, one of the state penitentiaries that still used chain gangs.

Max was also conspicuously absent, and no one blamed him. Of course, Eric hadn't been the one who broke Max's wrist, but he was partly responsible for what happened. It was unfortunate that Eric represented so many causes we thought of as righteous, since it so often put us in the position of defending him when some of us would have dearly liked to kick him. Even in this situation, we all felt we should make some token protest. For a while, we talked about petitions and marches, but finally decided to circulate buttons against the decision.

"How about 'Tanner, Change Your Manner'?" suggested Doug Robertson. He had recently become a teaching assistant in our department. Perhaps to suit the role, he had grown a wisp of a beard that I imagined he tugged at every night.

Mary Kay shook her bangs. "Sounds too British, and that's just what Eric doesn't need. We need something clear and American."

" 'No deportation without representation.'" It wasn't a bad line, but Joseph uttered this without inflection, the way he said most things. If he had had to scream, it would have come out in a monotone. And so his slogan sounded monotonous.

Andy the proprietor, wearing a cap that read "AARDVARKS UNITE," had been listening from behind the counter. "I've got some old 'Free Huey Newton' buttons you could use," he offered.

We finally decided on the prosaic "Support Lasker." A stationery store in town handled this kind of business, and we placed an order for a hundred blue-on-white buttons. Starting that Monday, we offered them in the Student Union for a dollar apiece and sold seven. Admittedly, this may have been because most of the students were gone. Max bought one, but altered it to "Support Finster." He was mending, but still bitter. And since in his condition he couldn't manage certain tasks alone, he had to rely more on others. He asked favors of Maxine, who was eager to oblige. I imagine this combination of magnetism and vulnerability was even more seductive than his usual display of strength. Maxine began hanging around his apartment, so I saw a lot of her, in both senses. Even fully clothed, Maxine wasn't fully containable, especially not during shorts and T-shirt season. She simply bulged in every direction.

Twice a week during his recuperation, Max went swimming in the pool at the gym, using a flutterboard and plastic bag arrangement to keep his cast dry. When the heat of June in Mississippi kicked in, I went there, too. I figured I could keep cool and get in some exercise at the same time. At some dim point in my past, I learned the proper strokes for the crawl, but I never got the breathing right. So I swam an old man's sidestroke, the way my father did. It wasn't flashy, but it was reliable, and it was exercise: after forty laps, I felt like I'd been beaten with a rubber hose.

Max's style was impossible to gauge since he was swimming in a sling. All I recall is that he had a swift scissors-kick and an urgent look as he propelled himself forward. Maxine swam in the adjoining lane, her broad body plowing through the water like a ship's hull. Most swimmers of any speed look as if they're cutting through the surface, but with Maxine the illusion was the opposite. Her great broad arms made it look as if she were pushing the whole pool backward in order to advance.

A bikini would never have contained such bulk, but even the largest available one-piece didn't provide full coverage. The reinforced elastic shoulder straps only barely restrained her breasts, and the fabric was like a second skin at the belly, contouring a navel like a great unwinking eye. Walking in the shallow end of the pool, she looked like some imperious queen nereid. Beads of water clung to her smooth white skin, the roll of her belly and buttocks riding the surface like a whale.

After they finished their laps, it was time to play. She would sit on the concrete edge of the pool, and when she stretched out her arms, Max came to her as if abasing himself before a goddess. Sometimes he would swim right into her, and she would trap him between her monumental thighs, huge columns of flesh as big around as other women's waists. A wisp of blue-black pubic hair showed against the huge pale whiteness when she spread herself for him. I caught a whiff of danger and stayed away—but not too far.

Beyond this point, I may not be the most objective reporter. I *know* what he saw in her.

As for what she saw in him, like most of Max's come-ons, it was a deliberate disguise. Maxine was an aspiring poet, so Max was an expert on prosody. I was an accomplice: soon after he met Maxine, he borrowed a book of mine on poetic form and meter. He also quizzed me on certain literary terms in that acquisitive manner of his. I felt my knowledge becoming his property, and I was half-worried, half-flattered. In fact, he really had published some verse in a few small-press magazines, the way he offhandedly seemed to have done everything at some point or other. He wrote Maxine a Petrarchan love sonnet, the kind that makes maidens blush. He let me see the poem, and it was then that I realized the affair had been consummated. I also gathered that he'd been sleeping at her place.

If he was a poet, he was also a critic—a rather tolerant one. He took her poetry in hand, caressed and stroked it, held it out and declaimed it and made it seem almost worth repeating. He hinted that he might get her a public reading somewhere. Privately, he showed the stuff to me and made nasty, clever jokes about it. I felt sorry for Maxine, but what was I supposed to do? Take her aside and tell her she was being taken in? She wouldn't buy it; she was infatuated with him. Take him aside and tell him to knock it off? He was on his great fleshly quest; he was, as Bateson commented half admiringly, in-fat-uated with her. So I did what I was perfectly wonderful at doing: standing by and doing nothing, getting my second-hand thrill like a contact buzz at a pot party.

There were days when I masturbated three or more times. Sometimes I did it in the bathroom and once daringly in my office, but the best spot was in my study because it was right next to Max's bedroom. Even though the peephole was blocked, even if the action had moved elsewhere, a sexy aura still clung to the wall. Call it metonymy. I would pull down my tight pants, exposing my paunch, and lie down on the carpet. My shirt hiked up, I'd massage my chest, grown puckery and soft. I'd gradually work my way downwards, inserting my fingers between the heavy crease in my belly and kneading my flesh. From there it was a short glide down the genital slope.

The more I did it, the more stimulation I needed to get myself off, and sometimes I'd call out Maxine's name or Max's. I'd press my flesh against the cool hard wall to excite myself more. And that's where I was when Susan walked in on me one afternoon.

"Don? Oh, God!"

Shit. Susan was usually at work at this hour, and I'd left the door of the study open. I struggled to pull up my pants, but they were too tight. The waistband stuck at mid-thigh and haltered my step as I tripped onto the carpet.

My opening line wasn't so good, either. "What are you doing here?"

"Me? What about you? Is this what you do—whack off to—to Max when I'm not around?" She was dressed for her typing job, and her heels made hard clicks on the floor outside the study. She hadn't stepped inside and didn't look as if she were going to. Sort of the way you keep clear of the monkey's cage at the zoo.

"I'm sorry, it's—it's not what you think." I writhed a bit. "Look, I know we've been having trouble lately."

"Thanks to Max."

"Leave Max out of it!"

"Well, you sure as hell have changed since you've known him!"

"Stop it! It's not that. I don't know what it is." Then I had an inspiration: female pity. "I just—" and here I broke down. It wasn't hard, especially since I was already mortified at being found out.

And Susan softened enough not to storm out of the apartment. I cried, I protested, I offered to go see a sex therapist, but she muttered that it wouldn't be necessary—which was good, since I had no intention of going. I knew what I wanted, and it was on the other side of the wall. Or would be one day soon, of that I had no doubt.

That night, in reparation, we made shy, tentative love, and I got enough of an erection to do something I'd never done before: fake an orgasm. Max had told me that women can't feel an ejaculation, anyway. And Susan was warily satisfied, so long as I kept my distance from our neighbor. I told her there were certain things I still didn't understand about myself, but I was trying to work them out. Half-truths are always best.

One day in early June, driving past a stretch of field in the middle of which was parked a rusted flatbed truck loaded with supermarket carts, each draped with a Confederate flag, I decided there were just too many things I didn't comprehend. It wasn't just sex, and I'd finally decided to blame the South. I'd never completely understand the enigma of Southern culture. Oh, I knew about whitewashed tire-fences and good old boys and bottle-trees, fried chicken and barbecue, Baptists and the blues, but to know about is not the same as to know. It's only the start. This is the problem with living in a different culture from the one you grew up in: it's a source of interest, not explanation. If Susan had been next to me, I might have nudged her and asked what all those supermarket carts were doing in the middle of a field and felt reassured, whether she knew or not.

But what about all the people from the region where I grew up? Max was someone from up my way, as several friends had pointed out. Mississippians tend to think all Northerners are alike, or at least all New Yorkers. I can understand the urge to classify, but the mind-set of a region is not the same as the make-up of an individual, especially someone as contradictory as Max. "One should always be a little improbable," wrote Oscar Wilde, a precept Max seemed to follow when he came down here. It's just that recently he had been acting dangerously. Something about the South had made him lose control. And maybe I'd been following. Southerners seem to deal with the South just fine, but it seems to warp people from elsewhere, or maybe just exaggerate their traits. At least that's how I rationalized it. I remembered what happened to the Irish Oscar Wilde in London and worried about Max's welfare. I wanted to warn him, to talk to him, to know what he was up to. If he'd tell me.

So I did something bold and uncharacteristic. I asked him out for a drink. You choose the place, I told him expansively. He agreed readily enough. We decided on Friday night, no wives or girlfriends allowed. Knowing how Susan felt about Max, I lied. I don't know what Max said to Maxine, but I told Susan it was one of Ed Schamley's weird night-time committees at Ted & Larry's. Since this had actually happened once before, it was semi-plausible.

Around nine-thirty, we got into Max's car and he drove straight to the one redneck bar in town, a place called Scottie's. It's halfway up the hill from the Polka Dot, with a large green door set into faded wood shingles. Fridays and Saturdays there are always a lot of pickups parked nearby, and occasionally you can hear rockabilly music out on the street. I'd never been inside.

Max parked his Mazda next to a Dodge Ram with a cracked windshield. The door opened onto a funk of cigarette smoke and beer. It was a little early, but there were people at the scarred wooden bar, and a few couples in booths. We paid a cover of three bucks at the door for the house band, and waded on in. A few looks settled on us and wandered away again. I felt more non-Southern than I had in a while. Max was wearing tight pegged jeans and something that looked like a polo shirt with a past. Never mind what I was wearing, but it started with beige slacks.

Max, at any rate, seemed to know his way around. He bellied right up to the bar. The woman bartending looked like someone who once had model aspirations and now had a weakness for fried food. Though her middle had softened, she displayed her fat cleavage aggressively. She nodded at Max, who nodded back. "How's business, Joan?"

"Business sucks. What'll ya have?"

"Two longnecks." I was waiting for Max to say what brand, assuming there was a choice. There wasn't. We got Budweiser, a beer I hate. But it was hot outside, and we were both thirsty, and we downed our bottles in a few long swigs. We immediately ordered two more and another round soon after, in the alcoholic equivalent of chain-smoking. Finally, Max put down his bottle. "Downstairs is a pool table," he told me. "There's two lesbians who play with a broom and can clean up most of the guys around here."

"I don't play pool," I told him. "Do you?"

He winked at me. "I fake it."

Sitting two seats down was a guy with a belly that looked as if it could use a seat of its own. He was hefting the bottle of Bud Light he'd just asked for. "Don't know why they call it light beer," he remarked to no one in particular. "Weighs the same, don't it?" A man in a black T-shirt with brawny arms was admiring his own biceps until a woman with bigger arms sat down heavily beside him. I sensed an arm-wrestling match in the air, but the man just took his beer to one of the booths.

It looked like a quiet night. The band was playing "You're So Vain," but no one was vain enough to dance. Budweiser longnecks were selling for a dollar. If you are what you drink, Max and I were a pair of maltheads that night. We turned our backs to the counter not to ignore our barmaid, though she was no Holly, but to survey anybody (or any body) that came in. Business was slow, as Joan had said. Two scrawny women I recognized as cashiers at Kroger's were talking about what sounded oddly like a mutual boyfriend. "Flatter Dan's ass off, that's what you do," said the one with peroxide hair, or maybe it was "flatten." The other one, a ropy brunette, muttered something about asses. They were speaking from one of the booths, and it was hard to hear. Anyway, they soon paid their bill and left.

I turned to Max and asked him how his prospects were. So he began describing someone he'd seen in here a week ago, a girl with a huge rear, her acid-washed denim shorts stretched to the screaming point around the inseam, her bare knees like boulders.

I took a swig at the latest bottle and leaned forward. "I meant with Maxine. What's going on with you two, anyhow?"

"The usual. For me, I mean."

Claiming that Max had a wandering eye would have been like accusing Machiavelli of pragmatism, so I didn't say that. But I did wonder out loud why he was looking if he was so satisfied with Maxine.

He gazed slightly to the right of me, as if some crossroads lay just beyond my ear. "The price of freedom is eternal vigilance," he quoted, then finished his bottle. "Said by John Philpot Curran, Thomas Jefferson, or Maxwell Finster, take your pick."

"Meaning what?"

"Meaning I have to keep looking to maintain my independence. Things that stop moving die."

"You're amazing," I sighed. But *amazing*, I realized later, is a tricky word. Look up the etymology sometime.

"No, I'm not." Max sounded annoyed. "I just know what I want. It's other people that are the problem."

"If you're not part of the problem, you're part of the solution." I thought for a beery moment. "I mean the other way around."

"Those who are not with me are against me."

"Malcolm X."

"Jesus Christ."

"No, I meant mine."

"You mean you don't write your own material either?"

I took another swig in lieu of a response. I was at the stage where any beer begins to taste like someone else's urine. I pushed my bottle across the counter like a knight's move in chess. "Just what do you do with Maxine in bed, anyway?"

"Re-enact the immaculate conception. Achieve holy bliss." He scratched his wrist, which was mostly healed again. No bruises— none visible, anyway. "Maybe we sit on each other's faces. Flail each other with bullwhips. What do you care, anyway?"

I considered the question. "I'm your friend."

"You're my friend." Max nodded. "Okay. All right. One way or another, one of these days, I'll let you know what goes on. But not right now." And he took out his paper wad to jot down a note to himself.

I tried one more approach. My tongue was thick, so the words didn't come out right. "Look," I said, leaning a little too far over the table, "where were you—what were you like in New York, anyway?"

He finished writing and looked up. "What was I *like*?"

I gestured clumsily. "I mean, were you then, were you always—"

"Was I always af-flict-ed with sat-y-ri-a-sis?" He spoke spondaically, maybe in line with his new poetic persona, more likely from alcohol. He leaned forward till our noses were almost touching. "I've always had fan-ta-sies, if that's what you mean. Is that what you mean?"

I thought about it. I thought about my hearsay evidence. "No, I have fantasies, too. I mean acting on them."

He tapped his forehead, almost tapping mine. "*That*. Takes courage. For a long time, I didn't do much. With anyone else. Oh, I lost my vir-gin-it-y after I got my driver's license, and all that. But it was dating stuff." He looked deep into the bar mirror beyond me, all the way to New York. "I even went through a period of cel-i-ba-cy in college—can you believe that?"

Max celibate? Hmm. Yes, I could see that, pursued with the same zeal as physical exercise.

"Of course, that doesn't include masturbation," he added. "Anyway, I made up for it in grad school—almost got into a lot of trouble, never mind how."

I nodded as if that were a given: both the trouble and the never-mind-how. "But why big women?" I realized this was a stupid question even as I asked it.

"Why big-titted women, why blondes, why six-foot models with prom-i-nent cheekbones? I like something to hold on to, that's all. If I wanted slim hips and a flat chest, I'd go out with a man." He sculpted Rubenesque curves in the air. "It took me long enough, but at least I know what I like. And finally how to get it."

"Which is?"

"You have to show them you're desperate enough." He leered at the woman bartender, who leered back with a laugh.

"But—"

"But what?" He took a last swig from his bottle and put it down with a thud. "Stop this line of questioning, okay?"

I realized I wasn't going to get any more information out of him. But that didn't prevent our hitting one more bar that night. In Oxford, owing to genteel blue laws, the bars have to stop serving at midnight, so anyone who wants to keep on drinking crosses the Tallahatchie River into the next county. They generally go to Fred's, a cowboy bar where the guys have just two words to say to the women: "Married?" and "Beer?" I thought it was Max's idea to go, and Max thought it was mine, and the truth is that when Max asked if I'd ever been, I said no, and he took that as a "yes, let's." So we went.

Fred's is decorated in Early Warehouse style, with a concrete floor and a lot of mismatched tables and chairs. A wooden stage to the side has a bad country rock band playing intermittently. You can get beer and Cokes from a cooler, and that's about it. Everything I could say about Scottie's went double for this place, maybe because it was a similar clientele in a later stage of inebriation. This time we parked between two pickups, one of which had a bumper sticker reading "YOU MESS WITH MY TRUCK, I'LL MESS YOU UP BAD."

Inside we found a couple of chairs detached from a table and bought ourselves two beers. Budweisers. I gave both to Max and wisely asked for a Coke instead. Max kept swiveling his head slowly like a gun turret, scoping the crowd. Some member of the Jukes family at the nearest table was describing how he swallowed a live catfish on a bet but then puked it up a moment later. "Well, it's no fucking wonder," said his inbred friend in a true Mississippi tmesis. "You gotta swaller it head first, or the fins go down the wrong way." A dry-run demonstration followed. Max got up and came back with two more beers and a Coke.

A guy with beefy forearms crossed in front of us, and I realized it was the same guy as in Scottie's. In fact, as I looked around me, bad as the lighting was, I saw the man with the semi-portable belly and at least five other of Scottie's finest. I also saw two frat boys I'd taught last semester, looking alternately cocky and scared. The cowboys were tough guys in tight jeans and boots working the few tables of women near the band. One of the women, a striking blonde at least six feet tall, kept getting to her feet to dance, only to crash back into her seat each time. The cowboys couldn't figure out what to do with her. "Look at her," said one of the frat boys hungrily. "She's so fried you could eat her off a plate."

"So get her to dance," said his good buddy. "Go ahead, ask her."

"Why'nt *you* ask her?"

"Too tall. I got my eye on the redhead down in front."

"I believe she's taken."

Good buddy squinted. "You may be right."

I had the feeling their conversation could go on all night. But for the most part, things *happened* at Fred's. Couples on the puny dance floor collided, women slapped men, and the arm-wrestling match that never materialized at Scottie's began in earnest a few tables down. The woman won after a painful-looking struggle, and the man promptly challenged her to a rematch. Greenbacks hit the table. At the pool hall in back, I actually did see a woman stroke a cue ball with a broom handle—did she travel with it, or just pick one up wherever she was? Max was right: she was damn good. I looked closer. It was Rita Pointz, the reference librarian. A few minutes later, she walked off arm in arm with one of the women the cowboys had their eyes on.

I lost track of her when a woman's body crashed against the edge of our table. "'Scuse me," she had the presence of mind to say to us before yelling, "Fuckin' bitch!" at whoever had pushed her.

"Keep your goddamn hands off Dan!" It was the two cashiers from Kroger's, no longer drinking pals. The peroxide woman launched herself at the brunette, and a crowd of men sprang up around them.

"That's it, honey, rip 'er teeth out!"

"Bust her a good one!"

"C'mon, honey, now quit that," said one of the cowboys with a droopy mustache. I figured he was Dan. But they kept tearing at each other, with a few solid thumps in between. They weren't just nail-scratching: the brunette smacked the other in the stomach. The blonde was bigger and got hold of the brunette under the armpits, forcing her against a table, but the brunette lashed out with a kick to the shin. The blonde shook her head like a horse and leveled her to the table again, pressing a knee against her chest. Then she shoved her denim thigh across the brunette's throat. The brunette flailed about like a crab, clawing the air. Finally she managed to connect with the blonde's right breast and squeezed hard. The blonde jerked around and hit her in the face. Max had just gotten up to get a better look when a bunch of the cowboys reluctantly separated the pair. The blonde rubbed her breast and spat. The brunette raised her hand in a "fuck you" gesture. Neither went back to Dan.

We had just settled down at our table again when two of the cowboys who had separated the women began to go at it themselves. I didn't see how this one started, either. It must have been something in the air. Or the beer. The fight quickly became a brawl, and I began looking for the way we came in. *"Now, Max,"* I said. "C'mon, let's get out of here."

"But it's getting interesting." Max's beery eyes were fixed on the center of the tumult, where a stocky son of a bitch had just gotten hit with a chair. Unlike those scenes in Westerns, the chair didn't break. But the man sat down suddenly on the floor, just a body's length away, and his head began to bleed.

"Then give me your keys," I told him, "Because I'm not staying around to get my teeth bashed in."

"Wait, I'll—." But he didn't finish his sentence because suddenly a pistol shot rang through the open space. A man who looked like the management had just fired through the roof. The fight froze. So did most of the people there. I grabbed Max's good hand like a child's and pulled him toward the red EXIT sign. Outside, I asked for the keys and got them. I drove away from there fast, though there wasn't any need to. Max stared back at the receding building. I felt relieved to be getting out of there, but also bothered that I so obviously wasn't a part of it. It does have a romantic side.

It's like all those county names you see on Mississippi license plates: Tishomingo, Yazoo, Sunflower, Itawamba, Chickasaw, Union, Humphreys, Coahama, Pontotoc, Senatobia, Tallahatchie, Choctaw. . . . Enough of them and you'd have a poem, but what do they mean? How does it feel to grow up in Natchez, and do you look down on those folks stupid enough to be born in Greenville? Along College Hill Road is a combination grocery store and laundromat that predicts the scores of every Rebel football game on their signboard, along with an appropriate biblical quotation. "VICTORY OVER THE BEAST REV 15-2, REBEL ROUT." Along Route 6 is an establishment called Fonsby's Hair World, with a huge hairy globe as a trademark. Would I ever learn to love this region? Or even understand some and forgive some?

I flipped on Max's tape deck and heard the tail-end of a rusty blues song. Most blues I knew were usually about my man who done left home. This was a scratchy recording, and the lyrics were hard to hear, but I made out a few: "When I feel so lonesome, you hear me when I moan . . . who been drivin' my Terraplane for you since I been gone. . . . I'm gon' hoist your hood, mama . . . I'm bound to check your oil." Another number called

"Milkcow Calf's Blues" was about a calf who needed a suck. I looked pointedly at Max, but he was fogging out. I drove on into the country gloom.

I felt profoundly isolated, like Ruth amid the alien vegetation. And then something happened I can't quite explain. I was doing about fifty, and feeling guilty as I felt the flying gravel chip away the paint job on the Mazda. Chipping away at us, is what it felt like. Damn country road. Those road signs that read "BEGIN STATE MAINTENANCE" always, predictably, mean bad paving. Kudzu lined both shoulders, black-green in the headlights, slowly encircling the trees in a fatal embrace. Halfway down the road, I saw a cloud of dust coming towards me. It turned out to be a rusted Chevy pickup with a warped fender, and some obscure piece of farm equipment on the truck-bed, briefly haloed in our bright beam.

Reflexively, I waved to the driver, whose figure I could barely see hunched over the wheel. He waved back, and I suddenly felt just right. I felt included—maybe all that Budweiser had something to do with it. The gravel continued to fling itself at the car, but so what? We could always go to the local autobody, and if they screwed up and painted it wrong, well, then, Max would have a more colorful automobile. It would make *us* more colorful. I found this thought liberating. It was as if part of feeling Southern was just relaxing into it, instead of walking around with your back up. I felt like an explorer persuaded by the natives to take off his spacesuit, who discovers that he can actually breathe outside.

All the way back, Max lay with his head pressed against the window like a lonesome tourist. As usual, I couldn't be sure what he was thinking. I sort of felt sorry for him, though, the way you pity a vagrant. The roads were stygian dark, but I knew the way. We were headed home.

26

The Southern feeling had faded by the time we got back. The blues tape had run out. It was late, we'd both had too much to drink, and we were still in Mississippi. Max had conked out against the window, and I had to nudge him awake.

"Whussat—Hattie? Darlene?" He spoke out of the corner of his mouth as if he were a gangster, or as if his lips were taped. His shoulders hunched together for company.

"No, Max, it's me." I looked into his thin face: membrane stretched over wire. His life lately seemed to be wearing layers off him.

"Think I'll go to sleep right here." He settled himself against the padded curve of the seat.

"Please, don't do that." If he did, the campus cops would probably flashlight him at three a.m. I got out of the car, opened his door, and reached around him. "C'mon, it's not far. I'll help you."

"I'm tired."

"I know. So am I."

"Tired of it all." Alcohol picks you up and puts you down, and right now Max was down. Without asking further, I hoisted him clear of the seat and the doorframe. He was surprisingly light. Or maybe it was just that I'd gotten beefier these past months. With him propped against my shoulder, I managed to kick the car door shut and slowly mounted the steps to the apartments. I stopped to catch my breath halfway up. Once or twice he shifted, and I had to carry him frontwards, his chest pressed against mine.

At the top of the stairs, I realized I needed his key. I fumbled in his pants pocket for a moment before I realized that the apartment key was on the same ring as the car keys. It looked as if I were groping his thigh, but he let me do it. I'm not sure he was that drunk, or just didn't want to wake up. Once inside, he gravitated naturally toward the bedroom, pulling me along. The bed was hastily made, with a strip of mattress showing. Five pillows lay scattered about, looking obscenely squashed. Neither of us bothered to turn the light on, but there was a half-moon that spilled milklight into patches of the room.

Max flopped down on the bed, spread-eagled. I sat on the side of the bed and waited, I'm not sure why. Then, as my night-vision got better, I saw the bungee cords hooked to the foot and head of the bed. A few were drawn taut; the rest looked like the snarl of an octopus. The roll of surgical tape gaped like a mouth by one of the pillows. A snapshot of one of Max's women as a roly-poly stripper lay propped on the dresser—Hattie or Mattie or Darlene. I stared at everything as if it might move. Max lay motionless an inch away. I reached out to twang one of the bungee cords and shifted my gaze to the wall. The Magritte now looked anchored to the wall with some sort of adhesive. For the damnedest moment, I wondered what it was like listening to Don on the other side.

Finally, I took off his shoes and placed them on the floor. Then I tiptoed out of his apartment and into mine. Susan was curled up on her side of the bed, and I crawled under the covers as quietly as I could.

I woke up the next morning to see Susan staring at me. Her lips were pressed into one hard line. Then she opened her mouth. "Friday night, and I'm home alone reading a book. I hope you two bastards had fun."

"What do you mean, 'you two'?"

"I saw you get into Max's car. And I saw you come back home." She sniggered. "Real sweet."

I shrugged. "Well, he was drunk."

"Uh-huh." We were still in bed, where all the best arguments start, only now she got up abruptly and started pacing about the bedroom. "You know, I was thinking of leaving you last night."

"Why?"

"I'm tired of competing with Max—"

"What is this thing you have about Max?"

"*You're* the one with a thing about him. I just—"

"But Max isn't—"

"Let me finish." Standing up made her taller than me, and even though she was wearing a floppy New Orleans T-shirt and tan bikini panties, she looked oddly assertive. She came over to my side of the bed. "I don't know what's going on between you and Max—I don't care, okay? But either you start paying more attention to me, or to hell with it." She looked down on me, her thighs a few inches from my face. I had the feeling she wanted to kiss me or strangle me. Me, I just felt small.

Maybe this was love, I figured. "I'm sorry, I really am. I've just been—distracted lately." I went on, apologizing and protesting my befuddlement. Susan sat down by my side. Finally I got back to Friday night.

"You wouldn't have enjoyed it. I'm not sure we did, either. Parts of it, maybe."

"Which parts?"

I told her a gappy version of the evening. Parts for wholes.

"I knew that about Rita Pointz," she commented when I got to that part. "Anyone could tell that." She took my chin in her hand, as if holding me up to the light. "Don, sometimes I think you don't see too well. Hanging out with Max isn't helping much, either."

"*He's a friend.*" As always, I was surprised to hear my own insistence.

"I know he is," said Susan softly, stroking my cheek. "But how about me? I'm your wife, remember?" And she kissed me, hard. I held her for a long moment and told her I'd try more from now on.

The bedroom confrontation shook me up more than I realized at first. Maybe I *was* spending a disproportionately large amount of time observing Max. Or was I just spending a disproportionately small amount of time with Susan? Now that she was working a full-time job, she and I saw each other less, though this wasn't entirely a bad thing. The problem of being with someone every day is that you have to put up with an awful lot of banality, not just from the other person, but from yourself, remarking for the hundredth time about the morning coffee, the item from today's newspaper, the shopping list. I found Max abrasive but not boring, and his one grand repetition was an obsession, which raised it to a different level.

So I watched and listened to Max, who enchanted me, while trying not to neglect Susan, who was merely my wife. Sometimes I'd see only Maxine, trudging along in her mammoth shorts and tent-shirt, and then from behind Max would emerge. After he'd convinced her that he adored her body, she let him do almost anything with it, occasionally in public. He patted her belly as if it were his own; he steered her by her bottom from Bondurant Hall to the library. And once, when they entered Bishop Hall together, he somehow merged into her side so they both fit abreast. "In order to form a more perfect union," he quipped. I was there, and I happened to have a camera with me, so I took a picture of them pressed together, squashed into one beast with two backs. I gave them copies when the film was developed. I still have the negative somewhere.

For a while, their relationship was all lovey-dovey, but for Maxine it wasn't just sex. Max had to praise her artistry, adore her womanliness, and in general stroke her ego—at least that's what you'd call it if Maxine were a man. With a woman, I guess the term would be bolstering her sense of self-worth, which could shrink or expand like Alice in Wonderland. She was convinced she was a poetic wonder but needed constant reassurance on the matter. She considered herself a fine cook, but Max told me he prepared all the dishes. She made jokes about some of the flat-chested women in the department but stormed out of the office when one of those women said something about installing a turnpike weigh station in the hall.

Fat people tend to look genial, even clownish. Think of what Julius Caesar said about the kind of men he wanted around him. Then think of what happened to Julius Caesar. Maxine wasn't a schemer, but she did have a temper. At one point, urged by Max, she tendered me three of her poems. "Max said you're a good reader," she ventured. No apology for intruding. The implication of my being a good reader, I suppose, was that I should therefore want to read good poetry, and here it was. I read it more as a favor to Max than anything else. I found mostly mawkish clichés, in the tradition a former professor of mine used to call Pastel Pastoral. Miracles of nature, sudden rapture—synthetic, confused, occasionally aspiring to pretension. The only interesting lines occurred when she compared her body to a landscape, which made for some strangely poignant verse.

Since I didn't want a confrontation, I wrote back a carefully worded note, the kind I append to student papers:

Maxine—

I think some of your lines work rather well, particularly the bodily images, though I wish you'd gone further. Too often, I think, you stick with the conventional, or you settle for too easy a word. Spring, for example: flowers, sunshine, and rebirth are all fine, but countless other poets have been there before you. You might want to read some Wordsworth.

I do think you have potential. And I'd be happy to look at anything else you want to show me.

I put in the last two lines to placate. But Maxine seized upon the Wordsworth reference and complained to Max that Professor Shapiro thought the only good poet was a dead one. And what's the use of being told you have potential if you think you're already there? It took Max a week to convince her that I had some redeeming qualities, though I can't recall what they were supposed to be. She took horribly to any kind of implied criticism. She never forgave Franklin for an innocent reference to a large corporation, for instance, even after he explained he was talking about Union Carbide.

Max cheerfully kept up the lies, partly because he liked acting, but mostly because he so enjoyed the sheer hyperbole of Maxine's girth. But there are other tropes that sabotage hyperbole: irony, for instance. And Max was a master at that, or mastered by it, which amounts to the same thing. He could only control his irony, not stop it; it was part of his character. He couldn't be with anyone too long without letting it show. Given time, he would undercut even himself. And Max's faculty status allowed him to say too much and get away with it. Meanwhile poor Maxine presented a huge, vulnerable target.

Let me qualify that. For Max, the target wasn't her body; it was her mind. How many times can you loyally mistake dross for poetry? How often can you praise what shouldn't even be condemned but simply ignored? One day in my earshot, he told her that her poetry was going nowhere, a statement that immediately turned her into a monstrous sullen child. Even Max looked alarmed. He soon took it back, cleverly explaining that you can't go higher than an apogee, but the words had obviously rankled. He was getting careless. When he tried to tickle her armpit a few minutes later, she clamped down on his arm, completely imprisoning it between her swelling breast and upper arm. He finally had to ask for his hand back.

Summer session at the university didn't help matters. She wasn't doing at all well in John Finley's Southern literature survey, and Roy Bateson had refused to take her for his creative writing class. Since Roy was known for maintaining a high standard of pulchritude among his female students, this was more a slap in the face than a slur on her writing. In fact, I heard him confessing to Elaine that he hadn't read Maxine's work at all. Elaine called Roy a pig, and Maxine complained that John was too wrapped up in divorce proceedings to give her the attention she deserved. Most of us felt for Maxine the same kind of mixed concern we showed with Eric. Because their cause was just and they were vulnerable, we tried to protect them. But it seemed at times a thankless task. Eric, incidentally, returned to England on July 1st, leaving over a dozen book cartons for someone else to take care of.

July 16th marked Maxine's twenty-sixth birthday, and to celebrate she decided to invite a group out to Darley's catfish place. Since she didn't know that many people in Oxford, half the guests were Max's acquaintances. Susan and I drove out there with Greg and Elaine in the back seat. Gina and Stanley made a great concession in coming because Gina absolutely detests the low Southern tradition that Darley's stands for. As it was, Gina wore a deep blue skirt and a chic silk blouse, which made Greg sigh—he'd warned her repeatedly about the greasy smoke. Five or six graduate students Maxine had met showed up, including Doug Robertson and Brad Sewell, though they sat in the corner, drank everyone else's wine, and talked about Franklin Forster all night. None of Max's former women was asked, though by an odd coincidence Marian was there when we arrived, nursing a cup of coffee at a table in the rear. She looked like a wraith, half-hidden in the shadows of the back room. I don't think anyone else noticed her, and when I looked back a few minutes later, she was gone.

Maxine sat in the middle of a large trestle table in front, taking up at least two seats' worth. Max sat opposite. The only trace of his injury was the slightly awkward angle at which his wrist rested on the table. Unfortunately, it had healed badly. The rest of us claimed seats wherever we found them, and I found myself next to Maxine. There were a dozen of us at the table, a tight fit. It wasn't so much cheek by jowl as ham to ham. It was as if we were sharing our buttocks. Maxine's body was yielding, but with a firmness underneath. So close up, she was intimidating, with thighs more than twice as wide as mine. She'd gotten even bigger than when I first met her. I smiled at her; she smiled anxiously at Max. I recognized that smile and worried for her sake. When Max's women began to fret about holding on to him, they invariably lost their grip.

There wasn't much fuss about ordering. At Darley's, you either got a filet platter, a bunch of three whole fish, or all you could eat. For the record, I will state that Darley's also offered battered shrimp, T-bone steaks, and fried bologna sandwiches, but no one ever descended to such depths. There were certain immutable laws of gastronomy in Lafayette county. You went to Jacky's Pit for barbecue. You went to Darley's to eat catfish.

Most people ordered the filet, except for Greg, who ordered the whole fish because, as he always explained, the fish tastes sweeter if fried with the bones in. Max and Maxine both ordered all you can eat. Gina put down her menu—except that there was no menu—and announced that she didn't care for anything. When the waitress came, she drew her over and asked if she could get a small salad.

"You won't like the dressing," Stanley warned.

"I know."

She approved of the wine only because she and Stanley had brought their own bottle, though the graduate students soon co-opted it. Most people had brought something to drink, though it was more along the lines of gallon jugs of white zinfandel that Gina said tasted like flat cream soda. Trying to ignore her surroundings, as she had for fifteen years, she sipped primly from her jelly glass of chardonnay.

Since it was a party, we wined before we dined. Numerous toasts were drunk to Maxine, or to Max and Maxine, which brought out smiles on both of them, though not of equal candor. Max kept jotting down notes, which began to annoy Maxine. He told her to have another glass of wine and poured more for both of them. By the time the catfish platters arrived, the graduate students were half-plastered. Max was on his fourth or fifth jelly glass of some North Carolina wine he and Maxine had brought. They'd brought four bottles of it. I had a taste, but it didn't seem to go with anything except itself. Maxine, for all her capacity, never drank much, but she did that night. It showed.

Alcohol is a funny substance. So many other drugs have specific effects: caffeine wakes you up, Valium quiets you down—but get two people drunk and you'll see two different reactions. It doesn't even have the same effect all the time with the same person. Max, usually a cheerful drinker, began sniping around his fourth glass of wine. And Maxine, who had few defenses when sober, became a huge sodden ten-year-old.

"Our poetess has a fine appetite tonight," he began. Maxine nodded, unsure how he meant that. "One fish at a time now," he added.

She stopped with her fork halfway to her mouth. "You ordered all you can eat, too."

"Have some more wine," I murmured, and sloshed the neck of the nearest bottle over her jelly glass. The scene would have made us uneasier if we hadn't been rather sodden ourselves. Several seats away, Greg had gotten into a long discussion with Elaine over the shape and size of French fries in the South. The graduate students had regressed to undergraduates and were tossing hushpuppies about. Gina was picking moodily at a clump of iceberg lettuce as she watched her husband dissect his catfish.

"I finished a new poem today," said Maxine bravely.

"My twenty-fifth year has flown . . . into the abyss of time." Max sounded as if he were reciting.

"Where did you read that?" She was plainly put out. "I haven't shown anyone yet."

"Everyone writes that after twenty-five. It's from *The Norton Anthology of Well-Worn Images*."

She reached for her purse, wedged against a table joist. "I thought I put it in here. . . ."

"To mourn over what was . . . tell me, is that such a crime?"

"What did I do with it?" She looked hard at Max. "What did *you* do with it?"

He stood up to declaim. "Give me your tired, your poor, your metered verses, yearning to be free!" He slowly circled the table until he was behind her broad back.

She swiveled around, no mean feat while seated on a bench. Her breasts rested against my shoulder, heavier than seemed possible. "*Where is that poem?*"

He reached into his back pocket and took out his paper wad. From the wad, he separated out a piece of typing paper. "Is this what you're looking for?"

"Give me that!" She grabbed for it with one pudgy hand, but he danced away, leaving her with outstretched arms, fearfully unbalanced. For a second, it looked as if she were going to tip over, but she stopped herself with her legs—wrapping her calf around mine. I gripped the table, and somehow we both stayed upright.

She got up abruptly, the leverage of her tremendous paunch almost upsetting the table. She waddled over to where Max was leaning against a wooden roof-post. "You're a thief, and—and a plagiarist."

"Plagiarism? For quoting this?" He held out the sheet tantalizingly.

This time when she reached for it, he put his hands behind the post, counting on her short reach. She forced him against the post through sheer weight. Those huge breasts surrounded his chest, his torso held fast in belly-flesh. They struggled for what seemed like a while—it was probably only a matter of seconds—until he was able to bring one hand around to tickle under her arm. She immediately let go, at which point he drew her back again and kissed her smack on the cheek. He held out the poem. "I apologize," he said wittily.

"Kiss my ass."

I couldn't tell how this was said—I had swiveled so far I was at risk of falling myself—but Max bent down and planted a double smooch on her titanic rump. He lingered there a moment, his hands gripping her sequoia thighs luxuriously. The sight of that angular face pressed against those mammoth resilient cheeks will probably stay with me forever. Then he folded the poem and stuffed it into the back pocket of her jeans, almost trapping his hand in the process.

"Don't be offended. I steal only what I like," he told her, and this mollified her somewhat. It was a half-lie: he also took what he particularly liked to hate. But he led her back to the table, and soon after that the cake came out, baked by Elaine and brought along in an old hatbox. It was an angel food cake with orange icing, and ringed around the edge were M&M's, standing for Max and Maxine. His own gift to her, Max hinted with a slight leer, lay waiting back at his apartment. There was still some wine left, including a bottle we'd completely overlooked, so we drank more toasts with that. Most were civil wishes for the coming year.

Then Max noticed Marian for the first time, sitting in back. She must have gone on an extended visit to the restroom. He stared at her for a moment, then raised a glass to her. She said nothing; she simply looked omniscient. Look what you gave up, her gaze seemed to say. Look at you now. Look what's happened to you.

No one said a word. The whole restaurant had grown silent. Max abruptly turned back to Maxine as if he'd made a decision. He raised his half-empty glass. "To a flesh-goddess," he proposed, patting her plumpness, "who has depths still unplumbed by any man."

When Maxine flushed at this, Max began to praise her physical charms at embarrassing length. Then he capped it all by suggesting they make love on the table, and Elaine couldn't stand it any longer and called Max a crass bastard. Which may have been a mistake, since it provoked Max to recite a few facts about her ex-lover

Nathaniel that surprised all of us, especially the financial aspect. "At least I get mine for free!" he shouted across the room. The graduate students, I noticed, had perked up considerably. Marian just watched in silence.

Someone should have shut Max up, but who? Susan later said she gave me a few kicks under the table, but either I didn't feel them or I thought it was just somebody's hiking boot. Anyway, Max seemed to know too much about everyone and was apt to lash out viciously. So he went on unchecked. He talked about the connection between inspiration and ejaculation, all the while squeezing Maxine's huge arm like an overripe melon. It was hard to tell whether he was angry at her or himself, but he was still magnificently insulting. He was drunk and they both knew it and that might have gotten him out of the situation. But her sad cow eyes must have goaded him on because he started to talk about poetry again. He made particular reference to what he called the Maxine Conklin school of verse.

"I always know it when I see it," he announced. "It's halfway between mediocrity and nowhere."

Maxine stiffened in her seat, a peculiar phenomenon to watch in someone so fat. "Is that your real opinion?" she asked slowly.

Max, flying high, beyond irony and pretense, answered simply. "Yes."

Maxine rose from the table and took him by the wrist—the bad one. "We're going home," she said quietly.

"God, yes! Let's go back to my place and make love, gigantic love."

"When I have you all to myself."

They walked out at that point, Maxine propelling Max forward against the flimsy screen door as he staggered slightly and cried, "Watch out! Make way!" That was about half a year ago, but I still recall Max's leer and Maxine's protruding lower lip, his hand in hers and the other trying to encompass the billowing curve of her waist. I can hear the gravel crunch as Max's Mazda drove off into the night.

"Well, happy birthday," muttered one of the graduate students, killing the last bottle. It was clearly time to go. We drove home soon after, dropping off Elaine and Greg on the way. I was tired and rather drunk myself, yet kept hyperconscious with one thought: the huge upcoming sex scene between Max and Maxine. All that naked flesh shifting about like Jell-O on springs. When we got back to the apartment, I told Susan I had to check something in my study. She looked at me warily, but started getting ready for bed. I shut the door and immediately went to the Wailing Wall. I put my ear against it. Blind but not deaf.

"Keep your arms up," I heard Max say, followed by an indistinct answer from Maxine and a countermanding "No, *this* way." The bed creaked nastily. I knew it was useless but checked my peephole anyway.

My God, it was open again. Max crouched shirtless in back of Maxine, attempting to take off her blouse and bra at the same time. This isn't easy even when the woman cooperates, and Maxine was moving only sluggishly. He'd gotten the buttons undone, as well as the three-hook bra clasp, but couldn't reach around for a good yank. The blouse parted in front, revealing a belly so vast it looked capable of supporting itself. But the blouse stuck at the armholes, so Max had to come around and push her thirty-inch upper arms back through the shirt. Her mountainous bosom, held only precariously by the confines of her bra, slid and rolled like a noiseless avalanche. He kissed her hard on the left breast as she reached out to pull him toward her, against her, into her.

He pulled back at the last moment. "Not yet!" he snapped.

"Stop giving orders. And—ow, stop pinching!" Max had nipped her on the side.

"You don't like it, you know what to do." He smirked. And pinched her again. Then he pushed her, hard.

Maxine frowned, shifting to the foot of the bed, reaching down for something outside my view.

"Don . . . Don!" I took my eye away from the hole. The voice came from the bedroom—my bedroom. My wife.

I said nothing. What could I say, when anything might be overheard? And anything I did, misunderstood. So I said nothing. I did nothing. In a moment came a knock on the door. I replaced the plug and rehung the picture, picking up a few papers from my desk on the way out.

Susan stood there in an ice-blue nightgown. "You coming to bed?" She placed her hands on her hips. "Or am I pulling you away from some fun?"

"No." I shut the door behind me. To show any hesitancy, I figured, would be fatal. "I was just about to join you."

"Good," she replied coolly, leading me down the hall. At first, making my feet move in that direction was hard. My body's spirit was elsewhere—hell, my libido was soaring around my study. But oddly, by the time I got to the bedroom, an immense lethargy had taken over. It was as if a heavy gray curtain had descended in front of me. I put on my pajamas barely able to see straight. I don't even remember getting into bed. I slept until nine the next morning, which as I recall was a bright and cloudless day.

There. I've told the story of Max Finster from all I knew about him. The rest of the story I got from the coroner's report.

27

Maxine at first wouldn't talk to the police. But when Elaine visited her in custody, she gave a sobbing account of what had happened that night. They had made love, going through their routine. This involved binding Max's wrists behind his back with surgical tape, and tying his ankles with bungee cords. They were both extremely drunk. She pulled him to her breasts, holding him fast against her; slowly slid him down her soft belly, couching him between her thighs. She forced him underneath her buttocks, sitting down on his face as he yelled, "More!" Then she passed out.

When she regained consciousness, he was still trapped underneath her, smothered. Burked. Ceremoniously pinned by hundreds of pounds of female flesh, unable to arch or even shift sideways, legs bucking drunkenly, weakening, finally losing his life below those slick, bulging sides. . . . Hideous, triumphant crucifixion.

"History Prof Dies in Accident," read *The Daily Mississippian*, complete with misspellings and no photos. No real story, either, just a paragraph brief as a tombstone. By then, Maxine was under psychiatric observation down in Jackson, where a few people from around here visited her from time to time. One of them was Greg, who was Catholic and therefore felt guilty about the whole business. Another was Elaine, who tended to see Maxine as a victim. Maxine spoke little to Greg, more to Elaine, who was trying to get her a good lawyer. But it was Greg who baked her peanut-butter cookies and persuaded her to eat a few, after a period when her appetite had deserted her. So had mine, in fact. I felt like hell.

I decided I couldn't bear to visit Maxine, in view of the circumstances, considering my connection with Max. And though I didn't see her, she visited me frequently—in my dreams. She would shine down on me like a full moon, trapping me in her beams whichever way I chose to run. Some nights I would wake up with the pillow over my face. I'd started sleeping apart from Susan, whom I couldn't forgive, just as I couldn't tell her what she'd done. If I'd been allowed to keep watching, if I could have seen what was happening, if only I could have done something before it was too late. Late was a long time ago. Now was hard to get through. All I could do was breathe deeply and wait for time to pass.

The coroner in his report noted that Max's wrist was broken. Given Max's previous condition, what this indicated wasn't at all clear. A lot of things about the case weren't clear. At first, the state was considering a charge of voluntary manslaughter, which involves the heat of passion. A preliminary public hearing was set up to determine probable cause. Involuntary manslaughter, or culpable negligence, was debated, as well as abetting a suicide. Maxine couldn't or wouldn't talk, but it never came to an arraignment. The case was dropped for lack of evidence and partly, I think, from sheer embarrassment. "The detestable and abominable crime against nature," runs the wording in Mississippi's anti-sodomy law, the issue of consent immaterial. They were even thinking of charging Max with sexual battery, posthumously. The particulars of the event, hazy as they were, affected people in odd ways.

Two weeks after the charges were dropped, I saw Marian emerging from Bryant Hall, where she was teaching a summer art course. She seemed to have regained some buoyancy since I'd last seen her, whether in flesh or spirit it was hard to say. At least she hadn't gotten any thinner. It was unnecessary to ask if she'd heard about Max: the incident surrounding the death couldn't be kept quiet forever. But there were powerful forces to contain it, from the chancellor on down. Eventually it assumed the proportions of a hushed-up scandal.

"I suppose you've heard about Max," I said superfluously.

"Of course." Her face changed. "I went to see Maxine two days ago."

"You did?" I made what Susan called a mouth-flap. "Why?"

"I had to."

I nodded as if I understood. "Did you find what you wanted?"

"In a way. They don't allow her much privacy up there."

"How much does she need?"

"You don't get the point, Don. They've been pushing her." She put her hands on my shoulders, and I thought she was going to embrace me. Her grip tightened. Her lips drew closer to mine. "If you push someone far enough, they'll push back." And she shoved me backwards, though she didn't let go of my shoulders. For someone Marian's size, her grip was strong, though of course the Marian of old had been significantly larger.

"You think Maxine was pushed?" Well, of course she was, but so what? A lot of people in life get pushed around, but they don't commit murder. Or abet it. "Or do you think Max pushed himself?"

"You know as well as I do," she said, letting go of me. "Why do you think they let her off?"

"Don't you feel at all sorry for Max?"

"I did, once. But that was a long time ago. Now, I think maybe he was a lucky son of a bitch. He got what he wanted, right?"

And when I couldn't answer this at once, she tousled my hair. "Poor Don," she murmured, and walked off.

What else can I tell you? Everything but the whole story. The problem with what critics call the narratorial stance is that it's limited. It's limited by what the narrator does, sees, feels, or is willing to describe. I study these aspects for a living. I can expatiate on them for an hour-long seminar or a twenty-page essay, whichever comes first. It's quite another thing to tell a story yourself. What do I know, and when did I know it, when in fact in retrospect I knew the whole sordid outcome?

I don't think I need to go into the actual details of the case. The police questioned all of us, and some of us tried to provide answers. Not me. All I can say is that after the state's hopes for a formal arraignment, all charges were suddenly dropped. This may have had something to do with a few of Max's temp-women, who showed up looking for him at his old apartment and got roped in to testify. Particularly Donna, the one who doused herself with eau de hell with it and tied men against her titanic cleavage. Or maybe Hattie, who buried candy bars in her vagina for her men to eat. I wouldn't say Max was any more sexually abased than his willing partners. Maxine underwent a course of therapy that may still be going on, for all I know, back in Wisconsin. The last time Elaine saw her before Maxine left Jackson, she said that Maxine had lost over seventy pounds and was cultivating an entirely new body image. I couldn't see it.

The history department hired a new assistant professor, and eventually apartment C-7 was filled by a bearded, sandy-haired man named Oliver Enfield. He was polite and discreet, and so utterly charming toward Susan that I thought he was after her, until she informed me that he was gay. Women seem to have a better sense of this than men do. Or maybe not, since Elaine soon started going out with him. Go, as my students sometimes say about a knotty problem in literature, figure.

As a sort of footnote: through a private detective agency, the Matts eventually tracked down their daughter Cheryl, who was living in Memphis. She hadn't entered a brothel and she wasn't even living in sin; she was working as a waitress. Her parents insisted she re-enter school this fall, and the father called me up to persuade her. I'm afraid I was rather rude to Mr. Matt, but he'll get over it.

Willy Tucker re-entered the hospital instead of school at the end of August, just as the fall semester was about to start. He had just been dressed by his full-time nurse and was sitting alone in his room when a blood clot entered his lungs. Unable to breathe, he lost consciousness and keeled over. He was found by his nurse about ten minutes later and flown to the medical center in Memphis. "Willy's a real fighter," said one of his former teammates in *The Daily Mississippian*. "He pulled through one crisis, and I know he'll pull through this." They operated to remove the clot, and for a week the paper issued daily reports on his status. But he never recovered consciousness, and he died from a massive pulmonary infection the day after he turned twenty-one. Since the Willy Tucker Fund had attracted national interest, his death was newsworthy, and *The New York Times* printed his obituary. Certainly his was the most talked-about death that summer in Oxford, far eclipsing the end of Max.

And so Max was phased out. No more news. But death doesn't stop literary scholars (except for their own demise, and even then they sometimes publish posthumously). In fact, only after death can a proper literary biography be written, when access to private papers is easier. A few months ago, they were cleaning out Max's old office. There wasn't much: a few books, class exams, and a desk-top datebook that the university gave to all the faculty. I hung around as a janitor and Henry Clay Spofford stuffed everything into a cardboard box.

The pages of the datebook were all blank—I explained to them that Max rarely worked in his office. Spofford picked it up in a pincers grip and dropped it into the box. He handled everything as if wearing white gloves. He'd suspected Max, he let it be known, from the beginning. They got to the desk drawers last and found a note pad, a jew's harp, and a chain of thick rubber bands. The drawers were swollen with humidity, hard to ease out, and the middle flat drawer wouldn't budge at all. After a double bout of tugging, they figured it didn't open at all.

The janitor prepared to close up. "You gon' stay?"

I hesitated, I don't know why. Spofford shrugged to the janitor, who passed the shrug back to him.

"Okay. I'll jus' fix the door so it locks on you." They walked out with the cardboard box between them, though it couldn't have weighed more than five pounds. Their slow footsteps passed out of the corridor towards Bishop Hall. I waited in that office for something, some sign, maybe a wink by Max from Beyond. It was hot. Nothing stirred. I eyed that desk until it started eyeing me. I had the clearest memory of seeing that middle drawer half-open, once. All of a sudden, I marched over to and yanked hard at it. Still stuck. When I tried it again, I noticed that it didn't go back all the way, that it could be pushed from underneath as well as pulled from the front. So I dropped down on my knees and pushed it. When I did that, the drawer slid out as smoothly as if it had wheels. Inside was a red spiral-bound notebook marked in neat block capitals, "NOTES."

I had always wondered what Max did with his wads of paper. Writing, after all, involves capturing and being captured. Though it would be just like him to have kept no written records at all, to trust in inspiration and memory. He was that odd combination of anal-expulsive, full of impulse and energy, ready to fling himself at the wall; and anal-retentive, keeping himself on a leash, holding himself in, preparing meticulously for a moment that might never come.

I see him as a sexual artist.

I shut the door, sat down in Max's desk chair, and began to read. I don't know how to classify it: it seemed a combination of observations, epigrams, expository paragraphs, puns both clean

and dirty, beginnings of essays, even a few ideas for inventions—
a programmable bumper sticker you could change according to
your mood, for example. It was a miscellany, a hodgepodge, an
olio, a gallimaufry. In short, notes. So this was what Max had been
scribbling on his wads of paper all the time. Only now he was
dead. I felt bequeathed. This is some of what I read:

————————

And the Word was made flesh. John 1:14.

Here I am again, sitting around waiting for me to happen to
someone.

There's a lot of power down here linked to religion, some of it
sexual, most of it repressed. The immaculate conception is a wonderful example of this: *noli me tangere*. If I'd been God, I would
have fucked the shit out of Mary.

Satyriasis is incurable. But what's the disease?

What if all human beings were anatomically the same?

Bleibtheit. Embonpoint. Zei-niku.

I like the South, I really do. There's no better place to hide things
than behind a good set of manners. In that respect, Mississippi is
the most seductive place I've ever been.

Marian isn't working out. She isn't eating properly and she's got
the wrong attitude. Don't worry: just think of her as a beginning.

Don is bright but academic, something I promised myself I'd
never be. I feel for him in a way I can't explain, as if he were my
sober black-suited superego. I never know how much I can talk to
him, though God knows I've let down a lot of the barriers. Not

all. Afterthought: I wonder if Don knows he's getting heavier, or if he understands why Susan's feeding him up. Or is that just my evil mind?

Can you torture a psychotic to confess anything meaningful? Can you force a psychopath to register emotion, or stir a catatonic with deliberate infliction of pain? What happens when one psychotic is forced to confront another?

Put on some of Marian's make-up before we did it last night, which made me feel like a slave. She said it was perverse, and I said that was the point.

Part for whole: definition of a fetish.

tribadism: the sexual act between lesbians. *burked*—now there's a useful word. Try out on Don?

How can the flesh be so dumb and yet so seductive?

Holly during the holidays wearing that tight purple pullover that makes her look like a Christmas pudding and me feel like a long spoon.

When I'm strapped in, I feel secure. I love the toe-clips on my bicycle, the seatbelts in Marian's Camaro, the hemp rope that I once got Holly to use. But nothing beats bungee cords, which allow just a twitch of freedom.

The reason my colleagues in the history department are so secretive is that they have nothing to conceal. Hiding one's light under a bushel isn't too illuminating, and I refuse to do it.

Historians who compare produce more interesting analyses than those who contrast. Apples and oranges are both fruit, after all.

Traditional genius is monomaniacal, with the capacity for bringing great concentration to bear on one subject while shutting all else out. So the chess prodigy knows nothing of baseball, the poet doesn't bother to vote in the election, and Einstein habitually mislaid his spectacles. But what about another genus of genius, the kind whose talent is always moving restlessly in polymathic pursuit? Or the rarest of breeds, the quiet ones who in their youth found they had the requisite genius but simply decided not to wreck their lives pursuing it. Too bad that history recognizes only the first kind.

Who broke Tucker's neck? That's what I want to know.

Cycling a hard thirty miles is a purge, a stripping down, an atonement, an offering the body makes to the spirit. It's easier than the old way of mortifying the flesh, at any rate.

Everyone cheats. But what are the ethical implications of this?

Male: "I've never kissed anyone." Female: "I've never been kissed by anyone."

fodgel; cf. *pyknic*

Am I pursuing a dream or pursued by a dream? Cunnilingus is as close as I'll ever get to rebirth. Butting my head against the gates.

"Don't worry about me, I'm keeping my nose clean."
"That's not the part of your anatomy I'm worried about."

Never, ever mess with your students. Forbidden fruit may be enticing, but it's deadly. As a professor at Ole Miss, I am not going to make the same mistake I made as a teaching assistant at Columbia.
I'm sure I'll make a different one, instead.

Idea for a café that serves coffee from beans roasted right on the premises and charges a premium price. Talk to Andy at the Polka Dot about this?

History fascinates me because it's such a record of atrocities, misdeeds, and cruelty. The same is true of literature. Niceness is for nursery tales.

The soldier searches out the enemy's weak spots to attack them. The lover searches out the loved one's weak spots to cherish them.
What's the difference?

Adam in *Paradise Lost* starts out feeling like God and ends up feeling like hell. We all have days like that but don't consider them worthy of epics. This sounds like something Don might say.

Don worries too much about defining his field. Literature is that hazy ground between language and reality.

sudatory: concerning sweat

She learned to dance so she could fuck men in public.

In Carville, Louisiana, is the last surviving leper colony in the United States. Fantasy of driving down with Holly so we can make love there in one of the wards.

The only way people will really hurt me the way I want is if I hurt them badly enough first. I don't see how that leaves me much choice. "Do unto others as you would have them do unto you."

Why does Helen use the same aperture for eating as she does for singing? There aren't enough orifices in human anatomy.

I have been straddled by love.

Some people want intimacy but not much conversation; others want a spouse and two kids; some just want a hot Saturday night. My idea of a perfect relationship is absolutely unspeakable.

[247

Vagina dentata, the grandmother of all castration anxiety. Once more, into the lion's mouth.

If humor is aggressive, what does it mean to laugh at someone's jokes?

Inside every thin woman is a fat one, aching to bust out and strut her stuff. I told this to Marian once, but she thought I was joking.

It isn't enough to hold tight or even rub together. The merging of the flesh is what's erotic. I have dreams of becoming a part of Maggie's belly, filling into Sylvia's thighs. To make the beast with two backs is only a step in the right direction: I want to be under, inside. Absorbed.

Just as Bibi turns off the shower, I crawl into the bathtub, lying lengthwise between her strong fat thighs. Once she gave me a golden shower, but it embarrassed her so much I had to make a joke out of it. "You know, you're really pissing me off," I said.
Got to work on my tickling technique.

If I were superstitious, I'd say Brother Jim put a hex on me. Or wanted to. What else can you expect from a God-fearing Christian? Anyway, he's wrong: it's better to burn than to marry.

Marjorie's gargantuan ass is one of the natural wonders of the world. I have the almost irresistible urge to slap a sign on it: THE END.

Rejection can be much easier to deal with than acceptance, from relationships to returned essays. That's it, it's done, try again. Acceptance, on the other hand, involves all sorts of further negotiation.

Aphorisms are too easy enclosures of human experience, but I still find them tempting.

Don is

a. shockingly naive.

b. extremely perceptive.

c. both of the above.

She's my cow-calved, thick-thighed, plump-placketed, wide-waisted, stout-stomached, broad-buttocked, big-bosomed, soft-shouldered dream-boat.

Sylvia, 215 lbs. Marjorie, 223 lbs. Alexandria, 157 lbs. Marian, 169 lbs. (at her heaviest). Holly, 187 lbs. Helen, 214 lbs. Bibi, 230 lbs.? Hattie, 267 lbs. I need to break the 300-lb. barrier. I have dreams of a woman so heavy she can barely move.

The difference between female and male masochism is the difference between passive suffering and a voice demanding, "Whip me!"

Story idea: a boy grows up in the suburbs of New York, well fed, well educated, and one day gets chased after by a big girl during recess. When she catches him, she sits on him. Five years later, he's furiously pressing weights in the gym.
Too obvious? Nope, too embarrassingly autobiographical.
The truth is, I've thought and I've thought, and I don't really know why abundance fuels my sexual urges. Or why it's grown so in the South. At least it makes more sense than a passion for scarcity. Excess is sexy; insufficiency is disappointing.

Swollen days, heavy nights.

First, I lightly run my forefinger up and down her bare arm, past the crook of the elbow, higher and higher each time. This tickles slightly, but it also feels wonderfully sensual. By the time I reach the plump flesh between her shoulder and breast, she's sighing like a steam engine. I steer her bedward, my hands moving over her vast breasts. At this point, she's all mine. I could step on her, and she'd just moan softly. Bending down, I slowly remove her shirt and pants, like the unveiling of some giant flesh sculpture. I have to reach around her to take off her bra and panties. The sound of elastic snapping against her endless side drives me slightly insane.

Beyond this point, I am hers.

She arranges herself on the bed, crooning to me to come closer, to wade into her arms. I obey. Then come the restraints. Sometimes she rubs my cheek against her arm, then pulls me against those mountainous breasts as if I were a baby. If I start to tickle her with my nose, her whole belly begins to jiggle, and if I get her really annoyed, she slips me under her armpit as punishment. Usually after suckling me, she rolls me around on top of her, slowly shifting me downward between her thighs to lick at her. Like forcing my way through an overgrown tunnel with my tongue. Or helpless as a quicksand victim as she crouches over me. I climax the sequence by squeezing under her bottom as she closes her thighs. There I am, over half my body spread underneath her global buttocks as she relaxes all her weight on me. I have to prod her more and more for that, sometimes nipping at her, pushing her. Whatever works. I'm planning an escape hatch through the mattress.

The Japanese on my wall reads *Issun saki wa yami*: "Darkness lies one inch ahead." Several people have asked me for a translation, but no one has ever asked me what it means.

The human body is a miracle of engineering. The human body is a frail vessel. Reconcile these two statements.

Complete bodily manipulation is so sexy that sometimes I ejaculate when Maggie is just slipping on the restraints.

What bothers me about Tuesday's training ride with Piggot is not that he rode away twice but that I could have hung on and didn't. I don't think I'm losing it in my legs, I think I'm losing it in my head.

Women with just a tummy bulge and a plump rear end sometimes excite me more than obese women because the gigantic women are already immobilized, but you can see the chubby ones vainly struggling as the flesh takes over. Sort of like kudzu on a tree trunk.

I can't decide which is the greater distraction, pleasure or pain.

I am getting tired of a lot of things, especially myself.

Frightening message found in a fortune cookie: "Your dearest wish will be granted."

———————

I could go on—Max certainly did. It was the record of a man obsessed, but an intelligent man, I insist. Some of his references were about me and Susan, and not always flattering, but I still regard Max as having been my friend. One of his later entries records a moonless night, boredom with the female species, and a sudden urge to go knock on my door. I was quite touched by that, even if he never did. I wish he had.

Here, let me tell you something I left out.

Max's parents came down soon after his death to go through his effects, but only what was left in his apartment. I carried away a few items myself before their visit, including Max's rather lewd statue. Still, I was in C-7 again that day, helping them out and guardedly answering questions, as well as appeasing my own curiosity. They were a fragile, short couple in their early sixties, the father and Max's stepmother. You could see a frail version of Max in Mr. Finster: the same wiry frame, twisted over time; the same blue eyes, now slightly dulled. When I asked what Max had been like as a child, Mr. Finster shrugged.

"Difficult," he said. "He read a lot and liked to show off what he knew, but he wouldn't take criticism." He bit his lip, sorrow welling in his eyes.

"Sensitive," suggested the stepmother, an unappealing thin woman with iron-gray hair. They showed me a picture of Max in his adolescence, chunky and scowling. He was heavy until his mid-twenties, his stepmother put in. It was then he had started cycling, and won his battle against the flesh. That's exactly the way she put it, "his battle against the flesh." Max's mother, I learned, had died of ovarian cancer when he was eight. I saw a picture of her, too: no balloon-lady, just a kind-looking woman who must have slowly wasted away. He was estranged from an older sister, who didn't bother to come down. I don't know if any of them were told the truth about Max's end, but I didn't ask, and I didn't think it was my place to tell them.

"Tell me," said Mr. Finster," clearing his throat uncomfortably, "did he mention us at all . . . before he died?"

Before he died? Near the end? What did they know, and when did they know it? The English teacher in me questioned the diction: wouldn't it have been odder if he made an utterance *after* he died? Actually, Max had never referred to his family, which was telling in itself. But that wasn't what Mr. and Mrs. Finster needed to hear, so I improvised. "He said . . . he said he loved you," I told them, feeling the air thicken around me. It was suddenly hard to breathe.

We were in the bedroom at this point, and I looked around for some familiar sight to steady me. I saw the Magritte on the wall, and I saw Max's stepmother looking away from it. With its breasts for eyes and pubes for a mouth, it did look obscene in an artful way. It buoyed my senses even as Mrs. Finster pointedly left the room. Mr. Finster walked after her.

I neared the painting. I'd plugged up my side of the hole with putty and spackling a while back, figuring that was enough. Now I looked at the wall and noticed that the painting was askew again, when I could have sworn that Max had finally glued it in place. I pushed it slightly, and when it gave I saw that Max had mounted it on a few springy loops of masking tape. It gave in either direction, just a bit. I pushed it to the left. I saw the hole, its outline ever so faint.

A bull's eye in pencil was drawn around it.

I took a deep breath. When that wasn't enough, I took another. So Max had known. But what had he known, and when had he known it? Assuming Max was Max, probably from the start, up to the end. "One way or another," he had said, "I'll let you know what goes on."

And that last night—I exhaled, unable to hold my breath any longer. What had he intended for me? The bull's eye looked as if it had been made by an amateur picture-hanger. It could have been an error.

Like hell it was.

I stared at the Magritte until it began to stare back at me. Finally I tiptoed out of the room to rejoin the Finsters, and I left soon after.

I didn't know what to say, what to think. About Max, about me, about what passed between us.

But I've been brooding on it since then, and these are my thoughts. Max's outrageous behavior and abasement weren't just a means to an end. They *were* the end for Max. Most women don't go for that kind of masochism in men—read Leopold von Sacher-Masoch's *Venus in Furs*, the seminal work on the subject, perched prominently on Max's bookshelf the day I visited his apartment. I looked up the book later in the library, and one of Sacher-Masoch's points is that most women find masterful men sexy; they don't go for cringers. Or if you prefer a woman's opinion, read Sylvia Plath writing that all women love a fascist. Well, Max was both, I think: the brute and the bruised. Or the snake and the worm, or the knight and the horse—take your pick of metaphors. That's why they call it sadomasochism: because the self-punishing behavior of the masochist one night can turn into biting sadism the next. It's no more paradoxical than the odd mixture of love and hate in most couples. I guess. And he wanted an audience, is that so terrible?

I reread Max's notes a few times and finally stored them in the flat drawer of my own office desk. Literature grows on me; it affects me in ways that real life can't. It was as if I'd absorbed the notes. I never showed them to Susan. She told me I'd grown distant, even more so now that Max was gone. We talked about our marriage, and eventually we decided to break up. She went back to Macon, taking half my life with her. It hurt like hell, but I confess I also felt a certain relief, as after an amputation necessary for your survival. This is a comparison from one of Max's entries. The journal has become a part of me.

At first, the spare time on my hands was numbing, and since I'm not much of a drinker, I couldn't kill the hours with a bottle. I reread Max's journal a lot. It seemed to contain more every time. Things began to happen. I bought a used ten-speed bike and started riding it around. Susan had taken the car, anyway. The first month, I dropped fifteen pounds. I'm still at it, quickening my pace, testing myself. "You look like a whole new Dr. Shapiro," said Mrs. Post the other day. That felt good but not quite as good as when three sorority girls in a Toyota slapped me on the ass during one of my rides and made a lewd suggestion. Do you know how many ripe women are floating around down here? Just waiting for someone to rein them in. I upped my mileage the next day. My legs feel powerful. When the pain gets to be intense, I push even harder.

I can't neatly enclose the other characters in my story because they run on, continuing to push and be pushed. Stanley is now working on an experiment linking sexual behavior and weight-gain in rodents. Meanwhile, his liberated rats still pop up around campus. They seem active and well-nourished, perfectly able to take care of themselves. According to *The Daily Mississippian*, several were uninvited guests at a recent sorority party. A follow-up letter to the editor called for campus-wide exterminations, but I don't think it'll happen. There'll always be rats around.

Gina is still on the trail of Faulkner's suicide. When she finally did get back to Mrs. Gar, the old woman recanted everything she had said earlier, so now Gina is back where she started. Recently, she took a trip to Vicksburg to see a man whose father went to the same sanatorium as Faulkner. I don't talk to her much about it anymore. I no longer believe that suicide is a definable category.

Fred Piggot trains alone again. The few times I've seen him, I momentarily mistake him for Max. I figure he could use a new riding partner, and any day now I'm planning to call him up.

Nathaniel is serving two years at Parchman. John Finley is now married again, with opinion divided on how long it'll last. Jane Forster is expecting, with Franklin expectant. Coincidentally, Elizabeth Hart is out for at least a semester, visiting an aunt in Vicksburg. At least until she gets rid of her condition. Life springs eternal, as Vernon Knowles might have said. He's now at a nursing home in Hattiesburg, where one afternoon is much like any other. Greg visited him there along with Dalrymple one weekend, but the era of salon Sundays is effectively over. Recently, Susan sent me a letter in which she told me she's begun attending church on that day.

I practice what little faith I have in private. I still teach my classes; I still carry out the daily chore of existence. But I'm directed now. I have plans and I keep a log. This Friday I'm taking the bus to Memphis and I don't intend to come back till Sunday. I've got a newfound confidence. Though I still have disturbing dreams. The other day, I unearthed that photograph of Max and Maxine merging through the doorway. The look in his eyes—is it possessor or possessed? Or both? And what happens when a man meets a woman who is both the immovable object and the irresistible force? All I can say with any certainty is that Max made his own choices. I hope I have the courage to make mine.

Thinking along these lines enables me to sleep better, especially now that I've installed Max's cracked statue of Priapus by my bed.

Nonetheless. There are nights when the vague pressure of my own hand gives way to a greater weight, the weight of a dream bearing down on me. I look up and see the ghost of a leer—is it Max's?—and the huge body just above, looming indistinct but massive, ready to receive me into the depths of the flesh.